MW00355264

Of Curses and Contempt

by

H. L. Hamilton

The contents of this work, including, but not limited to, the accuracy of events, people, and places depicted; opinions expressed are a work of fiction. Any similarity to real persons, living or dead, business establishments or events is purely coincidental.

Editing and formatting: Dorrance Publishing Co.

All Rights Reserved
Copyright © 2023 by H. L. Hamilton

Cover: Gigi Koa at Gigi Covers Haven

No part of this book may be reproduced or transmitted, downloaded, distributed, reverse engineered, or stored in or introduced into any information storage and retrieval system, in any form or by any means, including photocopying and recording, whether electronic or mechanical, now known or hereinafter invented without permission in writing from the author.

HB ISBN: 978-1-7380735-0-4
PB ISBN: 979-8-88729-036-2
eISBN: 979-8-88729-536-7

Trigger Warning:

This book contains themes that may be upsetting to some readers. These themes include descriptions of sexual assault, bullying (not by the love interest), suicidal thoughts or ideations, graphic sexual content, and violence.

Dedication

"To all those who have felt lost.
To all those who felt like they didn't belong.
To all those who suffered.
Who were bullied, beaten and downtrodden.
You are not alone. This is for you."

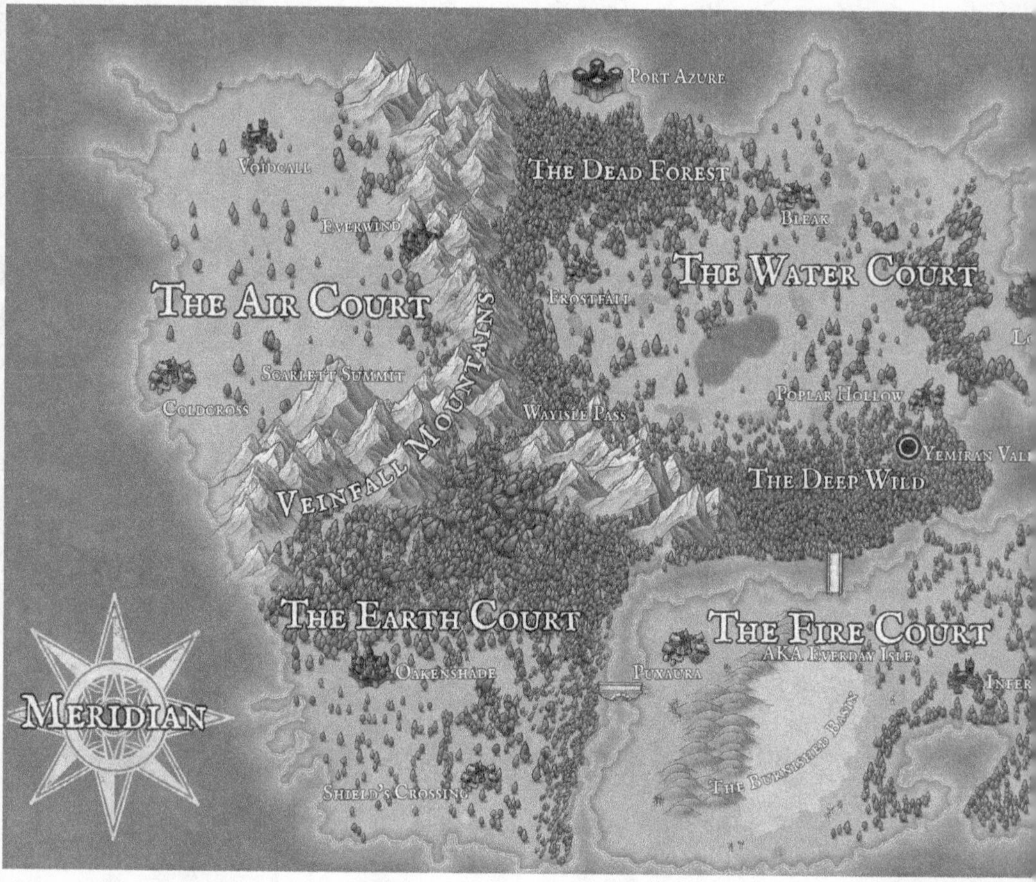
Port Azure
Voidcall
The Dead Forest
Bleak
Everwind
The Water Court
The Air Court
Frostfall
Scarlett Summit
Coldcross
Poplar Hollow
Wayisle Pass
Veinfall Mountains
The Deep Wild
The Earth Court
The Fire Court
AKA Everday Isle
Oakenshade
Puxaura
Meridian
The Burnished Basin
Shield's Crossing

Chapter One

I gazed at my father lying entirely too still on the makeshift cot in front of the hearth, the fresh logs that stirred the hot coals giving copious amounts of warmth. His eerie stillness was interspersed by bouts of chaotic shivering despite the roaring fire and the balmy temperature of the late summer morning. I couldn't suppress a shiver of my own that had nothing to do with the temperature. The morning would have been pleasant if not for the situation before me. I mopped his brow with a deep frown, ignoring the growing hollowness within me.

Eldan, the town healer and my father's oldest friend, snapped instructions at me as he checked my father's vitals, just as I had a dozen times over since he'd collapsed, his questions coming faster than I could keep up. *Which symptoms were first to manifest? How long has he been like this? His fever should have broken by now. What remedies have you tried so far?*

Three days. It had taken my father three days to deteriorate to this unrecognisable condition, leaving him gaunt and ashen skinned, laboring even to breathe.

Eldan checked my father again. I knew he was doing this to be thorough, but a small part of me grated against his lacking confidence in my abilities as his apprentice. But my annoyance softened and was quickly forgotten as my father coughed, blood pooling over his lip and down his now unshaven face. In an effort to be useful and busy, I checked the festering wound on his thigh for what must have been the seventh time in as many minutes. It was clearly the reason for his sickness; it was also something he hadn't thought to bring to anyone's attention until after he'd nearly collapsed from fever. The gash smelled putrid, filling the room with its scent, and yellow-green pus oozing from the wound. I gagged as I cleaned and re-covered it, and I wondered not for the first time how I could have possibly missed it. Eldan, the best healer this town had seen in Goddess knew how long, had trained me well. For the last five years, I devoted myself to learning what he could teach me: concocting poultices and tinctures, how to assess and treat injuries and ailments. And yet, when my father had returned from his hunt clearly exhausted and a little bloodied, I'd not noticed the signs. It wasn't uncommon for the blood not to be his. I was careless. And now I feared he was paying for that carelessness. I braced against the rising guilt, making my chest tighten and my lungs unable to take in enough oxygen.

"Lark." Eldan rose stiffly and cleared his throat. "A word." His pinched expression and stern tone told me it was not a request. I hastily joined him in the kitchen with my stomach souring. His dark eyes skewered me, making me pause mid-step, my pulse jittery and unsettled.

"Why was I not summoned sooner?" he demanded in a hushed whisper, his watchful eye remaining on his patient.

"I didn't even know about the wound until it was too late," I grumbled through clenched teeth. "The idiot thought to care for it himself. All of his symptoms I saw pointed to overexertion. You know how he is. How his leg bothers him even after all this time. I gave him miterwort and mintwater accordingly. Nothing suggested anything more dire until it was too late."

Eldan flashed me a look. Anger mixed with grim understanding. He knew all too well what my father, his closest friend, was like. Stubborn and independent.

"Like father, like daughter," He grumbled, but the bite in his voice was gone. "The fact is, girl, his situation is precarious at best. At this point, the medicines I have will not be sufficient to help him fight this infection. It may buy him time, but that is all."

"Fine. I'll ride into the neighbouring towns. There's that one to the west of us that has stock of most ingredients for apothecaries. I can ride fast."

He shook his head, dismantling my plan before it really even started to form.

Desperation clawed at me for the first real time as I looked at Eldan and my hitched voice dropped to a shaky whisper. "Just tell me what you need."

"Lark." His usual gruff voice held a gentleness he reserved for the most dire of situations. "It will take at least two days to get to Listwyne..." He trailed off, his eye contact breaking with it. His eyes wandered everywhere but to me, appearing to need a moment to say exactly what I knew he was about to. I sucked in a breath to brace myself. "I fear your father doesn't have that kind of time."

It was still like a punch to the gut. I felt the color drain from my face as an icy prickle of dread washed over me. I glanced at my father, forcing the lump in my throat back. He was all I had in the world. He was everything to me. I couldn't lose him. Certainly not because of my dereliction. That realization was crushing and somber and growing stronger with each breath.

"No," I whispered. "There has to be something. Eldan, you taught me there is always something. Give me something! Anything!"

"Lark... I can make him—" I cut him off.

"I swear to the Goddess, if you say the word comfortable... Don't treat me or him like we're just anyone. Don't give us that bullshit speech. Give me something I can do. *Please*."

I watched Eldan stroke his salt-and-pepper beard, wracking his brain for several heartbeats.

"There might be one plant that could save him," he said suddenly, startling me despite his hushed tone. "Have you ever heard of Aching Cress? No, of course you haven't," he muttered to himself before I could respond. I shook my head. "It grows only in places touched by strong magic."

"The Ruins of Calinor?" I asked, unsure what he meant by strong magic. The ruins, I knew, were a source of mystery and enchantment to the North of Poplar Hollow. There was a popular ghost story told in Poplar Hollow about a man and a woman from different courts meeting there and falling in love against all odds. According to our laws, relations between the four elemental courts must not happen. There were those that believed in keeping our Water magic as pure as possible. The purer the line, the more potent the magic, or so they believed.

When they were discovered to be seeing one another, they were told to renounce their love or face death for their crimes against their Courts. When they refused to renounce their love, they went into death together. It's said that their magic seeped into the ground, haunting it forevermore. To this day, they say you can hear the laugh of a woman and a silhouette of a man dressed in black, his face forever covered in shadow. Many people have gone searching for ghosts, but nobody I spoke to had ever actually seen them. There always seems to be the odd disappearance, or rumors of them, to keep the story alive among the town-folk.

"No, the ruins are not nearly powerful enough for Aching Cress to grow. We need a place of immense magical energy...." He grabbed a map from my father's desk in the office before returning to the kitchen where I sat. He slapped it on the counter and placed weights on the edges so we could observe it without holding it open. He scanned the map for a long moment before breathing a long and heavy sigh, and uttered three words I couldn't have predicted. "The Yemerian Vale."

A shocked gasp left me.

"You want to go to the Vale?" I didn't mean for my voice to come out as high pitched and shrill as it did.

I suppressed a cold shudder. I think I forgot to breathe for a moment, disbelieving what Eldan had just said. I'd heard myths about the Vale out in the Deep Wild. We all had. The problem was that nobody knew much about it. Nobody could seem to definitively separate fact from fiction, though collectively we could agree the Yemirian Vale was one of the most evil places in Meridian. Said to be home to deadly creatures that would curdle your blood just to see. They say the very magic there was far older and more potent. More wild. More unpredictable. Whether that was true or not, I didn't know. Few fae ever made the journey. Even fewer returned. And those who did… were never the same. As if the Vale had the power not just to fragment the mind, but the very soul as well until they eventually withered away. I recalled one such fae in my lifetime with a growing sense of dread. The hollowness in their eyes was something I'll never forget.

"No, Lark. I have to stay here."

With a look at my father, still shivering, he sighed. "He draws closer to the veil of death with each heartbeat. The herbs I have here can extend the time he has. Time enough for you to bring back the Aching Cress. You're stealthy and swift. Strong enough for such a task."

I felt my limbs trembling. The Yemerian Vale. I have to brave the Deep Wild *and* the Yemerian Vale. I glanced at my father. The sensible part of me knew there was no choice. The reasoning was sound. Of course, I would do it. For my father, who loved me beyond measure, even when it was disadvantageous. When he suffered such hardship for loving me as his daughter. Of course, I would do this. But every other part of me was screaming. I wrestled with the very idea of willingly going into such treacherous territory.

"The Yemirian Vale?" I murmured. Eldan's hard gaze landed on mine, a hand on my shoulder steadying me.

"You are one of the most capable fae I know, Lark. You are strong enough with a blade for this mission. Stealthy enough to avoid the creatures of the Deep Wild."

There was a moment I paused, gathering my courage and every scrap of iron will I had. I felt fear grasp at me, but instead I busied myself in grabbing a satchel for the journey, staying out of its reach for the time being.

"Aching Cress is the only thing that can save him now?" I prodded, hoping for another way while at the same time solidifying my resolve.

Eldan nodded grimly, the brutal honesty in eyes laid bare for me.

I sighed to cover the shudder the thought of the Vale elicited from me.

"Then I must not delay. I'll pack some supplies and I'll make my leave."

As I packed my satchel with food and water, as I strapped my weapons to me, Eldan marked my map with the best route to the Vale. He created drawings of the Aching Cress plant. An ugly, tall weed the color of blood. The smell, he said, was horrid enough to make your bones ache, partly how it got its name.

"It is a six-hour trek through the heavy brush of the Deep Wild or I would give you Haven," he said.

I glanced briefly at the map, taking note of the Vale's location and eyeing my first obstacle: The Deep Wild. There was a reason it served as a natural border between the Water Court and the Fire Court. It was a no-man's land where monsters roamed freely. Just a few miles out through the forested area of our hunting grounds, the foliage became incredibly dense and traveling wasn't just difficult, it was immensely stupid. It was where monsters made their nests and defended their turf. Worse, we became the prey in their hunting grounds.

Still, it wasn't unheard of for fae to travel through, despite the dangers. Common bandits and other lowlife scum routinely escaped justice by traversing through. But being light, swift, and stealthy with a keen sense of alertness was my key to getting through safely and unseen.

Unfortunately, the mare, although making my trek faster, wouldn't be ideal. The horse would likely not be able to make it through the heavy brush, moss, and gnarled root-covered forest floor.

"You have until tonight, Lark. Beyond that, I fear we may be too late." I saw the concern in his eyes, faint lines appearing as he glanced over my father's still form again.

"Then I won't fail." I knelt down by my father and squeezed his hand.

"I'm headed out to get some supplies, Father. I'll be back by nightfall." His head twitched in what could be considered a nod, barely awake enough to hear me, let alone respond. "I love you." I pressed my forehead to his. "Please get better." The small squeeze of his hand was the most reassuring thing he had done all day. He may as well have squeezed my heart. I bit back tears seeing my father, my hero, reduced to this. I looked to Eldan one last time and asked a question, my voice thick with emotion. "Take care of him?" He nodded.

"He will feel no pain. I will watch over him. Now go. Quickly!"

I raced out the front door, making my way through the lower cusp of the town before approaching the looming forest. Larkspur, my namesake flower, was scattered with other wildflowers along the well-trod walkway, its violet petals waving in the pleasantly scented breeze. I waved at a man in a sentry tower next to me. A single armed guard in case of a monster attack, usually a volunteer. He studiously ignored my presence with a scowl. Typical. I rolled my eyes.

Experience in the woods told me that the first few miles were generally inhabited by mundane wildlife. But every so often, a monster slipped into the territory where my people hunted from the Deep Wild. Bodies shredded to pieces were sometimes found later in the season, or they went missing altogether. Sometimes we could hear the baying screech of some creature in the trees a few miles out. Sirens or benevolent water nymphs were common wherever there was deep water. Being part of the Water Court, about a third of the territory was surrounded by or interlaced with water. Kelpies also liked making an unfriendly appearance to unsuspecting travelers. I had to stay one step ahead of them. Being born without magic in a magical world, that was a tall order. But something I'd been successful at so far.

I was a rare breed. I was the only fae in the Water Court, possibly in all the continent of Meridian, to be born without any form of magic in centuries. Perhaps longer. I suffered plenty of indignation at the hands of my peers at that, often coming home with injuries, seen as such easy prey even to those who had weak magic. I was prey to all. Eldan became quite familiar with my injuries after dressing them for what seemed like thousands of times. It was then that my father noticed and taught me how to fight. Not just with my fists, but with my blades. I fingered the blade strapped to my right thigh, finding comfort with the soft leather and sharpened steel. Somewhere between a short sword and a dagger, its presence was always bolstering as I walked into the sunless forest. It couldn't have looked more eerie if it tried.

A cool mist had spread itself through the trees, not enough to hideously impact my vision of my surroundings, but enough to whisper the dangers of the forest in my ear. It was too easy to spot eyes staring at me from every dark or misty crevice of the forest in my peripheral vision. I conjured my courage as I bounded through the forest's edge, refusing to let fear take over. I couldn't help but take a small look behind me at Poplar Hollow down below. It was once a pretty little town. The outpost that employed several crownguards had shut down and drifted to a larger town with a promise of better life, leaving many people struggling to find employment or basic necessities in my hometown.

There was an upper half and a lower half separated by a wide, red brick bridge that had seen better days. The upper half perched prettily on a ridge offered incredible views and the local market. The lower half stood in the shade of the ridge, protected from the elements. From here, I could see the smoke from the hearth of my cottage close to the bridge on the lower ridge, near the edge of the town. I forced my feet to move, taking out the map for reference. I needed to head southwest once I crossed the forest edge.

The ever-gloomy sky reached on ahead of me, peeking through the tree canopy and whispering ominously of an oncoming rain. I rubbed my dirt-crusted hands over my arms to salvage warmth as I shivered against the mist trying to rake its cool fingers down my neck, forging forward with a growing sense of dread. I'd been traveling much of the day based on the amount of light currently peeking through the clouds and I knew I was running out of time, despite miraculously not running into any monsters to slow me down. The Goddess was sending luck my way. I prayed for her continued favor.

My heart lurched as I unwittingly thought of my father again. I didn't know anything about the healing qualities of Aching Cress. Eldan gave me simple enough instructions, and a description of the plant. I grimly remembered I saw in his eyes he was unsure if I would make it in time. I felt yet another surge of anger at my father for hiding his condition from me, and even more so from Eldan.

I surveyed the amount of light and knew I needed to pick up my already brutal pace. I once again pictured my father's frail body on the cot in our modest home and shook the thought away, focusing instead on the ache in my legs at the slightly uphill trek. The Yemerian Vale was not far ahead according to the decrepit map I held in my hands. It was said that the Vale was one of the most beautiful places in the entire Kingdom, and the deadliest.

Sweat beaded on my neck despite the chill as I thought about what I may face in the Vale and wondered again how I'd avoided anything so far. A ravenous beast with blood-tipped fangs and gore on its murderous claws. Perhaps a Kelpie with teeth so sharp they could break bone with no effort, all while the Kelpie smiled. Or perhaps the worst of all; a Blood Wraith, silent and still as death as it stalks you. The rumor is that it forces you to watch your own death from its perspective so you can see the horror of your blood spilled and the light leave your eyes. I shuddered against the image.

Not for the first time since starting my grueling voyage, I fought against the panic creeping up my spine. My heart stopped a half beat before picking up double time as I dutifully distracted myself by marking my surroundings. Nothing looked familiar, suggesting I wasn't going in circles. According to the map, I should be there by now. The growing feeling of unease made me think I was definitely close. I wasn't sure if it were the distinct lack of wildlife, the absence of birds chirping, or the stillness and the thickness of the air that contributed more to that feeling. The air felt and smelled stale, as if it hadn't been used in centuries. Large bushes suddenly loomed ahead followed by light beyond, seemingly blinding compared to the relative twilight I'd been traveling in for some time now. I looked around, peeled away the layers of bramble, and I stepped to the edge of a clearing of the most beautiful place my fae eyes had ever seen. But also, the most unnerving. There was an air of warning in the air as if something were whispering that I was unwelcome. My skin prickled against the magic of this place, the very energy making my every nerve buzz and stand on high alert. It felt electric, the old magic did. If a magicless fae like me could feel it, it must be incredibly potent.

It had better be.

A still, silver pond almost glowed in the center of the clearing. Silver mist poured from it, giving it an almost ethereal glow. The trees, the sky, nothing that should have been reflected in the water's surface, did, giving me a strange sense of foreboding I couldn't explain. The water, murky within the pond, seemed to hint at menace underneath its surface. I didn't dare ponder too long about what could be watching me from beneath the waters. An unbidden thought of a grinning Kelpie made me shudder and made my feet stop moving in fear, but I shoved it down, reclaiming my nerve. Steeling myself, I swallowed a lump rising in my throat as I surveyed the rest of the clearing, all my senses straining for signs of danger.

The long untouched grasses and wildflowers I didn't recognize swayed in a gentle breeze I didn't think would be possible this far into the trees, their scent perplexing; one minute, smells of cinnamon and spice, reminding me of the bakery back home. In the next breath, the sweet smell of sunflowers and honeysuckle that made me inhale deeply in appreciation. The next breath made me gag: rot and desiccation. There was almost no sound other than the rustle of the grasses. Still no birds chirped and there were no discernable animal tracks leading to the water. I couldn't help but find that deeply unsettling. I kept low in the brambles as I further took stock of what was around me. I had clearly made it to the Yemerian Vale. *It seems almost too easy*, I thought to myself. I furrowed my brow. The stories said that once found, the dangers of the Vale often found you quickly in return.

I closed my eyes, not wanting to be reliant solely on visual aids, listening closely for any signs of danger before I headed into the clearing in search of the flowering red creeper vine known as Aching Cress. Eldan said it grew close to the water's edge. I scanned the perimeter of the pool, noting a distinct absence of any vegetation. I cast my gaze a few meters outward from the perimeter, and as if placed there by the Goddess herself, the red vines Eldan had described came to view: long, winding vines covered with blood-red flowers cascading over a massive fallen tree trunk, long hollowed out and emitting an earthy smell of damp and decay even from my place in the bushes. A distant howl in the background sounded, and I ground my jaw together.

I shifted my weight to stand, eyes scanning the clearing still. One step. Then another. When no danger revealed itself, no growl or snarl from an unidentified monster, I scurried to the fallen tree with my dagger in hand.

With minimal effort, I sheared as much of the Aching Cress as I could, fighting the urge to gag at the smell and feel of the plant. It indeed reeked enough to make one's bones ache. I could now attest. My bones sang—no, *shrieked*—at the alien sensation. I ignored it to the best of my ability as I sheered the grotesque vine. It stank like rot and the liquid that flowed from my cuts to the vine flowed thick and red like blood. I worked quickly, taking as much of the flowering vine I could stuff in my pack, red now staining the bottom of the material. When I was certain I had gathered enough, I returned my now-full satchel to its place on my back. Somewhere in the forest I heard a noise.

I glanced around, not seeing an obvious threat. But the chill dragging down my spine was hard to ignore. I gingerly crept into the hollow tree trunk and crouched down onto my knees, damp with spongey moss. I was about to dismiss the danger had passed when I heard the noise again. Footsteps. Loud ones. And... voices?

From my place inside the hollow tree, I could see the pool through a few holes in the wood. I watched as two women emerged from the forest, either unaware or uncaring of the dangers here. Or, I thought to myself with a shudder, maybe they are one of the dangers of the Yemerian Vale.

I watched a white-clothed woman emerged from the forest into the clearing first. She did not hesitate as she walked to the water's edge and knelt, gazing intently into the opaque water, as if inspecting something I couldn't see. Her white robes weren't that white, I realized. The bottom was dirty and dishevelled from clearly a long journey on foot not unlike my own. Her dress fit her slender waist and torso well, covering up to her neck. A simple silver circlet atop her auburn head failed to attract much attention in the dim light.

Following her was the most beautiful and terrifying woman I've ever seen. Vibrant red hair that seemed bright even in the dim, color washing light tumbled down her slender shoulders to the small of her back. She wore a blue tunic, the material obviously very fine even from my position, with golden plates of light armor along her chest and lower arms. Her legs were outfitted with fine leggings and boots that were no doubt far more comfortable and drier than my own. A large golden diadem adorned her head with a deep blue jewel in the center of her forehead which could only mean one thing: she was a member of the Zodiac, the

Meridian kingdom's royal family of sorts. The Zodiac Kinship, they were called. The land of Meridian was divided into four courts—Water, Fire, Earth, and Air—and the people born to a court had the elemental gifts of that court. Being born into Water, I supposedly had access to water elemental magic, like all people in my Court did. The thought tasted bitter to me, knowing I had no magic. The Zodiac Kinship acted as our sovereignty and leaders of the Guard of Meridian. There was only one female member currently of the Zodiac Kinship of the Water Court.

I was acutely aware of who the woman in front of me was. Terror seized me, paralyzing me at who was in front of me. I saw her endlessly dark eyes, black as night interspersing the natural vivid green glancing coldly at the woman near the water. As she walked nearer, my horror grew. What bare skin on her upper arms showed, revealed writhing black runes inked into her skin, like shadows incarnate. The kind of magic enhancement spells you can only undertake if you're a Zodiac, or at least as strong as one. The color of the runes depended on the magic you wielded. The inky black runes encircling her arms confirmed my worst fear, despite my trying to deny it. The woman in front of me was worse than any monster I could have come across in the Vale.

I was staring at Scorpio, the Barbaric Queen of the Water Court in the flesh. The Wielder of Black Magic. The Cursed One, herself. Black magic was so incredibly rare. So few fae traversed to the Echo Isles of the Shadow Realm. So few risked the curses, insanity, or even death to wield the shadows. So few were strong enough to survive it. And yet the Queen did. She survived. One had only look into those poison green eyes to see the madness that lay there. And the havoc she wreaked with her magic and her rule has left the court in shattered shambles. She was the most dangerous faerie in our realm—no.

She was the most dangerous faerie in all four courts. And she was in front of me. I went completely still, barely daring to breathe, lest she hear me. The Barbaric Queen was ruthless, cutthroat, and whatever she was up to here in the Yemerian Vale, she didn't want witnesses. There were no visible Guards. I scanned the perimeter of the Vale again in confusion. The Crown Guard were usually an ever-present protective force in her presence. I gulped. They were notably absent. No, whatever it was the Queen of the Water Court was doing, she wanted as few people to know about it as possible. Which meant if I were discovered, I was as good as dead.

I watched the scene unfold with bated breath as Scorpio barked orders to her subservient, who I gleaned was a prophetess and seer named Amaya. Amaya stepped lightly into the almost opaque silver water, softly chanting as she did so in a language I didn't recognize. My guess was the old language. The language of magic. Of spells.

When she was waist deep in the water, her hands fell into the water at her sides and she began chanting in earnest, louder and more forcefully, with an air of command. The water responded to her whim, and suddenly there were ripples flowing outward from her to the edge of the pool where Scorpio waited with impatience on her face.

Suddenly the chanting, that had been rising in candor, stopped and the water stilled once more. From my position in the tree I could see half of her face, which sent me cold. Her eyes, once a dark brown, were now swirling silver like the water she stood in. She turned to face Scorpio with an impassive face, appearing to be waiting for something.

She didn't have to wait long, as Scorpio barked at her a single question.

"Prophetess, tell me, how do I break the curse at long last?"

Amaya's back stiffened and straightened to the point I thought it might break, her head rolled back, mouth open in a silent scream. What gentle ripples that came from her before were now violent waves lapping at the shore, some of the water now dangerously close to my hiding place. When Amaya spoke at last, it wasn't her voice that came out. It was a distant, angry rasp, that caused the wind around us to whip and spike violently. Even from the relative protection of my hiding place, my golden braid was thrown around and the icy wind bit at my clothing.

"*In a pure moonlight pond,*
Shows the way to break the bond,
A curse so terrible a Queen even quakes.
To right it, the death of one by her will make.
The most powerful fae
One born the way the Queen was made"

A chill I couldn't explain came over me at the prophecy from the seer's lips. As if someone had dumped icy water over me. I watched as the mist in Amaya's eyes became as turbulent as the waters she stood in, growing larger by the second. Scorpio gazed impassively as Amaya began thrashing in the water, as if trying to move to shore, but her feet were stuck to the ground. Her face quickly becoming panicked as Scorpio opened her mouth to speak once more.

"Where can I find the most powerful fae? Who are they?" Amaya's head whipped back, and her mouth opened in a horrid, grotesque expression. Her features became gaunt and pale, her bloodless lips now moved.

> *"In her veins lay fire*
> *That grows when her fate becomes dire,*
> *In her heart lay water and ice*
> *Turbulent and strong in times of strife.*
> *Upon her lips read words of air*
> *Underestimate her and beware.*
> *The Earth itself trembles before her*
> *She knows not her own power"*

As Amaya spoke, her voice grew hoarse, as if it were a great effort to speak. Scorpio didn't seem impressed, her scowl deepened as her eyes blazed. Amaya tried weakly to swim to the shore, but her feet remained rooted to the spot.

"Who is this girl?" Scorpio asked. "Where can I find her?" Amaya whimpered but said nothing. Scorpio tsked and sneered before repeated her question. Still, Amaya didn't speak. Amaya's head suddenly went under the water, as if dragged. I could see her struggling to get to the surface, succeeding for a few precious moments before she was under again.

Scorpio's rage wasn't hot or explosive like an inferno. It wasn't deadly or volatile like a lightning strike. It was as lethal as being trapped outside on the coldest night. It was a subtle but terrifying thing. Her sneer twisted into something not even describable as fae as she looked to Amaya, who seemed to be slowly drowning, a silent plea on her face. My heart was pounding and I let out a breath I hadn't realized I'd been holding when my lungs demanded air. Scorpio was killing her. The black tattoos glowed in the light. Scorpio's hands were encased in shadow as she stared at the girl in the water who was fighting for her life against something I couldn't see or understand. Amaya wasn't going to live through this, I knew with absolute certainty. I was witnessing this fae's last moments. She resurfaced then. Her skin was snow white and looked like canvas stretched thinly over bone. Scorpio hissed and asked again with a voice like razor wire where the most powerful fae could be found.

Amaya only wailed unintelligibly as if the liquid around her were acid instead of water, still thrashing. It made my blood run cold. I came to the realization that I was about to witness a murder. This confirmed in my mind why the crown guards were missing, Scorpio didn't want anybody alive to hear the prophecy but her. She asked her question again. Amaya didn't answer, too busy fighting off whatever was in the water with her. Or perhaps she was fighting the water itself. Maybe it really was Scorpio's doing. It was hard to tell what was really happening. Scorpio watched callously as Amaya's tortured screams turned into desperate whimpers and pleas, before at last she slumped and went silent in the pool. All at once, as if a line had been cut with Amaya's life, the silver pool returned to its pristine, opaque state, Amaya's body slumped face down, bobbing in the silver water. Scorpio huffed, as if inconvenienced. Horror and rage flared within me on behalf of Amaya who was discarded so easily like trash. That kind of indignation undeserved by anybody, except for perhaps the Barbaric Queen, whose victim list was longer than anybody who had ever walked Meridian.

I hadn't realized I'd been trembling. I almost didn't notice the Barbaric Queen turn on her heel and leave. Leave Amaya in the water, like her life had meant nothing. I barely remembered getting out of my hiding spot. And I didn't remember making the decision to go into the water and try to haul the girl to shore.

I looked at her now half on land, both of us so waterlogged I couldn't possibly drag her out any further. Her body, and mine, soaked the ground beneath us in viscus silver liquid. But at least she was face up, looking at the sky, rather than at whatever terrors lurked below. My eyes moist and my heart heavy, I felt for a pulse. At first there was nothing, as I expected. I closed her eyes, the final thing I could do for her. I recognized that I had lingered here too long. Too many threats could be closing in and had to get back to my father.

Just as I had decided to stand up her eyes flew open, back to that terrible silver churning I saw when she was in the pool. I screeched in alarm and threw myself backwards, reaching for my knife. She only weakly turned her head to me with a ghost of a smile on her face.

"I'm glad you're okay." Her voice hoarse, barely above a choked whisper. *She knew.* Shock barrelled through me like a battering ram, leaving me speechless and in shambles before her. She knew the whole time that I was there and specifically didn't tell the Queen I was there. She saved my life. The gratitude I tried to voice wouldn't come out. I took her hand in mine and held it as I watched her eyes darken through my own tears.

"I'm so sorry," I whispered, my voice fracturing. "Why did you protect me? It may have helped you to—"A sob cut off the end of my question. She squeezed my hand, her reply barely more than a rasp.

"Because my fate was already sealed. But yours was not. I would not give up an innocent life, not to her. I knew when I went into the Moonlight Pool that I would not come out. Thank you for having mercy and pulling me from it. It means the Goddess will have my soul after all."

She choked on her breath as I choked out another sob that wracked my entire body as I clung to her hand, desperate to make sure she knew she wasn't going to spend her last moments alone. In this moment I would've given nearly anything to see the Queen burn for all she'd done to my kingdom. To poor, broken Amaya. My hatred for the monarch was overwhelmed only by my gratitude to Amaya.

"It's all right," she said, seemingly reading my mind. Maybe she was, I mused. She was a seer after all. Goddess only knew what other powers she might possess. "You need to leave. Now that the power of the Queen has left, the terrors that haunt this land will be coming. I don't have much time."

"I don't want to leave you," I choked out. "Let me stay with you, at least." She smiled, a genuine smile that reached her eyes for the barest of moments.

"I'm already dead, Lark." I gasped, shock now feeling like my constant companion today, felt like lightning carving its way through me as she breathed my name. "You have no idea the kindness you've done me. So, I will do you this one last kindness." Her eyes began to darken as she whispered, "You will hear my voice again when the time comes and you need it most. Your choices will decide the fate of Meridian."

"What are you talking about? How do you know me?" I stammered. But the light in her eyes had left, and I watched as her final breath huffed from her body, lying eerily still. Then, I was alone in the Vale once again. I let my posture sag, as I mourned Amaya, a fae I didn't know. I let the sobs consume me for a brief moment. I closed her eyes once again and placed her small hands over her heart. I looked around the Vale and saw the wildflowers that scented the breeze. I picked some with the most vibrant colors. Scarlet. Magenta. Saffron. Orange. Violet. I picked them with care before returning to Amaya and placing them in her hands over her heart.

"Rest well, Amaya. May you meet the Goddess in kindness. Until we meet again." I said the words of the funeral Rite, marking the symbol on her forehead so that the Goddess would accept her with open arms in the afterlife. I stood slowly, knowing I had lingered too long.

And then I heard a twig snap.

Chapter Two

I whirled around to face the threat, my hand going to the dagger at my side. I was startled, faced not with a fearsome beast, but instead I was face to face with the most striking man I'd ever seen. Black hair atop his head so dark it looked like color disappeared around him. Longer tendrils fell into his eyes, giving him a slightly boyish look. And his eyes... His blue eyes were like nothing I'd ever seen. The deepest shade of sapphire. With gold flecks around the irises. It reminded me of soft, buttery sunlight glistening on the surface of the ocean on a warm day.

He was dressed similarly to Scorpio, which sent a flare of alarm racing down my spine. Broad shoulders were showcased by a fine, deep blue tunic and encased in light armor, a weathered chest plate and gauntlets that looked like they were once a proud golden color. But instead of looking dishevelled, or faded out, he looked menacing and dangerous. Strapped to his back was a sword, that he didn't bother drawing despite my dagger pointed at him. Mirth danced in his deep blue eyes and a smirk tugged on the corners of his mouth, pulling me immediately from my reverie.

"Who are you?" I said simply, forcing a bravado I scarcely felt. I tried and failed to come up with something more threatening, to sound more intimidating than I was. After all, when you come across a dangerous animal and you have no other options, you're supposed to be as big as possible to seem like a bigger threat. Though by the look of dark amusement on his face and his casual, unhurried stance, I guessed that all the posturing in the world wouldn't save my life if he decided to end it. My pulse skittered as he looked me up and down. There was an amused lilt to his voice when he replied.

"You don't know?" He snickered at me after getting over his moment of surprise.

"You'd think a blank look and me asking would've made that obvious," I snapped. He barked a surprised laugh I didn't think either of us were expecting.

"If you don't know who I am, then I think indulging you that information would be more of a disservice to you." He smirked as if he knew something I didn't, which was likely the case. He took a casual stride towards me, then another. I raised my dagger and sank into a defensive stance as my father had shown me. His advance didn't stop, as if he didn't notice it, but I suspected it was because he didn't care.

I spared a look around me, but there was no way I could likely outrun him. There was nowhere to go where he wouldn't undoubtedly catch me, gauging from the athletic physique. I refused to back up a step as he stalked toward me, not dissimilar to a cat toying with its prey. I smoothly switched my grip on my blade to my backhand, and it didn't go unnoticed. Quirking an eyebrow, he asked, "Do you have any skill with that blade?"

I shrugged, aiming for the picture of nonchalance, although pretty sure I was fooling nobody. "More than most women see in a lifetime."

Not a lie. My father taught me the basics as a child and I'd practiced what little I did know, but I'd only ever spared with my father.

An argument could be said that I'd defended myself against aggressors in the past, but they were just my peers from Poplar Hollow. Peers with violent streaks and a vendetta against fae they saw as so much weaker than them. How much weaker could I be, being without magic?

In any case, I'd never gone up against someone with skill. But he didn't need to know that.

"If I were you, I'd keep my distance, unless you'd like my dagger to find a new sheath," I warned, trying my hardest to keep my voice level and my pounding heart calm. His eyes lazily raked me up and down, making me wish for more clothing as he did so. I realized with dismay that he was sizing me up.

And by the look on his face, he'd found me wanting.

"Put your dagger away." There was the tiniest scoff in his voice that made my face flush with indignation and something else. "If I want to kill you, that dagger won't do a thing to stop me."

My mouth pressed into a thin line. I knew being bold was probably a bad move, and yet I couldn't seem to stop myself.

"I've never let anyone tell me what to do and I'm not about to start now with you." His eyebrow quirked my retort. My patience was beginning to wear thin as I craned my neck to observe the sun's position in the sky through the tree canopy. I needed to get back to Poplar Hollow. Now. "What do you want? If it's all the same to you, I have to be going, so if you're done ogling, I'll be taking my leave." I squared my shoulders and kept my gaze on his, daring him to challenge me. I knew better than to turn my back on someone like this.

A full, toothy grin graced his features, lighting up his eyes for just a moment, coupled with just a hint of glittering madness. The kind of smile that told me he knew something I didn't.

"It's not all the same to me actually," he drawled, taking his time on each word. "I watched you hiding in that fallen tree. I know what you witnessed." He paused, looking pleased with himself. I hadn't had any idea that someone was there. Where could he had been hiding? I had looked everywhere before moving into the clearing. "You look shocked. You really should check your surroundings more carefully. You never know who might bump into." He paused, most likely for dramatic flair. "Do you know what the Queen does to witnesses?" he asked with a look that said he was going to savor my reaction.

"You're another one of the Zodiac," I whispered, the realization dawning on me. He grinned, malice overtaking the softness of his features. Was he Pisces or... Cancer? The Crowned Assassin? The Water Court's dwelling nightmare. Either way, he was right. My dagger wouldn't protect me from him if he decided to kill me. I likely wouldn't be fast enough even to try to evade his attack. I gauged him, looking for signs. There was no sigil on the breast that would usually identify him. Both Pisces and Cancer were known for their intuition, cunning, and their ability to be cutthroat. I had nothing further to go on to determine who I was speaking with.

I straightened my spine and squared my shoulders again, my back feeling ramrod straight. I tried to ignore the icy chill churning in the pit of my stomach. Everything inside me was screaming at me to run. But I held my feet firmly in place. I willed my fear not to show on my face, and I hoped I had some success with my bravado. That hope died when I saw amusement grow on his features as he pulled his sword out of its sheath with the grace that only a well-trained killer could achieve. The sound reverberating through my bones. That well-trained killer was currently stalking his prey—me.

"Well, I assume you're going to tell me or do you just enjoy building the suspense?" Again, forcing a boldness, while fighting the fear that had firmly taken hold of my pounding heart and sweaty palms. I almost lost my grip on my knife, suddenly feeling like a very heavy weight in my hand. I didn't dare glance at Amaya, still just a few feet away. My gaze remained fixed on him, waiting for any sign of movement. His eyes narrowed at me, that taunting grin never leaving his face. A dry chuckle came from him, clearly amused.

Don't back down, I reminded myself, gathering my resolve. For what I didn't know. A fight? A chase? More extremely unwitty banter? *Never show fear,* my father's voice echoed in my ear, further bracing me. *Assess the situation,* my father had taught me. I took him in with wide eyes. He had a sword he played with in his hands, sharp and lethal looking. I had my long dagger in my hand at the ready. Point: him. I had two more daggers hidden in my boots that he didn't know about. Point: me. I stood a chance if he rushed me. I let my gaze flick to his armor, looking for any weak spots. Beneath the arm was common.

"I'd make it quick, you know," he said, interrupting my thoughts. He busied himself with running his fingers up his blade with all the tenderness he might caress a woman. His eyes solely focused on me. "After what you did for Amaya, you don't deserve to feel pain. You were just in the wrong place at the wrong time."

Panic gripped me fully then. But not for me. *Not here. Not now. My father needed the Aching Cress. I've already lost so much time and daylight. I can't die here.*

"Please," I begged, feeling sick. I abandoned my bravado. I let him see me now. Really see me. The girl who was desperate to get home to her ailing father. "Not here." I took my satchel from my bag to display the contents, the bottom now thoroughly stained with red.

He looked at me unfazed but didn't move.

"My father is extremely ill. We have a healer who swears he can make an antidote from this Aching Cress. I've traveled so far to get it. I'm running out of time. He's running out of time and he's counting on me. If you must take my life, take it after I've delivered the medicine to my father. Please."

"Interesting. You beg not for your own life but for your father's. You are the only one who can save your father? What of your siblings?"

"I'm an only child, and my mother died when I was born. I'm all he has. I'm his only hope for survival. Please," I begged again, the words turning to bile in my mouth. I couldn't help the dirty feeling as I did so and fighting the urge to clench my teeth over the words to stop them from coming out. Begging went against everything in my nature.

To his credit, he did look like he considered my proposal. "How far away is your home?"

I pointed to the north-east, towards home.

"About a five-hour hike if we move swiftly." The sun was getting to a position where it would be at my back on my way home. The forest would be cast in a perpetual twilight, shadows getting longer, more sinister, and dancing as if to taunt me for my rotten luck.

"I will escort you to your village. Then you can make your preparations. I will not disobey my Queen. I will do you this mercy. Do not make me regret it."

Warning tipped his last sentence and I knew there was no escape for me. At least my father would be okay. Using that small condolence to comfort me, I shouldered my backpack. My lack of horror at this faerie telling me that I would soon die gave me pause. I should be terrified. I was sure once we got closer I would be. But now I had some time to figure a way out of this.

Or maybe, if given the opportunity, I could kill him first. That thought bothered me. I tightened my grip on the knife I refused to re-sheath, my knuckles blanching. Could I do that? Take life? After a moment where guilt pulled at me, I admitted to myself that perhaps I could. He looked at me with narrowed eyes, as if he knew the direction my thoughts had taken. I glared at him.

"Then I hope you can keep up, it is a long walk, and I'm not stopping because you're tired."

"Glad to see your impending doom hasn't impacted your attitude problem."

I whirled on him, taking him aback. A flicker of delight lit his eyes.

"Attitude problem? I'm sorry if you're used to women kneeling before you and nobody ever telling you the word 'no.' I'm sorry nobody has ever informed you that you're a jackass. Or maybe your fancy looks got you far in life, but not everyone is mesmerized by nice hair and some muscles. I'd be more impressed if there were signs of a brain or a personality in that pretty head of yours." I flipped my blond braid back over my shoulder in a huff and marched on at a tempo that suggested I thought I could outpace him, my irritation making me forget my dread temporarily. A booming laugh came from somewhere behind me.

"I can't assure you all those things are true, though I'm glad to know you like my nice hair and muscles." I could hear the shit-eating grin on his voice and it grated on my every nerve. He was literally going to kill me and it was necessary to annoy the ever-loving Goddess out of me? Is that ethical? I might actually die of irritation. I briefly wondered if it were possible. I used that irritation to force my legs into a brutal pace, eager not only to get home, but to put at least some distance between him and myself. My lungs burned in competition with my aching feet and calves. Each breath I dragged into me felt like shards of glass in my body. I half expected blood to show up. I liked the pain. It distracted me from my building sense of dread.

"Who taught you to fight with a blade?"

His sudden change in topic spun me. I forced my feet to move faster still as I answered him between labored breaths. "My father. He's the only one in the village who would."

"Why do you say that?" I considered not answering. But he was going to kill me either way.

"I was born without magic," I said, showing my unease. "I've had to survive defending myself against those who would harm me just because I was an easy target." I saw his eyes dip subtly to my thinly scarred forearms. I almost scoffed. The scars on my back were worse, not that I'd show him. "My father, five years ago, right before Scorpio's reign, was a member of the Crown Guard. A member of the Elite."

"He was a Crown Guard?" I nodded. His face flickered with surprise. Crown Guards, especially members of the Elite, don't usually settle down in a backwater town such as Poplar Hollow. So I explained.

"Not long before Scorpio took up the throne, a monster attacked Loc Valen." He nodded, clearly remembering. I wondered if he were in that fight. Or perhaps he was off on... assignment somewhere. I shuddered. "The castle was breeched by a lone monster. My father said it had left a trail of bodies leading to the Keep. They theorized that a traitor had let it into the castle. My father was severely injured when the monster tried to tear his throat out. He barely survived. His leg was also crushed in the battle." I thought of the scars that adorned my father's neck. He wore them proudly. Unashamedly. He thought they were testament to all he'd overcome that day.

"I remember. That was the day the King died."

"Were you there?"

His face darkened. He looked to be reliving a memory most unpleasant.

"I was too late getting back from a mission. I arrived in time to watch the king perish."

"I'm sorry. Were you close?"

"Not particularly." His voice was dry. I believed him.

I remained quiet after that. I took the lead, stepping further in front of him. My back to him made my spine tingle in the worst way, like there was an alarm going off in my body, screaming at me to keep him in my line of sight.

When I turned my gaze to him, he was gone. I couldn't even hear his footsteps. The most unsettling feeling came over me. It reminded me of the time a giant morcasia spider crawled into my room. I went to find something to dispose of it, but it was gone when I returned. Morcasia spiders were poisonous. It took three days of searching to find and dispose of it. All the while, it felt like I was being watched.

This man wasn't a spider. He was a member of the Zodiac Kinship. Stronger, faster, and had far keener senses than normal fae like me. More access to magic than normal fae as well. Whoever this was, Pisces or Cancer, I was in serious danger. It was eerily unsettling not to be able to see him, but I knew he was there, watching. Waiting for me to panic and flee perhaps. I didn't know if I'd get the opportunity. When I got home, when I gave Eldan the Aching Cress, when I said goodbye to my father, I would grab his sword and make a stand, I decided. I'd likely get cut to bits, but I'd go down fighting. Not fleeing like a coward.

I tried hard to not think about the stinging kiss of his sword I would no doubt experience in a few short hours. My brain worked itself around that thought. My life would be over in just a few hours. He'd promised it wouldn't hurt. The terror I hadn't felt earlier began to creep into my heart, toying with what little calm I had left. I clutched my knife with my now-shaking hands, fighting the tears and the bubbling fear by pushing another gear of speed I didn't know I'd possessed, my body howling for a break. My thoughts drifted to Amaya. I hoped I'd made things better for her. I saw the pain she was in, even if I couldn't understand the source of it. Was there something in the water with her? Something I couldn't see?

I felt, rather than heard, his presence behind me suddenly. It was as if the trees whispered his presence to me. There was a crackling in the energy when he was near. Like the air was electrified. It made the hair on the back of my neck stand on end in warning. I turned to acknowledge him, glad he was back in my line of vision again.

"Hasn't anyone told you the dropping down behind a lady is unseemly? Or creepy?"

He blinked, incredulously. "I don't think anyone has ever called me creepy before. Not with this nice hair and muscles." I glared at him. "What? Your words, not mine." His crooked grin had to be the single most irritating thing I'd ever seen. I had to resist the urge to smack him, hard. It was a battle I knew I wouldn't win. "You did a good thing for Amaya," he said, his voice losing the edge it held. I felt the surprise on my face I didn't have the forethought to hide. His feet stopped moving, drawing my own to a halt. I felt his gaze boring into mine with an intensity that wasn't there before. He stepped slightly into my personal space, but not enough to make me retreat. "Do you even understand what you witnessed? What you did? Do you have any idea?" he quizzed.

"Not really," I confessed. "I've heard rumors of the Vale but so many fae talk. I'm not entirely certain what I witnessed with—" I choked on my next words, not bothering hiding my disdain for the Queen.

"The Moonlight Pool isn't so named because of the color," he started, ignoring my tone. "It's actual moonlight, trapped in liquid form by magic."

That explains that silver color and strange consistency.

He continued, "It offers intensified visions for those with The Sight, like Amaya. But at great cost. The pool slowly drains your magic, and once it's gone, it starts on your life. You must not let the pool drain all of your magic or certain death is yours, like what you saw today. Decades of training is needed for seers to use it well, and even then it's risky and dangerous. Skilled seers seldom do unless the need is dire."

"Was Amaya skilled or experienced? Why would she do that?" I was almost scared to ask, fearing I knew the answer; she wasn't. The Cursed Queen had used and killed any seer worth their salt years ago. Now she was tracking down any seer regardless of their skill level and using them and their visions to find a way to break her curse. If the seer weren't experienced or didn't have enough practice wielding their magic, she quickly discarded them. Seers had to have a certain amount of control over their magic to have accurate or clear visions or prophecies. Entire towns had been razed to the ground after the seers Scorpio found for her cause were getting younger and younger in age. Townspeople died protecting their children, their families and neighbors going beyond the Veil of death for their retaliation. The Queen would publicly execute those who openly opposed her, calling them 'demonstrations.' I shuddered, hating the Queen. I hated the rest of the Zodiacs by extension. I caught myself thinking back to what Amaya said to me after I fished her out. The man's face stayed impassive.

"No, Amaya was not particularly experienced. Her visions had greatly disappointed Her Majesty. Amaya unfortunately didn't have a choice besides getting in the moonlight pool. Amaya was told the Pool would be her last chance. Brave the Pool and win, live to fight another day. To get a vision that aided Queen Scorpio. But she wasn't skilled enough to fight off the Pool's magic for long."

So either Amaya gave Scorpio a decent vision and lived, or the magic of the Moonlight Pool killed her. Poor Amaya had somehow accomplished the impossible. She gave the Queen the vision she'd wanted. And the Queen let her die anyway. Made her stay in the pool until it was too late. If she required those with the sight, why would she let one of the few remaining die?

A chilling thought rolled through me. For the same reason that she didn't have any Crownguards with her. No witnesses. Magic could only stop you from talking so much. Witnesses stayed perfectly silent if they were dead. My heart dropped for Amaya. She must have been so scared. That was when the coldness of realization began to sink into my bones.

I was a witness who was about to die too.

"There are far worse deaths that she could've endured, I can assure you, Lark." So he'd heard Amaya speak my name.

"Well, if you know my name, that puts me at a disadvantage," I said, keeping my voice even. He regarded me out of the side of his eye. "You're going to kill me. What harm could it possibly do to tell me your name?" He remained stubbornly silent, as if weighing his options. "I know you're one of the Zodiac, which names you either Pisces or Cancer. So tell me. Who do I have the displeasure of speaking with?" A slight chuckle came from him.

"My name is Lachlan. Or Locke. But most people know me as Cancer, the Prince of the Water Court and the Crowned Assassin, at your service." He added an exaggerated flourish of his hands as if to properly punctuate his title. A smirk graced his features as the color drained from mine.

"The Prince? And the Assassin? Isn't that a conflict of interest?" I said, trying to hide the fact that my mind was reeling. My luck couldn't have been worse. So he was Prince Cancer. The torturer and assassin for the Water Court. I didn't dare look at him as I didn't know what my face would show. He laughed at my reaction and his grin was downright sinister. His expression sent gooseflesh alight over my body. I pushed my nerves to the side as I continued to assess him.

I knew what he was. I'd heard the stories from travelers and merchants passing through our town. He was a walking nightmare, devoid of empathy, compassion, or love. All the things the Cancer sign ironically stood for. But you couldn't have any of those things and be an assassin, especially for what he had done. He'd taken part in the Queen's demonstrations, taking innocent lives because they dared questioned their Queen to the wrong person. They dared defended their family member or friend who happened to having the powers of a seer.

The Barbaric Queen was bad enough. Everyone knew why she did what she did. She was hellbent on breaking the curse upon her. Cancer was arguably worse. It was said he took great pleasure in torturing his victims for Scorpio.

"So I'm going to be another victim to the Nightmare Assassin." I kept my tone frigid, hoping to hide the wavering of my voice.

"You know, I really hate that title. I sounds like I fight nightmares, rather than cause them. It's really false advertising." The grin on his face was as lax as his languid posture, as if we were discussing the weather. Disgust radiated through me.

"Yeah, yeah, I get it. You'll huff and you'll puff and you'll blow the house down and kill everyone inside. Like the monster you are." I bit at him in a dry tone. He blinked, my dismissive tone taking him off guard. I rolled my eyes and resumed my pace in silence. Though, my thoughts were anything but silent. If he expected me to fear him… Well, I would, but I would be damned before I showed him and gave the bastard what he wanted.

An ever-present chill lingered at the edge of my thoughts. *Why was he even here?* He mostly targeted the many threats to the capitol city, Loc Valen, which took him out of our own court often. Given how often the demonstrations were happening, I had a feeling he'd be within our own borders much more. I doubted he would spend much time in the surrounding villages on the outermost circle of our territory. But here he was, walking next to me, staring at me with an expression I couldn't place. Curiosity, perhaps? He gripped my shoulder and spun me to face him, a wicked gleam in his eyes. In the evening light, his face was half shrouded in shadow, making him look every bit the Nightmare Assassin.

"A monster?" he asked with genuine amusement on his shadowed face. "My darling Lark. You've no idea how monstrous I can be." A very real shiver made its way down my back. I knew I wasn't able to hide it. I kept my eyes locked on his, refusing to give in. Goddess damn him, I would not be intimidated. Or at least I wouldn't show him I was intimidated. His gaze was intensely feral as he observed me, drinking in my unease. I bit my lip, a nervous habit. Acid filled my mouth as I raised my lip in a snarl.

"Killing an innocent girl gives me some idea," I spat with venom laced in each word. The words struck true, seeing the flicker of emotion behind the mask for just a heartbeat. His face returned to a cool mask of indifference then as he spoke.

"You were in the wrong place, at the wrong time. Her Majesty's orders are to kill witnesses. I obey my orders."

"So you're a dog on a leash," I challenged, "unable to think on your own." I should care that I was prodding one of the most dangerous fae in the realm, but my irritation had run away with my mouth.

"I know what battles to pick," he said. "I haven't been alive this long by ignoring orders."

"How long is that?"

"A little rude to ask, but 379 years."

It was staggering how old he was. And yet he looked not much older than me at twenty-two years. Members of the Zodiac also had one fun thing: they were immortal. They stopped aging after reaching maturity after being recruited for training in the very secretive Zodiac Guild. Regular fae like me could live for hundreds of years, but we would eventually grow old and die. The Zodiac could on forever without aging provided they weren't killed.

"Anyway," he continued, "the souls of those who die in the pool are trapped within the lake, destined to feed on the next victims who end up trapped in the Moon water. When you pulled her out, you saved her soul from that fate."

He looked at me, brushing back a section of black hair falling into his eyes. "You really had no idea…"

I shook my head. I didn't know why I pulled her from the water. I only knew I couldn't leave her that way, face down like discarded trash. That's why she said the Goddess would claim her soul, after all. I hadn't known what she'd meant at the time. I didn't know Amaya, but something tells me she deserved far better than the end she'd been given. There was a kindness in her eyes that was haunting me still, and I was certain I'd never forget as long as I lived. A predatory smile arranged itself on Locke's face as he looked behind us. His eyes glittered with the promise of pain. He became a hunter.

"I think you're going to get to see that monstrous side of me after all, love." His voice was barely above a whisper. His words sent a thrill of alarm down my spine. I looked around, straining my ears for any sign of danger. Locke placed his hand on the hilt of his sword casually just as I heard the voice behind me.

"Don't move!" said the voice. "And give me your satchel, wench!" I whipped around to find a ghastly, large man behind me. Locke was pinning the owner of that voice with a withering glare that went unheeded. "And maybe hand over your clothes too." His gaze traveling over me in a way that made me feel naked already, grinning at my disgust. Locke opened his mouth to speak but I beat him to it.

"Or," I began, "you can fuck off, and you get to live." I noted Locke's eyebrow raised at me out of the corner of my eye. A ghost of a smirk started to raise the corner of his lips. "I'm in a hurry so you'd best be on your way if you value your lives." I felt, rather than saw, Locke's surprise at my language. Even amusement. My words causing our assailants to bellow a great laugh, hands still on their weapons.

"Looks like we got a live one, boys!" Their answering grins were telling of their intentions that my blood went cold. They had no intentions of leaving. There was four of them and two of us. They clearly didn't see me as a threat and they thought they could overpower Locke with their numbers. I couldn't say I was surprised by my lack of intimidation skills. Nothing about me was particularly intimidating. I knew what they saw: blond hair, green eyes too big for my face, slender, and short of stature. They thought me meek. I looked like the perfect prey. Locke looked like a sure death waiting in the wings, and the look on his face promised a slow, bitter end. But still they persisted. A bad decision on their part.

One of the bandits in front of me stepped forward, ensnaring my attention. His long facial hair looked unwashed and his body and clothing were poorly and unkempt. Three other men fell in behind him, drawing their blades. Their eyes roamed my body freely, making me fight the urge to retch. I reached for my dagger by my side, earning a few more laughs. My irritation flared over my fear as I flourished my blade, ready for their assault. The first man stepped into arm's reach with jeers and threats, clearly not threatened by me. Though he seemed to keep half an eye on Locke. Their smell was an affront to all fae everywhere. I struck in a flurry of razor-sharp steel and fury. He parried the blow at the last second, but my knife dragged slightly. When I brought my knife back to regroup, I noticed I'd left a shallow nick over his cheek. I couldn't help the small grin of satisfaction as he swore and regrouped, leaving me some breathing room.

"Definitely a live one," he said in a low voice, readying his weapon again. "Oh, I'm going to enjoy this."

"Don't you worry, baby doll," said the filthy one from behind him. "I promise I can be real gentle." I heard him whisper to his friend about how he'd bet I was a virgin. I grimaced, not bothering to hide my disgust.

"Who do you think you're talking to? I suggest you learn to speak to a lady with more respect," Locke said, his voice smoother than silk as he stepped forward in front of me. My lack of fear was evident, and I let them see my annoyance with their inconvenience. Fury crossed the leaders face as he sputtered, clearly not used to a woman showing no fear. And clearly not used to anyone talking back when staring down the business end of his blade.

Locke slowly drew his sword, the blade kissing the sheath as he did so. The leader stepped forward again, beginning to close the gap between them. The wind picked that moment to send an array of leaves into the current around his feet before blowing away. Locke looked like an angel of death standing there with his sword drawn. Even the leaves fled before him.

One of the men charged at Locke. The one that promised to be gentle with me. Locke smiled, driving his sword into his skull with a savage grace. The movement was so fast I didn't think any of us saw it until the grunt fell to the forest floor in a heap of gore and blood. I felt something wet splatter on my clothing and I didn't dare look down to inspect, fighting the rising urge to be sick.

I tried not to show my uneasiness with the blood, now soaking the ground beneath our feet. Hunting was one thing, helping the injured was one thing, fae blood through violence I witnessed myself was another altogether. Some healer's apprentice I was. Locke didn't seem to mind; he didn't even slip on the now slick ground as he pirouetted, attacked, and dodged oncoming attacks. He reminded me of a jungle cat. Coil, strike. Coil, strike. He took out each of the bandits, one by one, very quickly and with very little effort. He was about to deal the killing blow to the last thug when I blurted out, "Wait!"

Locke immediately stayed his hand, head cocked my way. The grim amusement on his face falling away into an unreadable expression. The man whimpering his thanks to me, cowering on his knees. I looked at him with as much disdain as I felt. "Locke, make sure he's roughed up enough that he remembers well the day he disrespected a Lady. And his Prince." The man paled when he realized who Locke was. He began stuttering apologies to us both.

"Y-yes, m'lady. Sincerest apologies, m'lady. You're right, I should never have— I mean—Oh Goddess… Your Highness! I meant no harm to you! I swear it! I—" He didn't get to finish stumbling through his apology when Locke hit him hard on the head with the butt of his sword, dropping him to the ground; the sound enough to make me rub my own head in sympathy.

"I don't envy the headache he'll have when he wakes up," I murmured. Locke cleaned the blade of blood before re-sheathing it. My discomfort with the blood must have been evident on my face.

"You can sass someone threatening to assault you, but you're afraid of a little blood?" His voice hard over the word assault. I gave a small, sheepish smile and shrugged. He rolled his eyes, shaking his head with a bewildered look on his face as we kept moving. "You don't suppose those bandits had horses, do you? Anything that could get us to my town any faster?" He regarded me with an odd look, but after a moment, he just shook his head.

"I didn't smell horses on them. We'll be traveling on foot only." Our feet began moving quickly, once again in the direction of Poplar Hollow. I glanced at the darkening sky. Dusk was closing in. I was running out of time. I glanced at Locke, curiosity getting the better of me.

He must have felt the questioning look I gave him because he continued. "Zodiacs have a few other powers and abilities above other fae," he explained. "We have enhanced senses, speed, strength, and each one of us have our own unique abilities depending on our title."

"And what is your unique ability?" He looked at me a long moment as if deciding if it's a good idea to tell me, when he eventually answered.

"As Cancer, I'm particularly in tune with other's emotions. It's not mindreading, but it's pretty close. It comes in handy during interrogations."

"So what emotions am I feeling?" I asked, not even sure if knew the answer myself.

"You're worried." His voice took on a softness I didn't expect from him. "About your father. You haven't even given yourself much time to think about your fate upon returning to your home. Or maybe you're refusing to acknowledge it yet. But you're confused by me. You don't know what to think about me. I felt your horror in the Vale, and I felt your sorrow for Amaya, your desperation to help her. What I can't understand is why? Why did you want to help her so badly when you didn't even know her?" His answer took me by surprise with its accuracy, but with regards to his question, I wasn't sure I knew the answer.

"Amaya was fae like you and me. She was an individual, with thoughts, feelings, hopes, a family. Loss of life and suffering is an awful thing in and of itself. Amaya deserved the kindness I could give her, even if I didn't fully understand what it was I was doing. And besides, I would want someone to do that kindness for my loved ones. Or for me."

He looked at me like he was genuinely considering what I'd said before he stated, "I also hate lives being taken needlessly."

I sputtered and glanced back at the men we'd left behind only moments ago, set to call him on his lie.

"Those men were going to rape and sell you in the trafficking market. Those deaths were not needless. And you were merciful on the last one, even if I didn't agree with it," he finished dryly.

"You're an assassin, isn't death part of a regular day for you? What about the demonstrations?" I couldn't keep the disgust out of my question. His glare zeroed in on me, his gaze was hard on mine. I returned it with equal fervor.

"It is, but only the deaths of those who truly deserve it. And as far as the demonstrations, my hands are tied. The Queen gives her orders and I must carry them out. It's not like I have any choice in it."

At my surprised look, he continued. "I know the rumors about me," he said with a dry amusement, hinting he wasn't keen on those rumors. I couldn't say I wasn't surprised given his earlier comment about causing nightmares and false advertising. He noted my very palpable surprise as he continued with a long sigh, looking very genuine for the first time. "I know the monster Meridian makes me out to be. Like later, when you return home. Your death will not be easy on me, and I will make it quick." I bristled, something he chose to ignore as he spoke. "You don't deserve to feel pain." His deep blue irises swirled as if dealing with conflicting emotions; listen to his Queen and take an innocent life—my life—or let me go and hope the Queen doesn't find out, for which her wrath would be like no other. Or perhaps I was being foolish and looking for compassion where there wasn't any. I regarded him with a somber, sorrowful expression, not knowing how to respond. My words failed me, but I knew he understood how I felt.

After a few more hours, it was truly dark in the forest, but from the hilly vantage point poking out, I could just see my town at the bottom of the hill. I was almost out. Which was good, because I nearly out of time. Night had nearly fallen. The very last vestiges of sunlight bled from just beyond the horizon.

From here, a short way's past the edge of the Deep Wild, Poplar Hollow looked like a single ember on the wind. With the border of the Deep Wild behind us, the likelihood of running into something hideously unpleasant decreased drastically. I felt my body soften, relax in the relative safety in view of Poplar Hollow. *Home.* A thought that warmed me greatly and chilled me to the bone. I broke into a run, the satchel thumping heavily on my back. My entire body ached, screaming and begging me to stop moving, but home was so close. Locke remained close, keeping pace with me at all times, even if he weren't necessarily in sight. He often went to scout ahead to make sure we weren't running into danger. Now he rushed back in my direction, a finger to his lips. I started to whisper what was wrong, when his hand came to my lips, quashing the sound. Before I could pull away, I felt a tingle of magic around us, as he put his arms around me. I balked at the contact and thrashed against him, ready to curse him out. His hands were gentle but unyielding.

"Trust me. Close your eyes," he whispered against my ear as he cast a strong concealment spell, blurring us in the inky shadows against a tree. I closed my eyes, as instructed, feeling his hand move from my mouth to cross over my eyes as if to keep them closed. The other remained on my waist. I felt every inch we connected, searing heat along where my back met his front far too intimately for my liking.

There were a few heartbeats where all I heard were our breaths and the pounding of my heart. This was so… close. I was about to object again when I heard the most haunting of sounds. Something that made the blood in my veins chill to ice. Something that made the hair stand up on the nape of my neck. Something I'd only heard from the relative safety of my home. From right in front of me. The screech of a Blood Wraith. It rattled the trees and I felt it echo in my bones. My heart thrashed in an effort to break down my ribs, or lodge in my throat. Panic spiked. If it weren't for Locke, I knew I would have opened my eyes and screamed. If it weren't for Locke and his grip now tightening on my waist, I was sure my knees would have buckled. It wasn't common for them to be this close to Poplar Hollow. It did happen, but…

My thoughts scattered when I heard it searching through the brush only feet ahead of us, sniffing and searching the air for our scent. I heard the grumble that I knew usually proceeded a roar. There was a strange clicking I heard as it moved. I felt nauseous at the sucking sounds of its movements, like wet snapping sounds, like breaking bones repeatedly.

I couldn't suppress my shudder and I held my breath, falling perfectly still, noticing Prince Cancer did the same. Based on the sound, it couldn't have been more than ten feet away. I prayed the Prince's concealment spell held, because if not… the fate awaiting us would be entirely worse than death.

Another ear-piercing scream, loud enough that I knew my family would have heard it back home. Would Eldan be wondering where I was? My lungs burned in my chest, crying out for air, but I held my breath still. As did Locke. At long last, when I thought my lungs were going to burst, I heard the footfalls far too close to us for comfort walk off at last. It had moved on. I allowed myself one single shuddering breath. I held it once more, my heart throbbing against my ribs. I listened until I couldn't hear it anymore, and even then, I waited several moments before relieving my lungs once more. When I felt Locke disentangle himself from me, I asked him why I needed to cover my eyes. His answer haunted me to the bone: "There are just some monsters you don't come back from after seeing."

Now that my town was so close, I was filled with desperation to get the Aching Cress home and it fueled me with an anxious energy. Energy enough to force my exhausted body to hustle despite my muscles crying out for reprieve. I prayed to the Goddess that the lack of any residual sunset didn't mean that I was too late. That Eldan could still save the only family I had in the world. That all would be well. *Until he had to bury me.* The thought came uninvited and I stamped it down as far as it could go. I forced my feet to carry me as fast as they could, leaving Locke behind. Right now I just needed to keep on moving one foot in front of the other and focus on making sure my father lived.

When I arrived at the familiar house, small for this town, modest, but well kept, I hurriedly shouldered my way inside. A warm fire blazed in the hearth, driving away the cold in my limbs and soothing to my aching legs. Eldan waited in the chair opposite it, my father on a cot close to the fire, visibly shivering even from my place at the door.

Eldan gaped at me as if unable to believe I was there. I dropped my backpack to one arm, holding it to display the contents: the Aching Cress. He took it without a word and took it to the makeshift alchemy lab in our kitchen straight away, everything prepared for my arrival. My legs began shaking as they carried me over to my father. He looked paler and more gaunt than he even had this morning. I reached out for his hand and gripped it firmly, so he knew I was there. His eyes opened all too briefly with what looked to be considerable effort that made my heart squeeze.

"I'm here, Father. I made it back. I got the Aching Cress. Everything is going to be okay. You're going to feel better soon, you'll see." Pouring all my hope into the words, I hoped he'd take heart too. Though looking at him it was so hard to reconcile the man in front of me with my hero. The man he'd be again once he got better. He gave me a weak and waning smile in response, his strength failing to allow him to do more. I couldn't let my father die. He was all I had in the world, the thought of me being too late so abhorrent I dashed it away. The anxiety lingered while Eldan continued wordlessly preparing the Aching Cress in the kitchen. I squeezed my father's hand again gently, not letting go for anything. "I love you, Papa." I hadn't called him Papa since I was a small child, nearly a decade ago. Tears welled in my eyes. Sniffling, I refused to let them fall.

Chapter Three

A strange smell began emanating from the kitchen a short while later. I wrinkled my nose against the unpleasant aroma.

"If that medicine tastes anything like it smells, Papa, then I'm so sorry." I smiled weakly at his unconscious form. As much as I wanted to check on the medicine's progress, I couldn't bear to leave my father's side. On some level, I was aware that my body was aching from head to toe and my stomach was letting me know that it would be ignored no longer. I didn't feel the pain from either. It was like someone else was experiencing these troubles.

After what seemed like an eternity later, Eldan emerged from the kitchen smelling of the foulness of the Aching Cress with a vial of rank-smelling red liquid, looking quite exhausted himself. I moved out of the way as the Eldan tried to wake my father. My heart sunk when he couldn't. It plummeted through my body when my father didn't so much as stir. Even with prodding, and gentle slapping of his cheeks, he didn't so much as flinch. I felt the world fall out from under my feet. But Eldan reassured me that he was still breathing, still with us, and I came back to reality, though my knotted-up stomach stubbornly remained in my throat.

We coaxed small amounts of medicine into my father, gently rubbing his throat to initiate his swallow reflex. He gagged even in his sleep on the medicine, which would have been funny if not for our dire situation. When at long last the medicine was ingested and my father slept fitfully, Eldan finally turned to me with heavy eyes.

"Now we wait. You were very close to the time limit, Lark," he said neither with disapproval or disappointment. Only stating a fact. But it still felt like a sucker punch to the gut.

"How long before we can tell?"

"Hopefully by sunup. Maybe midday. It is hard to tell. But if he is not better by then, you have some hard choices to make." Like what to do with the body. I shuddered. I had been taking on the world with my father since I was born. I couldn't imagine having nobody left, being alone. Alone in a world full of fae that preyed on those weaker than them. And me being without any power, I was the weakest of them all.

"Will you stay?" I asked, hoping he could help me take care of him through the night. I knew I'd avoided my deal with Locke long enough. He only nodded as I pointed him towards my cot. He gave me a questioning glance. I told him I'd sleep next to my father by the fire. That was answer enough.

I rose on legs that felt numb, tingling, and sore all at once, barely feeling like my own as I made my way to the main bedroom that was my father's. I strode into the closet, rummaging around until I found what I'd been looking for: his sword.

It was a fine sword of excellent craftsmanship, or so he'd told me with pride one time. Despite its significant lack of use in recent years, it was razor sharp as I removed it from its sheath to inspect it. The hilt was gold—real gold, I knew. The words "Crown Guard" inscribed lovingly on it. There was a red gem on either side of the hilt, glinting in the limited light of my father's room. I held the sword away from me, checking its weight and finding it exceptionally balanced. I re-sheathed it briskly and crept on silent feet to the front door.

I swallowed the lump in my throat and stood, possibly for the last time. He promised me it'd be quick, and I held to that, not remembering any lie in his eyes. I could go into death if I had to knowing I had saved my father. But I sure as hell wasn't going down without a fight. I mustered up all of my courage and stalked to the door feeling an energy I'd never experienced before and steeling myself for what was to come.

Locke was waiting silently outside the veranda, eyeing me patiently from the shadows.

"How long have you been out here?" I asked, feeling bad that I didn't let him in where it was warm. I knew he was going to kill me, but where were my manners?

"You really need to notice your surroundings better." He pinched his nose in mock annoyance. He was… teasing me? "I was in the shadows in the corner of your living room. The whole time. With you. I've only been out here a short while."

"How could I not see you? I don't understand."

"That's the thing about shadows; it's easy to hide what you don't expect to be there." He showed me a faintly glowing, navy-colored rune on his forearm. "This allows me to blend into shadows seamlessly. With this power, those that see me only can because I willed it to be so."

"Then why didn't you show yourself to me?" He looked at me with a sober expression, one of real sympathy. The first real emotion he'd given me.

"You needed to be with your father. Really with him. Not thinking about me or our deal. You didn't need that distraction at the time." *But the time has come,* were the words he didn't say. I nodded, lifting my sword.

"Why bother with the kindness? You're going to try to kill me anyways," I said, more to myself. Before he could react, I continued. "You're deluded if you think I'm going to make this easy for you." Of all things, he smiled. A real, genuine smile that stopped me in my tracks. He had a dimple on each cheek, faint, but present.

"I expected nothing less from you, Lark," he said with a tinge of... approval? His voice was like velvet as it washed over me. "But not here." He looked towards the edge of the forest where we had just come from and we both walked together. This was it. My final walk. I looked up at the stars I'd soon be joining, basking in their beauty one last time. One final look through the living room window. The firelight allowed me to see my father sleeping. Still, except for the steady rise and fall of his chest. Was it just my imagination or was it looking better? Less shaky? If I felt his pulse right now, would it be strong under my fingers or would it still feel thready?

I shook those thoughts away. My father was safe. That was all that mattered. With a strange sense of calm, or perhaps it was numbness, I followed Locke into the tree line, the full moon above dissolving more than enough of the shadows that seeing wasn't an issue. My feet fell into step behind him as we disappeared into the trees. Locke walked to the center of a small clearing as if he'd scouted it out earlier and turned towards me. A warm, sweet-smelling breeze bristled around the wildflowers underfoot. I drew my sword. The clang sound it made was deafening in the quiet night air. My eyes focused on him, waiting for even the tiniest of movements, not sure what to expect. I remembered how fast he'd been before. I knew I wasn't going to have to just react to his movements but predict them if I wanted to leave here with my life. I entered the clearing and observed my surroundings briefly before coming to a stop a few feet in front of him. *How did we begin? One, two, three, go? Do we shake hands or something?*

"I guess I'll find out after all if you have any real skill with a blade," he murmured as much to himself as to me. I adjusted my grip on my blade the way my father had taught me and sank into a readied stance.

"You're small and slight," my father had said to me when I held a sword that first day. It was almost too heavy for me to hold it, let alone be effective with it. My lack of strength gave me pause, making me doubt being able to learn, but I listened to my father's words. "You won't be using brute force to attack. Instead, you'll be focusing on dodging and slashing your enemy. Wearing them down, attacking when they're tired. Staying one step ahead of them."

"But what if there's more than one?" I had asked then.

"You keep as much distance between them and you, and if they beat you, you go down fighting like a champion. And take one of them with you if you can," he had said.

Those were my words to live by.

I had practiced the twirls, pirouettes, combinations, slices, stabs, and strikes many times. But never against an opponent other than my father until somewhat recently. Some of my peers felt it necessary to attack me and try to claim my life simply for not having magic to deter them, but because of my father's training, I stopped them with naught but my blade. I remembered that fight. I remembered how victory had felt when I staved off their attacks and sent them all packing. There was a magic all its own in swordsmanship. I clung to that belief as I joined Locke in the clearing, who fluidly drew his own sword.

I looked at Locke standing with his sword drawn in the moonlight, shadows shrouding him dangerously, like death incarnate. His black hair was just long enough to blow on the breeze, eyes black in the light, unreadable. His jaw set in a hard line, determined.

I stalked towards him. I needed to harness that calm from earlier. I needed to focus. I raised my blade, testing the weight of it. Locke strode towards me. He made a lazy strike in my direction, one that was meant to be easy to evade or counter. I chose the latter, and countered the attack, flinching inwardly at the metal on metal screech. He smiled. Another strike, this one a bit more straightforward and a bit faster. Another counter, but not as easy. And another, and another. Faster, and faster, forcing me to move my feet. Much more and I was going to have to fall into evasion mode. I scanned the footing around me, looking for something I could use to my advantage, but the look cost me. He charged, making almost no sound as he did so. I leapt to my left, hitting my shoulder on the ground harder than I'd expected but letting my momentum roll me to my feet.

"So you've had some tuition, then," he said, seeming slightly impressed.

"I told you as much," I said simply, not wanting to break my concentration. Another strike, harder this time. Another counter. The reverberation of the blow made my hand vibrate enough I nearly dropped the sword. I couldn't keep this up, I realized, dodging another strike. My lungs burned from the effort of keeping up with him. I needed to get on the offensive.

I saw my opening and attacked, slicing my blade near his chest. It was countered with such speed my eyes couldn't follow the movement. I felt my eyes widen as I realized the insanity of this. The inevitability. I felt the fear rise up and try to consume me not for the first time, but mirrored my anger into my movements instead. I channeled my anger, my sorrow, my determination, and I let it fuel me as I refused to be taken without a fight. I rushed at him with all my might, determined to block a sword attack and body check him to the ground if I could.

The sword strike happened just the way I expected it to, and I countered it perfectly. I picked up speed and slammed my body into him with all the muscle I had. Which was none. It was like hitting a brick wall. I landed lightly on my feet and spun to dart away.

Too late.

I gulped as I understood the gravity of my mistake and I felt his arms wrap around me, one around my wrist, squeezing until I dropped my sword with a hiss, and his sword stung my throat, the cold blade icy on my sensitive skin. Suppressing a shudder, I raised my head high and looked at him over my shoulder, but his back was to the moon now, his face nearly fully engulfed in shadow. The cold sting of his sword still kissing my throat, we stayed locked like that a moment. I wasn't even sure I breathed, waiting for him to slit my throat. For death's embrace. To meet my mother for the first time. Would she meet me at the Veil? His hands were deathly still, perfect contrast to my pounding heart. I closed my eyes waiting for the pain to come.

But nothing happened. The only sounds were our haggard breathing. The anticipation was killing me more than he was. Hot anger seethed and churned in my veins in a hot rush unlike anything I'd known until I was too hot.

"If you're going to do it, then do it already," I snapped, my voice sounding far away and unlike my own. This woman sounded wild. Angry. Strong. Unbreakable. A sound somewhere between a gasp and a sigh came from Locke and he released me, his sword no longer on my neck.

I was free.

I blinked; he was now standing a few feet away, not taking his eyes off me. Staring at me with an intensity I'd never seen before. Like I was the most curious puzzle, but somehow also dangerous. The most beautiful, most venomous snake.

"I don't understand," I said.

"Have your hands ever done that before?" I looked down and saw red glowing runes tracing their way along my hands. Bright, but not glowing like his, the runes churned lazily over my skin. Or, I couldn't deny what I was seeing, within my skin. The runes were a part of me. One with me. I couldn't take my eyes off them. They were beautiful, swirling lines curving their way from my fingertip to my wrists and ending at my elbows. My attention to them made them glow and steam was released from my hands. No, not steam, I realized in terror, smoke.

But that's impossible! That's fire magic. My thoughts became jumbled and came at me too fast to process. But there were a few things of which I was certain: I was born of the Water Court. I should have water magic.

Until this very moment, I'd been magicless despite every effort. Only Fire Fae had fire magic. This isn't possible.

I looked at Locke with horror, my breath coming in rapid gasps as I shook my head, struggling to understand. But the flames that began to lick their way up my arms didn't seem to understand that they shouldn't exist. Popping and hissing sounds blended in with my frantic breaths and shouts of alarm. In a faraway, distant part of my brain, I realized that while I felt extreme heat, I did not feel pain. But that part of my brain was too rational, too quiet, for the not rational scenario unfolding. The shock and the panic. Locke regarded me wearily, as if I were a wounded animal. One he was unsure whether to feed or kill.

"I thought you said you were magicless." His voice was hard and accusing. "How do you have fire magic? Much less Fire Runes? Only the Zodiac are generally strong enough to undergo the rune trials and survive…" I looked at him, my eyes wide. The fire started churning its way up my arms towards my head. It began spreading down my body to the ground, causing the wildflowers to catch. In a matter of seconds, the flames were all around me.

"I don't know! How do I get rid of them? This has never happened before!" I yelled at him, his eyes searching mine from under a furrowed brow for a long moment before he approached me. I looked around, eyeing my sword and gauging the distance between it and me, when he caught my hand, flinching at the heat they were emitting. I felt the cold at the same time his whirling blue runes ran over his skin, emitting a soft blue light. My hands felt immediately colder as he summoned water to soothe my hands.

"I need you to look at me." His tone was firm, but surprisingly gentle. I peeled my eyes away from my hands to his eyes, now tinged with alarm. Alarm for me. "Fire magic is strong, and is directly tied to your emotions, more than any other element. It is the most volatile of the elements. I need you to restore your sense of calm. Take a breath with me." I filled my lungs with air as much as I could, holding it there a moment before letting it go, Locke breathing in time with me. "Good, Lark," he praised. "Again."

We stayed like that for a full minute before I felt my emotions bottom out. When Locke dropped my hands, I looked down to see the runes had disappeared entirely. The flames had also disappeared from both my body and the ground at my feet. I looked up in time to see Locke sheath his sword that I didn't realize he'd dropped to help me. Through the entire motion, he never took his eyes off me. I blinked and blurted, "Aren't you going to need that?"

"For what?"

"To… finish me off," I stammered out, my voice breaking slightly.

He stepped closely towards me; I could touch him. I looked away, unsure what was about to happen. He reached a hand to my chin, and with a devastating gentleness, he tipped my head up to look at him.

"Oh, Lark, love," he drawled with a wicked gleam in his eyes "I think it's gotten far too interesting for that." A lopsided half smirk tugged one corner of his mouth, while his eyes held a thousand questions directed at me. Questions I didn't have an answer to. My heart skittered for a second before picking up double time at his proximity. I felt the heat from his body, warming me despite the night air, now feeling frigid after being so close to flames. I could smell him, like smoldering ashes, musk, and the faintest tinge of something sharp. It took me a moment to place it. Pine. I bit my lip and began to look away, but his hand didn't leave my chin, holding me fast in place. I felt the question expressed on my face. And I wondered what I would do if he closed the distance between us.

With a breath that sounded like a sigh, he released my chin and stepped away, stealing back the warmth from my body. Fighting the urge to frown at the loss of contact, I scolded myself for acting like a lovesick puppy. I felt my cheeks flush as I looked away, anywhere but at him.

"So what happens now?" I heard the smallness of my voice and cleared my throat. The epitome of *"act natural."*

"I guess nothing." His voice was calm, level. Nothing to suggest we had almost kissed moments ago. Or that I'd just fought for my life against him. Or that I'd accidentally somehow had fire magic. "My Queen doesn't necessarily know you were there. My orders are to kill all witnesses. But no harm, no foul, if she doesn't know you were there. It'll be like our little secret." He grinned at our shared secret and held my gaze firm as if to make a silent deal. I couldn't help but grin back.

"Were you really going to kill me?" I asked. He bristled at the question, looking conflicted as he answered.

"When I first saw you hiding in that log, I had every intention of doing so," he admitted with a stony voice. When I didn't break eye contact, he continued. "But I saw what you did for Amaya, and I knew I probably wouldn't be able to complete my mission. I tried several times today to carry out my Queen's orders, but I just couldn't do it."

"Then why the sword fight?" I asked in an exasperated tone.

"I just wanted to see if you had any skill!" He winked at me. *An actual wink!* I gaped at him, my mouth hanging open. He let me think that he was going to kill me all day! Anger rose in me. Before I could stop myself, I grabbed a rock from the ground and threw it at him with all my might. He plucked it out of the air as if it were nothing, increasing my rising fury.

"You let me think I was going to die this whole time! That I was walking up here to my death!" Another stone. "You fought me. Had your sword against my throat. And you never thought to tell me you weren't going to kill me?" Another stone that didn't inflict any damage. His grin widened, seeming to enjoy himself.

"You have every right to be angry. But would you have fought like that if you knew your life wasn't on the line? Would you have discovered your fire magic?" He frowned then before adding, "How do you even have fire magic? Much less runes?" At his question, the stone I held in my hand ready to throw stilled. I almost had forgotten about my summoning of fire magic and the manifestation of the runes up my arms. "Who are you?"

"I have no idea. I've never been able to access magic before in any capacity, let alone an element that isn't my own Court!" I stammered, shifting my weight from one foot to the other.

"Interesting," replied Locke, his brow furrowing.

Interesting? Interesting how?

"And the plot thickens." He certainly had a flare for the dramatics. "You've never been to Everday Isle?" I shook my head. I'd never left my own Court. I had scarcely left Poplar Hollow or the immediate surrounding area.

"You can't tell anyone about this," he said. "But ask your father about your history. Anything he may have not told you. Something isn't right."

"And when he asks why I'm suddenly so very interested in my family history?"

"I don't know, make something up. But you shouldn't ever reveal what transpired just now to anyone. Your life depends upon this remaining a secret."

"You really expect me to never talk about this? Cancer, I've never had access to magic before! I've been marked as prey because of it. And suddenly I do? Suddenly I have the means to put a stop to that once and for all and I can't?" His huge body loomed over me. In the moonlight, I saw his features pinched with annoyance. But his eyes spoke softly of sympathy.

"I understand it's difficult. But if you value your life, you will keep it a secret. Because if word gets out, your life will be over."

"Why?" I challenged again.

"Because fae hunt those significantly more powerful. Or prey upon those born without magic, as you well know." I flinched. "Having more than one element makes you extremely powerful. I have been sent to Fae who have become too powerful to control before. Until you can control your magic enough to fight off the Crowned Assassin, you need to lie low." He leaned in close to me, our faces too close for my liking, but I refused to back up. "I wouldn't be able to save you like I did today if I were commissioned to kill you."

I gulped, thinking of the people in my town. I had very few people I could trust. I could absolutely see any of the citizens of Poplar Hollow selling me out if I were a perceived threat. The somber look that came over my face must have convinced him I understood the danger. Or perhaps he could sense it in my emotions.

"How am I supposed to get better at my magic?" I asked. "If I'm not supposed to tell anyone."

"I know a place. It's far from here," he answered after a pause. "You would have to come with me. I didn't immediately offer because I didn't think you would come. I saw the way you looked at your father. I know you look after him." I cut him a look to show him how right he was. "Would you come with me long term to learn your magic? I can promise you safety."

The ache in my heart was a pain unlike anything I'd ever experienced. I wanted to. I wanted to so badly it was like a visceral need. To learn my magic. To wield it and protect myself. But I thought of my father alone at our cottage and I knew I couldn't leave him. And Father would never leave. I thought of Mother's grave in a meadow not far from here. Resting beneath a great oak tree and surrounded by larkspur. He visited her daily still. Still placed purple wildflowers on her grave. Her favorite color. No. He'd never leave to come with me if I left. And if I did leave, he would be left in a bad spot. My work as Eldan's assistant was what kept us alive. My father and I both hunted to supplement our food stores. But with his injuries, it was unlikely he could take up a steady income without his body breaking down severely. He needed me. I sighed and shook my head, recanting my thoughts to him. He nodded, seeming to understand, sensing my emotions that were currently at war with themselves.

"Then you need to find a place that's secret to practice your magic. Somewhere without prying eyes."

I nodded, knowing full well I couldn't trust anybody in Poplar Hollow. I felt the wheels in my head turn. *Perhaps soon I could take a trip to the Fire Court. Perhaps they could teach me my fire magic.*

"This is where I leave you, Lark. Be safe," he warned.

"Thank you," I said, sobering myself. "For everything." He nodded and turned his back to me starting to stride away. "Wait!" He stopped, his head tipped towards me. "Would you like something to eat, or a place to sleep for the night? It's late, and dark, and I wouldn't want you to come across something in the forest."

A smile that didn't meet his eyes made an appearance.

"I am the thing creatures of the forest hope not to come across, Lark." From anybody else I would have dismissed his comment as posturing. But I'd heard the legends. I'd seen him kill. I'd seen a taste of his magic. I saw the hard edge of him and knew that his statement rang true. As he strode away, I watched a moment before turning and headed back to the town. I didn't get more than one or two steps when he spoke again, turning abruptly to face me. "Oh, and Lark?"

"Yes?"

"Practice your swordsmanship." He winked at me again. With a snicker and his trademark smirk, he turned from me a final time and disappeared in a cloud of mist and shadow. I was left alone at the forest's edge. I put my arms around myself, took in a deep breath, and looked at the sky. I admired the stars that not long ago I was so certain I'd be joining. It was a moment of peace in an otherwise chaotic day. *Or a chaotic life*, a bitter sentiment I forced away as quickly as it had arisen. The soft wind brushed the blond fly-aways of my braid and toyed with my frayed, dirty tunic.

As I walked back to our cottage, I untied my hair from its braid, half falling out to restore some order and re-braid it before I got to the front door. I brushed the dirt and debris off my tunic as best I could not to alert my father of the battle for my life I experienced only moments before.

The fire was dim, its embers dying down, but it was still cozy and warm when I returned. I silently closed and locked the front door, stoked the embers of the fire, added two logs to keep it burning overnight, and curled up with a blanket next to my father. Too exhausted to even wash my face. His breathing had evened out since I'd been gone, chest rising and falling steadily, easily. His breath sounded deeper and less hoarse than it had in over a week. I checked his pulse. A strong thumping under my index and middle fingers answered me. It was the most reassuring thing. Everything that happened today was worth it. My father was going to be okay.

I finally took stock of my body. As hungry as I knew I was, my body needed sleep, exhaustion clawing at me and winning the battle. I ached right down to my bones from my journey today, the warmth of the fire soothing me until my consciousness drifted. I was asleep in moments, dreaming of swirling runes from a long-dead language and eyes of sapphire blue.

Chapter Four

I woke up with a nauseating pain in my stomach. I groaned against the discomfort and the bright morning sunlight prying beneath my eyelids in the most intrusive manner. With a yawn indicating how unready to wake I was, I looked over my surroundings, still blinking away the vestiges of sleep that clung to me. The fire had burnt out, the logs I added last night reduced to a fine ash. But the most important thing I noticed was that my father was not on his cot next to the fire. My eyes widened as I took in the empty, disheveled sheets that he hadn't left in a couple of days since he first took ill.

My eyes darted around the room, but my ears found him first. There was a clinking of dishes that caught my attention. A weak laugh started from the kitchen, followed by a cough, less harsh than before. I leapt to my feet, now fully awake, to find Eldan standing at the wood stove, stirring something in a pot that called to my now angrily growling stomach. The aching discomfort reminding me I hadn't eaten since yesterday morning. I didn't care about that; I stared at my father sitting at the table. They both turned to look at me with warm smiles.

I released a breath I didn't realize I'd been holding as I looked at my father. He looked better. He had slight color to his cheeks again. His eyes, though clearly weary and lined with dark circles, had a lightness to them that hadn't been there since he took ill. My heart flooded with so much love and relief I ran to him and threw my arms around him, not caring that my eyes were burning with tears of joy. A small laugh, slight compared to his usual loud, booming raucous, surrounded as his arms encircled me.

"Papa…" I heard the croaking in my voice, the dam breaking before the tears began. I hadn't allowed myself to cry the entire time he'd been sick. I hadn't cried in a long time for that matter. But it felt so good to let the frustrations of the whole week pour out in my tears.

"Lark." His voice was soft and soothing as he rubbed my back. "I understand I have you to thank for my being here today." His voice was so proud it brought a massive grin to my face, lips turning upwards to reveal my teeth. "My brave Lark."

"I'm just so relieved you're all right, Papa. I've been so worried." I looked over at Eldan, his eyes lined with crow's feet from a lifetime of genuine smiles, the one on his face no different. When he smiled, his eyes smiled too. "The Aching Cress worked? He's for sure going to be okay?"

He nodded as he stirred the contents of the pot again. "Everything seems to have been successful. You brought the aching cress in at the last possible moment, but you made it in time. Your father is very lucky, both to be alive and for you to have done what you did to keep him so."

"Leave it to Lark to make a dramatic, last-minute entrance," my father goaded and I giggled at how normal this all was. I allowed myself to enjoy the moment, bask in the normal. Last night I wasn't sure if I would still be here, much less if my father would. The anxious tension in my body began to relax and my stomach began to un-knot itself at last.

My thoughts strayed back to Prince Cancer, to Locke. The Crowned Assassin. I could not for the life of me believe everything that happened. It seemed so surreal. The Vale, the prophecy, The Prince, the trek home, the sword fight, my magic. our proximity, our goodbye… There was so much to process.

But then there was the issue of the fire magic. Fire *rune* magic, no less. Where on Earth had I gotten runes? Rune magic was largely reserved for those who successfully completed and survived the runes trials. I'd done no such thing. Those in the Zodiac Kinships of any court would wield the power of runes. And perhaps few others. My understanding was that they appeared tattooed on one's skin as a show of power once they'd passed the tests of the trials. Mundane fae couldn't be powerful enough to withstand them. Survive them. How could I have runes?

I couldn't say I didn't attempt to summon flames a few times on my way back to my cottage, but no flames came. I reached within me for a sign that I could somehow access or use magic on some level but found nothing. But the evidence last night was irrefutable. I absolutely had magic somewhere. I was the spitting image of my father, sharing his green eyes, blond hair and bone structure. I couldn't be adopted, so that didn't explain anything. *What if,* the thought came unbidden, *I had two elements. Water and Fire?* Very few fae in existence today that

I could recall had multiple elements. The laws about inter-court breeding wouldn't allow for it. But it had happened nonetheless. Occasionally, two star-struck fae fancying themselves soulmates collided and created an unfortunate heir. None of the myths of fae with multiple elements had happy endings, I realized with a chill. Was it possible I'd simply been well hidden? Poplar Hollow was the last stop for traveling merchants, extremely removed and out of the way. Was our living here by design? Why my father refused to move? Why I wasn't allowed to leave for long periods of time?

I shuddered, thinking of Queen Scorpio who commanded the allegiance of both Water and Black magic.

There must be another way to have multiple elements. There must be, I decided. Perhaps the Library of Aramithia would know more about this. Perhaps I could travel to Loc Valen. It had the biggest and oldest library in the entire Court, possibly even Meridian. I couldn't help the tiny thrill at the idea of seeing Locke again, too, knowing he most likely resided there. As much as I wanted to search out answers, I couldn't deny there were a set of sapphire blue eyes and robust shoulders I wanted to see again too. The library has books dating back to the Creation period where fae had been the most powerful. Before the Courts, when our kind were feral. Maybe I would find my answers there. The warning in Locke's eyes was sincere when he warned me not to speak of the fire magic to anybody. He said my life depended on it. I trusted him, but how could speaking to my father about this put me in danger? Or perhaps it might somehow put him in danger, the thought was hard and unyielding in its effort to take root in my mind. No, the library would be the best place to seek information.

My stomach growled in longing, bringing me back to the present where my father watched me, something flickering in his eye that seemed strange to me. The healer chuckled quietly,

"It's almost ready, Lark." His eyes softened with a touch of concern. "You really should eat more. All that traveling and excitement yesterday and you barely ate. If you keep that up you're going to end up my patient like your father."

I knew he was right, especially with winter coming. Game for hunting already getting scarce as the herds moved on to warming climates for the winter, towards the Fire Court. With any luck, my father would recover from his sickness before the fall came fully and we could stock up on meat for the winter. It was easier to do with both of us hunting.

The beast that had originally wounded my father's leg five years ago was killed, but not before taking several men with it and wounding several others like my father. The day of the attack of Loc Valen. The King was killed and Scorpio was ascended as Queen. I still remember when they came to the door and told me the news. I remember dropping the ingredients I had picked for supper that night in the foyer and letting them whisk me away to the outpost where healers were tending to him. They had carted him home from the capitol well before his rotation had finished, certain he'd die. I could still smell the coppery blood. Eldan had pulled off a miracle saving my father's life and his leg.

His leg was in tatters, gore dripping around him despite the healers' best efforts to staunch the bleeding. His neck had claw marks raked down one side, though the healer assured me that they were just flesh wounds. I was reminded of the horror every time I saw the faint scars on his face. They told me his leg had been crushed by the weight of the beast when it'd mauled him, trying to bring my father with it in death. They were able to clearly see two separate fractures, but Eldan said it was likely there were more. It had taken a lot of time, coin, healing magic, and a lot of potions and herbs, but his leg now a little more than five years later was functional, even though he'd always have a limp. They told us even magic could only do so much.

But my father was a stubborn man, like me I'd supposed, and wanted to rejoin the guard. He enjoyed the work, he'd said, and I couldn't deny his pay was much better than the meager income I had of bringing healing herbs and supplies to Eldan. For him to rejoin the guard, he had to become physically fit again, to hold a sword and fight without pain. It was some time after Scorpio ascended as Queen that my father became well enough to think about returning to the crownguard. He still had a ways to go, and he'd likely never be as effective as he once was, but defending our sovereignty was something my father considered a high honor. An honor he wanted bestowed upon him again if he could. Though even he had serious reservations about serving in Scorpio's Guard after rumors of her viciousness echoed in our town, of her razing whole towns to the ground, searching for talented seers who had no choice of serving her. Fae, entire families, going missing. Streets of towns whose fae defied her running with blood, the public demonstrations of what happens when fae disobey her. Question her. Defy her. Whispers of a rebellion gathering, fae fleeing into the neighboring courts.

It had been so much time, and my father devoted every waking hour he wasn't hunting for our dinner to strengthening his leg. It was during this time my father had taught me the basics of swordplay. But then, early this week, the sickness came. It had been mild at first, nothing he couldn't handle. But then it didn't go away. He'd refused my recommendation of a healer. Instead, it festered insidiously in him and continued to tax his health until finally he was unable to move from his bed. The wound he received while hunting recently became infected and made his sickness even worse. I had sent for Eldan to see to him immediately after his collapse.

Aching Cress was poison, plain and simple. I thumbed through Eldan's notes on the counter on the herb with trepidation. It could heal in the right parameters but only a skilled healer, gifted with magic and a strong alchemy skillset, could make it happen. I glanced at our family friend as he spooned whatever stew he'd made. My mouth began watering over the chunks of venison, carrots, potatoes, and seasoning, pulling me once again back to reality.

I ate without tasting my first bite, practically inhaling the contents. I disregarded the burning of my tongue in favor of lessening the cries of my stomach. When it was finally silent, I reached for a second bowl. I was able to slow down this time and truly savor my meal. I wasn't the only one starving. My father and Eldan gorged themselves as well. It wasn't until now, sitting and eating with my family and friend, that I realized I wasn't the only one suffering while my father was ill. Eldan had been here every day, eating and sleeping and replenishing his magic when he could. My father had barely eaten anything more than broth in several days and fell on his stew like a ravenous beast.

We sat around the fire talking well into the afternoon, our bellies finally content. We played dice games into the evening. I couldn't help but fall back to a time when life was so much simpler. I laughed for the first time in weeks, watching my father seeming to get better by the hour. His cough was all but gone and light had returned to his eyes. Color rose to his face again, replacing his parchment-pale complexion from earlier and it made my heart sing, the normalcy of the evening a far cry from the desperation of the night before. Of the last week. Normalcy that if things had gone differently, I might not have been here to witness.

In my mind's eye I saw Locke in the clearing, features half shrouded in the darkness and unveiled by moonlight. The moon traced the edges of his armor and lit a halo of light within his black hair that fell ever so slightly into his face. I recalled his sapphire eyes. The casual grace with which he withdrew his sword. He'd asked me to go with him, likely to Loc Valen to train to use my magic. Saying no was likely the hardest decision I'd ever made, but looking at my father, I knew it was the right one. I couldn't leave him long term. He needed me.

Eldan took his leave not long after, he and my father exchanging a few words I couldn't hear. I met Eldan at the door with promises to be ready by daybreak tomorrow to gather supplies for him. His eyes were soft when he put his hand on my shoulder in a kind gesture before walking out the front door. I watched as he turned the cobblestone corner and went out of sight.

My father and I sat together in a comfortable silence for some time, neither feeling the need to speak. Just happy to be near each other in peace for the first time in over a week.

"Are you going to tell me what happened in the forest when you went to get the Aching Cress?" My father said out of the blue. I looked at him, keeping my face carefully blank.

"What do you mean?" He eyed me with a look that told me he wasn't buying it.

"You've been quiet, more so than usual since your return. You keep looking out the window. I can't tell if you're searching for something or waiting for something. Or someone," he added. There wasn't judgement or disapproval in his voice. He knew I was well old enough to make my own decisions.

"There's nothing really to report, Papa," I cajoled, not wanting to tell him about Cancer. Locke, I corrected myself. A crowned Prince of our Court and a famous assassin. Legends and tavern tales alike painted him to be a monster, but after last night I wasn't entirely convinced. There were times he regarded me with genuine concern, even if for only a moment. He'd stopped those thugs from hurting me. And worse, he went against his Queen's orders and let me live. But I wasn't ready to tell my father about him yet, wanting to keep the tale to myself. Besides, how would Father react if I told him I'd traveled with the Crowned

Assassin? Especially the part where he tried to kill me? As a former Crownguard, he would've seen Locke in passing, or even protected him. A part of me wanted to think he'd be proud, but I was certain horror would be the predominant emotion. If I told him about Locke, I'd be too tempted to tell him about my magic. Locke told me not to tell, and for now I would listen.

"It was a very long trek to the Yemerian Vale," I said. "There were a lot of things I'd rather not see again." I thought of how Locke had destroyed those bandits, and the proximity of the blood wraith. I knew it showed on my face. "But I'm fine, and you're fine. That's what matters to me. Everything is worth it because you're okay."

"Then why is my sword by the front door?"

Shit! I hadn't put that away yet?

"I took it with me for protection to the Vale," I lied smoothly, feeling icky for doing so. I hated lying to my father. For not telling him any of this and feeling like I could not confide in him. I planned to tell him about it once I had returned from Loc Valen—with hopefully more answers than I had now. I did not want to worry him after he had been so ill; it wouldn't help anybody. "I do want to discuss something with you though, Papa." He quirked an eyebrow, waiting for me to continue. "I'm going to visit Loc Valen. I want to go to the library." He choked on his tea.

"Why would you need to go all the way to Loc Valen for that? We have a library here that's perfectly good!" he sputtered. I almost laughed thinking of the library in my town, if you could even call it that. It was a collection of books that were written by locals. I'd read most of them, very few on anything scholarly. None of them carrying anything close to the information I sought. I used that to my advantage in what felt like a budding argument with my father.

"You know as well as I do that our library has little on scholarly literature," I started, wheels in my head turning as quickly as I could manage. I didn't want to lie, but I wasn't ready to give the truth yet either. "There are some areas of study I'd like to investigate. Medicine being one of them." Not entirely untrue. There was a reason I was an errand girl for Eldan. To be a good healer, you must have knowledge of the body, alchemy for potions, and botany for healing herbs. A great healer could utilize magic as well. Eldan was a great healer. Under Eldan's guidance, that was to be my future as well. Minus the magic part. Well, *maybe not now*. It was amazing how that little thought perked me up with such glee. I felt a brightness about my future I didn't think I'd ever felt before, filling me to the brim with hope. Yes, I would do some reading up on the subjects in the library of Aramithia. But first, I needed to look up the history of magic in the Courts.

My father considered a long moment, taking long sips of his tea. My own cup was by my feet, cold and forgotten about until now.

"How long would you be gone for?" he asked slowly, appraising my reaction.

"You'd need a horse." I lit up. Riding was my favorite pastime and he knew it. Eldan let me ride his horse when there was need.

"It's a two-day journey, so probably a week? Perhaps longer if my research goes well?"

"What will you do for lodgings?"

"I've been saving as much as possible from my work with Eldan. I have enough to be comfortable for a few days in Loc Valen." It was true. My father had done odd jobs around the town to make extra money, but with his ruined leg, these weren't the sort of jobs that paid well. Or often. To make a meager profit, he often had to complete multiple to make it worth his time. It pained me to see him sore after every day of hard work, but with his extra income, the money I had saved could be stretched to allow me to go to Loc Valen. With food and housing paid for each month, I would put away any spare money in a small cupboard I fashioned out of a floorboard next to my cot. It wasn't much, but enough for this.

"I understand you want to do this." He smiled tightly. His brow deeply furrowed, the telltale face of my father's disapproval. "But it's dangerous. The monsters are getting out of hand with the Guard having fewer outposts, the bandits are running rampant and there are growing whispers of the rebellion. Civil war, Lark. I don't think you should go."

"Papa, do you have any idea what perils I faced yesterday?" I tried to keep my voice composed. "Do you notice how I'm still here, unscathed, I might add?"

"You forget your training with a blade is limited, Lark!" he snapped, the scars along his eyes seeming to jump off his face at me with his scowl.

"I don't want to argue with you, Father. I'm going to Loc Valen. I'm old enough to make my own decisions and I'm strong and capable enough to see them through."

"What are you looking for? What's in Loc Valen that you have such urgency to go?"

"You taking sick and me not having a clue how to help you certainly lit a fire in me!" I snapped and I hated as I watched his gaze fill with sorrow and guilt. I hated having to play the guilt card. "I refuse to watch you, my only family, almost die again." I gentled my voice. "I'm going to the court's capitol for my education. You were always the one who told me education opens all doors magic can't."

He considered what I was saying. His eyes were restless as they took me in. It was like he was seeing a woman standing before him and not his helpless daughter who came home covered in bruises and cuts from the latest harassment.

"Perhaps I should accompany you."

No! I wanted to scream.

"I'll ride faster with just me," I said gently. I needed answers to my questions and I didn't need him snooping around and asking questions of his own. And if by some miracle I saw Locke, perhaps he could give me a few lessons while I'm in town.

"Lark, I don't like this one bit," he said with a note of exasperation that let me know I'd won. "I don't think it's safe, not remotely. But I also know I can't truly stop you or change your mind once it's set on something. It's truly set then?" I nodded. "All right, then. Grab your blades, we're going to go over some drills."

The drills lasted well into the evening, the twilight sky bleeding sunset orange and painted pink with hues of blue. By the time we finished, I was sweating and exhausted, my father more so, but the lessons he'd given me were worth it. Guilt lit me up, seeing how weak he still was, and how much his leg still pained him.

He'd always taught me heavily on how to defend myself, focusing less on my offense. He wanted me to be more proficient in my attacking skills, such as takedowns, swordplay, and my footwork. All things I had to have proficiency in due to not having any other way to defend myself. It was what kept me alive sometimes. He wanted me fully prepared for my journey tomorrow. For whatever I might face.

We settled in for the night after making a list of preparations for the coming week with me being away for the next few days. First, I had to deal with Eldan. I yawned and fell asleep, planning how that conversation would go in the morning.

I was up before sunrise, full of energy for the first time in weeks. I washed my face in the basin, looking in the mirror at my reflection, light in my green eyes for the first time in a long time. I wrangled my long blond hair into a braid that fell over my shoulder. My green tunic belted with a worn brown leather sheath that had seen better days but did the job of holding my dagger by my side. Legs crammed into leggings and brown leather boots equally as worn. I grabbed a black overcoat to fight against the early morning chill. I added a log to the fire and stirred the embers quickly for Father before I quietly exited the front door.

Eldan was waiting for me as I arrived at daybreak, like I had promised. My father had used a lot of his resources during the past week, so I knew I was in for a long day. I greeted him with as much cheer as I could muster this early on a chilly morning, my breath hanging in the air. He returned his greeting with a piece of parchment, bigger than usual. I opened it to find an extensive list of herbs and resources. I gawked at it before looking up at him, unable to contain my surprise. He grinned at me.

"My stores are nearly spent. Your father was not my only patient this week," he said. "You brought back enough Aching Cress to last a long time though." I hoped for forever.

"Can I discuss a matter with you before I head out?" When he nodded, I explained that I needed to go to the library in Loc Valen, citing medical tutelage as the reason. Not entirely a lie, I reminded myself to feel better about the half-truth. I asked about borrowing Haven, his lovely black mare. He often let me borrow her for pleasure rides and to help keep her exercised, but my asking to borrow her for such a journey... I knew this was a large ask. He opened his mouth to respond, but I wasn't finished yet with all the reasons he should let me go.

"I promise I'll work extra hours, go further for more rare ingredients." The words were tumbling out of me. "In fact, I could pick some along the way and I could stop by the botanist in the city. They will have stores of items harder to find here."

"I know how much you want to be a healer," he said slowly and thoughtfully. "You realize you need magic to be as effective as you want to be." It was somehow both a question and a statement.

"It helps. But I've saved lives without it." I reminded him. It took all my willpower not to tell him about the fire magic. If I had fire magic, I could do healing spells. In theory anyway. I just needed to learn *how*. His eyes were hard, missing nothing. He knew, I realized in that moment that he knew I wasn't telling him everything. "Eldan." I looked him straight in the eyes, beseeching him, "I wouldn't be asking if it weren't of the utmost importance." A long moment of silent communication passed between us. All I could hear was the blood rushing in my ears. I eyed his deliberately blank face with dismay. It was the look he gave me when he was going to let me down. He was going to say no.

"How important is this?" His sharp eyes studied my reaction, missing nothing. "What happened in that forest yesterday, Lark? You've been different ever since you came back. What did you see in the Vale?"

"It's one of the most important things in my life," I said honestly. "If I don't go, I may never amount to all I can be." And that was the truth. I picked my words carefully. A small part of me wanted to know if I truly could be a powerful fae of this generation. All the fae I could help if I were. And if I could get a handle on my magic, I could make something of myself. A healer, or even something greater. And beyond that, I thought the words at last I'd been too afraid to think, I'd never have to be a victim again.

"There are a lot of risks. Bandits and raiders. The Barbaric Queen herself. Refugees fleeing, neighboring towns pillaged. There are whispers of civil unrest, possibly even war," Eldan explained, echoing my father's words from yesterday. War in the Court would be devastating if it happened upon our little slice of Earth. But so close to the edge of the realm, Poplar Hollow was relatively safe.

"I can take care of myself, Eldan." A hard edge to my voice. *I'm capable,* I reminded myself. *You have no idea how much I proved it last night,* I mentally added, reliving those moments I crossed blades with Locke. I knew Locke wasn't really trying, but the Crown Assassin hardly compared to what I'd likely see out there. I truly felt I would be okay.

"All right. Haven will see you there safely. Goddess knows she likes you more than me at this point. That horse forgets who feeds her." He rolled his eyes. "When will you leave?"

"As soon as your supplies have been restored." The lilt in my voice betrayed my excitement, my enthusiasm. I bounded towards him and threw my arms around him, barely giving him a moment to return it as I flew off his patio before he could change his mind. "Thank you!" I hollered over my shoulder, the sound of a rare burst of laughter from him following me as I went.

I threw myself into my labor with a vigor I hadn't known in a while, forgetting to even eat my lunch of dried venison, some bread I attempted to bake myself (and failed), and an apple. The sweat collecting on my brow drove the chill away from me. My hands were cramping by the noontime hour from carefully picking flowers listed on the parchment Eldan had given me. Flowers, berries, roots, certain grasses even. Some needed to be dried and ground down to a powder. These in turn would be used in potions to cure various ailments.

During my moments of travel and looking for herbs, after glancing around surreptitiously to make certain I was alone, I stuck my hand out, willing the flames to erupt. I reached deep within myself, searching for the fire that I tried so hard to banish before. But no flames came. I tried to not to let the disappointment sting, but that was another thing I failed at.

I had finished gathering many of the herbs requested by the time the mid-afternoon sun began beating down in earnest. I had done this for so long for Eldan that I knew where all the best growing places for each herb and it made for a quick job these days. When I first began working as his apprentice, this task would take me hours more, if not days. By dusk I had finished preparing the herbs for medicinal use and had painstakingly put them away in Eldan's jars and his apothecary cabinet, my hands cramping and ached from the fine work and using the mortar and pestle for long hours. I grunted as I put the various herbs and ingredients away in each of their overly tidy little jars and drawers, all labelled in Eldan's perfect cursive writing.

Eldan nodded his approval at my handiwork and gave me the go-ahead to leave when I was ready. I thanked him again and promised him I'd bring home ingredients, potions, and whatever else he wanted. He gave me a coin purse, a list, and a warning that he'd be looking for a receipt for all the things I bought on his behalf. *As if I'd spend his money,* I bristled at the accusation. After deciding to leave the next morning with the sun, I promised to bring Haven home happy, healthy, and sound, and I ran out before he could say anything further. Though I did hear some grumbling behind me as I left that sounded an awful lot like a prayer to the Goddess for my safety. I tried to not let the chill creep down my spine as I headed for home. The fire glowed through the front window when I arrived on the front porch, giving an image of warmth and comfort. I smiled as I walked through the door to see my father assembling supper onto two plates, and two cups of water.

"Perfect timing," my father chimed as he invited me inside. My body thrummed, exhausted and starving from the last forty-eight hours of work and travel. I plopped inelegantly into my seat with him and ate eagerly.

As we ate, I told my father of Eldan's approval of my journey and that I'd be leaving the next day.

"Are you sure this is a good idea? What of the tutors here in the village? Surely, they are capable of teaching you what you want to know." He stopped when he realized that we'd tried the tutors here. I told him that if a good healer that didn't use magic existed, there would be record of them in the Library of Aramithia. My entire life I had tried to use magic. Element magic, even the most basic of spells I couldn't perform. I thought back bitterly to all those times, all those classes when my classmates were able to use spells, craft water and ice, and I sat awkwardly in the back trying to avoid notice, completely unable to participate, no matter how hard I tried.

But when I recounted the fire magic, I remembered it had been easier than breathing. Stopping was the harder part. And that Locke so easily shrouded us against the Blood Wraith. Had so easily summoned water, even cooled the temperature of it to calm the heat coming from my palms. I remembered how disturbed he had looked at my display of magic. A display I hadn't been able to do since, and it was time I got an explanation.

"It's my best bet at bettering my healing abilities." I hated that I was lying to my father. I had never kept secrets from him, but Locke's warning about his safety rang in the back of my head like a warning bell. "This town can't help me more than it already had in that regard. If I'm going to help fae, our townfae, I must learn from the best."

I didn't tell him my fears. I didn't tell him about the fire magic. I didn't tell him about Locke. And I prayed that was the right choice.

"How long will your journey be?"

"I only plan to be gone a week at most."

"Be sure that it is only a week, Lark," he said, his eyes soft, but his voice had an odd edge to it. "You're needed here and have great responsibility."

I set out after a night of fitful sleep. I packed obsessively, trying to plan for any eventuality. I brought with me food and coin for the journey, hidden in various hidden pockets I'd sewn into my satchel and into Haven's saddle pad. My father's sword sheathed on my back, like I'd seen Locke do before, my trademark dagger still belted on my hip. I placed a small, sheathed knife inside each of my knee-high boots at my father's behest. "You never know when a hidden weapon may come in handy." His words made me put another sheathed knife in my other boot. I wore a green tunic and riding pants, fine enough to blend into the city, but not so fine as to attract attention. I braided the front of my blond hair into a crown on my head and left the remainder to fall free so I could feel the wind of it when Haven and I galloped down the road. I was about to wear my usual faded black overcoat when my father approached me with a box in his hands.

"What's this?" I asked, eyeing the box with curiosity.

"Open it and see for yourself." His voice was soft and his eyes said he was somewhere else. Somewhere in a memory. "This was your mother's," he said at last.

I took a sobering breath. My father barely spoke of my mother, much less gave me her things. I knew so little about her. Father simply told me that she'd passed beyond the veil during childbirth. He always looked so heartbroken and tormented whenever I brought up questions. I couldn't bear to see my father like that, so over time I stopped asking. My heart thudded in my chest, curiosity eating me as I wondered what was inside. In the box was a thick cloak of the most beautiful emerald green. When I donned it, placing the cape over my head, I witnessed something I'd never seen in the two decades I'd been on this earth: a tear misting in my father's eye. "You look so like your mother," he said, wiping that single tear before it could fall. My breath felt as if it had been wrenched from my lungs. This was the first time he'd ever said that. But I also didn't get it. I thought I resembled my father. Though I supposed I'd never actually seen a picture of my mother, so I truly had no frame of reference. "You look beautiful." I wrapped my arms around my father and his encircled me as well as I whispered my thanks. When I pulled back he said, "This cloak becomes you. Your eyes look even more green with it on. I'm sorry, Lark, I should've given it to you a long time ago. I know she would have wanted to you have it for the journey though." My eyes welled with tears as I told my father it wasn't his fault. I knew he wasn't ready.

"There's one more thing," he said, looking into the box again and pulling out a hair pin. The pin itself was gold and decorated with an intricate design of leaves made of what looked to be some sort of green crystal. They couldn't be emerald:

our family was much too poor to afford such an item. But it glimmered in the sun nonetheless as I pulled my hood down and pinned it where my braided crown met the back of my head. "You're ready," he finally murmured as he walked with me to the veranda where he said goodbye to me again.

"Papa I'm only going to be a couple of days," I admonished him his excessive caution.

"Let an old man worry about his only daughter, would you?" he teased, a twinkle in his eye. "It's the first time you've gone away from home by yourself for this length of time. I know you're capable, Lark," he added quickly, "but it's my job to worry. After all you've done for me, let me fuss." He handed me a large skein of water for the road, which I took gratefully.

"I love you, Papa," I said, squeezing his hand.

"I love you too, Lark. Just a couple of days, right?" I nodded my promise to him. I turned and walked towards Eldan's stables before my emotions got the better of me and I called this whole thing off. I squared my shoulders, feeling the determination.

Haven waited for me in her stall. Her tack set out by Eldan for me near the cross ties. I sent up a silent thank you to him as Haven nickered to me. With a pat and a carrot as my payment, I began preparing her for the journey ahead.

The sun had well risen when I led Haven out of the stable and mounted up, careful to not jab myself or the horse with any of my weapons. Once seated comfortably in the saddle, I didn't need to push her on, she left toward the main road in an excited trot that had me sitting back in the saddle.

"Easy, girl," I crooned, patting her neck. "We'll be on the open road soon." I settled my cloak around me as we walked. I had to admit the color was even more stunning in the sunlight against an ink-black horse. Every so often, I had to remind Haven we were only supposed to be walking at this point, much to her irritation, which she pointed out to me by pinning her ears. I grinned. This was going to be a fun ride.

I turned her toward the open road and I lengthened the reins, letting her go, thundering hooves carrying me swiftly towards my destination. It would be the farthest away from home I'd ever been, and for the longest amount of time. I couldn't wait. And I couldn't tell if I were selfish for that or not.

But I was ready to get out of Poplar Hollow, even if only for a few days.

Chapter Five

Loc Valen. The city I couldn't wait to experience and explore lay ahead of me. It was picturesque from my position on the hill. There was a large descent down the hill and then back upwards, as if the city itself forced the ground around it to lower to admire its greatness. And it truly was great. Magnificent even. The pleasantness of salty sea air toyed with my hair; the sea just beyond the city seemed to spread as far as my eye could see. The alabaster walls around the perimeter were fortress-like and well guarded. Looming spires in the distance caught my eye—the massive, sprawling castle, Castle Ari'inor. Where the Zodiac Kinship resided, where Cancer resided, ascended far ahead in the exact center of the sprawling city, the towers of the castle taller than any other building in the whole of Loc Valen. A heavy mist blanketed everything despite the sunlight, giving the city a haunted appearance. The guards' patrolling presence along the battlements did nothing to dispel that illusion. Looking at it and seeing very little of the surroundings made me feel like a page in a book yet unwritten.

A single cobblestone causeway inclined gently to the main gate, seemingly connecting the city with the lower terrain perfectly. Maybe causeway was the wrong term. It felt more like a bridge with the sea as the backdrop. People often said the capital of the Water Court was a jewel in and of itself. And they were correct. The skyline of this city was pure perfection.

Loc Valen's swooping architecture was even more striking up close. I had never seen anything like the heart of the Water Court: long cobblestone roads teeming with all varieties of life. Merchants loudly, even obnoxiously, advertising their wares, fae of all walks of life bustling about on foot, all seeming to be in a hurry. Horses or teams of oxen pulling heavy carts drove by, surprisingly quick despite their size. The picturesque streets were lined with towering pale brick buildings that seemed to be reflecting the sunlight, making the city seem to glow. There was one true showstopper in the city though. Something old and unique to the city of Loc Valen were the waterways that made up the main arteries of the city. Fae in boats of various sizes, from a couple in a long rowboat to several in a large boat, luxuriously dining in view of the city. Over top intermittently were wide stone walkways for pedestrian travel, made of the same pale cobblestone as the buildings. The sun shone pleasantly on the crystal-clear blue water, the mist from beyond the walls nonexistent here.

I arrived at a town square that seemed to be a common gathering point. There were fae dining at various cafes or restaurants lining the perimeter, more merchants begging for attention for their kiosk, lost travelers wandering aimlessly, and entertainers cracking jokes with, or making jokes of, the general public much to the amusement of onlookers. There were shop fronts for various businesses; from here I spied the signs for a jeweller, a blacksmith, and an alchemist.

I urged Haven to walk towards a hitching post I spied in the center of the square, where she could get some rest and sustenance, and I could get better acquainted with my whereabouts. I dismounted, removed her bridle, and replaced it with her halter. I led her to a hitching post lined with hay and fresh water, and looked to have soft footing with shelter from the sun. All things she was definitely in need of. I sought out the guard charged with the safety of the horses and inquired about cost.

"It's usually five coins," he said with a smile that made me feel dirty. I kept my face pleasant as I felt his eyes rake up and down my body, pausing briefly near my chest. "But for you, let us make it three."

"And you'll take care of her and everything on her?" I asked. He nodded, giving Haven a pat. I handed over the three coins with thanks.

"If you want, you can place your saddle on the saddle rack in front of her trough." He pointed to it. "I keep my men on the look-out for the horses and their riders' belongings. I promise nothing will go missing." Indeed, there were seven makeshift stalls, and three horses, now four including Haven, were happily munching away looking content. Their tack neatly placed on the saddle racks, four large fae guarding them from their places close by, spread out to attack any threat or thief that dared present itself. I untacked Haven, who shook her body in delight of losing her saddle and drank deeply from her water trough. I grabbed my satchel with the coin and gave Haven a parting pet, telling her what a good girl she was. She huffed in response. I laughed before turning to the man again.

"Where can I find lodgings for myself and Haven for the night? Perhaps two? And I'm also looking for the Library of Aramithia. Could you please point me in that direction?"

"There's an inn practically on every block, lady." He half scowled. "You must be new to the city?"

"I'm here on business," I said flatly, though not rudely. He eyed me up and down again, eyes going to my sword and my knife as if noticing them for the first time.

"What kind of business?"

"My business is my own." My tone was hard, shutting down the conversation. "Just the direction of the nearest accommodations for myself and my horse will be all I require from this interaction." His eyes went up in surprise before muttering an apology and pointing west, towards the corner of the square.

"Close to where that minstrel is performing," he said, stuttering an apology again.

"Just take care of Haven," I said, softening my tone before walking in the direction he pointed me in. Lofty buildings loomed impossibly far overhead as I took in my surroundings and the fae around me. There was so much beauty here, even the fae were beautiful. Not dirty or disheveled from long days of work like back home. Here, I had doubt that most of the females, so beautifully dressed, had calloused hands or knew of such labor. The minstrel that had been pointed out to me was singing love ballads, receiving a coin in his hat from time to time by appreciative ears. Fae women were dancing in dazzling gowns of chiffon and silk, clearly a Loc Valen custom, these dresses. I looked down at my traveling attire and realized if not for the elegant cloak my father had gifted me, I would be sticking out like a sore thumb. I thumbed the soft material of the cloak further around me as if to hide my plainness in it. I quickly crossed the street at the first lull of equine and pedestrian traffic until I stood in the inn's entrance.

The interior's smell his me first: stale ale, mead, and something stronger, mixed with the earthy smell of roasting vegetables. A homey smell, if you also had a bar in your kitchen that was spilled. Often. There was a hint of a lemon-scented cleaner as well. It seemed out of place with the other assorted smells. Patrons busied themselves with their drinks and conversation, paying me no mind as I walked to the counter.

The woman behind the bar addressed me as she wiped down the counter in front of her.

"What'll you have, miss?" There was the slightest lilting accent to her voice I couldn't place.

"I'm looking for lodging for myself and my horse. Do you have accommodations?" She nodded and I inquired about the price. Twenty coins for a night. Twenty? That seemed steep and I had half the thought of trying someplace else, but I had the coin to cover it and then some for later. Maybe I'd buy one of those pretty dresses so I could move about without sticking out so much. Blend in more. I paid my fare and ordered a drink while she fetched my room key. I was extremely parched from the journey, my skein long since empty, and I drank deeply when it arrived in front of me.

She showed me to my room so I could drop off my satchels. I dropped my bags down on the bed with an exasperated sigh. The bed was calling for me. And I wanted nothing more than to lie my head down among the pillow and blankets after two days on the road, but I knew that would have to wait.

The bar maid showed me the barn next. Like the temporary rest stop Haven was currently in, this place was also guarded. Four of its six exceptionally large stalls were currently occupied. One of the stable hands got to work preparing Haven's stall with soft bedding, hay, and more fresh water. Haven would be very pleased. I turned back to the woman and asked for directions to the library, and ideas on where to go shopping. With a wide grin, she gave me my directions to the library and told me if I wanted to wait for her to get done work in a few hours, she would be happy to take me shopping herself. I searched her face for trickery but her offer seemed genuine, so I accepted. I told her I didn't know exactly when I'd be back from my business at the library, but I'd meet her as soon as I could. She dismissed me, telling me she'd find me when I got back.

"My name is Lark, by the way," I said awkwardly, realizing I'd not introduced myself. She smiled, brightening up her face.

"Lorelei," she replied. "It's nice to meet you, Lark. You're clearly not from here, what are your plans while you're in Loc Valen?"

"I'm just here on errands for our town healer, and to do some personal research," I said being as vague as I could, while also trying to be friendly. She seemed to get the hint and she changed the topic. We chatted animatedly about various tourist places in Loc Valen I should see while I was there.

She'd grown up here, and the inn was her family's. It didn't take long to like Lorelei. Her grin was contagious and her enthusiasm sparked one conversation after another. I couldn't help but think how nice it was to be treated like a regular person and not like a "freak" for not having magic. It felt liberating to know that nobody in Loc Valen knew of my lack of magic and how I could be a whole other person in this city; not who I was back home. I relished the conversation.

When a handful of new patrons came in, she bade me farewell until the evening. She pointed the way to the library before she left but cautioned the long walk. I made my way back to my room, waiting the rest of the hour before I moved Haven to her stall at the inn.

I looked in the mirror and gaped at the reflection in front of me. Though my eyes seemed bright and alert, the long ride had clearly exhausted me. I was dirty and dishevelled. I eyed the bathroom of the unit longingly. *I have time*, I thought to myself, looking at the various sweetly scented soaps along the bathtub's rim. I succumbed to the promise of luxury. I filled the bath with piping hot water, adding some of the bubble bath. I was greeted by the lovely scent of vanilla and chamomile. I didn't even realize how much my limbs were heavy and aching until I set my body into the hot water. I quickly tied the rest of my hair up before lowering myself slowly, so as not to scald my skin. I settled in and realized I never wanted to leave the tub, luxuriating in the foamy and pleasantly smelling bubbles. I quickly washed, careful not to wet my hair. It took great effort not to let my eyes fall shut and let sleep claim me.

The third bell of the hour chimed from the clock in the main bedroom and I knew I had to leave the warm water's embrace. With a groan of longing, I pulled the plug, grabbed the towel, and quickly dried myself off. I dressed in a change of clothes much like what I'd been wearing: a long tunic, this one a deep blue, black pants and my brown boots. As always, my knife belted to my side, I tucked my two knives back into my boots and my sword on my back. I dragged a brush through my hair quickly. I smiled at myself in the mirror, looking more presentable than I had in weeks. I donned my cloak, lovingly fingering the material.

I made it back to Haven just as my time was up. I saddled Haven who snorted her disgust at her vacation being interrupted. I laughed as I rode her with just her halter and lead, her bridle slung over my shoulder. I didn't miss the men's surprised looks and raised eyebrows as I walked away towards the inn.

I deposited Haven in her stall; she quickly laid down and rolled in the straw, happy as a clam, before she got to her feet again and munched on her dinner. I wished I could give her grassy pastures to wander while we were here, but safe, comfortable, and fed were good enough. I gave her a long, affectionate scratch along her withers, her favorite spot. I grinned, watching her upper lip lift to show her teeth in a very equine smile.

The trek to the library was pleasant taking the ferry as Lorelei suggested. It was only a single coin, and you got a piece of paper allowing all-day use. I marveled at the beauty of the city, the impossibly tall buildings, the mountains that made up the boundary between Air Court and ours occasionally peeking through gaps in the buildings. I had never been to a city like this before, never seen this many people in one place. Fae were everywhere. I couldn't get over the loudness of it. Talking, yelling, riding, eating. All seeming to be in such a hurry, as I observed them from my spot on the ferry. And then I saw the library.

It was recognizable just by the sheer size of the building, one of the largest in all of Meridian. Scholars in long robes of various colors teemed the premises. I assumed the different colored robes meant something; whether rank or title or a specific academy they attended, I wasn't sure.

I disembarked from the ferry thanking the driver, who ignored me, and walked giddily towards my destination. I felt a tingle of excitement run down my back at the anticipation. *I'm really here! I'm going to find what I'm looking for.* Nobody paid me any attention as I approached the main doors with awe in my expression I couldn't hold in. The building seemed to stretch upwards forever with lovely curving architecture sweeping in intricate designs. I thought it gave the building an incredibly aristocratic look: elegant, majestic, imposing, and timeless. Age hadn't seemed to wear on the building; instead, the building seemed to wear it like a mark of honor, vines tumbling down the one side of the far wall.

I entered through massive wooden doors with metal reinforcements and heavy locks the size of my head. For a moment, I thought it seemed excessive but understood the measures taken. A building of this size must hold a wealth of knowledge. I couldn't stop my heart from pounding with excitement as I took in the library. The massive atrium boasted an entire ceiling made of crystal-clear glass, allowing for light to flood in. The scent of old parchment reached me, earthy and comforting. An old Faerie stood at a desk lined with parchment papers and countless books stacked in messy piles. As I watched, it seemed to me that he somehow knew where everything was, scarcely looking up from his task to get something. *This is the very definition of organized chaos,* I thought with amusement. The room behind him caught my attention, my eyes falling away from him for a moment. The room was inconceivably large, stretching on and on. The room split into two levels that I could see; to the right was upstairs and downstairs to the left with bookshelves so tall, massive ladders were used to reach the majority of the books, towering multiple stories. The sweeping, curving architecture from outside was continued inside and the ceiling was a giant window allowing for cascades of light. Fire posts and sconces burned every few feet, obviously spelled to never burn anything it wasn't supposed to, casting light where the windows failed, nary a shadow in sight. I gaped, seeing fire magic in here. I knew using magic of all courts was common in the main arteries of Meridian, but I'd never seen fire magic outside of the Everday Isle used so casually. Here, and in other main cities in the Courts, working together as a unit was more common than in the outermost towns like my own. The old Faerie at the desk adjusted his eyeglass and looked at me with a drawn look.

"Can I help you find something, dearie?" His voice was gruff but not entirely unkind. The voice of someone who had once loved their job but was now completely exhausted. I didn't want to think about how much time he'd spent working here, how many years.

"Yes please, sir," I responded with my brightest smile, which did seem to soften his gaze a little. "I'm doing some research on the history of Meridian. And I need to go as far back as your resources allow. I'm also looking for volumes on magic use and dark magic as well." He gave me a long, strange look, and I wondered if I'd said something wrong. I tried not to look guilty of something and just stared straight ahead, making eye contact. He seemed satisfied I wasn't up to anything I shouldn't be, though his gaze remained sharp as he instructed me to go down to the lower level—*not a basement,* I noted, the lower level flooded with light still, and turn to the right. The archive room would be through there.

"There are different sections for various ages and subjects in that time period," he explained. "Depending on what you're looking for, you may have to go quite a way back into the sections. There should be someone of staff near the entrance of the archives, so if you require further assistance, please let them know. Collections on magic use can be brought to you. Though I fear dark magic collections will be limited as it's not a subject the scholars in Meridian know very much about." I thanked him kindly for his guidance with a smile, which he almost seemed to return before dismissing me for the papers in front of him.

I began my trek, speed-walking in my haste to get to the lower level, my excitement beginning to get the better of me. I glided down the stairs trying to keep my pace casual, smiling at fae as they walked by. As I got into the archive room, I smiled at the librarian who was working diligently and barely acknowledged me. I noticed the humdrum of foot traffic had begun to slow, and eventually as I reached further into the archives, I realized I was all alone.

I began my search at the back and I figured I'd work my way forward in time. It was darker all the way back here, where the light from the windows didn't reach well. Spelled firelight worked well enough but gave the room an ominous glow to everything. I looked along the shelves that were becoming scarcer with books than previous ones, and I clung to the hope that answers would be found here. How could a fae have more than one element? Had it happened before? Could they control it? I thought back to feeling out of control with my fire magic and how terrifying it would be if that happened again if Locke weren't there. A librarian had dropped off a few titles most relevant to my search and asked me to let her know if it needed more information before leaving.

What would have happened if Locke hadn't been there? I shuddered despite remembering the heat of my hands. Not enough to burn me, but it did burn Locke. I saw his blistered hands afterwards. What if I did that to someone like my father? To Eldan?

My eyes scanned titles of various volumes; *Meridian's History Through the Ages: An Objective View of Various Social and Political Issues, Magic Systems, Volume One* and *A Look Through Time: Before the Courts* all piqued my interest as I pulled them through the shelf. It took some time scouring through the shelves but eventually I had two other titles that showed promise. I brought them to a small table lit by spelled firelight and began flipping through relevant chapters.

The first book was a total bust. It discussed various wars throughout Meridian's existence, racism against various types of fae, and how they were driven out of their lands. It spoke of poverty in the outer rims of some of the Courts, but nothing from before the courts being formed.

Magic Systems was helpful in its own right. It explained how to use each type of magic. I found myself taking notes on fire and water. Locke was correct when he told me fire magic was strongly linked to emotion, specifically strong, volatile emotions. Thinking back, I didn't understand how this hadn't happened before. I had experienced strong emotions before. *But my life hadn't been in danger*, I reminded myself. Locke was trying to take my life. That had to be a factor. But he didn't. He spared me against his orders. A debt I may never be able to repay.

My life had been in jeopardy many times before. I didn't understand what was different that night. I let my mind wander to Locke briefly. I wondered if he were in Loc Valen or if he were on a mission in one of the other Courts, or even the faraway kingdoms. I knew I couldn't exactly look him up or knock on the castle doors, but it would've been nice to see him again, under better circumstances. Or perhaps seeing me again may force his hand, something I hadn't considered before now. He spared me once. Maybe he wouldn't be able to if I saw him again. I swallowed thickly thinking of that notion. I shook it off reminding myself that he was Prince Cancer, the Crowned Prince and Court Assassin. Firstly, he was very busy dealing with real threats to the Court, and secondly, he would have no way knowing I was here. I nodded to myself to affirm this.

I poured myself into my research. I learned that water magic was also tied to emotions, but it also ran deeper than that. There was a practical side to water magic that my brain could scarcely comprehend. It felt like the equivalent of hopping up and down, alternating feet, while patting your head, rubbing your tummy and singing on key all at the same time. One or two of those things seemed doable, but water magic required effort and training to control and conjure. Fire magic was more explosive and required control of a different kind. The magics being opposites and similar in so many ways. The book titled *A Look Through Time: Before the Courts*, I dug into last. It was a thick book, bigger than the others. It was old and dusty, as if nobody had touched it in decades. Dust plumed out of the musty-smelling pages when I opened it, finding some of the writing illegible from age. Looking through this beast of a book was going to take some time.

It took two hours, but I finally found a passage that made my heart stop altogether:

> "...the years before the existence of the courts, when Meridian was a more feral land, Faeries of all elements intermingled at will. Fire, Air, Water, and Earth coexisted in one realm together. In many cases, most offspring of such unions held one element, though it wasn't entirely uncommon to see a child of two elements discovered as a result of inter-element breeding."

A child of two elements. I'd seen my father use water magic. But... my mother died in childbirth. Was it possible my mother was from Everday Isle? The Fire Court?

I read on further as quickly as I skimmed, finding precious little else but a single other paragraph mentioning "children of two worlds." It mentioned that they weren't as common a thing as you'd think. And that in today's society, they were illegal. That thought was chilling with its implications. I swallowed the lump in my throat as I continued skimming the pages of the large tome.

As the decades, centuries passed, and the four elemental courts were instilled as a system of sovereignty, marriages, and interbreeding of elements between different types of fae in Meridian became illegal, according to the book. Citing that the offspring were so much more powerful than their predecessors, and were often difficult to control and thus hunted for it. The book cited a few stories of children born of multiple magics stricken down for their power. *Feared even as children...* I read on. Different elements could be neighbors, friends even. But alliances and romantic involvement were strictly prohibited, and children who were born of these unions, accidental or otherwise, were most commonly either hidden, or disposed of—I shuddered at the thought—in effort to hide the relationship. Supposedly, these laws were put in place to keep magic at its purest. The more pure the magic, the more potent the power of the element. This was in line to what I'd been told back home as well. The book went on to discuss the Zodiac Kinship of each court and their duties to their respective realms. For Water, the titles were Cancer, Pieces, and Scorpio. Air signs were Libra, Aquarius, and Gemini. Fire signs were Leo, Sagittarius, and Aries, and Earth was made up of Taurus, Virgo, and Capricorn.

The fae with the strongest powers, shown in their tutelage, was given the throne as king or queen. The others were bestowed the titles of prince or princess. The book spoke a little about the Zodiacs. They were appointed by a very elusive council called the Zodiac Guild. They were in charge of finding, testing, and training candidates for their potential role as a Zodiac. They pass or fail rune trials. I quirked a brow. The book didn't go much into detail, but I got the gist. Either you passed the Rune Trials by living or you didn't, and death was your punishment. I shuddered thinking of the Barbaric Queen, Scorpio, and her black magic. Had she turned to black magic to keep herself in power? Did she go insane as the black magic took hold or long before that?

The hour was getting late, if the decreasing amount of natural light were anything to go by. I frowned, looking up at the far away windows, wondering how the day had gotten away from me when I heard someone clear their throat behind me.

"Are you stalking me now?" The voice came as a surprise and I whirled around to see Prince Cancer—Locke—standing in front of me, leaning against the door with crossed arms. The picture of sophistication and grace. Casual and elegant in a blue shirt with polished but well-worn black leather armor studded with black and gold adorning his wide shoulders and arms. His feet adorned with fine black boots. His black hair, as always, slightly falling into his face. And those blue and golden eyes staring intently at me.

I felt like a fish, my mouth opening and closing repeatedly trying to come up with the words to speak. *How had he found me? How did he even know I was here?* I looked around the library but there was nobody else this far into the archives. Amusement flickered in his gaze as he watched me squirm.

"I went back to Poplar Hollow. You weren't there."

"How could you have possibly even known I was here?" I hissed a whisper, even though there was nobody around. Library habits die hard.

"I didn't," he said simply. And didn't seem to care to elaborate, adding to my irritation. He didn't necessarily seem pleased to see me either, which might've hurt more than I wanted to admit.

"Then what's with the attitude?" I asked. When his gaze sharpened on me like a blade, I felt a tingle of danger and I straightened my spine. "Am I in trouble?" His lips turned upwards into a ghost of a humorless smirk, sending a small shiver up my spine.

"Take a guess."

"No?"

"Take another guess." Something flickered in his eyes I couldn't read. There was no scrape of amusement in his gaze.

"Wow. Is it because I didn't swoon at the sight of you, perhaps?" I worked to keep my voice light and unbothered. The tick in his eyebrow told me I might not have been as successful as I might have hoped.

"Your swooning could do with a little work," he mused. "What are you doing in Loc Valen? It isn't safe for you here." His eyes shifted around, neck craning to listen for sounds of life I couldn't have heard. Satisfied there was nobody, he stepped closer to me.

I straightened my back, hackles up, and I glared at him.

"Not safe? How on earth do you figure? I think you're just annoyed that you currently have a reminder that you disobeyed the Queen running around and you're worried I'm going to spill that little secret, is that it?"

His jaw ticked. I must have hit a nerve. His eyes didn't leave mine as he stepped closer still. Another step closer and he'd be in my personal space again. Electricity buzzed in the air between us, making my hair stand on end once more.

"Do you really not understand the risk you took by coming here?" he asked. "You have more than one element. Neither of which you have any control over. That makes you one of, if not *the*, most powerful fae in Meridian. Even if you're not trained, you're a threat to the Queen. If she discovers you, if anyone loyal to her, or afraid of her, were to discover this, you'd be dead. And I wouldn't be able to lift a finger to help you. I—" He cut himself off, looking away, very real anger on his face. "What are you doing here?" he finished, replacing his anger with a cold mask of indifference. That calm face he had before. Though his voice still held a tremor of irritation.

Indignation snapped.

"First off, all we know is I have my fire element. We know nothing about whether or not I have water. A magic I've not been able to access since then, by the way. Secondly, you're the one who told me not to tell a soul about that little predicament. I'm here to learn more about my magic, how to control it, anything I can find." I didn't realize how much that frustrated me until I stepped into his personal space and poked him in the chest, earning a bewildered look for a moment.

"You're the one who said my life is in danger if I tell anyone." I wasn't convinced challenging him was the best idea, but maybe I could irritate him into giving me something. "I haven't told a soul. Not even my father. But I still need answers, and you left. I didn't exactly think you were going to come back and visit." His answering glare was telling. But then, didn't he just say he looked for me at Poplar Hollow? "I came here to get answers, if there were any to get. The library of Aramithia is one of the biggest in Meridian! It has texts dating back to before the Courts. Before the Zodiac even," I spat. "If anyone is in trouble, Locke, it's you. For dropping a bomb on me and leaving me to deal with it myself without anyone to trust or speak to!"

"There is a lot you don't know, Lark. About the Court, about the Queen, or about me." The intensity in his gaze made me pause, completely unsure what to say.

"Then tell me," I implored. I tried not to feel the hurt when he withdrew from me, his eyes flashing with something I couldn't comprehend. This man was a complete mystery to me. I couldn't read him any more than I could read the worn-away text in that book, illegible with age. "Let me understand what's going on. What danger I'm in. What can I do about it? Not just for me, but for those I love around me."

"You don't understand," he said darkly. "These things aren't common knowledge. These are secrets of the Court. You knowing them will get you killed. I can't tell you unless you understand the risks to you and possibly your family."

"I'm already in danger, Locke," I said gently. When he looked at me I could see the war within himself. I could see he wanted to tell me. "What's holding you back?"

"The curse…" he whispered, eyes beseeching mine in a way I hadn't seen. Like he was telling me everything through his eyes. He looked like he was trying to decide what he could tell me. "Scorpio isn't the only one who is cursed." I looked at him and saw the emotion on his face. "Scorpio wasn't always as you see her now," he continued. "She was kind. She was funny. Fiercely protective of her kingdom and her family alike. One day her brother caught sick. Her only real family. It wasn't curable and he was on death's doorstep. She decided she wasn't going to lose him, and there was no stopping her. I *tried* to stop her." His voice lowered to barely a whisper and I could hear the dread and regret in it. "I got there too late. I got to the Echo Isles of the Shadow Realm too late and was cursed alongside her when she asked for black magic enough to save him. That curse is the danger to you, Lark. And a very real danger I can't protect you from." His voice regaining that hard edge. "That's all I can tell you for now. Nobody else in all of Meridian knows this. Nobody knows that the Prince of the Water Court is cursed, nor why the Queen is. And you need not to breathe a word of it to anybody. I don't want your name on my list."

His kill list was the word he didn't say. He'd had to kill fae that knew too much, I realized with my heart giving a little squeeze for him. There was pain in his eyes. The slightest flicker that was gone so fast I couldn't be entirely sure, but I was sure enough that my heart ached for him. I reached for his hand one more time, grasping with a gentle squeeze.

"I'm not afraid of you or your curse. Or the Queen for that matter." His head lifted at that. "I don't know what your curse is, and I can see you're not ready to tell me. I hope you will at some point. But I'm not afraid of you." He didn't say anything at first and I was content just squeezing his hand reassuringly. I wasn't sure what I was doing, but I had the feeling Locke had been alone for a long time.

"You need to stay away from me, Lark," he ground out, with great effort after a long pause. I saw his jaw tick again, and his sapphire-blue eyes intense, the color rotating inside his irises. It sounded like a warning and an invitation.

"You're the one that found me in the library," I reminded him sternly.

"Maybe it wasn't you I was reminding." His voice was low and husky in a way I hadn't heard before. His scent was all around me, filling my senses. My heart beat wildly in my ears and I was certain he could hear it. I hadn't even noticed he'd backed me up a few steps to the wall until his arms came up on either side of my head, effectively blocking my escape. His eyes whispered of danger and dark promises as they locked on mine. I felt my face flush as I bit my lip, peeking up from beneath my lashes, suddenly more than a little self-conscious.

He was so close. Our breaths mingled in what little space there was between us. There was a darkness glinting in his eyes, and my bones ached with how much I wanted him to close the distance between us. Another breath, a question in his eyes, a question that was echoed in my own rather than answered. And when he finally did close the distance, my nerves were set alight. My very blood heated within my veins. Or maybe ignited would be a better word, for it felt like hellfire was coursing through me the moment his lips lowered to mine.

His lips were hesitant at first, giving me room to pull away. But I was having no part of that. I fisted my hands in his shirt, then his hair, dragging him closer to me. My fingers grazed the solid cords of muscle with enthusiasm and curiosity that surprised even myself. I wasn't like this, but my body didn't seem to care and my thoughts were quickly scattering under his touch. He was like hard stone under my hands, but warm to the touch. And he was kissing me.

Any cool control he seemed to have was gone in a flash of heat as his body came to press against mine against the library shelves. There was no place we weren't touching. His mouth slanting on mine in a now feverish pace that had me burning. His tongue came to expertly work between my lips, prying them open to taste me, to battle for dominance with my own. My nerves rattled, my heart raced and my blood hummed under his touch. I'd been kissed before. But Locke was claiming me with his kiss in a way I'd never felt before, and I felt like he'd forever marked a small part of me. No, I'd never been kissed like this.

He bit my lip. My breath left me in surprise and I felt him smirk against my lips. He slowly, achingly, did it again. A bit harder, while simultaneously pushing himself against me in a way that set fireworks along my nerves. My heart fluttered and my lungs forgot how to breathe. Feelings of closeness, and a resulting fear of that closeness, whispered at the frayed edges of my mind, but I was too far gone to care, lost entirely in the feel of him. A moan of longing escaped me, followed my a breathy sound that sounded like it was supposed to be his name. It sounded like both a strangled curse and a plea. It sounded like an invitation.

When he finally pulled away, I drew in a shaky breath and worked to steady myself. His eyes on mine with a flicker of vulnerability before he stamped it and all the other emotions in his gaze back down and his face was, while a bit flushed, was the picture of cool and collected.

"How do you expect me to stay away after that?" My breathlessness betrayed how affected I was. He didn't answer me initially as he untangled himself from me with a frown.

"I'm sorry. I shouldn't have done that. We can't—" I cut him off.

"Let me guess, for my own safety?" His eyes snapped up at the hard, steely edge to my voice. I'd been used and discarded once before, and I'd not allow it again. I shirked away from the memory feeling so achingly similar to the position I was in right now.

"I know you don't believe me. I can sense the betrayal in you. I am trying to protect you. Let me do that for you at least." My eyes shot to him. "I'm not discarding you, but we don't have the luxury of choice."

"No, you're taking away my choice. You won't even give me all the factors and let me make the decision myself. How is that fair?" My fists were now shaking at my sides, my fingernails cutting into the flesh of my palm. I hardly noticed as my blood began to boil.

"What kind of relationship do you think we can have?" he growled, taking me aback. "A cursed Prince and Assassin and a towns girl who can barely control her magic. Who the Queen requires her death. I couldn't court you, not the way I want to. I can't take you for meals, take you dancing, show you Loc Valen at night, or introduce you to my family. Tell me, Lark, how is that any fairer too you? To either of us?"

"Wait," I said, not fully understanding, "the Queen requires my death? Why?" His eyes widened as he realized his accidental admission, but his mouth pressed into a firm line. "What aren't you telling me?"

He let out a ragged breath and dragged a hand through his black hair, clearly torn. His next admission shattered me in a way I didn't think was possible.

"I happened upon you in the archives today because I was researching black magic. Because I have reason to believe the prophecy you overheard in the Vale that day? You're the one who's death will break the Queen's curse. The prophecy is about you."

Chapter Six

My mind whirled, trying to keep up with my own thoughts. *I was the one Amaya had spoken of?* She not only knew I was there, she purposefully didn't tell Scorpio that the one she had to kill was fifteen feet away hiding in a tree trunk. Her kindness to me knew no bounds as I found more ways all the time to be grateful to her.

"Does that mean I have the other two elements? Air and Earth?"

"If I'm correct, it does."

"But as far as I know, I've only Fire, and theoretically I have Water. I just read in that book"—I pointed to the desk I'd been working at before—"that a child of two courts could inherit both powers from their parents. Could that not be possible?" He gave me a long look. "Could it not be possible?" I repeated with an edge of desperation to my voice, willing that to be true. My thoughts turned to a specific passage of the prophecy, the words seeming to suffocate me.

A curse so terrible even a Queen quakes
To right it, the death of one by her will make

"The only one that can answer this for you is your father," Locke said, chewing over his words and bringing me back to the present moment. "He'll be able to tell you about your heritage," he finished softly.

"What about you?" I asked. "How do we break your curse? Do I have to die for your curse to be broken too?"

His voice was pained when he answered. "Our curses are different. My curse must be lived to completion and cannot be broken."

"Lived to completion?"

"Please, Lark. Please don't ask me about that. I can't go there." His voice had the tiniest raw edge to it. Of hurt. But it was gone before I'd even fully processed it.

"So, what now?" I asked lamely changing the topic, for which I could see his gratitude.

"You go home and speak with your father." And I knew that was true. I needed to know if I were a Child of Two Courts. Or something else. *One born the way the Queen was made.*

A shiver tangled with my spine at the remembrance of those words. The Queen was made.... Was that line referring to her being cursed with black magic? If so, I had a connection with black magic. I couldn't see my father turning to such methods. But perhaps love and grief weren't the only reasons he didn't speak of my mother.

"Will you teach me magic?" I blurted out. He looked at me.

"I will," he said with a sudden gravity. "That was why I went back to Poplar Hollow. I was going to ask you once more to come with me. I have friends in the other Courts that can teach you the ways of the other elements, as well. If we're right about this."

I was stunned. My emotions hitting me at once, too fast. So instead I was numb while I processed this information. He was going to train me. Really teach me how to use my powers.

"Why?"

"I wanted to try once more to convince you to come with me. The reality is you need to be able to protect yourself from the dangers you'll face. And if the Queen catches you, you'll need all the power you can muster."

"Why?" I asked, suddenly suspicious. "You're Cancer, the Crown Prince of the Water Court. The Crowned Assassin. Who doesn't wear a crown, I might add." I pointed out a lack of jewelry adorning his head. "Why do you want to protect me, when my death will ultimately break the Queen's curse?"

His head snapped up, pressing a finger to his lips and I realized that we must not be alone. I frowned. Rotten timing. I strained hard for signs of life beyond our little area but heard and saw nothing. He pointed down the hallway, where indeed noises of casual conversation began to reach my ears. I felt confident nobody had heard us though. But as I glanced back to Locke, he had vanished. I looked around for evidence of where he could have been or what direction he went, but there was nothing. And I was left alone in the archives.

I half ran out of the library. It was like I was watching myself as an objective outsider when the thought occurred to me, at least I'd gotten my answers I'd come for.

Even if those answers hurt more, scared me more, than I could ever have imagined. I was the missing piece in the Queen's grand plan to break her curse. The pillaging, the seers, the demonstrations to ensure enough fear that people report seers, the death, it was all a mad way to search for me. To kill me. And she'd been so close that day in the Vale and neither of us knew it. The irony hit me like a thousand bricks. But now one question remained.

How was I supposed to live knowing that my death would save thousands? More? It would put a stop to the demonstrations. The killing. The senselessness. Even the civil war that there were whispers of. Peace could once again be attained. The last five years could be a blight we as a realm recovered from. What did it say about me if I didn't want to die?

I scarcely remembered the ferry ride back to where the inn was, as emotionally numb as I was. I hopped off the boat and wandered back to the inn in a daze. Lorelei greeted me and let me know she'd be off work soon. I asked her if it were okay if we went out tomorrow, as I was feeling unwell, citing something I ate on the way to the library as the cause. She seemed empathetic and told me a bowl of hot stew would be sent up to my room.

"On the house," she told me with a wink. She tried to banish me to bed, but I told her I had to see Haven first. Make sure she was okay. She nodded and said she'd bring me the stew in about an hour and she'd check on me then. I thanked her earnestly. I don't know how I'd gotten so lucky to meet Lorelei. I decided I'd tell her so as well when she came back upstairs.

Haven was resting in her oversized stall, lying in the hay and munching, looking every bit the pampered queen of nonchalance. I offered her an apple from my satchel and she greedily accepted but made me come down to her level. "At least someone is enjoying themselves," I mused to her, petting her neck affectionately, earning myself a snort in response. I shook my head with a grin. Mares.

I left a few kisses on her velvet nose, which she accepted with very little enthusiasm if the flat expression on her face were anything to go by. I chuckled at the horse, gave her one last pat and left for my room upstairs. As soon as I closed the door to my room, I looked around for something, anything, to take my mind off everything. I decided a second bath wouldn't be such a bad thing and I filled the tub again, using the soaps and oils lining the tub again. Fresh flowers in a lovely vase had been added to the bathroom. Obviously housekeeping had been in. I checked to make sure nothing was taken while the tub filled. Everything was in its place, giving my mind a sense of ease and security, especially as I checked the lock on the door.

I eased into the hot water gingerly, allowing my skin to adjust to the near scalding temperature. Once I was in, my mind began to drift to what Locke had said to me today. About the Queen and him being cursed. How I needed to die to break her curse. But not his apparently. Something about that conversation had clearly disturbed him. I knew he didn't want to tell me any of this. And there was still so much to know. Was I a Child of Two Courts, or was I really the one from the prophecy? If I were, what did that mean for how I came to be? Who was my mother? What happened to me? How had I truly not even questioned any of this until now? Was Locke the only one who was keeping secrets? Why was Locke not delivering me in handcuffs to the Queen when he was the Prince of the Court? I brooded over those questions as I washed my long hair in the sweet-smelling soap. I wasn't sure how long had passed when I heard a knock on the front door.

That'll be Lorelei with the stew, I remembered. My stomach grumbled in response and anticipation of food. I called out to her that I'd be at the door in just a moment. I towel-dried myself in record time and threw a robe on over my body. My hair hung damply around my shoulders. I unlocked the door and opened it, smiling at Lorelei. Only it wasn't Lorelei. It was Locke. And he was holding a bowl of stew, his eyes surprised to see me in this disorganized state. I didn't miss the way his eyes traced the boundary of where my robe met my skin, ever so briefly, as if he couldn't help it. His gaze heated, reminding me of the library, calling to my blood in response. He cleared his throat abruptly and the moment was obliterated.

I looked at him bewildered and I pulled my robe tighter over my body, my face flushed. Something passed over his face, amusement? But he'd schooled it back, for my benefit I was certain. Only a hint of his amusement was evident in his eyes. I wanted to punch him.

"What are you doing here?"

"A girl was about to bring this up to you. I told her I could do that for her. So... um. Here." He looked so domestic and wildly out of his element. I supposed having a Prince hand-deliver you dinner was likely some great honor or something. I laughed in his face and it was his turn to look bewildered and uncomfortable, at least for a moment. I stepped aside to allow him in and closed the door behind him, a laugh still falling from my lips.

"If you want to set that down on the table, I'm just going to run about and put a few more clothes on. I apologize, I wasn't expecting you and I just got out of the bath." I wasn't sure why I was explaining. I felt my face going warm and my voice small and squeaky. His raised eyebrow and smirk that told me he didn't mind the state of my dress.

I all but ran to the bathroom again with a fistful of my clothing and dressed in record time. I stared at my reflection dressed in a tunic and leggings with a frown. I probably should own more dresses, I thought to myself. For just such occasions as this one. I smoothed my damp hair so that it fell somewhat nicely around my face and at least didn't look like a tumbleweed before I stepped out to see Locke sitting at the table in the dining nook, seeming now completely at ease in my room. One ankle crossed over his knee, reclining back in his chair. The picture of self-assurance. I nearly gaped at him for it, because I certainly couldn't say I felt as calm. He looked at me as if he knew, that trademark smirk making a quick reappearance, lifting one side of his mouth. Hell, he probably did. He said he could read emotions.

"Why did you come here?" I asked. "Better yet, how on Earth did you know where I was staying?"

"I'm the Crowned Assassin." He scoffed with an air of derision. "You think my targets tell me where they are? I'm pretty good at finding people who don't want to be found. Finding a girl who wasn't trying to cover her tracks is a cakewalk." It wasn't necessarily boastful as the words seemed to dictate but rather a calm explanation. Though there was a twinkle in his blue eyes, the slight upwards tilt of his head, that made me think he was showing off just a bit. Self-assured, indeed. I rolled my eyes.

"You realize rolling your eyes at a Prince is a grave insult?" he asked, a deliberately slow grin picking up the corners of his lips again. "Do it to the wrong Prince and you might find yourself in trouble. Or thrown off a bridge. You know, the usual stuff. A typical Tuesday these days, really." I deliberately sauntered up to him, crouched down to his level, looked deeply into his eyes, and grinned as I rolled my eyes so far back into my head, I was surprised I couldn't see my brain. He barked a laugh, mischief bright in his eyes. We grinned widely at each other for a long moment. Before I remembered the time and place and our earlier discussion. I felt my smile fall away and his faltered in return.

"Why are you here, Locke?" I asked him again, my smile fading into sobriety. He looked at me, all trace of his earlier amusement falling away. Standing before me wasn't just Locke anymore, but a regal Prince of my Court. A Prince in a mid budget inn, seeming way too big for the space. Too grand.

"You asked me before why I wanted to train you. You asked me why I wasn't going to turn you in to Scorpio. You asked me before why you should trust me. I'm here to tell you, if you'll allow me."

He was giving me a choice. Leaving it up to me. I nodded and gestured for him to continue.

"Before we continue, I need to know I can trust you in return. What I'm about to disclose is dangerous information to us both, even more so than telling you about my curse. I'm going to need you to undergo a swear spell." My jaw dropped. This must be serious if I were to take a swear spell. When a swear spell is broken, the fae who breaks it is in for a rough go. A swear spell is usually sworn on someone or something incredibly important to the one undertaking the vow. It doesn't work if what you swear on isn't valued enough by the one taking the vow. If you're to break it, pain, sickness or even death can happen to the one you swore on. I couldn't deny I was nervous. I'd never done a swear spell. It was commonly used by fae with something to hide. Something serious. Possibly even criminal. The Prince of the Water Court looked at me calmly. But even I could read the smallest bit of unease in his too stiff posture, unsure what my response would be. He placed the ball in my court. There was the slightest moment of trepidation, but I met his gaze with a steady look of my own, seeing no trace of deceit, something I was good at sniffing out.

"How do I do it?" I asked. He regarded me with a look that told me he was both surprised and impressed. He took my hand, causing my pulse to skitter a beat, and bade me to think of the most important person to me and repeat after him. I gasped as I felt his magic pour into me from our connection, the feeling strange and unfamiliar. I nearly dropped his hand, but he held on, interlacing our fingers. I calmed myself with a breath and focused on the instructions, ignoring the strange, oddly intimate, feeling of his magic filling me. I thought immediately of my father. I would swear on my father. Locke's voice was gentle as he spoke again.

"It's very simple. Repeat after me; I promise and swear on—whoever you decide to swear on—that I will closely guard the information Prince Cancer gives me. I will not reveal secrets told to me until my lord releases me or under pain of death." I felt his magic flare to life with just the smallest urge from me. It ignited my insides. I felt the same thrumming in my veins as I did that night when I'd accidentally summoned fire. He was giving me his magic so I could take the oath. Or perhaps he was unblocking whatever kept my magic from me.

"I promise and swear on my father's life that I will closely guard the secrets of Prince Cancer. I will not reveal his secrets until my lord releases me or under pain of death." Where our hands united, there was a flash of white light, sealing the vow.

"You didn't even hesitate," he commented as he withdrew his hands from mine. I shrugged.

"I wouldn't have betrayed you. If you needed some magic promise-keeper spell for your peace of mind, then that's fine with me." I smiled at him.

"You should eat your stew." My stomach growled at the mention of it and he chuckled, low and hearty, before pulling a chair out of me, gesturing me to sit. "Before it gets cold." I sat in the chair and he pushed it in for me, ever the gentleman, and returned to his seat opposite me.

"You asked me before why you should trust me," he repeated. When I didn't make a move for my food, he gave me a pointed look. "Eat," he commanded me, his voice firm. I picked up a spoonful of broth, beef, and carrot and took a bite, my face silently asking, *Are you happy now?*

Seeming satisfied, he continued: "You don't know what it's like. Being forced to do her bidding. Because she's the Queen. You think I don't know what she's called?" he asked, his voice low and heavy, and clearly listening for other fae in the vicinity. "The Mad Queen or the Barbaric Queen. You think I don't know she deserves that title? The Water Court is my home. I don't enjoy being sent to kill innocent people. I don't enjoy having my hand forced. I don't want to see bloodshed when the fae eventually have enough and revolt. She's killing fae in droves, searching for the person who can tell her what can end her curse. And now that she'd heard the prophecy from the vale, she's getting closer. Which means she's getting closer to you. But with your power, assuming you learn how to control and harness it, it's possible we can stop her. Save the Water Court. That's why I want to help you. I need you. I think you may be the key to stopping all of it. While staying alive," he added quickly at my expression. "I think you may be the key to our salvation. Not just because of your powers. Because of your strength as well."

It all fell into place. How could I not have seen it? The shock must have appeared on my face because his answering grin was chilling.

"You're the rebellion." My voice was barely above a whisper, though inside me was a maelstrom. "The rebellion that's been growing its numbers, saving survivors from the Queen's "demonstrations" and you're planning an attack."

"Guilty as charged." A smirk on his face. "Although I wouldn't use the word 'attack.' We can't kill someone who's invulnerable. We're going to capture her and put someone else on the throne."

"Someone like you, you mean?" My tone far was more biting than I'd meant. He gave me a dry look.

"I have no desire for the throne, love. They're terribly uncomfortable. Being a prince is exhausting as it is." He grinned at my shocked expression.

"You mentioned my strength before. What do you mean by that?"

"You witnessed something horrible in the Vale. Most people would have fled as soon as they could have, but you stayed and saved Amaya. The kindness you showed in that moment towards a stranger was exceedingly rare. You were faced with death by my hand. You didn't beg for your life or cower. You asked me to spare you long enough to save your Father's life. Then you met me at the edge of the forest, with a sword. You held up your end of the deal, but you were going to fight like hell to save your life against a trained assassin. You did quite well, by the way," he commended and I heard a twinge of respect in his voice. "You wanted so badly to come with me that night to gain control over your magic, but you couldn't leave your father, no matter what that meant for you. That's the kind of character and strength you're going to need going up against Scorpio." The assessment of my character left me speechless. I had just thought I'd done what anyone would have done.

"No, most people would not have done the same. I would know." I could tell in his mind he was seeing all those who'd begged and bargained for their lives, those he hadn't granted such clemency to. I could see the weight of all those lives on him. He took them with him all the time. My heart went out to him.

"I thought you said you couldn't read minds."

"But I can read emotions. I can feel other's emotions. But beyond that, your thoughts are written on your face plain as day." I schooled my face into a casual nonchalance, to which he grinned, the amusement sparking in his eyes, and I knew I'd succeeded in making myself look constipated.

"What of my father? Will he be safe? Will he be okay without me? Or should he just come with me?"

"I've already arranged for him to remain safely in Poplar Hollow. He will have enough money and resources to remain comfortable while you're away. He's a welcome guest with us if he chooses, but he will have to undergo the swear spell as well, regardless of if he stays or comes with us."

"He won't tell anyone," I began to protest but he shook his head.

"The fewer loose ends, the better. And it is safer for you and him if he does the spell." I knew Locke was right. And I knew my answer I would give him. I could learn to use my magic and help stop the Barbaric Queen. I thought of Amaya and all she must have gone through. A flutter of hatred for the Queen settled in me. For her, I would strike at the Queen where it hurts. Take her power, her throne and she wouldn't be able to hurt anyone else. For my family. My court. For me.

"When do we start training?" His answering grin told me sooner than I would've liked. I warned him that I was going shopping with Lorelei in the morning. He balked.

"You mean to tell me that you want to be trained in your magic so that you can help overthrow a violent, insane monarch, but you have to go shopping first?" His face was a mix between amusement and incredulousness. I burst out laughing and tsked him.

"What was that old saying? A girl can conquer the world in the right outfit, or something like that. I'm just trying to make sure I'm thoroughly prepared." He rolled his eyes while shaking his head at me, an exasperated sigh coming from him.

"What does it mean if you roll your eyes at me?" He laughed, an easy sound.

"It means that you better get used to it. I feel like it'll happen often." I had the childish urge to stick out my tongue at him.

"Eat your damned stew." His words were soft.

"I feel rude eating when you don't have anything to eat too," I admitted sheepishly. He laughed.

"Is that what this was about? Why didn't you say so?" He turned and walked out the door without another word, closing it behind him. I gaped at the door where I'd last seen time. What was he doing?

A minute later he walked back into the room, knocking twice before entering, holding another steaming bowl of stew. He set it down at his place at the table and tucked into it, completely at home. He was everything his surroundings were not: elegant, handsome, grand, and yet here he was eating stew out of a wooden bowl like a commoner. Well, if you could overlook the perfect table manners and obsessively straight posture. I gaped at him a long moment. He looked up at me, eyes bright with mirth.

"I'd better not hear any more excuses. Your stomach is growling. I can hear it from here, that's why I want you to eat. It's very loud." I covered my stomach in embarrassment. Oh Goddess, kill me now. He chuckled.

I spooned another mouthful. We spoke over our meager dinner of various things. It was homey and comforting, and I began to genuinely relax and enjoy myself. I found myself smiling at him a lot, and I realized I was blushing from time to time too. I wasn't particularly shy, but I felt shy with him for a reason I didn't want to ponder too much, especially if he could read emotions.

"What's it like to read emotions?" I asked him, also distracting myself. "Is it like a sign above our heads telling you what we're feeling or are you just very intuitive?"

"Water Zodiacs are highly attuned to the emotions of others, though my title, Cancer, is attributed as being the most in tune of all the zodiac signs," he explained. "When I look at a person their emotions are like an aura around them. When they're happy, they might have a light red aura, deep blue, or almost purple for extreme sorrow. Orange if they're mistrustful. And so on."

"What color am I?"

"Green, with a bit of blue, some light red," he said.

"What do those colors mean?"

"Green, in this shade anyway, is hopeful." He was looking at me carefully, exposing my emotions but giving nothing away. "Light blue excitement and uncertainty. You're worried about your father. But you're happy in this moment. It's the first time I've seen red in your aura since you saw that your father was going to live."

"To be fair, you've only generally interacted with me when I was under great stress." He nodded his agreement, but if there were more wanted to say, he didn't.

"Do you ever see your own aura?"

"What?"

I broke out into a wide grin he at the bewildered look he gave me.

"You know how you can always see your nose, but your brain ignores it? Is that what it's like? Or do you do you not even see it? What about if you look in the mirror?" He looked like he didn't know whether to shove his face into his palms or laugh. He proceeded to do both before answering, his shoulders shaking as he laughed off the rest of his amusement.

"I don't think anyone has ever asked me that before." His voice was low as he dragged his fingers through his hair and his eyes found me again. He returned my widening grin for a moment. "I largely ignore it, but I can see my own emotions if I choose to. I seldom do. Experiencing them firsthand is quite enough." He continued in a more sobered tone before I could ask another ridiculous question.

"What time should I collect you tomorrow? For training."

I suggested midday, and I hoped Lorelei would be okay still to shop in the morning. He laid a small purse on the table in front of me. It felt like the finest moleskin, soft to the touch. When I opened it, there was more coin than I'd made in a year inside. I balked before handing it back to him.

"I don't want your money," I said, trying to not take offence. "I worked hard for my own. I'm capable of taking care of myself."

"I understand that. Consider this a 'thank you' for all that we're planning on doing. Buy yourself something you love. You deserve it. From me." I began strongly protesting when he caught my hand with the coin purse as I was about to give it to him. "I insist." He lowered my hand to the table and took my fingers, forcing me to drop the purse.

He still held my hand. I looked down at it and asked from beneath my lashes, "What was it you were saying about me staying away from you?"

He chuckled and leaned down so his breath was in my ear.

"I think we both know that I'm the one who can't stay away." His breath, hot on my neck, made me shiver.

"Maybe I don't want you to." My voice barely above a hushed whisper, not daring to look at him. I was vaguely aware of my lip between my teeth, feeling the warmth in my cheeks at my admission. My heart stopped—I wondered if I'd gone too far. Shown too much of my hand. He looked down at me, an unexpected heat in his gaze that made my knees shaky.

"You're doing that wrong." His voice low and silky smooth with that aristocratic lilt. Looking the picture of arrogance as he loomed over me.

"Doing what wrong?" I blinked up at him in confusion. The heat in his gaze, reminiscent of the library, held mine steady. That prickling heat spread throughout my body, dancing a tango with my nerve endings. My toes curled. My breath caught in my throat that paired with a strange fluttering in my stomach. He grinned wickedly at me, knowing exactly the effect he was having on me.

"This," and before I could process what was happening, his lips were on mine again, my lower lip caught between his teeth. He bit down gently, sending warm feelings all over my body and settling in my core. He licked my lower lip before kissing me again, sweeter this time. Unhurried. I bit his lip in retaliation. His hands tangled themselves in my still slightly damp hair, holding me in place as he upped his assault on my mouth.

His tongue darted in to play with mine, stoking my rising desire. I ran my hands over his body in appreciation, loving the shudder that went through him as I did so. I was hot and cold at the same time; my heart was pounding so much it was making my head rush. I felt him back us up towards the bare wall behind me. I felt myself yield to his lips and kiss him back, matching his enthusiasm, reaching up to loop my arms around his neck. The hard plains of his body were suddenly against mine as he grabbed my hands from their resting place and held them above my head with one hand, forcing me to arch into him slightly. His other hand raked deliberately slow streaks upwards from my hip, making my hypersensitive skin flush and sending a shiver down my spine and coil lower still.

This kiss wasn't sweet. This kiss was fiery and intense and desperate and spoke of a passion we'd barely explored. It was heated. He bit my lip enough that it made me gasp. I felt him smirk against my mouth as he kissed and licked away the small hurt, earning a breathy moan from me. His hands came around to my thighs and lifted me roughly against the wall. I couldn't even feel bad for anybody beyond the wall as I wrapped my legs around his waist, his hands supporting me, firmly cupping my behind. I tangled my hands in his hair, not being gentle as I tugged, earning myself a growl of approval. His stubble sanded the sensitive skin of my lips, but I wanted more. As my tongue warred for dominance with his, I bit his lip again, loving the second growl I elicited from him.

He pushed me hard against the wall again with his solid body, matching me kiss for feverish kiss. And then I felt the hard length of him through his pants; I groaned as I ground shamelessly against him, my head tipping back. He pressed himself firmly against me and held me there with his hands and the wall as his lips traveled, leaving little nips along my jaw, along my neck, and I breathlessly arched into him, a silent plea for more. There was a breathy version of his name that came from me, a less silent demand. He gave me a chuckle that vibrated against my neck that led me to believe he was just getting warmed up.

"You're a greedy thing, aren't you?" he teased as he pushed his body to mine again in the most delicious way, eliciting something between a sigh and a moan. I wanted more of him. I wanted all of him. I hadn't realized I'd wanted this since I met him. But soon this feeling was going to devour me. I reached a hand down between us, intending to palm the length of him. I wanted to touch him too. To drive him as feral as he was driving me. To chase away his thoughts as he was chasing away mine. But he chuckled again, claiming my hand. I locked my ankles tighter around his waist as he kept my hands from him one handed while his lips did the talking along my neck. His other hand reached between our bodies to my breasts. He moved my cup of my bra aside from the outside of my shirt and ran his fingers in agonizingly slow circles around the taut bud of my nipple, making me pant and grind against him harder. I let out an expletive when he pinched gently, his lips traveling back up my neck to my lips. He reached under my shirt but hovered at the hem. His lust-filled gaze caught mine with a single question in them, as if to give me a moment to reconsider what we were about to do. I nodded and reclaimed his mouth with mine, my hands raking over the swell of his biceps, hating the clothing between us. With that, he reached down, pulled my shirt over my head, leaving my arms pinned in the sleeves, and palmed my breast under my bra, causing me to arch into him. His lips left mine as he quickly began slow, searing kisses down my neck. Insanity, heat, and want were claiming me all in equal measure as his kiss seared away all rational thought. He trailed his tongue, teeth, and lips down to my collarbone until at last he pulled my bra away as his mouth reached my breast.

I gasped at the hot of his mouth of my skin. I whimpered his name as he bit gently down before licking over the small pain, giving me full-body shivers. The way his tongue was moving I knew exactly what would happen if he went any further south. His arms tensed then, the only warning I had before he hoisted me away from the wall. He brought me over to the bed, placing me down on it carefully, as if I were the most delicate thing.

His fingers roamed the hem of my leggings, toying with me a moment. I decided I didn't have the patience for that. I lifted my hips off the bed to allow him to slide them and my panties off me with very little effort. I removed the rest of my shirt and discarded... somewhere. I didn't care. All I could care about was that his lips were back on mine. His hand traced slow circles along my abdomen, igniting an inferno of desire within me. That searing touch slowly made its way lower, so slowly I wanted to force his hand down to where I needed it, but his warning growl and nip told me I was exactly where he wanted me.

When at long last his hand dipped down between us, I made a strangled sound I'd never made before. He let out an expletive as his fingers found the slickness waiting there for him. I moaned his name as he slid two fingers along my entrance but never giving me what I wanted, teasing me. The ache in my core growing, I bucked my hips in effort to take what I wanted from his hand, but it made no difference. His lips broke apart from mine, his fingers still caressing me achingly slowly, his thumb ever so gently whispering over and over my most sensitive spot I so desperately wanted him to touch.

He looked me over with his gaze dark, blue eyes swirling with emotion. I felt my cheeks heat when he uttered one single word.

"Beg."

"Please," I whimpered, the heat in his gaze intensifying as he at last sank his fingers into me, his thumb finally giving friction to the apex of my thighs. As I was about to cry out, his other hand came over my mouth and stifled my moans as he pumped me, pressure within me already beginning to build.

"Fuck, I want to taste you" he growled in my ear in a tone that made me breathless. He began planting scorching-hot kisses down my body while his hands kept up their punishing pace. My breathing quickened as his tongue finally traveling to apex of my thighs, lightly caressing it once. He gave a groan of appreciation before circling his tongue over it again. My every thought scattered at the contact. I couldn't help the loud moan that he elicited from me. I think I begged him again. And I don't think I was quiet about it. He chuckled against my skin, the vibration driving me wild, my hips moving of their own accord. That building within me was becoming a force, driving me higher and impossibly higher, and I knew it wouldn't be long until I shattered. "You're in an inn, Lark. You have neighbors. You're going to have to be a lot quieter than that." I blushed, and he grinned wickedly at me, a promise of something sensual in his gaze.

I felt a glimmer of magic in the air. I was about to ask what it was when his tongue, now almost ice cold, found that hypersensitive spot again, rendering me incapable of most speech or thought. I cried out, neighbors be damned, my back arching off the bed at the shocking, cold sensation of his tongue, my hips moving again against him. He grinned, knowing exactly what he was doing, and I was lost to the slow pace of his cold, skilled tongue paired with the feverish pace of his fingers. My hands were clutching the sheets as if I'd fall off the earth if I didn't. It only took a final glance down my body to see his eyes locked on mine. He let me see in his gaze how much he was enjoying this, enjoying me, and it was my undoing. I found my release loudly with his name on my lips. His unoccupied hand absorbing much of the loud moans as his still cold tongue and opposite hand rode me through it, chasing every shuddering, delicious aftershock. When rational thought returned to my brain, I found him standing over me, his pants down and the considerable hard length of him free. I felt his weight dip the bed on either side of me when I glanced up. My mouth went dry at the thought of taking him—all of him—in. He was only inches from me. "What is it you want, Lark?" he ground out with some effort, positioning himself just outside of me. I could feel him right on the precipice. It would take the smallest movement for him to be where I wanted him.

"I want you. I want this." My breaths came out in pants. I meant those words. I couldn't believe how much I wanted this. That grin again.

"Use your words. What do you want?" he teased, refusing to give me what I needed just yet. I was going to explode from this crackling inferno between us.

"I want your shirt off," I managed to say with a steady breath. He obliged, taking it off swiftly and discarding it to the floor, revealing muscled shoulders and arms covered in swirling inky blue and black runes that were currently leaning over me. My hungry eyes devoured the sight of the hard plains of his abdomen all on full display to me now. I let my gaze trail south, down to where we were so close to being joined. Feeling emboldened by seeing how much our encounter was affecting him, I whispered, "I want you inside me." I begged him, "Please."

He groaned and I was rewarded as he filled me. In and in, inch by inch. He breached me slowly, gently, allowing my body a moment to adjust to him until he was sheathed to the hilt. I moaned an expletive as my body struggled for a moment to accommodate all of him.

"You can take it, love," he whispered, his forehead to mine, eyes watching, waiting for the moment I was ready. The effort of his restraint was evident. A couple heart beats passed before my body relaxed.

I reached up to kiss him, my hands raking his biceps once, twice, before pulling him closer, a silent cue for more. He reached down and pulled my leg over his shoulder, before leaning into my embrace again. I shuddered, my head falling back, at the deeper position. He drew out and back in with that delicious slowness that had my head spinning and his name on my lips.

"Quiet, love," he reprimanded between kisses, and he picked up his pace, making his request almost impossible. I moaned in response but made a herculean effort to stifle it. I clung to him, my nails raking into the flesh of his back, his arms, tugging his hair, all were met with growls of approval. I met him thrust for thrust and he ploughed into me harder. I felt the telltale quickening of my body, that building of pressure, and bit on my lip to keep from crying out. He upped his pace, bringing his hand to my mouth to stifle my loud volume right on cue as I found my release again. I moaned his name repeatedly and he rode me through it again, not once slowing down, but instead rearing up and his fingers finding that spot between my thighs again and I was falling unexpectedly for the third time, this one rocking me to my core and setting fireworks off in my body and behind my eyes. He kept barreling into me at the most bruising pace through each aftershock. I clutched him, I clutched the bed, the sheets, anything I could not to fall off the earth as he pounded into me. I was breathless when I felt him get impossibly thicker within me, harder, before he, too, found his release, growling my name before collapsing over me, thick arms holding his weight off me.

When the world returned to normal, when my sense came back to me and I was capable of stringing more than a few random scraps of thought together, I reached up to cup his face and kiss him again, sweetly this time. And maybe a bit shyly as my head returned to me and I realized what we'd just done. I bit my lip, feeling far too exposed suddenly. My eyes darted around the room as I searched for my clothes immediately.

Locke barked a laugh at my awkwardness and pulled my naked body to his. He pulled the covers over us to offer me the covering I wanted so much and wrapped his arms around me, settling me close to him, my back to his front. His warmth and his scent was comforting, and when I half turned and looked back, I saw him smile at me. A real, genuine, honest-to-goodness smile, his dimples peeking out at me. His expression light, carefree. It made my breath hitch, and his hands reached up to catch my chin and hold me still while he planted a soft, sweet kiss on my lips that made my heart ache. I smiled back at him. I wanted him to see that what we'd done meant something to me. I kissed him back with all that emotion. I felt him shudder.

"What am I doing?" he asked himself more than me.

"If this is you telling me that was your first time then I can't wait to see what happens when you get more experienced." He burst out laughing against my neck, planting a kiss there.

"For someone who looks as innocent as you do, you have an awfully dirty mouth."

"Maybe next time I'll show you just how incredibly useful too." His eyebrow quirked up, giving me a full-toothed grin.

"Lark, you surprise me more all the time." I grinned despite myself. I wondered if my entire aura were light red. With the way I was feeling, it surely had to be. "It pretty much is," he answered me out loud. How did he keep doing that? I believed he was performing a fast one on me, and he absolutely could read minds. He grinned against my neck. "No, love." He drawled, kissing my neck again. "You're just very easy for me to read."

"Really?" I asked, my voice sickly sweet. "Can you read this?" I shot him an obscene hand gesture and he chortled in response, his hot breath on my ear making me shudder.

"Go to sleep," he said. "After shopping, you're going to have a long day."

"The lights are still on." I started to get up when he held me in the bed. He got up and got the lights for us, and settled back behind me, enveloping me. I didn't remember the last time I felt this happy. This whole. This blissful. This *safe*. I basked in the warmth and scent and comfort of him before my eyes felt heavy. And as I was drifting off to sleep I heard him whisper, "My aura is all red too."

I smiled as his weight settled in for the night behind me.

Chapter Seven

When my eyes cracked open, Locke was gone, his side of the bed neatly made. Of course he was a neat freak. I rolled my eyes but couldn't help the smile that came to my face. On his side of the bed was a carefully folded note that read:

Lark,

Have fun shopping this morning. I ran into Lorelei downstairs. She's going to meet you in your unit when she's ready. See you later. Be ready.

Locke.

PS: Eat your breakfast!

Breakfast? When I scanned the room, it didn't take long to see what he was referring to; beckoning to me from atop the dining table was a basket filled with various goodies. Croissants paired with butter and fresh jam, a jar full of cheese cubes, another jar full of grapes, and something warm underneath. I lifted the food out and lifted the tray lid inside the basket to reveal a bowl of warm oatmeal with a jar of honey and fresh strawberries and two strips of bacon. My mouth watered immediately, not remembering the last time I'd had bacon. I fell on my meal like a wild animal, thankful that Locke was not present to witness my lack of manners. My heart tugged a bit that he'd gone out of his way to get me a breakfast. A good breakfast at that. Another smile came to my lips as I finished off the cubes of cheese, beginning to feel full.

I quickly dressed in my usual attire and ran a brush carefully through my long hair in the mirror. My eyes were brighter than they usually were, more like emeralds than their usual mossy green. My cheeks were more flushed too, and my lips seemed permanently turned ever so slightly upwards. I was unsure if it were because of Locke in general or because of last night. I bit my lip at the memory, my blood heating up for a moment. I saw my reflection in the mirror light up. A delicious soreness still ached between my legs, a not unpleasant reminder of where he'd been. Definitely because of last night, I decided.

It took a few minutes of coaxing, but finally my hair fell in loose, sunlit waves down my back. I was considering braiding the front pieces of my hair into a crown atop my head when there was a knock on the door.

When I hurried to answer it, I saw Lorelei beaming at me, her thick, dark brown hair tied back in a loose braid with a pretty blue bow at the end of it. Loose tendrils framed her face. She was wearing a light blue dress that ended at her ankles, with matching flats. Her dress was feminine and pretty, like those I saw upon my arrival to the city yesterday. The skirt and sleeves were made of chiffon, while the square neckline bodice made of silk with delicate buttons on the front.

I offered her a genuine smile and an apology for the unexpected rain check last night. She offered me a conspiratorial grin.

"I would have rain checked too with… you know." She winked at me. I felt my cheeks go red and she giggled. "Your secret is safe with me, Lark." She smiled and hooked my arm in hers. "I hope you're ready to shop till you drop! I can tell you've never been to Loc Valen. I'm going to make certain you never forget today."

She meant it. By near midday I swore my feet were ready to fall off and I had purchased three new dresses and tried on countless others, Lorelei helping me decide which colors looked best one me. We decided that with my pale complexion, bright green eyes, and blond hair that jewel tones were best: greens, blues, reds, and purples. And Lorelei insisted that every girl is required to have a black dress.

My black dress was a showstopper, even for Loc Valen. It felt like a waste of money because I had no idea where I'd wear something like this. A glittering black fabric that sucked in my waist and gently flared out to the floor. The bodice a corset which showed off my bust line and my curves. Chiffon cap sleeves glittered on my shoulders. The skirt had a scandalous slit in the side of it, revealing my legs when I walked. Instead of looking promiscuous or lowly, I looked empowered, strong, sensual. I looked beautiful. Even though I had no place to wear it, Lorelei insisted I buy it and she was taking no prisoners. And if I were being honest with myself, I absolutely loved the dress and parting with it might have been viscerally painful. We moved onto shoes, as Lorelei insisted my boots did not work with any of my dresses and helped me pick out three pairs of flats: black, nude, and blue.

I begged Lorelei to help me find a store where I could find new leather boots, citing the fact that mine were falling apart in places. She escorted me up a frightfully busy pedestrian walkway to a leather store where I picked out a pair of knee-high, brown leather boots. I fingered the soft, supple leather and I knew I wouldn't even need to break them in. When I looked at the price tag, my stomach dropped. They'd cost more money than I'd brought with me, and I'd had to dip into the coin purse Locke had given me. I tried not to feel cheap as I handed over the money, but I desperately needed new boots. And boots made this well would likely outlast me if I cared for them well.

We passed by several other stores, including a few stores for Eldan and his list. As we walked down the busy street full of colorful storefronts, I glanced around me and wondered if the foot traffic ever really ceased. Even late last night I heard the telltale signs of hustle and bustle. I saw a sign that made my thoughts stop in their tracks. A smile donned my face. Lorelei threw me a questioning glance as I picked up my pace and hauled her into the bookstore. I took a deep breath to inhale the new-book smell and lined parchment. My heart soared looking at all the stories lined up on the shelves. I walked out of the store with about nine different books, excitement making me giddy. We didn't have a bookstore back home. The closest thing we had was that Goddess-forsaken library, which I'd read every book in. This gave me some new adventure to experience.

By the time we made it back to the inn, the sun had made significant progress in the sky. I collapsed against my door, dropping my bags inelegantly. My feet and calves were aching and I was completely exhausted. I wanted nothing more than to curl up on my bed and have a nap. Or a bath to soothe my aching legs. Lorelei had laughed at me, and honestly her laugh was infectious. I had a great morning with her. She showed me around Loc Valen while moving us from boutique to boutique. She pointed out various attractions: places to see plays, the local art district, a pedestrian-only street called the Merchant Mill. It was a place for fae to sell wares of all kinds: everything from silk and satin and other lovely fabrics, exotic spices, charms and paused spells, potions, rare ingredients, fragrant foods, and everything in between. Walking through, I felt every eye on me—the odd girl who gawked at everything with absolute wonder. There were various restaurants and eateries, well-stocked taverns, and even giant monuments to the Zodiac Kinship. I looked up at the statue of Locke with a look I'd hoped passed for casual interest, but the knowing glint in Lorelei's eye told me she'd caught it. The city was a bustling hive, fae going to and fro and as fast a pace as possible. It was the kind of place it would be easy to get lost in or lose your bearings but Lorelei kept her arm hooked in mine and led me around, never once seeming to lose her place.

Before I knew it, I felt myself falling in love with Loc Valen. With its vibrancy. Its energy. Its easy anonymity. It was so much more exciting and fun than my small town. I found myself wanting to extend my stay, but I knew in my heart I couldn't. My mood took a slight downturn when I thought of the conversation I knew I'd have to have with my father when I got home. I frowned, not looking forward to it. I decided that to avoid settling in for a nap, I would pay Haven a visit. She deserved a good pampering session with my grooming kit. I bought an apple from Lorelei at the bar on my way out. She laughed at me when I teased her about exhausting me this morning and told me she'd see me later. I was so glad I'd met her. I really liked Lorelei. Her eyes crinkled with a smile when I told her so.

Haven stamped her hoof impatiently as I arrived, letting me know that being cooped up in a stall was beginning to wear on her. I noticed the stable was full this afternoon, clearly some new patrons at the inn. I couldn't resist saying hello to some of the more friendly geldings popping their heads out of their stalls for some affection. I laughed when Haven snorted in disgust at my betrayal. I led her into the crossties and bribed her with the apple, which she accepted greedily, still giving me the side eye. Though after a thorough brushing, I was certain she'd forgive me. Especially if I could convince Locke to take me out of the city to train so Haven could stretch her legs. I began running the curry comb over her shoulders, Haven sighing her appreciation.

Locke found me in the stable murmuring to Haven and petting her neck. Her velvety soft nose nudged my pockets, looking for more apples, causing me to laugh at old "greedy gut," earning myself a derisive snort from the mare.

"You really love that horse," Locke said. I turned and smiled at him. I beckoned him over to meet Haven, my best friend in the world.

"There was a time she was all I had besides my father," I explained, not taking my hand off her neck. I began scratching her favorite spot along her neck at the base of her mane. Haven wiggled her upper lip in appreciation. "Eldan has let me ride her for five years now and she's become my best partner. Growing up, the other fae would hold races, some even with jumping obstacles. Haven and I are the reigning champs," I said with more than a touch of pride in my voice. "Can we do our training outside the city? I know she'd love to stretch her legs."

"I was going to suggest the same thing," he said with a smirk, and he walked over to one of the other horses in the barn. One of the new arrivals. A dappled gray steed nickered to him as Locke let himself into his stall. My eyes perked up. When had he brought a horse?

"I bought him this morning," he said, answering my question I hadn't voiced. I narrowed my eyes at him. How certain was I that he couldn't read minds? "My usual partner is in the palace stables and I don't want to alert Scorpio that I'm not just aimlessly brooding somewhere in Loc Valen. He doesn't have a name yet." His voice was soft. "Would you like to help me name him?"

Excitement exploded through me and I knew just what to name him.

"Aristocrat," I said, watching him paw the air. "Fit for a Prince." His eyes widened in surprise and a small smile came to his face. He pet the horse gently, murmuring his new name in his a few times.

"I like it," he said, turning to me as he brushed Ari out. "It suits him." I couldn't help my wide answering smile.

Locke tacked up quickly, me following suit with Haven. I didn't miss how gentle he was with Ari. How kind. I didn't miss the scrubbing of Ari's withers. How deft his hands were as he saddled his horse, clearly having been around horses often. He caught me eyeing him at one point as I was bridling Haven and I was forced to quickly avert my gaze. Though I also didn't miss the half grin lifting the one corner of his mouth as he finished tacking up.

We led our horses out, Haven half dancing in place, and mounted. I walked over to the mounting block outside the stable door on account of being short and Haven... not. Locke barked a laugh and smothered it unsuccessfully when I gave him a glare.

We headed down the street at an easy trot, though holding Haven back from a faster pace was an effort. I followed Locke and Aristocrat to the main gates of the city and over the causeway, guards pressing to the sides to be out of our way with respectful bows to their Prince. It was impossible not to look down the long, narrow bridge. Going up to the city, it was easy to focus on the shining city itself in all its splendor. Coming out of the city felt like descending into a darker realm. A realm you could accidentally fall to your death to. "Where are we going?" I asked finally. Even Haven seemed happy to carefully place her feet, despite the considerable width of the stone structure.

"Nowhere in particular," he said, "just away from the city. Away from any potential witnesses or casualties." He made it sound like he was going to murder me rather than train me. I voiced this opinion for him to laugh heartily. I opened my mouth to speak again when he continued. "See if you can keep up," and he urged Ari on to a full gallop. But Haven wouldn't be outdone, and without any encouragement, she was off after the pair as if Hell itself were snapping at her hooves.

We matched strides with them easily enough. I had to hold Haven back a bit. I couldn't pull ahead without knowing where we were going. We surged on ahead together, Locke and I and our horses.

"Is that all the speed you've got?" I taunted, ready to let Haven kick in another gear. He smirked in answer and gave Ari his head as he took off at what had to be full speed. I followed suit and the world fell away as it tended to do. Suddenly it was like Locke wasn't there. Just me and Haven running free. I relished the rush of adrenaline and the wind playing with my hair. The feeling of freedom.

"Ease up!" Locke called after some time. I sat in my saddle and murmured softly to Haven, pulling her up to a trot. She was breathing heavily from the exertion, her chest heaving, but I could tell how much we both enjoyed that. I gave her a hearty pat and told her in a gentle murmur that she was a good girl. She tossed her head as if in agreement, bringing another smile to my face.

We were on a somewhat well-traveled road. I thought it lucky, or perhaps strange, we hadn't happened upon anybody on the road with the speed we were traveling. One side of the road was open field where crops grew and wild grasses overtook the shoulder. The lovely scent of wildflowers fragranced the air. The other side appeared to be tangled, dense forest, which casted intermittent shadow on the road. I kept my eye on the treeline expecting to see someone or something looking out at me. Locke pointed at a path in the forest and turned us towards it.

Or what could sort of be called a path, I guess. The horses had about a foot of space on either side of them with how close the trees were, my foot one spook away from being crushed against a tree trunk. We walked down the trail for some time in companionable silence before it opened into a clearing.

It was a meadow with a single apple tree in the midst of knee-high wildflowers blowing softly in the wind. A stream towards the northern edge of the meadow trickled faintly in the distance. The sun poured down over the trees, making everything incredibly picturesque. The meadow was clearly untouched by fae, or industry.

Locke dismounted and I followed suit, switching Haven's bridle for a halter. Though I had no idea where to put her.

I felt a glimmer of magic again. Like static in the air, and Locke pressed his hands to the ground. Suddenly the trickle of water was more of a rush and a river ran around the perimeter of the meadow, wide and deep. I gaped at him. He did this? He could do something like this?

He smirked at me, more than a little boastful. "You can let her go. It's too deep for the horses. They won't try to cross it." It was true. For all Haven's amazing traits, she wasn't a fan of moving water. Once I tried to take her swimming in a lake and ended up on my ass when she reared up and bolted. It took me three hours to try and catch her that day. I had told Eldan I had gotten lost, but I knew he didn't believe me. Though I'd hoped he just thought I'd selfishly extended my ride rather than almost lose his horse.

Haven seemed happy to be free, galloping, bucking, rolling, and otherwise gallivanting. Ari seemed content to just graze by the river's edge in her presence. Locke and I strode into the center of the clearing to stand under the shade of the apple tree. I turned to face him with an expectant look. I was ready for my first lesson.

"Now what?"

"Water magic doesn't just give you power over water in just its liquid form." He started straight into it without any preamble. "You can control steam and ice as well. Even if you can't see it. For example, I could freeze the water in your body and stop you from moving. For as long as I wanted," he said, his voice hard edged. "But if your magic is stronger than mine, if your control over the element is stronger than your opponent's, then they can't control it. You do. Not unlike the game tug-of-war. Almost everything has water of some kind in it. For starters, I want you to simply conjure water to your hands."

I held my hands out and willed water to my hands. Nothing. I searched within me, looking for the well of power I assumed to be in there somewhere. I closed my eyes and pictured water in my hands. I felt the air around me stir, but still nothing. I blinked up at Locke, unsure what I was doing wrong.

"Remember water magic is akin to fire magic in the sense that it relies on emotion. While fire magic relies on volatile emotions, water magic depends on large and steady emotions. It can be happiness or sadness, for example. The stronger the emotion, the stronger the magic. Think, Lark, to the happiest you've ever been. Or the saddest. And remember, you're a beginner. If you can't do it the first time, that's pretty expected. Let's just see how far we get today."

I considered. The first time I won the race with Haven came to mind. Or when I realized my father wasn't going to die. Haven and I mid-run, my hands fisted in her black mane, her breath snorting on the wind in every stride. I focused on that feeling of total freedom. Away from the fae back home. That was when I felt the wetness in my hands.

I looked down in shock to see water pouring from my hands and quickly looked up at Locke in awe flashing a disbelieving grin. I was using water magic successfully for the first time I could remember! I blasted the grass around me with water, the feeling so good to finally do something I should always have been able to do. When I finally stopped, I saw Locke watching me, his expression unreadable.

I tried doing something my dad was good at. It was the reason I couldn't sneak in or out of the cottage, even if I'd wanted to. I tried casting my awareness outside of myself, feeling for signs of life. I'd never been able to do it before, but then again, I'd never been able to use water or fire magic.

I felt the water on the grass. I sucked in a disbelieving breath and the moment was shattered, but I'd done it! Something about Loc Valen must be waking my magic up. I selfishly never wanted to leave the city or the surrounding area if it meant I could finally be who I was supposed to be. If it meant I could use my magic.

"Good. The ground around you is waterlogged, as you no doubt could tell from what you just did. I want you to extract the water and move it into a ball.

Like this." His hands made a motion and the water seemed to drip upwards from the ground to the spot above his right palm. I gaped in amazement as the water I had conjured formed into a sphere between his hands, seemingly without any effort. I wasn't amazed that he did this. This was a common enough display of power. Most water fae could do this. I was amazed that there might be a good chance that I could as well for the first time in my life. He released his hold on the magic and just as easily as he'd gathered the water to a ball, he dispersed it, sending it to the ground once more with a challenging look on his face.

Not to be outdone, I raised my hands the way I'd watched him do, albeit with a degree of uncertainty. I felt for the water around me. When he suggested it may be easier to place a hand on the ground and cast my magic outwards so I could feel where the water was, I listened. I crouched down, with my hands on the damp earth. I cast my awareness around me like I did before and was surprised the I could indeed feel the water in a way I couldn't explain. But I could feel every drop as surely as I felt the moist earth beneath my hands. I felt the circular mote Locke had made to keep the horses from wondering off. Feeling more like a thunderous waterfall on the edge of my consciousness than the light misting that was the water spilled on the ground.

It was odd that after just ten minutes of instruction from Locke I was able to use magic in a way that I hadn't in my entire life. And it wasn't from lack of trying throughout the years. I tried at my school lessons alongside my peers, but it'd always shamefully eluded me. Even the simplest of things every fae could do was impossible for me. Even simple spells, magic without an element, didn't seem to come as easily to me as it had today. I couldn't believe that simply harnessing my emotions was the entirety of it. There had to be something more. Perhaps having such a powerful tutor? Perhaps when he'd given me his magic for the swear spell, he unlocked something. Or got rid of something within me. Because for the first time I searched for the magic sleeping within me and I balked when I found it sleepily waiting for me.

I felt for the water around me and pulled upwards, a strange sensation I'd never done before, and felt slow and sticky. The water responded sluggishly by coming towards my outstretched hand. I gasped in my excitement and as if I scared the magic away, it vanished, my concentration momentarily lapsing.

Locke chuckled and bade me to try again. I bristled at the challenge, and I refused not to rise to meet it head on. I cast my awareness out again, felt for the water, conjured the memory of Haven and I galloping, and pulled hard. The water did as I commanded and flew to me, and I nearly drenched myself as I focused hard on forming it into a sphere between my hands.

Okay, maybe it wasn't a very good sphere. Maybe it was sphere-*ish*. Heavy on the *ish*. But I was so excited I was making headway. I refused to lose my concentration again and I beamed up at Locke with a small, prideful grin on his own face.

"Now freeze it over," he said, freezing my ball over in an instant. I caught it before it could land on the ground, regretting it immediately, and set it down, the cold so intense my hands burned as I huffed on them to warm them. Frost grew on the ice ball. A perfect sphere without cracks or lines in the ice. I couldn't deny how pretty it was, especially when the direct sunlight hit it casting rivulets of fractured light everywhere.

He unfroze it and I spent a full minute bringing the water back to a sphere between my hands again. I pictured cold. I closed my eyes as I concentrated hard, unsure how to proceed. I pictured the snowstorm last winter that kept my father and me stuck in our home for three days straight. I willed the sensation of the deep cold to my hands. I became the memory of the freezing snow and indeed the temperature around me dropped. I heard a thud at my boots and I cracked my eyes open. I had succeeded in freezing the water, but I had also succeeded in casting ice around me ten feet in any given direction. A gentle snow falling directly over me, light, barely there even. The cool temperature was enough to give me pause and rub my arms together. I looked at Locke's surprised expression. Had I done this?

His face seemed at war, like he wasn't sure whether he was impressed or shocked, both emotions showing clearly on his face.

"I thought you weren't able to summon water magic? You can't tell me you've never done this before and expect me to believe it," he questioned finally. "This isn't the work of someone who's never used magic."

But that was the truth. I hadn't. I expressed my thoughts again, and he frowned.

"It's something that I don't understand," he admitted at last. "You're so strong, and this is only our first lesson. How have you never been able to do this before? Was this at all difficult?" I shook my head. No. It wasn't. And that thought for some reason was deeply unsettling.

"I want to try something," he said. He conjured ice, or rather water, from the ground and froze it, in the shape on a stalagmite. "I want you to thaw this ice." He pointed at the ice when he continued. "With your fire magic"

I shuddered. I hadn't been able to conjure the flames since that day in my village, when Locke had promised to kill me. I had tried my best not to think about it, but the thoughts lingered on the corner of my mind, waiting for the moment they could take center stage.

I gaped at him, nervousness settling in my limbs.

"Are you sure? Last time…" I remembered his blistered hands.

He nodded, his expression blank. He was placing his trust in me. I supposed I knew how to dampen the fire now. Conjure water. The thought made me feel slightly better. He murmured to me about fire magic. To think of memories of strong emotions: anger, fear, intense happiness, extreme sorrow, and dread. I briefly wondered if all the fire magic bearers were depressed with all those negative emotions before drawing on my own. The bullying I had suffered from the other fae my age for being unable to wield magic. The embarrassment. The shame. The ridicule. The ice shards they threw at me of their own magic, a constant reminder of all I couldn't do. *Look at you now*, I thought to myself remembering the ice I'd conjured. *I'd best them all now.* I felt heat in my blood at the thought of beating them all at their own games and proving myself finally. I thought of how far I had fought to keep us alive when my father was injured. I thought about when those I'd thought were my friends tried to kill me. About my fear when I thought Locke was going to kill me. The remembered panic stirred in my thoughts but didn't affect me further. I choked down my anger at my memories until I was channeling it. I didn't know what I was channeling it to, only that the heat inside me was rising. Instead of running from the internal inferno, I threw myself into it and allowed myself to burn.

When I looked down, the fire wasn't just in me. My hands were surrounded by molten red flame licking up to my forearms, where it should have burned. By all rights, it should've hurt. It hurt last time. I remembered the panic, the fear, and the heat last time. But no such burn scalded me this time. Was it my control, perhaps? But I felt nothing of the heat as I faced the wall of ice ahead of me. I walked up to it and placed my hands on it, reducing it to a puddle in a matter of seconds, my fire burning hotter and hotter as my resentment from the memory fuelled it. I couldn't remember a time where I felt more powerful than I was right now. I felt strong for the first time in my life. No longer powerless, and it was a heady feeling. I knew in that moment I would never be a victim again. I cast a look to Locke to gauge his reaction.

His eyes grew dark, a touch of concern on his face, evident in the stark contrast of the firelight. But I didn't know from what.

"Can you douse the flame? Think of calming thoughts," he asked. I focused on my hands. Thinking of the easiest moments of my life. Haven and me. Locke and me right before I fell asleep last night. The thought came unbidden, but I remembered the contentment I'd felt in that moment. "That's it, Lark!" he encouraged me. "Whatever memory you're channeling, keep doing it." I looked down at my hands, merely glowing embers now, the fire runes snaking lazily up my hands and forearms. I focused on that moment of peace last night, allowing the memory to fill me. Reliving it even. And I felt my hands cool and return to normal. With a sigh I fell to my knees, suddenly exhausted. As if I'd run a thousand miles. I struggled to catch my breath.

"Your power is even more considerable than I could've imagined," he said softly, almost as if he were speaking to himself more than me.

"Am I stronger than you?" He looked me dead in the eye with an expression that sent shivers down my spine in a way that felt ominous.

"The fact you hold more than one element makes you the strongest fae in existence at the moment. We don't know of anyone else alive that does. I've had the displeasure of personally seeing to that," he grimaced. I didn't even want to ponder the meaning of that, but the look of disgust and heartbreak on his face was gut-wrenching.

"Is the magic I hold over the element of water stronger than yours?" I asked, flipping a switch.

His voice was calm and his face aristocratic and arrogant.

"No. Not by a longshot."

"But it could be one day?" I pressed, giving into the challenge in his voice. He didn't answer. His gaze was dark as he seemed to consider the possibilities.

"One thing is for sure," he said. "We need to have a chat with your father." We. Not "I." Which meant he had questions of his own. Questions I could see lurking ominously behind those eyes. More and more I was getting the feeling that my life was about to be forever changed by this conversation.

The ride back to Loc Valen was slow and quiet and without much conversation. Locke seemed to be in a dark mood, with a lot of thoughts on his mind. A few times I attempted to talk to him and lighten the mood, but all I got in return were wry smiles and a few humorless laughs. Haven seemed content to walk alongside Aristocrat, having apparently made pasture buddies with him. This kept me close to Locke's side while he was brooding, and I wasn't having it. *I am not entirely sure what I did wrong, but I'll be damned if I'm going to apologize because I am stronger than him,* I pondered to myself. *Or because I have two elements. I didn't ask for this!*

I looked up at him, a challenge in my eye. He looked at me and I clucked to Haven, giving her head with the reins, and she was off like a shot. I let her go, really go. I felt her leap into another gear and an impossible speed still, her long strides pacing across the distance to Loc Valen. I heard Aristocrat pick up a gallop behind us, Locke shouting for me to wait. I dared look under my arm behind me and saw they were quite a bit behind us. But I wasn't going to rein Haven in. Not yet. I wanted my blood to pump in my veins. Maybe a gallop would make him feel better too.

I lost myself in the thunderous pace Haven set, her hooves pounding along the shaded ground. When I looked behind me again, I couldn't see Locke anymore. I cooed to Haven to let up and set our new pace to a slow canter, which she didn't seem happy about. After a moment, Locke still wasn't behind us. Did I miss a turn back to the city? Haven was fast but she wasn't *that* fast. I slowed her further to a walk. He was galloping behind us, so he would catch up shortly. I moved Haven to the side of the road in case we got near the upcoming bend and were out of sight to the galloping pair. I shuddered at the idea of a collision.

Rounding the bend, my blood froze. Five fae men on foot adorned in decrepit leather armor unsheathed their swords and pounced at me as I noticed them huddled against the tree line. Two grabbed the reins of Haven who loudly half reared in fright, the whites of her eyes showing. I didn't even get a chance to reach for any of my three blades before the other two grabbed my leg and arm hard and roughly pulled me from my mount. My body fell heavily to the ground. Pain radiated from my shoulder where I landed. The fifth sauntered up to me, a haughty leer on his face. I scowled at him, putting my rage into it. He plucked my dagger from its sheath and toyed with it, making sure I watched as he fingered the fine blade. I simmered.

"Look at the pretty pony," the one crooned. "She'll be nice for breeding."

"So will the girl," the one who seemed to be the leader jeered in response. His men laughed and I gritted my teeth as I struggled against the two men as they tied my hands behind my back and forced me to my knees. I couldn't get to my daggers in my boot. I thought back to my lesson earlier when I shaped water and froze it. *What if I don't need my dagger?* I tugged on the well of magic within me, still feeling fairly depleted from doing so much after a lifetime of not using magic. But it answered nonetheless. That felt reassuring in the face of a dire situation. I narrowed my eyes at the lot of them. I would wait for my moment to strike. I stopped resisting. One of them would try to get me alone, likely the leader who was busy undressing me with his eyes. I could take them one at a time. I stared at him defiantly and spat at him as he approached me with a repulsive expression.

"Take her to my tent," he snapped. "You're going to wish you had some manners, girl." He clamped a hand down on my chin, as if to get a good look at my face. I bit his thumb and he drove his hand across my cheek, splitting my lip. I bit back any sound, refusing to give him the satisfaction. I stared at him in the eye, a quiet smirk on my face. He had the good sense to look slightly unsettled.

"Crazy bitch," I heard him say as his orders were carried out and I was hauled to my feet and away. *Where is Locke?* I looked into the trees but didn't see any sign of him. My heart plummeted. *I can do this,* I thought. My plan was messy, but it was a plan.

The two men dragged me to an encampment not far from the road but hidden in the shrubbery. It was easy to see how they'd gone undetected in the thick brush and brambles. And with how quickly they'd gotten ahold of Haven and me, I'd guess they'd been doing this a long time and were good at it. I guessed there were probably misdirection spells in place too.

They monitored me, forcing me to kneel in the center of the tent. They insisted on making suggestive jokes and taunts until their leader arrived, despite my lack of acknowledgement of them. He barked at them, and like dogs they left but not without one last lazy glare at me. Their leader, a towering man of at least 6'5" and muscular build, paced around me like a hawk circling its prey and waiting for the right moment to strike. I formed my plan in my mind and remained calm. I was also still sure that Locke would show up at any minute and render my plan needless, but if they had him too, maybe I would be the one doing the rescuing. Remembering back to those bandits outside the Vale, I shuddered. I seriously doubted that. The leader's smirk widened, thinking my shudder was a sign of fear.

"You're right to be afraid, girl," he chortled at me. I glared up at him, not that he cared. "Nobody here is going to be gentle with you. You're going to be in for a long night. And when me and the boys have had enough of you, there's a market for pretty girls like you. So I hope you get used to being on your knees, sweetheart. You look good there."

The first bit of real fear hit me, realizing how much I had to lose. I couldn't mess this plan up. Horrible visions of my possible fate came to my mind's eye, but I stamped it down with pure grit and determination. My sudden fear must have flickered on my face because he smirked as he moved behind me.

"I wonder what a grand price a beautiful thing like you would fetch? I'd wager a handsome sum indeed. But I do enjoy testing out the goods. Quality assurance and all, you understand." He continued to circle me, wondering aloud who would bid on me before lifting me by the hem of my leggings and positioning me kneeling off the edge of his bed. I fought back panic, my heartbeat thrashing in my rib cage. I knew the type of market he was referring to. Where men and women were sold in auction to the highest bidder. Sex slaves, hard and dangerous laborers, bodies for sadistic torture or even worse appetites, the list of cruelty went on.

He began unbuckling his pants behind me and suddenly my plan fell into place. The opportunity I'd been waiting—hoping—for was about to present itself perfectly. I knew exactly what to do. I smirked. I heard the soft sound of linen falling the floor and I knew he was naked from the waist down. My smirk grew to a grin and I almost laughed. This was going to be even better than what I could have hoped. He gripped my head by my hair, shoving it into his filthy makeshift bed as he fumbled one-handed with my clothing.

"You smell so good," he groaned out.

"You don't," I bit at him. He tugged my hair roughly at my remark, making me hiss and curse at him.

"I'm going to make this slow," he said. "But don't think for a second it won't be rough. And when you're spent and in pain, my boys will have a go at you. And they don't mind sharing." His hand fondled my ass, fingers dangerously close to my center, and I decided I'd heard enough. I angled my palms towards his body, which was starting to press up against mine. I gagged feeling the solid warmth of him. He looked down in surprise. "You little whore," he said with surprise through gritted teeth. He pressed into my hands and I called on my magic. It sputtered a moment as I willed it to work. Come on…

"You like this, don't you? You want my cock in your hand, you little whore? You want it inside you? Are you drenched for me and my boys?" His hands roughly yanked at the front of my pants to try to see. *Please,* I begged my magic, panic starting to set in. *Work for me!* "Should I call them in here now and let you service us? You—" he cut off with a scream as I finally conjured a long blade of sharp ice that erupted from my hands. I wasn't sure where I stabbed, but I had a pretty good guess.

"The only one being penetrated here tonight is you," I said, allowing the malice to creep into my voice. I got to my feet, readjusting my clothing, and turned as he writhed on the ground, my makeshift blade sticking out of him around a gaping wound through his groin. There was so much blood. My feet reversed as the blood pooled around him, seeming to come towards me. My knowledge of anatomy told me that with this amount of blood it was likely I'd hit the femoral artery and possibly nicked a few other major ones. He would likely bleed out soon. I looked into his eyes and smiled. He sputtered helplessly as I created another blade from ice, gritting my teeth in concentration, and severed the ties to my hands and freeing myself. I looked down at him spasming on the ground. "The world will be a better place without you in it," I spat at him, pouring my hatred into it. I heard commotion from outside, my only warning for what happened next. His friends burst into the tent, having heard the scream. I froze the ground, causing them to slip, and I catapulted myself over top of them, my magic running very low. I felt my magic sputter like a kinked hose. I didn't even necessarily know how to replenish it, I realized. I'd never used magic, much less in this capacity. With a lot of effort, I gathered my magic to me. I blasted it at them with the intention of forcing them back with a powerful torrent of water. But my magic fizzled uncooperatively and all I did was soak them while they were on the ground and struggling to find their feet. One of the men laughed and threw a flurry of razor-sharp, deadly ice daggers at me. I was forced to dive out of the way to avoid the brunt of the attack. I felt the running cuts over my body and knew I was lucky only to have lacerations. I felt the blood drip down my body. I pushed my panic and pain aside as I took in my widely grinning opponents.

"That all you got, *Princess*?" he taunted, and I smirked widely. I remembered what Locke had said earlier.

I could freeze the water within you to stop you from moving.

Locke's words from earlier trickled into my mind. An idea came to me. I cast my awareness out and felt my control waning over what little magic I had left. If I was going to do this, I'd have to be fast. I felt the water within their bodies. In their blood. I gathered every scrap of magic from within me and I froze it. They wailed as spider webs of frost formed over their skin and their breath came out in puffs of cold air. Their movements were sluggish, but they weren't immobile entirely. This was the best chance I had.

I knew it wouldn't hold them long, that it was buying me seconds only, and they were going to be mad as hell if they caught me. They had my one blade, but they didn't know about the blades in my boots. I unsheathed one and held it on my back hand as I ran to where they had tied Haven.

I didn't hesitate, and I sliced through the rope securing her to the tree. I was mounting up when a hand gripped my shoulder and pulled. I tumbled to the ground with my assailant. A scream bubbled in my throat as he landed on top of me, the frost already beginning to fade. He was saying something. But my blood was roaring in my ears as I grappled with him, struggling to get free. I managed to wrench my one arm free, the side with my dagger in hand. He didn't even see it as I brought it savagely over his back. My aim struck true as the scream assaulted my ears, though I scarcely heard it. I didn't know where my blade hit, but he went still not long after the garbled scream. I didn't give myself even a second. I couldn't. I heard the voices of the others close behind. I shoved the corpse off of me, not acknowledging the fact I was now drenched in blood. I mounted Haven and spurred her on in the direction I'd come from, erupting in a full gallop down what little trail there was and finding the road quickly. *Where is Locke?* I'd hoped he wasn't hurt. Taken by surprise and the group of bandits having the numbers…

I didn't make it far before I heard more screaming behind me from where I'd just come from. I pulled up Haven. This screaming wasn't just pain. It was fear. There was only one thing I could think of that would make my captors that afraid. Had Locke found me? Or perhaps a Blood Wraith attracted to the scent of the spilled blood. I rode back cautiously, giving the trees a wide berth lest one of the remaining bandits try to ambush me again.

But they didn't, though their screaming became louder and more insistent. I dismounted silently, keeping my blade available in my hand. I left Haven's reins looped over a branch as I crouched and crept towards the source of the screams until I heard distinct words. Peeking through the trees, I saw what made the bandits scream.

"Where is she?" a voice drawled, both familiar and foreign. A lazy smile that didn't reach his eyes twisted on Locke's mouth. No, not Locke. Cancer, the Crowned Assassin. There wasn't much of the Locke I had come to know in his expression. His smile was nothing like the smiles I'd seen from him. Not the soft, easy smiles I got. Not even the arrogant, aristocratic smirks. This was perverse. Twisted. Touched with malice and promises of suffering. In his hand he held a dagger. His sword remained undrawn at his back. I could tell this game of cat and mouse came easily to him and it made my stomach twist.

The three men I'd frozen to the ground lay in a bloody heap at his feet, all of them leaking significantly from wounds I did not give them. Their skin was blotchy and purple from frostbite. Their legs bent at unnatural angles, making my stomach heave. One was actively weeping. The other stared silently. The third was begging piteously for his life in a horrible wail that grated on the ears.

"We didn't know she was with you, Your Highness," he sobbed. "Please have mercy on us."

"Like you were going to have 'mercy' on her?" It was Locke's turn to circle his prey, as I'd seen him do to me. "I'll ask you again. Where is she?" His blade swung across a random leg, spurting blood and eliciting a scream of torment from the victim. I couldn't help the wince. All that blood…

"We don't know," the crying one whined piteously. "She killed at least one of our men. My guess is she managed to get to her horse and took off."

"Then I suppose you filth don't need to crawl the earth anymore if you don't know anything." The savagery in his voice was at odds with the calmness of his features, as if he were simply having a conversation about the weather with them. The opposition was the most frightening thing of all. All three men started begging for their lives. It was horrible to watch. I stepped through the briars at that moment, the men pointing at me.

"S-see? She's safe! J-just like we said!" the one bandit stammered out. The other two following suit, saying something similar. I looked at Locke—no, I reminded myself of who it was currently in front of me. The Crowned Assassin's face changed into the blank mask I'd seen a thousand times from him. His eyes raked me, looking for signs of injury. I saw his anger boil over as he took in the lacerations on my skin. They were starting to hurt now that the immediate danger had passed. I was covered in blood, much of it not my own. He turned his wrath-filled gaze to the men beneath him with a snarl.

"I was wondering what happened to you," I said to him, giving him my attention. I saw the hope on the men's faces as Locke turned back to me. My face pulled into a grim smile like his. "Please don't stop on my account, Your Highness," I crooned, unable to resist calling him by his title, realizing for the first time I never had. His eyebrow quirked as I nearly stumbled over the unfamiliar words. As he fixed his stare on the bandits a slow, deliberate smile dragged the corners of his mouth up in a sinister way.

I gestured to the men who all seemed to realize their fates were set in stone. That I wouldn't help them. The crying one began praying that his death would be quick. But by the look in Locke's eyes, I highly doubted it. I leaned down to them, all my rage seeping into my voice until I was nearly shouting at them.

"You should know that if you had managed to take me, he would've tracked you down," I hissed venomously. "If you were able to enact the things you wanted, your screams would have been enough to topple mountains." I knew what they had wanted. It had made my blood run cold. As I said the words, I saw the set line of Locke's jaw. I knew that was true. I could see the barely contained fury in his eyes, that same fury echoed in my own. Fury mixing with horror but not being outweighed by it. As much as I wasn't a fan of violence, I couldn't deny the world without these men staining it would be a better place.

The man in the middle, the silent one, his hands went for my hair and tried to put me in a chokehold, my guess was to gain leverage on Locke in a frantic bid to save his own hide. But I was faster, my apparently unnoticed blade in my backhand grip already. I shifted my weight and plunged my dagger into his stomach, driving downwards. Hideous sucking noises came from his body as his diaphragm spasmed, trying to take in air and he went limp, his scream dying with him.

"Anyone else?" I snarled, my head pivoting between the two of them. I flashed my dagger and bared my teeth at them both. Neither moved nor dared even to breathe as I stood. I was covered in the blood of their kin. I tried not to show how disturbed I felt as I looked at the Prince, who was clearly impressed with my kill. He approached me, putting a hand on my arm.

"Go wait with Haven," he said, his voice and touch gentle. "You're not going to want to see this." His eyes slipped to the men cowering uselessly at our feet. They knew running was useless, and they were likely too injured to do so. *Dead men walking. Err... sitting.*

"Locke?"

He raised an eyebrow in question.

"Make it hurt." His answering grin was downright horrifying. It was enough to make me want to turn and run.

"With pleasure, love." His drawled words had such malice to them. He turned on them with the intentional slowness of a jungle cat, making a show of slowly drawing his sword from his sheath. I listened to it sing as I walked away. I shuddered knowing full well I wasn't going to want to witness what he was about to do. There was a time I would have asked for mercy on their behalf. That I, in fact, had asked for mercy on behalf of another bandit. Remembering the fear tingling down my spine when they caught me and thinking of their plans for me, I stamped the merciful thoughts down hard. I knew if they were allowed to live, they would certainly have hurt some other unsuspecting fae. My legs gave out as I reached Haven. I looked down, my clothing soaked in blood. My eyes prickled with tears as reality crashed down on me with a crushing weight. I had really killed someone. A few someones. I knew they were bad fae. All of them were. I knew they were all in self-defense and I would be in a rough situation if I hadn't, or I'd be dead. But the guilt and ache in my heart was enough to make the tears fall. Now that the adrenaline was filtering out of my system, the horror of it all fully kicked in. I recalled my father warning of bandits when I was leaving. I remembered disregarding the warning, thinking foolishly that I could take care of myself. Even in my worst fears, I imagined daring escapes without actually having to kill anybody. My hands were shaking. No, not my hands. My whole body was shaking from the wracking sobs. Haven's head reached for me, gentle and reassuring. My hand touched her velvety nose, but the sobbing wouldn't stop. I heard the screaming not far off and the sobbing still wouldn't stop. I slipped into the memory of stabbing those men, the feeling of my blade easily penetrating flesh and sinew. Of that moment in the tent I didn't think my magic was going to work. I became trapped as I helplessly became victim to my own mind. Once again I lived how easily my knife, ice or steel, had sliced into their flesh. How quickly, as if through butter. How their warm blood had soaked my clothing. I suppressed the urge to be sick and I wrapped my arms around myself.

I wasn't sure how long I lay there listening to the screams, but I knew some time had passed. I wasn't sure if they vindicated me or filled me with dread. Neither? Both perhaps? Haven didn't move. She stayed with me as if understanding my fragile state. There were several minutes of no sound. Nothing but the wind in the tree canopy and Haven's even breathing at my side.

Footsteps crunched softly and I watched Locke approach me. He had blood splattered all over him, once again bringing up mixed feelings within me. It also brought the sobs back. He knelt beside me and pulled me into his arms as I cried. He didn't speak a word to me. Just calmly rubbed my back. He dragged his fingers through my hair in a steady rhythm, soothing me. From my forehead to the ends of my hair. Eventually, my sobs turned into hiccups before finally stopping altogether. I leaned back and saw the tear stains on his shirt, miraculously between bloodstains.

"I'm sorry," I whispered, unsure of why I was sorry, but I was. How was I supposed to help in a rebellion against someone called the Barbaric Queen when I sobbed my heart out when I killed deserving bandits in self-defense?

He gave me a patient look.

"There isn't anything you need to be sorry for," he explained firmly. "I'm very proud of you. I know your training with a blade isn't substantial, but you'd never have known it by what I saw. And you fashioned a sword made of ice on the leader." I flinched at the memory. He frowned, placing his hand on my shoulder. "You did what you had to survive. There is no shame in that."

"Then why do I feel like such a monster?" I whispered. "I always thought I could defend myself. I never thought I'd have to kill to fight for my life. Not to be able to show mercy. I never thought I'd truly get taken by surprise like that. I thought I was stronger and smarter than to get caught in a situation like that." Tears continued flowing over my cheeks and I briefly wondered if they would ever stop. If the guilt would stop.

"You fought like a warrior, Lark," he said, his voice devastatingly gentle. "You were incredible. And I can feel your emotions, so trust me when I say this: I know you feel horrible for killing them. For having to. I know what they had in mind for you. I know it terrified you. I know you feel grateful for their deaths. And I also know you feel bad for being grateful for their deaths. I know you feel like a monster." I bit back another sob. "That doesn't make you a monster. It makes you, you. Those fae were going to do unspeakable things to you and you still on some level regret their deaths. That makes you a good fae. The opposite of a monster. You're better than me. I detest taking innocent lives. I don't kill unless I have to." His voice took on a sudden edge. "But I admit when I killed those bastards I felt a lot of things. Remorse was not one of them. When I caught the scent of your blood… they were dead as soon as I found them. But when I couldn't find you… I knew I'd make their deaths hurt. It won't ever be enough for what they were going to do to you. You don't deserve that. Nobody does. When I saw you come through the trees, I've never known relief like that."

I looked up at him through red-rimmed eyes and finally asked the question. "What happened to you?"

He only nodded clearly expecting it, but there was pain on his face.

"When you took off at a gallop, I was about to go after you when they struck. There was a small army of them. They stopped Ari from moving—don't worry, he's safe," he said when he saw my concern for the horse. "They overwhelmed me for only a moment, but it was enough that we were separated. I finished most of them off. Many had the good sense to run. Some might still be frozen in place. I didn't know how far you'd gotten or if you'd gotten away. But as I was tracking you, I smelled your blood and I was able to follow the scent."

His face twisted as he caressed my split lip, which I then realized was swollen. There was a slight tingle, and the swelling went down. Healing magic. Not something everyone could do. He shrugged at my shock and showed me the rune on his left forearm. "It's not like I can patch serious wounds. But I can fix those pretty lips of yours." Of all things, I blushed and murmured a thank you. I was grateful for his help. He proceeded to heal the cuts from the ice daggers. One was deep so it required a fair bit of his concentration. He apologized, informing me I'd likely have a scar, due to healing magic not being a skill set of his. I thanked him again for healing me and a scar was a small price to pay.

"You had escaped by the time I got there," he continued his story. "You didn't need a knight in shining armor. Or even the Crowned Assassin. You said you thought you could take care of yourself. I'd say you did a hell of a job." His words resonated somewhere deep within me, finally vindicating me. I finally smiled at him. Soft, barely there, he smiled back, his hand covering mine. "I even was able to get this for you." He presented the blade those bandit bastards had stripped from me. I looked at him, realization dawning over me. There was something grimly satisfying that he'd used my blade to hurt them. I couldn't believe I hadn't noticed. I smiled again and took it, sheathing it into its rightful home at my hip, the heavy weight of it a comfort.

"Now let's get back to the inn and get both of us cleaned up. You look a fright," he teased.

"And if you looked half as good as me, it'd be an improvement," I shot back. But my heart and usual bite weren't in it. He chuckled anyway. I grabbed Haven's reins, planted a kiss on her nose, and followed Locke to where he left Ari tied to a tree. We mounted up and began the ride back to Loc Valen.

Chapter Eight

Locke left me at the inn. He told me to rest tonight and head back to my home in the morning, and that he'd meet me there when he could as he had some business to take care of first at castle Ari'inor. The nonchalance with which he said that made my head spin. It made me self-conscious of the four-room house I called home.

"Is there any way you could hide me until we get to my room?" I asked. He gave me a questioning gaze. I gestured to my blood-covered clothing.

"Ah." He nodded. "Yes, of course. I need you to hold onto me." He brought my hands around his neck and I interlocked my fingers. He swept an arm under my knees, knocking me off balance and catching me under my shoulders. "Don't make a sound." His eyes were bright as he coiled the shadows around us, veiling us from sight, much like he did with the Blood Wraith that first day. I wondered if shrouding was something he'd always been able to do or if this were a black magic perk. I decided I'd ask him about it sometime as he whisked me at a breakneck pace up the stairs and deposited me at my door.

"Why did my hands need to be around your neck?" He grinned at me, unabashed, arm leaning against the door frame.

"They didn't. I just liked them there." I gaped at him, my eyes wide at his audacity. He laughed as I tsked him with a casual swat to his shoulder. I opened the door and went inside but waited on the threshold. "It's painfully easy to make you blush," he said to me. I turned my head away, not letting him see the color rising in my cheeks.

"Are you sure you don't want to come inside?"

"I really do have things to take care of at the castle. The kind of things that if I don't do them, we might end up in some trouble." At my quirked eyebrow he continued with amusement, "Why does everyone think a Prince can do whatever he wants? Of course I have duties that must be taken care of, but I'll meet you tomorrow at your home," he said. "You'll be okay. I know you're hurting, and I'm sorry I can't stay."

"I'm fine," I said, and honestly, I was okay right now. I didn't know how I'd feel once I got into bed. *When I closed my eyes, would I see all the blood? Would I feel my blade cutting into flesh?* He squeezed my hand, placed a chaste kiss on my forehead, and walked away. I closed the door with a heavy sigh and ran a bubble bath again. I threw my clothes in the trash, not envying the fright the poor housekeeping staff were about to get. I figured I should write a note but stamped the thought out in the same breath, because what on Earth would it even say? Different drafts came to mind, each one more ridiculous than the next, and I laughed without even a trace of humor.

After my bath, I dressed in my night clothes and rummaged through my purchases at the bookstore today, looking for a story to take my mind off where I was and lull me to sleep until the sunrise. I was content to read until unconsciousness claimed me. My pulse hammered each time I closed my heavy eyes. Blood. So much blood. It was hot on my skin as I fought for my life against a faceless assailant. My heart pounded adrenaline-laced blood through me and I quickly opened my eyes, content with my original plan to read until I couldn't any longer. I needed the distraction to calm my racing thoughts. I picked a book and began reading, snuggled up warm in bed, the fire blazing in the hearth. The warmth of the fire wasn't quite enough to drive away the cold horror that remained just underneath the surface of my skin.

I don't know how much time passed, a few hours anyway, when I heard a knock on the door. I eyed the door suspiciously. At this hour? My hackles went up as I moved silently to the door and looked through the peephole.

I opened the door and Locke strode into the room. I saw him for the first time without his armor on. Just a fitted blue shirt, a black jacket, fitted black pants, and boots, which he kicked off by the door.

"What are you doing here?"

"I know you're less okay now than you were. So, I brought my work here." He gestured to the box of papers, ledgers, and Goddess knew what else. "The thing is, the closer I am to someone, the bigger the distance I can feel their emotions. I could feel your hesitancy to sleep. I'm going to do as much of my work here tonight as I can. You're safe." He led me to the bed and tucked me in. "You're safe," he repeated. "I'm not going anywhere. I'm so sorry I left in the first place. I shouldn't have."

"You didn't have to do this," I said, my voice cracking. "I was okay."

"Then why do you sound like you're going to cry?" He led me to the bed and pulled the covers back in invitation.

I knew why. I wasn't used to such kindness from anyone but my father and Eldan. Not that I'd voice that aloud, so I said nothing. The look on his face told me I didn't need to, as he brought the covers up to my chin.

He moved the dining table over so that it was right next to the bed. His chair was close enough that I could reach out and touch him if the urge struck me. He kissed my forehead and bade me goodnight as he took out his ledgers and several papers. He reminded me once more that I was safe as he pried the book from my hands and bade me to rest. I meant to ask him about what he was doing. I meant to ask him what kind of duties he had as a Prince. But I was out cold when my head hit the pillow, lost to the world in a dreamless, deep sleep.

Sunlight filtered through the blinds, against my weary eyes before they were ready to take on the day. I had apparently forgotten to close them last night. Locke was gone, of course, all evidence that he'd been there, gone as well. Another note in the spot I'd last seen him.

> *Lark,*
>
> *From the obnoxious snoring I heard, I trust you slept well. From you murmuring my name over and over, I trust you had pleasant dreams ;).*
>
> *Go ahead and begin traveling home. I have a few of those previously mentioned time-sensitive errands I must do before I catch up to you. I'll meet you there as soon as possible. Try not to cause trouble or run into it.*
>
> *Travel safely,*
>
> *Locke.*

I. *So.* Didn't. Snore!

Okay, maybe if I were exhausted. But I did talk in my sleep. I didn't remember any dreams at all, let alone any involving him, so I was roughly seventy percent certain he was joking. It was enough to calm the redness in my face and make me roll my eyes with a huff. I began packing my things, wondering how I was going to bring all my wonderful new things back home. I stuffed everything inelegantly inside my satchels and forced them closed, but they were all packed so tightly I began worrying about the stitching of my bags.

I carried my things down to the tavern where Lorelei was once again working the bar, chatting cheerfully with a few patrons. She smiled at me before approaching to bid me farewell. I handed her a coin purse with the total for the room for the duration of my stay. She shook her head and pushed the purse back to me, informing me that my tab and already been paid in full.

Of course it had. It only took half a thought to know who was behind that.

Lorelei shrugged and gave me a departure hug.

"Come back again if you're ever in Loc Valen," she said. "It was so nice meeting you!" My heart warmed as I looked at her, her face full of genuine kindness. I smiled at her.

"It was really nice being here. Meeting you was a pleasure and I feel lucky to have made such a good friend here." She beamed before a demanding patron had her rushing to return to her work behind the bar.

I walked to the stables to see Haven looking quite happy to still be in her stall. She was lounging with her eyes half closed until I came in. Instead of her ears perking up, she swished her tail and pinned her ears. Not recovered from yesterday's frantic gallop and getaway yesterday, then. I let myself into her stall, offering her an apple. She took it without a second thought, her expression softening a bit, and I knew all was forgiven. I took my time and great care grooming her for Eldan, her ebony coat gleaming when I was done. I patted her neck before tacking up and attaching my saddle bags, notably heavier this time around. She huffed at me as if she were over it.

The sun was well into the sky and the city busy by the time I was mounted on the street and headed for the gates of the city, Haven's hooves on the cobblestone comforting as I silently said my goodbyes to my new favorite place. I was going to miss the busy streets, the intricate architecture, the shops, even the fae as they perpetually hurried to and fro. My thoughts drifted to Lorelei. I would definitely come back and visit if only to go exploring Loc Valen with her again. Because of

Locke, I was coming home with more coin than I'd started with, not that I was planning on telling anybody about that. But it meant I could come back. And I'd probably have to if I were going to keep training with Locke. I thought of the prophecy as we walked over the bridge connecting the city to the rest of the world and urged Haven to an easy canter at the bottom. The prophecy was an ugly stain on an otherwise wonderful trip. If Scorpio found out who I was, and that I was within her city, that would go very badly for me. Thinking about it made me understand why Locke was mad at me in the library. He needed my assistance in the rebellion and here I was throwing myself in harm's way. I smiled despite myself. Sounds about right.

A lot hinged on what my father revealed to me upon my return, I realized. It would change the course of my entire life, and I could feel the heaviness of that settling on my shoulders and making my chest feel tight. Whether my mother was from the Fire Court and I was a child of two worlds... or if I had other elements. How could I have come to be? It wasn't by accident. And if that were the case, my father, the only family I had, had been lying to me for my entire life.

One born the way the Queen was made.

Who knew one single sentence could bring so many questions to the forefront? Questions I'd never thought to ask before. Who was my mother? And what connection did she have to black magic?

The way back to Poplar Hollow was long and arduous but ultimately uneventful. After the events from the previous day, I was heavily on my guard, but it turned out to be for naught. The road was well traveled, making it difficult for bandits to sneak up on people. Haven had to detour around slower going pedestrians, carts, and occasionally other horses.

I dropped Haven off at Eldan's first. I peeked my head into his cottage, but he wasn't home to say hello to. Given my rising anxiety about speaking to my father and the oncoming confrontation, I didn't look too hard either. I placed his coin and his ingredients I purchased on his behalf on his desk and promptly left. I untacked Haven and let her go in the pasture where she proceeded to roll in the nearest mud puddle, losing the lovely gleam to her coat I'd so lovingly given her. Typical, I smirked at all four hooves up in the air as she rolled over like a dog. I carefully put her tack away, hoisted my bags over my shoulder, and turned towards home.

Now that I was home, I realized how much I'd changed. How small my village felt. How stifling and small minded the fae here can be. I eyed one of my peers making eyes at me as if he might approach me. I dared him with my eyes. I straightened my spine, showing no fear. I almost laughed as it made him second-guess himself. That had happened a lot since last time when I'd been forced to draw blood and wound his friends in self-defense. Everyone was weary about my blade that never left my side, now that they were privy to the fact that I knew how to use it.

I turned my back to him, an insult, and walked away giving him no mind; I did not have time for a confrontation and he wasn't worth my breath. But I'd cast my awareness out behind me for several minutes, making sure he didn't try to ambush me. Nobody did. A victory in and of itself.

My small feeling of victory was short lived. I was acutely aware that I had no idea what to say to my father. "*Hey, Father! Guess what? I'm going to join the rebel army because they can teach me how to use my magic I suddenly have. Oh! And bonus! I have fire and water magic. Got any ideas about that?*" I sighed anxiously, my chest feeling tight again. My heartbeat picked up with each step I took until my own cottage nestled on the corner of the street at the edge of village came into view. The wind picked that moment to blow by carrying with it the homey scent of fresh bread from somewhere down the street. I inhaled greedily, allowing the scent to give me bracing comfort before stepping up on the veranda, trying to ignore my shaky knees.

I entered the cottage, seeing a fire warming the space, but it did nothing to drive the cold from my body as I saw my father's head pick up and smile in greeting. He was up immediately to help me with my things and ask how my trip was. But I couldn't do it. I couldn't do the niceties. I slammed my things down, looking him hard in the eye. The man who raised me stopped abruptly, confusion and concern written on his face.

"Father," I began. I didn't know how to start. How does one begin a conversation like this? I decided to go straight for the heart of it and cut through any bullshit. "I found some interesting things in my studies."

"Oh?" His eyes were a little wide, clearly not understanding the connection yet between my words and my disposition.

"Where was Mother from?"

"Why would you ask?" he asked, eyeing me cautiously. "I thought you were studying medicine." A deflection. Okay. If that were how he wanted to play, then this ought to cut to the chase. I allowed the feeling that had been bouncing around the fringes of my mind, but I had never allowed it to take root. I let betrayal in, the hurt of being lied to over and over again and a flame kicked its way up my palms, winding in a serpentine fashion around my arms, doing as I wished. My excitement mixed with horror as I realized the flames now came easily, almost naturally. It took very little effort this time. My father watched the fire runes run over my wrists, my arms glowing as if my body under my skin were a living flame. He gasped in shock, staring widely now at me. At my magic. My magic that wasn't of my court. But I wasn't done. I doused my hands, drawing on my replenished well of magic deep within me. I willed the ice flow out from my feet in a perfect circle, proving my dual magic.

"I'll ask again, Father." My voice was nearly as cold as the ice I stood on. "Where was Mother from?"

His shock never stopped from his face; it was like a veil had been lifted in his eyes. He looked different somehow. Not more like my Papa, more like a stranger. The thought filled me with dread. Long ago, my father had told me about the love story between him and my mother. It had been beautiful, sweet, romantic. All the things you'd want in your own love story. It created the foundation for how I wanted to love someone one day. But what if it were a farce like everything else? The betrayal surged within me, making my magic sputter, but I leashed it quickly, not taking my eyes off my father.

"You might as well sit down." He gestured towards the couch as he thawed my ice before it ruined the floor. "It's a long and complicated story."

"You lied to me," I said, not hiding the anger and venom in my voice. My whole life my father and I had one rule: never lie to each other. He would have my back against anything and stand with me against any foe. So long as I didn't lie to him. I thought back to my childhood, when I was teased and bullied for having no magic. When I came home with bruises, cuts, and other assorted injuries because of it. My father told me to finish my fights, but if he ever found out I started them, he wouldn't stand with me. He would not abandon me so long as I never lied to him. The cruel irony laughed in my face. I could tell he was thinking of the same rules.

"I had no choice. This will all make sense if you let me tell you everything." Anger flared, and my palms lit up. The flames danced with my temper as they blazed dangerously towards the ceiling. I doused them immediately. He wanted to tell me everything now that the cat was out of the bag? I sat with my leg crossed over my knee and my arms folded as I rested on the couch, waiting for him to continue. The glance at my hands didn't go unnoticed by me and I couldn't help but feel a twinge of satisfaction that I'd made him nervous. He launched into the story, barely pausing for breath.

"Your mother was not from the Fire Court," he began. I lifted my eyebrow, about to speak when he cut me off, leveling me with a firm tone. "Do you want to hear your heritage or not?" I settled again with a huff, awaiting his continuing. He didn't keep me waiting long.

"Your mother was from another village not unlike this one. I, as you know, grew up here my whole life. We met, fell madly in love, and were married after a year of courting. We wanted to start a family desperately." I heard the touch of heartache in his voice. My anger softened to see how much he missed mother. "We tried and we tried. For years. And we never had success. And it wore on her. All she wanted in the world was to be a mom. And she would be so proud of you," he said, true pride on his face. "I was working so much that at first I didn't notice the changes in her. The moodiness, the anxiety, the trouble sleeping, the nightmares. I thought it was a benign issue. But then she told me she was pregnant, and I thought it a miracle. I didn't even guess how, and I wouldn't look too closely under that rock." His face fell. "But I should have. I should've asked questions. Because long story short, your mother suffered from madness. At the fault of black magic." It was my turn to be shocked. At first I'd thought he was going to tell me he wasn't my real father. She'd used black magic to conceive me? What did that mean? Was I cursed? Did I have... a fifth element? "I didn't find out until you were almost born, and by then, there was nothing I could do," he continued. "I didn't know what deal she struck with the darkness. Only that when you were born, runes of white, blue, red, and gold appeared on your body." When a fae is born, the runes of their court surface momentarily on their flesh, showing the whole world who they were. Blue for Water, Red for Fire, White for Air, and Gold for Earth. And I had all four.

"The *most powerful fae, one born the way the Queen was made*," the prophecy from the Vale... The Queen made a deal with the darkness to save her brother and the darkness made her into the cursed monster she is. But I was born of it. With all four elements.

"Why do I have all four elements? What deal did Mother make?"

"Because your mother foolishly wished for you to be powerful so that you could make a name for yourself. So you'd never be a victim." The irony was like a swift punch in the gut. My father too, looked wounded as he continued. He looked like the words were hurting and sharp on his tongue. "The darkness never grants your wish in the way that you want. It grants it in a twisted and perverse way, so you spend your time wishing you'd never struck the deal. In this case, the darkness made you the most powerful fae in existence. And if that fact were discovered, you'd be hunted your entire life. So, Eldan helped us. He cast a spell to weaken your magic. And eventually seal it off. Even your Water magic. The potion is ingested thrice weekly. We couldn't dose you this week because you only ate and drank sparingly due to my illness and then you went off to Loc Valen. I had hopes that even though you theoretically could use magic, you wouldn't notice because you never had before. And even if it did reveal itself to you, it would most likely be water magic. You would've written it off as a fluke." He paused a moment, taking in a shuddering breath. Then a second before continuing.

"I'm not sure the specifics of what she offered the shadows... she never told me. But all she wanted was to make sure you'd never be a victim, as she was. She had magic, but it was weak. She didn't want you to go through what she did. And she ended up putting you through so much worse. And worst of all, her life was taken by the darkness she'd sought help from!" My father's voice was laced with an agony that even after over twenty years had still not healed. His broken, un-mended heart lay bare before me. My mind froze, unable to process what I was discovering. My mother died so that I wouldn't be a victim? My blood boiled at the pointlessness. Fate had mocked me. And her. As for my magic... I couldn't deny the Goddess-awful sting of betrayal from my father. He was why I was seldom allowed outside of the village for extended periods growing up. Because he needed to keep dosing me. Poisoning me. Walling me from my magic. My face twisted in horror.

"Well, I didn't discover it alone," I ground out, chewing over every word. "I found my Fire magic when I was fighting for my life against Prince Cancer, the Crowned Assassin. I also recently discovered my water magic."

"One of the Zodiac kinship knows… about you?" he stammered, panic streaking across his face. "We have to get you out of here! You must hide! Run!" He stepped towards me, trying to usher me, to where I wasn't sure. I shook my head at him.

"He's on his way here," I said, not moving another muscle. "He's training me. Something you should have done a long time ago."

"I did it to protect you." His voice faltered, fracturing into sobs.

"And there was a time for that," I agreed. My voice turned hard-edged and sharp. "But that time ended when I grew up. I'm not a child. You should have respected me enough to tell me the truth. Because not knowing almost cost me my life!" I yelled. I knew I should stop when I saw the pain flash in his eyes. The deep sorrow and regret. I knew later these words would haunt me, but years of betrayal were speaking through me as I said, "You should have known better. You asked me what I learned in the Vale. I met Cancer. And he was going to kill me." I left out the part about Scorpio in deference to Cancer. "I begged to bring you the Aching Cress first and that I would fight for my life and he agreed to my conditions. And after the medicine was administered, after I saw you were going to live, I stole your sword and went to face my death." He paled further with every word, his tear-filled eyes not leaving mine. "I fought bravely. You would've been proud. Cancer was. His blade kissed my throat and the fire saved me. Fire he wasn't expecting. Except neither was I and I couldn't control it. It nearly killed both of us if he hadn't taught me to control it." His eyes were wide as he took in this information. I didn't pause to let him process. I kept going.

"Cancer seemed to think that it was because my life was in immediate danger that I summoned fire. But controlling it wasn't something I understood. I couldn't use any magic before. Why didn't you tell me? Train me? Teach me how to use it?" I kept talking instead of letting him answer. "All those times I came home beaten to a pulp. For the times Eldan had to heal me or bring me home unconscious. How many times had I nearly died from my injuries? All those times I couldn't defend myself, because I never had magic. I was easy prey. And you knew the whole time!"

"Because I don't know how to teach you anything other than Water magic and I don't know anything about the other elements!" he snapped, his guilt and his horror finally coming to a head.

"I couldn't just tell you half the truth. I couldn't unlock only some of your magic. It was all or none. And if you had your magic and lost control of any other element, you'd be hunted the rest of your life. You'd have been killed. All those days you came home unable to defend yourself from magical onslaughts of your classmates? I died with you every single time! I hated doing to you what I did. But it was this, or death. Because everyone loses control when they begin learning magic. You couldn't afford it. You still can't."

There was a knock at the door. Three loud whacks. I knew who it was. I called to them to enter. I wasn't surprised to see Locke dressed in his shiny black armor at my doorstep, with the Cancer constellation, his sigil, on his breast. But my father was. His face shone with surprise and recognition. Locke's face seemed cool and confident as he faced my father by the hearth. My father had beaded sweat along his brow, as he bowed low.

"Y-your Highness," he stammered. He looked at me beseechingly. He wanted me to bow to him, I realized. The thought was so ridiculous I bit back my laughter. I turned to Locke, amusement dancing in his eyes as he clearly came to the same conclusion. My father watched us, perplexed.

"I will never bow to you. That's way too weird," I said to Locke. He shrugged, the picture of nonchalance, clearly enjoying my game and happy to play along.

"Good thing I don't expect you to," he said, eyes still bright with amusement. "I'm not sure anyone could make you bow, with that stick up your—" I cursed at him as I smacked him in the arm with a mock glare and he chuckled. My father rose from his bow with a look of uncertainty. The Crowned Assassin, Prince Cancer, stood in his living room, bantering with his daughter. His daughter did not bow to him. His daughter fought for her life against him, and now they were... friends? Allies? It was clear he didn't understand our dynamic and it made me laugh. It took some convincing from me, but I had Father fill in Locke as I boiled some water for tea. Locke's face remained carefully blank and he sat still as a statue as he listened to my father's story. He didn't say anything a long while afterwards, creating an awkward and uncomfortable silence. My father looked downright terrified, something I'd never seen before. I thought he looked like he'd just confessed his sins to the enemy and was now afraid for both of us. Which, in his mind, is exactly what had happened. I placed my hand on his shoulder, offering a half smile. One he did not return as I glanced back at Locke.

"He's not our enemy," I told him in an attempt to be reassuring.

"He's a Zodiac! He's the right-hand man of the Mad Queen herself! What's to stop him from betraying us? Our lives rest on this information staying secret," he whispered.

Prince Cancer snorted derisively from his place on our dilapidated couch.

"The majority of what you told me I already knew. The magic suppressant I didn't know for sure, but I suspected. If I had wanted to turn you in, I would have." Father looked at me, confused.

"He has super hearing," I said, reading his thoughts. "It's a Zodiac thing. You get used to it." Or did I misread his confusion? He was a Crownguard. He would be familiar with Zodiac hearing. Perhaps he was just processing everything.

"And you're okay?" he said, looking at me. "You're okay with him?" Locke bristled at the thinly veiled accusation, gritted his teeth but said nothing. I whirled on him.

"Okay? He's saved my life on more than one occasion. And he's teaching me my magic. I trust him more than I trust anyone else right now." A low blow and we all knew it. Even Locke looked surprised at my hostility. Hostility I would come to regret later, I was sure, but at this moment I couldn't bring myself to care. I would apologize later. I felt the need to get out of my house, the cramped cottage walls slowly caving in on me. "I'm going to get some air. Don't come looking for me." I didn't wait for a reply as I stomped out the door and headed... somewhere. I didn't have a destination in mind. I just needed to go. The angry energy around me was nearly a physical thing, snapping whips at me and forcing me to move.

I turned to the trees. I ran into them and I didn't stop until my lungs cried for air and my legs ached fiercely. Birds chirped around me as I sat down to stew in my own hurt. I wanted to cry out my anger, my frustration, and betrayal, but no tears came. I knew I needed time. Time to process what Father had said. It was by this point that I was already beginning to feel badly for what I had said right before I left. *Papa had just wanted a good life for me and how could I have that if we were on the run? If I were hunted by the very fae training me? If I'd been named on his kill list?*

On the other hand, being the village punching bag because I was an easy target wasn't exactly a hoot either. Maybe that was one of the things I had loved about Loc Valen. The anonymity. The fact that nobody knew me. I could blend in seamlessly. Nobody knew that I couldn't perform magic and there was little reason to ask. But after years under Eldan's tutelage as a healer, I could move there and open an apothecary supply store. I could do that. I didn't have to stay in this Goddess-forsaken village.

The more I thought about what my father said, the guiltier I felt. I understood what he'd been trying to do. The sting of the lies cut deep, but my understanding of his perspective made me contemplative and broody, rather than angry and spiteful. He could've told me a few years ago. But he chose not to. That was what I couldn't understand, or forgive. At least not yet. I got to my feet and stalked back towards the cottage, needing to burn off a little more steam. I knew I'd need time. Probably a lot of it.

I thought back to all the days I came home with bruises and marks on me, unable to defend myself against magical attacks. I eventually learned how to fight back with my fists. My father told me to grab the biggest one and break their nose. It had worked and I remembered the feel of his nose crumpling under my fist. I stared at my hand, remembering my dad helping me ice it after, a huge smile on both our faces. A rare victory. But it meant that I was dealing with ranged attacks from then on, and there was nothing I could do about them other than learn not to get hit. He could've helped me. He could've let me use my magic. The tears came then. Hot and streaming down my face. No sobs, just tears. All that pain. All the humiliation. Feeling hopeless and defenseless. It could've been avoided. I was so much stronger than them. But nobody knew. How ironic was that?

I couldn't take it anymore. I let out a scream. My anger, my despair, took hold of me in the form of ice. Frost I scarcely felt the cold of raced in a tingling rush past my fingers and into the ground. The ground became a solid sheet of ice, quickly fanning out around me and coating everything in crystal-clear ice. It encased all it touched in a shimmering glass. I didn't stop. I pushed my ice magic into the trees around me, coating them, frost collecting on the boughs around me, until I'd created an entire area of solid ice. It looked like a winter fantasy. Bright sunlight cascaded through the trees and glittered on the glass-like coating on the trees. I heavily dragged air into my lungs, genuinely wondering if I'd breathed in the last minute. My hands on my knees felt like the only things keeping me upright.

When the tears began to stop finally, I stood again. The shadows along the ground had lengthened. *How long have I been out here?* I began the walk back to my cottage feeling drained and practicing my apology to my Father. I'd tell him I was sorry, that I understood what he'd tried to do. I understand he couldn't have known what would happen. But I'd also tell him that I'd need a bit of time to get over the hurt. That I was going with Locke to train. That the time would be good for us. Locke had promised that my father would be taken care of if he decided to remain here, which for now I hoped he did. I had a lot to process before I lived with him again. For the first real time, I felt no angst over leaving. I needed to step into who I could truly become. Perhaps when I'd healed, he could join me. We could be a family then, with a fresh start, and we could finally leave Poplar Hollow behind.

I heard shouts ahead of me and in the very next breath there was smoke on the wind. I looked up, trying to see through the trees, but to no avail. Upwind of my current position was my home. Something was wrong. Had someone seen my display of fire magic back home? I thought back, but there was simply no way.

I pushed my legs into a run as I held panic at bay, the smoke in the air getting stronger with every breath until it was a knife in my lungs. I coughed as I made my way closer. For the smoke to be this thick, it had to be one of the homes on our street. Chills licked down the back of my neck. Or perhaps intuition. I knew before I got to the edge of the forest which house had caught fire.

Flames licked their way along the roof, climbing higher still. Black smoke was choking out the sunlight and giving the immediate area a twilight effect. My legs carried me to the door before I even made the decision. Where was Papa? Locke? I flung the door open and flames rushed to greet me. I expected the rush of heat, and as subtly as I could, I pushed the flames back, though they were far greater than my power and limited training could control. I couldn't put the fire out. I could only buy myself seconds. A minute at most. I called out for my father, hearing the flames snap in response. I walked into the living room watching everything engulfed in flames. I felt the strain on my magic as I struggled to keep the flames at bay. The smoke rushed in with each breath, trying to choke me. I sputtered and coughed as I made my way through the rooms. I ran to my cot in the next room, filled with smoke but not yet fire. I grabbed the bags of my belongings I'd brought from Loc Valen including the coin and flung the pack over my shoulder and attached it. I saw no sign of anybody being in here. I called out for my father again. For Locke, once again receiving no reply. I couldn't check my father's room. It was an inferno, as if Hell itself had crawled up here to take that part of the home.

I was out of time. My magic was spent and I couldn't stay here any longer. I scanned the room once more for signs of life and left with tears on my face. My home... I ran through the front door for the final time with dread gripping my heart. The air outside the inferno was comparatively cool, the sweat on my body feeling freezing moving away from the flames. It was then that I saw my father.

He wasn't there when I'd entered the house. He lay face down on the ground not far from the house, unmoving. A puddle of what could only be blood under him. I had helped Eldan heal massive injuries to know how much blood one could stand to lose. Under my father was well beyond that, the red liquid catching the fire light and giving it an even more grotesque look. He was eerily still, his blank eyes staring, fire dancing in his pale gaze. Bile rose in my throat as I screamed. I saw the rest of the picture then. To see Locke kneeling over my father's body, knife in hand and blood spattered on his armor and face. My world zeroed in on that scene. My father's body lying still and Locke kneeling with the blood-soaked weapon that killed him, his hands roaming his body as if searching it. Locke was covered in his blood. I heard white noise in my ears and the perimeter of my vision faded to black as if to frame a snapshot of the worst moment of my life.

No, no, no, no, was the only coherent thought I had. It echoed inside my head back and forth. I couldn't move. Could barely breathe. Someone far away was screaming. Locke looked up at me, eyes wide with horror. He'd been caught. My father was supposed to be safe. He'd promised. Yet, he'd killed him himself. Betrayal flared through me, hot and red and unlike anything I'd ever known.

Waves of wrath crested within me, each larger than the last. I didn't remember reaching for the blade at my side, nor the other in my boot. I didn't remember making the decision to fight. I was getting flashes of what was happening. It was like a play, and I was watching in third person, my body acting of its own accord. I hacked and slashed my knife crudely at Locke, which he blocked without effort. He continued blocking and evading my attacks, though never landing a blow. Something wet on my cheek. I realized I was sobbing as I attacked. Locke's expression was hard and unreadable.

"Lark, please stop," he said, and I saw the moment his front fell away. His eyes were wide, beseeching, hopeful. And a touch of something else. Remorse? Acceptance?

"Did my father ask you to stop before you slaughtered him?" I spat the words out, putting as much venom into them as I could. I didn't stop as I drove my fist forward, crudely stabbing with the knife with everything I had. Locke sidestepped it easily, but I whirled on him fluidly and struck again. And again.

"Please, Lark, you don't understand what—"

"Oh, I'm pretty sure I understand just fine. Did my father ask too many questions? Did he not want you to train me? Are you not used to the word 'no'?" I snarled, my voice taking on an edge of something wild. "What did he do that he deserved this? I'll never get to apologize to him for what I said. Because of you!" I switched my knife to my backhand and in one motion spun and stabbed at him, giving myself more leverage than stabbing forward. There was a high-pitched screech as it made contact with his chest plate, but it skidded inelegantly to the side, harmless. I threw myself into the fight, blindly attacking. I knew if I didn't have my knives I'd be coming at him with my nails and teeth.

"It's not what you think." His voice was pleading with me, but it had taken on a darker edge. He was almost at his tolerance level with me. Good. Then maybe we could end this. Because I was done too. The only family, the only ally I truly had, was gone. The only fae on this earth that loved me was dead and I didn't know how to move forward. I screamed at him to fight me, to fight back. But he kept refusing. On the edge of my awareness, I knew people had started to come to help, both with the fire and with the body. Everyone's attention was on the fire that was now burning out of control and was catching neighboring cottages. They didn't notice or pay any mind to the skirmish across the street in the treeline. We were set back from the road to be easily noticeable. And I was too far gone to care. Locke turned and fled into the trees, and I followed him, a snarl loosing from my lips.

He stopped a few minutes into the trees and whirled to face me under the boughs of the forest. A dark blue aura surrounding him, giving him a dangerous, ethereal look. His dagger in his hand held perpendicular to the ground and chest level in a defensive position. His black hair falling into his hard eyes. He looked every bit the predator I knew he was. I just never expected him to take the life of the only person I'd ever cared for. Instead of seeing an ally, a friend, possibly more, I saw him for who he truly was: Cancer, the Crowned Assassin in all his deadly glory. And it hurt. It hurt so fiercely, this hole now gaping in my chest. I'd started to like this monster. I'd started to care.

Never again.

"Lark." His voice was low, rough, as if under great strain. "I don't want to fight you. I don't want to hurt you!"

"Tough," was my only response. I was determined to finish this. I tried my backhand spin again, this time aiming purposefully somewhere more exposed. As our blades crossed repeatedly, I felt hot. There was a heartbeat where I saw why. My blades were engulfed in flame, the meadow around me had burst into flames. I was surrounded by fire. I looked at my hands and saw the flames writhe on my skin. I kept attacking, using this magic I didn't even conjure consciously. I was landing hits, his cheek openly bleeding from a wound I inflicted. I tried my backhand spin again, and the world went cold.

Strong hands encircled both my wrists, squeezing until I dropped both knives. And then he pressed me to his chest. I tried to summon water, ice, fire, anything, but my magic was tapped out from controlling the flames inside the burning house, and whatever explosion of magic I just did in the meadow. I struggled weakly against him, though I knew it was useless.

"Lark. Please."

I snarled a curse back at him and struggled for all I was worth. I bit, kicked, screamed, and I struggled, but Locke held on. I felt a savage satisfaction at the hiss of pain he emitted when I head-butted him, drawing blood. I bit down hard on his hand but he didn't let go. He refused. Nothing I did was going to get me out of this situation. I cursed him loudly. The tears threatened to fall down my face as my body stopped fighting. Recognizing it had lost, and was completely spent, I sagged. If not for Locke holding me up, I would've fallen to the ground. I hated him in that moment. He was still covered in my father's blood and he had the nerve to touch me? I finally realized I was sobbing uncontrollably, tears and other things pouring down my face. He didn't let me go. I had no idea what to do from here. How could I go on without my father? I was too young, I had so much more to learn from him. He was my only family. He was everything to me. And he was dead. The images of him glassy-eyed in death over an impossible amount of blood came into my thoughts unwittingly, sending me into another wracking sob.

Eventually the sobs turned into hiccups. And then into nothing. My body was utterly spent. I couldn't even protest as Locke put an arm under my knees, tipped me backwards, and caught me under the shoulders. I heard him mutter something I couldn't understand. I felt a tingle of magic. My eyelids immediately grew heavy and I didn't remember leaving the safety of the trees. My eyes closed and I was bombarded with memories from today—the worst day of my life.

Chapter Nine

"Papa, you're so pretty!" I squealed in excitement. My papa laughed as he took in his reflection in the looking glass. He wouldn't let me use animal fat to do his hair, but he did let me use as many hair ties as I could find to "spike" his hair. My papa had more than enough hair for the style, his blond locks falling to his chin, now separated into roughly thirty tiny individual ponytails, the hair ties wound several times around the smallest bunches of hair.

"Yes, darling Lark. Pretty is the gold standard I strive to achieve every day." My papa chuckled, planting a kiss on my forehead, earning a squeal from me.

"Why can't I use hair product?" I pointed to the animal fat. My father grimaced, dramatically.

"Because Papa likes his hair to smell good," he said, lifting me up and placing me on his shoulders. "Let's go for a walk and get a treat. My hair looks so good, others should see what a great job you did." I beamed at him. My papa bounced on each foot as he walked, jostling me with every step, making me giggle with delight. Around us, fae stared. Some looked emotionless. Others looked on in disgust. But any time I began to notice, Papa would bring my attention back to him, jostling me harder and making me laugh.

We were led to the bakery by the increasingly enticing scent of cinnamon and warm sugar. Once inside even I could notice that we were the recipients of more hostile glares. But on some level, I knew nobody would harm me if I were with my powerful, magic wielding father, the Crownguard. My papa was purchasing a favorite treat: sweet honey cinnamon bread. I was beside him at the counter when a small child, maybe a year or so younger than me, approached me. I eyed him wearily, but smiled nonetheless.

"Hi!" I said in greeting. He smiled at me, wide and toothy, and returned my hello.

Finally, someone who might talk to me and not shy away from me. "What's your favorite color?" he asked me.

"Teal," I said excitedly. "What's yours?" He told me red with an innocent excitement, matching my enthusiasm. He asked me my name, his smile widening. "Lark! What's yours?" He opened his mouth to tell me. It was then that his mother broke from her conversation and noticed who her child was talking to.

"Gael! Get away from her. She's beneath you." She hissed at me. "Noquim," she spat at me. Gael looked up, confusion easily read on his young face, looking back and forth between his mother and me. My father's head snapped up and fixed on the fae before she could say whatever else she was gearing up for. He said something to her in that tone that often alerted me to trouble. The tone of voice that made hair stand up on your neck. Pure venom. I couldn't hear the words. But I watched as the offending woman's face visibly paled at whatever he said. He turned back towards me with a smile that seemed a bit tight as we walked out together with our treats. I looked back at the boy—Gael— but found he would no longer meet my eye. I turned my attention to my bread that my papa placed in my hands. The smell was like heaven, allowing me to at least pretend to ignore the stares of the village fae around me. Worthless. Noquim in the old tongue meant worthless. My peers made sure I knew that. Papa told me to ignore them. I tried. I tried so hard. But it wasn't just a small group of fae. It was the entire town. How do you ignore an entire town?

"Never let them see that they hurt you," Papa said to me on the way home, when I asked him why everyone was always so mean to me. "Fae are fickle, cruel, and if they think they can get a reaction out of you, they will do so. So never give them a reason."

"Why can't we just go some place else?" I frowned as he guided me back home amid more stares. Papa's hand softened on my shoulder.

"Because nothing will ever change, pumpkin. No matter where we go, when fae discover you don't have magic, it'll be more of the same. I'm sorry. I wish it wasn't like this. It's not fair to you."

"Me too," I said.

"You know I love you, right? You're the best thing that ever happened to me. Magic, or no magic. I'm so incredibly proud of you. I'm proud to be your papa." He said it loud enough that all the fae around us could hear, and I didn't miss the stare he directed to everyone looking over to us.

When my eyes fluttered open, I was lying on a soft bed with numerous pillows. My eyes were still heavy, requiring more sleep, and slipped closed again. Before I remembered what had happened—the fire, the blood, the fighting—I bolted into an upright position and took in my surroundings. I was in a small room, the walls a creamy, soft white like the sleep clothes I was currently wearing. Furniture in dark wood tones broke up the stark white on white motif. Next to me was a fully stocked bookcase, my singed satchels I'd rescued from the fire waiting for me next to it. There was a large, comfortable-looking chair in the corner of the room. Locke sat elegantly in it, one ankle crossing his knee, his eyes wearily on me. He cocked his head as I sat up, his lips thinly pursed. I glared at him, my expression like that of a wounded animal. I instinctively reached for my knives, but of course they were missing.

"Why?" My voice was hoarse. It was a question, an accusation, and a demand. Bile rose in my throat looking at him. He'd cleaned himself off and changed his clothes. Were we back in Loc Valen? The only window in the room couldn't answer my question at the angle I was currently viewing it.

"Why do you think I killed him?" he challenged with his chin raised against the accusation. I turned my body towards him abruptly, making hard eye contact with him. I was only aware of my tightly curled fingers into fists by the sharpness of my nails biting into my palms.

"I saw you with the knife in my hand. Don't try to confuse me. I saw his blood on you. I saw you searching his body."

"Do you not know me well enough by now to know I don't spill innocent blood unless I have no other option?"

"All that means is you think my father was guilty of something," I sniffed. I looked down at my now raw-feeling hands, realizing I'd begun wringing them at some point during the conversation but genuinely having no idea when. Doubt, however unwelcome, crept into my mind. Could my father had been hiding something else? Something sinister? But I'd thought of him making pancakes on Christmas. Of him reading to me every night before bed as a child. Of him comforting every sorrow away. I knew that couldn't be the case. I saw his eyes yesterday before I left to cool off. He had been stripped bare, no more secrets to show me, and I knew not to doubt myself. Locke didn't answer at first, his eyes sharp as he took in every movement. I wondered if he could feel my hatred. I wondered what color it was. I wondered if black were too obvious an answer. And I wondered if I'd ever ask him.

"You didn't see me kill your father. Yet you're so certain I did it."

"There was nobody else around, Locke!" I shouted at him scornfully through a clenched jaw. "Don't try to gaslight me into believing you're innocent. I know what I saw. Who else could it possibly have been?" His features turned glacial.

"Believe whatever you want. Consider it motivation, then, for training."

"If you think for one second I'm training with you still—"

"Oh? And where do you plan on going?" A cruel smile that didn't reach his eyes spread across his face. That must have been why he killed him. To ensure I had no real place to go. I could stay with Eldan I supposed, if I ever got out of here. And for that, I realized with dread and disgust, I had to train. I had nowhere near the magical resources to take Locke on, or anyone under his employ. And while I give myself credit for being scrappy, I wasn't up to snuff with a blade either, at least against anyone with any real skill or multiple opponents. I looked down at myself, flexing my muscles, searching for signs of injury. I found none. Surprise rippled through me. Locke never attacked me yesterday, remembering flashes of our battle. Flashes that were hazy, like remembering a dream. Locke had evaded, blocked, and eventually disarmed me, but he never attacked me. That should have been enough to put me at ease, but it didn't. I glowered at him with distaste, resisting the urge to spit at him.

"I'll be back shortly with some food. I'll give you a tour after you've finished eating and we'll go over your schedule." I refused to acknowledge him. "Please try not to get into trouble. I don't want to fight with you."

"Then let me go! I have no desire to be your prisoner." His head snapped towards me.

"Is that what you think this is? You think you've been kidnapped?" he asked incredulously before shaking his head. "Your father is dead, Lark! If I let you go now, there is nothing for you. This is where you agreed for me to train you not too long ago. Remember when you said you wanted to take down the Queen? If you go out there right now, with your emotions as they are, you're going to lose control. Maybe not right away, but you will." My memory snapped to the flames in the meadow. The out-of-control inferno as I fought Locke.

"You might even hurt someone, you might kill someone. Do you want that on your conscience? But worse, you'll reveal yourself for what you are, the most powerful fae ever to cross the earth. So much power, but no training to control it. How long do you think you'd last when the Queen realized who you were? A whole Court coming mercilessly for you? Multiple Courts even, if Scorpio plays her cards right, which she usually does. How else do you think the other courts have allowed her to slaughter her own people all these years?

* *
* * *   Of Curses and Contempt   * * *

"There would be no place safe for you. Nowhere but here right now. Once you've mastered your elements well enough, I will not stop you if you still wish to leave and never see my face again. But until then, you're my guest here." His voiced grated over the word "guest' to emphasize it. "Is that perfectly clear?" I gaped at him. I'd never heard him speak so much, or so passionately. Like he'd meant every word he said. "I know you don't trust me. I know you don't believe me. But I've never done anything that wasn't in your best interest since meeting you." I couldn't bite back a snide reply, though my sneer was likely more than enough.

"Fuck you," I said, leveling my glare in his direction. He body position shifted as he fully faced me, leaning against the door frame with his hip. His arms crossed. His eyes met mine and I saw the fiery challenge that lay there. And the darkest humor. His eyebrow raised and a ghost of a smirk graced his features.

"You're always welcome to." I balked at the unabashed look on his face, a complete contrast to what you could almost call compassion that was just there. His smile was sinful when he added in a husky voice, "I remember our time at the inn fondly."

"You make me sick!" I gasped. "You kill my father, kidnap me, and now you have the balls to suggest I sleep with you?" I was incredulous. "You're a monster," I choked out. He'd used me, I realized, and the hurt of it was palpable. I'd slept with him because I'd wanted to, yes. But I'd also found myself liking Locke. A lot. What we'd done in the inn had meant something to me. It was clear that those feelings were a one-way street. I felt it. The revulsion. The nausea. The urge to crawl into a ball. Be small. I'd thought for a moment he wasn't like the others. For just a moment. My eyes burned but not just with sorrow or despair. With hate. Rage. They burned but I'd never let him have the satisfaction of my tears. Goddess, I loathed him.

The dry smile on his face didn't reach his eyes. His voice picked up an even dryer lilt. "Good. Glad to hear it. Welcome home, Lark."

"This is never going to be my home." The venom poured from my lips. "I hate you."

"And your words wound me greatly," he said in a carefree way that made me think the opposite. I saw the quick, unfocused look he donned when assessing emotions, but it was gone before I could form some nasty retort. He turned to the door quickly then, and just like that he was out the door, closing it softly behind him. I jumped to my feet and ran to the window to get a better view of my surroundings. We must have been somewhere at least partially underground, because this window looked like a little pop up. I saw roots overhanging the window that suggested that this window was hidden to the outside from under a tree. Earth magic or strategic design? That made me think that wherever I was, the location was a secret. Not necessarily Loc Valen then. But I knew now that the window wasn't a viable escape plan. Except... as much as I hated and resented it with all my being... he was right. I was a ticking time bomb if I didn't learn to control my magic. The meadow where I fought Locke was proof of that.

So I'd do it. I'd learn. I'd let him teach me the ways of the elements. The ways of the sword and shield. Of dagger and bow. And then I'd look him in the eyes as I kill him. I'd make him regret the day he killed my father. A needless, unnecessary death. But something felt off about it. He refused to tell me why. I couldn't be sure of why, but it definitely made me infinitely more suspicious of him.

There was a light knock on the door some time later and Locke opened it without waiting for an invitation from me. I threw the closest thing to hand at his face, a book, which he caught easily.

"I'm ready for you. I'm not going to let my guard down."

"Good to know my knocking before entering alerted you to my presence, then. You know, the exact opposite of being stealthy." He rolled his eyes. His tone was dry as he tossed a wry smirk at me. I rolled my eyes in return, my contempt for this man almost overwhelming. I could feel the heat itching to ignite along my palms. I couldn't believe I once liked him. That I was even potentially starting to care for him. My glare alone should have been enough to make him wither away under the heat of it. Red runes were slowly flickering to the surface along my arms and hands, the first sign of my control of my magic slipping. I expected Locke to say something about it.

But instead, he presented me with food in a basket, much like that morning at the inn. In it was a variety of foods, all of which got me salivating: roasted chicken, carrots, buttered mashed potatoes, fluffy dinner rolls, fragrant gravy, and a pitcher of water. Of course, he knew my favorite meal. I couldn't hide my stomach growling. I glared my displeasure at his half smirk. I wanted to wipe it off his stupid face. I took the basket and stared at him, hoping he'd leave. On cue, he turned towards the door, granting my wish.

"When you've finished, come find me in the arena. Just turn left and follow the hall. You won't be able to miss it. We have much to discuss." His tone felt overly formal and business-like, as if I were dealing with the Prince for the first time rather than Locke. Before I could tell him to fuck off, he was gone. He didn't even await a response from me as he left and closed the door behind him. I waited for his footsteps to fade down the hall before falling on my food. Not surprisingly, it was delicious. Of course it was, I thought as I devoured it, flavor exploding over my tongue. Why did it have to be so good?

When my belly was sated, I waited some time. If he thought I was going to be given orders, he was absolutely mistaken. So instead, I examined the books in the bookcase. Back at the inn, when we'd chatted over soup we'd discussed favorite books. I had read all the ones in our library at home. As I looked over the titles, I realized they were the ones I'd mentioned as my favorites. And several others that seemed to have a similar feel to them. There had to be fifty books here, and the whole top row were the ones I'd listed as my favorite. It was hard not to feel touched by his remembrance as I fingered the spines delicately.

I wasn't surprised at the loud knock on my door some time later. I looked up from my book with a huff of annoyance as a pretty fae with dark blond hair with a flower crown opened it and let herself in. Locke's girlfriend, maybe? His treachery really did know no bounds. Goddess, I hated him. Possibly more even than the Queen.

The girl smiled at me despite the anger and mistrust that must have been apparent on my features. "Hi! I'm Lenore. Locke asked me to bring you to the arena for training." I rolled my eyes and shifted my gaze back to my book.

"I have no interest in doing what he tells me to do. Tell him he can fuck right off. And tell him he doesn't need to send his girlfriend in the future." She laughed, in no way put out by my hostile mood.

"He said you might see things that way. First, if you're asking if he's single, he is." She accented that with a wink. I hated the flush that came to my face. "Second, he told me to tell you that if you don't follow me, he'll tell everyone about what happened at the inn." I looked at her in horror. He wouldn't dare. She narrowed her eyes at me, still smiling. "I don't know what happened at the inn, but you sure seem to want to keep it that way, gauging by your expression. But he also said he's content to sling you over his shoulder and carry you out if he has to. And he'll have fun with it. Just come down for training and meet everyone, Lark. Right now, you're only making things difficult on yourself."

"I'm not a child, so maybe don't address me like one," I snapped, putting some venom into it. I glared at her in what I hoped was a vicious expression. My temper thrummed in my veins. If he wanted me, the bastard could come collect me himself.

"Then stop acting like one."

I flipped her off and made a show of dismissing her by returning my attention once again to my book when another girl who looked like Lenore's identical twin popped her head into the room, scolding Lenore.

"No wonder she doesn't want to come with you." She elbowed her way in front. "You're being such a bitch." She turned and faced me with a bright smile. Lenore bristled at her comment but said nothing. I almost laughed.

"Sorry about her. We may be twins but I've always been better with others. She can be a bit rough around the edges, but we all mean well. I'm Lennox. My sister and I are two of Locke's Knights." I just stared at her, unsure what to do. "Look," she sighed, sitting down onto the edge of my bed, "I know what you're feeling. We've all been here before. I know you don't trust Locke. You might even hate him." She smiled brightly and reached her hand across to take mine, which was still clutched in an angry fist. She gave me the kind of smile that lit up a room. The contagious kind. "But I haven't done anything to you. Will you just come with me to the arena? It would make all our lives easier if you did. Yours included."

I sighed, resigning myself to Lennox and to training. I told myself I was only going because Lennox asked so nicely.

I rose on shaky legs that I was pretty sure I hid well. I inclined my chin and stared down my nose with what I hoped was haughtiness and hostility at both of them. I put one foot in front of the other, making it out the door with a twin on either side of me. I bristled at how close they were. At all of this.

"I know you hate him, but Locke is a really good fae," said Lennox gently. "He looks after all of us. And I know he cares about you."

"Killing my father is a funny way of showing any of that," I countered spitefully as we moved down the hallway. Others stopped and stared as we approached and passed by. I inclined my head at all of them, daring them to make a move against me.

"Why do you think he killed your father?" asked Lenore, bringing my attention back to her. "Despite his title, he's not exactly prone to unnecessary violence. You might want to consider what your dear old dad was doing that might have gotten him killed."

Lennox scoffed at her sister. But I didn't even think. I didn't even remember making the decision to act. My hand flew of its own accord.

I punched Lenore in the face.

Lennox grabbed Lenore before she could do anything in retaliation aside from laugh. I had no idea that a laugh could sound so menacing. I knew by the dark look on her face that Lennox might've just saved my life. When you punch someone in the face and make them bleed and all they do is laugh... that's enough to know you're dead meat later. I knew I was going to have to watch my back. I couldn't help the small bit of grim satisfaction rippled within me when I saw Lenore's bloody nose. It helped with the fact that my hand hurt like hell. But it did nothing to quell my fury.

"You don't know anything about my father." My voice was callous and deathly calm. Beneath it was a violent undercurrent of anger raging against the restraints I'd placed over it. My limited control slipped before I knew it. I couldn't leash my powers any longer and fire erupted over my clenched fists at my side. The twins both froze. Both gaped at me a moment before Lennox bade Lenore to go up ahead to the arena, and that she'd take care of me from here on. I watched Lenore go with my lip curled up in a growl, curse words on the tip of my tongue. My fiery palms begged me to hit her again. To be unleashed upon her and everyone here. I took a calming breath. Then two. And a third. My more volatile emotions coming back into a manageable territory. Though my flames continued to beg, to thrum addictively under the surface of my skin, I wrestled them under control and doused the flames. I savored Lennox's unsure reaction. Despite her earlier shock, Lenore seemed cool as a cucumber when she walked off, seeming unfazed entirely by the encounter. Lennox only sighed, schooling her face back into a calm mask. But I'd seen a flicker of surprise her in eyes. Of caution. Good. "Well, that could've gone better." A smug, uncaring grin toyed with my features at her dismay.

"Really? I've had worse introductions." I tossed my hair over my shoulder and sauntered after Lenore. I kept my head tall and my eyes up, seeing that everyone nearby had stopped to watch me. Some wore nervous expressions. Some looked ready to fight me. *Do it*, I thought, in both warning and invitation. I had no qualms about going down in a bloody fight. My knuckles still sang after I punched Lenore. And I was itching to do it again, my muscles and magic alike begging for a release. My magic coiling and exploding just beneath the surface of my skin.

After a few minutes, we opened into the arena. A coliseum was a better word for it as I eyed the stadium seating around the perimeter. It was easily as big as the town square of Poplar Hollow, but three times as tall. It seemed to be set up for various stations: close combat and ranged attacks for the fighting side, and magic wielding. The close combat section was outfitted with a wide assortment of weapons: swords, spears and glaives, battle axes, maces and Morningstars all hung delicately as if artwork on display. Also close by were punching bags, mats, and various weights.

The ranged station was more limited; an assortment of different types of bows, throwing daggers and stars, and a few throwing spears lined up over here. Even a chain scythe. There were targets of all shapes sizes and distances away. Various fae trained and sparred under supervision and order of... a drill sergeant? A commander? I wasn't sure.

The magic area of the arena had a small circular podium in the center, I assumed for the tutor to give instruction. Around it was a moat of water, I assumed as a source so nobody was wasting magic creating water. Being in the Water Court, I supposed that made sense. Around the perimeter of the entire arena was a running track. This place really covered all the bases and there was still so much room.

Locke was in the close combat station sparring with someone. Locke held a sword and his opponent a sword and a dagger. He didn't even notice me come in so I waited on the sidelines, watching him move, feigning disinterest. He'd discarded his shirt somewhere and I saw the bulging of his biceps and the hard angles of his abdomen, suddenly feeling very soft in comparison. I blushed, remembering those hard abs against my body. I chastised myself as I watched him, damning him for being ridiculously handsome. I could hate him and know he was hot. I swear I saw him smirk as he sparred, but it could have been unrelated to me. His eyes never left his sparring partner.

I watched as they went through what looked like a choreographed routine, it was all so fast, so reactive. Instinctive. But I knew it was just years, decades really, of devoted study and practice. I watched as they slashed, pirouetted, crossed blades, and danced around each other until finally Locke got the upper hand at last and disarmed his opponent, forcing him to yield.

They clasped forearms with wide grins and easy laughs. They looked like old friends, brothers even. I wondered briefly if I were looking at Pisces, our realm's third Zodiac. I scanned his body for telltale runes, but found none. What I found instead was Locke approaching me with an easy smile, hard eyes, and the grace of a cat. And still no shirt on.

It took great effort not to stare at his body, covered in various runes, and keep my eyes on his as he approached me. Locke's body was…. It's not like I hadn't seen it before. In the inn. It wasn't like I didn't see when he was sparring that he had a good body, but… with his swaggering step approaching me, I got a long look at the angles of him. Lightly bronzed skin hinted at training outside as well. I flushed. The damned faerie was cut. Seriously cut. The way the light accented him was very flattering to him, the shadows outlining and defining his muscles favourably. The planes of a broad, tattooed chest, abs, even the swell of his black and blue rune-lined biceps spoke of an impressive fitness regimen.

He cleared his throat as he got closer and I hastily brought my eyes back to his face with a sneer. His face now donned a shit-eating grin. The kind of grin that told me he knew exactly where my thoughts had drifted to, and he was quite content in his smug amusement. I scowled at him. Asshole. He may have been hot, but he was still an asshole. A murderous, kidnapping lunatic.

I watched as Locke strode through the space, closing the remainder of the distance between us with the grace and confidence of someone who's always been assured of his place in the world. All others parted for him and he moved through them all without a cursory glance, looking every bit like the rock water flowed around. He spared nobody attention, his eyes zeroed in on his target: me.

I deepened my withering look, content to show him my displeasure. At him. The entire situation. At being summoned like a dog. His entire being. I hoped he could read the loathing in my stare. It was the kind of look I'd honed over the years to make others think twice before approaching me. Attacking me. But it only served to amuse him further, that smirk widening as he reached us. Bastard. His eyes dipped to my lip and I realized I'd started chewing it. They darkened, clearly remembering the last time I did that. I shuddered, effectively ending the moment.

"Thanks for finally making an appearance." His voice grated on every nerve. "Welcome," he said lightly, " to Hell's Gate." I glanced around, seeing a lot of the fae were leaving until only us, Locke's sparring partner, and a handful of others remained. Though the latter paid us no mind. The tall, blond stranger Locke disarmed strode over to us. His long strides ate up ground quickly as he made his way over behind Locke. His smile seeming a permanent fixture on his face.

"This is Aspen. He's my second in command here. If you can't find me and you need anything, Aspen will be close by and can help you." Aspen seemed like Locke's exact opposite in many ways. They had the same piercing blue eyes, but Aspen's looked bright and unhindered, where Locke's always carried a haunted look that said some of the ghosts of his past had nearly caught him. Aspen was all light where Locke was dark. Sandy blond hair left long enough to be up in a bun; a five o'clock shadow dusting his chin; a lean, muscled body; and a smile of perfect teeth that seemed like it never faltered. He had a light, easy energy about him. I liked him immediately. He reached his hand out to me. I stared at him a moment as if he might bite me before returning his handshake. He didn't seem fazed by my hesitation.

"I know he subtle brags a lot. 'I have a second in command,'" he mocked teasingly with an exaggerated eye roll. His hand was warm and firm in mine as he shook it. "If you tune it out, he does eventually stop and go away." He winked at me and I honestly couldn't fight the rising grin despite myself. Locke gave him a fake wounded expression and I actually laughed for a second before I caught myself.

"I'll consider that lesson number one," I said, finding a scape of humor for the first time. "Got any other tips on that?" Aspen chuckled and proceeded to list a few things. Apparently, he was allergic to fish oil and it made him break out. He liked his skin flawless, so if I wanted to be rid of him, all I had to do was threaten him with it and he'd run screaming for the hills. Locke protested.

"Hey! That was one time!"

I gave him a pointed look and grinned savagely, daydreaming about getting my hands on fish oil and putting it all over his pillow. Maybe I could irritate him enough to let me go. I could be the worst captive and annoy them all into kicking me out. That could be effective.

Locke finally cleared his throat, effectively ending my reverie and my improving mood. I dragged my eyes to him, seriously wishing he'd put a shirt on. Keeping my eyes up was not easy, and I wasn't loving the memories his bare chest was bringing up. *Why did I have to sleep with him?* I groaned internally. And why had it had to be so good that even though I hated him I still liked the memory of us together? Locke cocked an eyebrow at me but didn't acknowledge my train of emotions further. Thank the Goddess.

"Every morning at eight a.m., breakfast will be delivered to your door. By ten a.m. sharp, you'll have weapons training and physical enhancement here in Hell's Gate with Aspen. So I'm glad you like him now. You likely won't once we start tomorrow." Tomorrow? That soon? Aspen wiggled his eyebrows at my incredulous look. He continued, not giving me a second to ask. "You'll have lunch after you bathe. You'll have a few hours of rest, or personal time, and at four p.m., you'll have magic lessons. Dinner will be right after that, and you'll have personal time again."

"How long does it take for people to harness their powers?"

"It's different with everyone," Aspen said, rubbing the back of his neck with a shrug. "Learning the intricacies of one element takes months on its own. You have four. I don't know what your timeline is, Lark. I'm sorry. That's why we're practicing every day."

"And where is 'here' exactly? Where am I?"

"You're still in the Water Realm," he said. "The most northern city of the Water Court, Port Azure. Welcome to the Court of Rebels." He grinned. "Though I hoped to bring you here under happier circumstances. But the Queen won't find you here. There are enough misdirection wards around us that unless one of us leads you in, you won't get in. Same with getting out." There was a slight warning in his tone. I feigned innocence I was certain he didn't buy.

I glanced over that in an effort to make it look like I wasn't planning to escape at my first opportunity. "Can she be beaten?"

"Well, that depends on your definition of 'beaten,'" he said seriously. "Can we kill her? No, we, and others, have tried over the years. She's invulnerable. It's part of her curse. She's cursed with a hellish existence she cannot die from. But if we lay waste to her defenses, we can capture her and dethrone her that way. If we all train hard, we amass larger numbers, and we're lucky, then yes, she can be beaten."

"What if we break her curse?" I asked. Both of them stilled. Locke was the first to speak.

"That requires you dying."

"I'm well aware," I said dryly.

"Well, it's out of the question. There's no need for you to throw your life away. You're more valuable alive."

"Really? Tell that to the people whose towns have been destroyed? Their families? Their livelihoods? How do you think it feels knowing your death might be the only thing that stops the cycle."

"Assuming we let you die, which we won't," he growled, showing his impassivity on the matter, "ending her curse doesn't kill her. It restores her sanity and ends her eternal suffering. There's no guarantee she'd stop or be any easier to kill. Scorpio didn't just become the Queen by accident. She's strong, both a skilled fighter and can wield magic better than almost anyone I know. You dying doesn't make sense." Aspen looked horrified and a little sad.

"I think I'm ready for that personal time that was promised?" I yawned, ready and eager to get out of here. I was suddenly feeling hot and stuffy and claustrophobic despite the large area. I just wanted to be back on the bed I woke up in. I wanted a book and some tea and my blankets. I want to cry. I missed my father.

Father...

A wave of grief hit me. I grit my teeth against it and forced it back. I refused to give any of these fae the slightest bit of ammunition against me.

"I'll escort you back," Locke volunteered. I waved him off and turned on my heel. He followed me but not before finally snatching his shirt where he'd discarded it before my arrival. He donned it before leaving the arena.

"Glad to see you know how to wear a shirt," I said dryly as he reached my side.

"You didn't seem too upset when it was off. In fact, your aura told me you liked the show." I laughed with out a trace of humor. He was just so damned self-assured.

"Did my aura also tell you I tend to like my men with a bit more substance then just nice muscles?" I asked with a sugary-sweet voice. "Too bad your brains and personality are all in your biceps, or you might actually be interesting."

"So you admit my muscles are nice." I snorted and rolled my eyes. "That's not a no," he said as we arrived at my door.

"No, but this is." I opened my door, slipped inside, closed it quickly, and locked it. There was silence on the other side, but I didn't hear footsteps. He was still on the other side of the door.

"I hope you enjoy the books," he said softly through the door. Almost... shyly? "We can get more. Let one of us know if you want or need anything and we can acquire it. I know it doesn't feel like it now, but... I want to make this your home for as long as you're here. Whatever you need to make you feel at home, just ask." I didn't respond. I stared wearily at the door. I heard him let out a heavy breath of resignation and finally walk away. I didn't know what to do with any of this information. I didn't understand his attempt at kindness. My guess was to assuage his guilt? Assuming he felt any? Perhaps to attempt to win my loyalty for the upcoming war I was sure he was going to wage.

I didn't understand his ability to get under my skin. I had every intention of lying down with a book, but instead I lay down on my bed and let my mind wander. I thought of my father. I wanted to remember how he was making breakfast in the morning, but now every time I thought of him, I thought of that damned puddle of blood under him. The expression on his face, immortalized in death. It was like he was telling me to run from beyond the grave. Perhaps I should have.

It wasn't long before I was crying again, fat tears running down my dampened cheeks. I curled into a ball, feeling small and fragile and everything I couldn't afford to be right now. I cried myself to sleep that night. Every time I closed my eyes to try to sleep, all I saw was the nightmare of my father's death. Next to him was Locke covered in his blood. The pain, the loss, the dread, the betrayal all came back, as fresh as it was yesterday. I brought my knees to my chest into an even tighter ball and sobbed, soaking the pillow beneath my head. I mourned. I not only mourned my father's death, I mourned what could've been between Locke and me. If only his feelings had been real like mine were. If only he hadn't killed the only person I ever cared about. How could I have been so stupid? So fucking stupid?

That stupidity is what killed my father. I was just as guilty as Locke was. And I knew I'd never forgive either of us.

I hissed in pain as my father brushed passed me, his shoulder collapsing into mine. He didn't mean to. His leg still gave out occasionally, his leg muscles not rehabilitated well enough yet to support him from his brush with death in Loc Valen, despite the passing seasons.

"Lark?" my father asked me, looking me up and down with suspicion. "What's wrong?" Before my father's eyes could find anything, I turned away, walking into the kitchen, biting my lip to choke down another sharp intake of breath.

"Nothing, Father. I stubbed my toe. Sorry, I didn't mean to get in your way. Eldan should be here soon. Would you like a cup of tea if I make some?" But I was lying. I wasn't okay. I felt the blood oozing on my stomach from a wound made by a blade. He'd gotten me just enough to wound me, not kill me. But that didn't stop it from hurting and bleeding incessantly. They'd found me mostly unarmed, finding herbs for Eldan in the forest. They found me, and a golden opportunity. I finally lost them after an hour of blindly running and being chased by to the edge of the Deep Wild, attacked, injured, and left for dead. The trek back had been arduous and slow going. And terrifying. Baying howls could still be heard from the forest outside, looking for the source of blood I was leaving behind. My long sleeves covered the majority of my wounds on my arms—mostly superficial lacerations from running through thorny brambles. But a few were from deadly sharp icy projectiles they'd tossed at me. Some I barely got out of the way from.

I had slammed my medical kit closed and shrieked into my pillow as to not alert my father to my current state. He'd only worry or get angry. His seeking retribution every time this happened came from a good place but ultimately only served to aggravate my aggressors. I glanced down at my shirt, the wound open and leaking through my new shirt now. I had no thread left to stitch it closed. I sighed mournfully, so irritated with myself for not restocking my first aid supply and I was left to use the only thing I had: large quantities of tape and a few small pieces of fabric to bind my wounds. But it wasn't effective. Even now I felt the wound leaking a bit. Even moving was difficult. I was going to ask Eldan in secret for a healing spell, not for the first time. My father eyed me, his eyes narrowing. He read me like a book, knowing the signs all too well.

"What happened?" he asked, his voice firm, but kind. He sighed. "Another attack?" My father told me to never lie to him. We couldn't have trust if we lied. So I said nothing as I prepared the kettle to boil. "Show me," he said.

"There are too many," was all I said. My father's voice shook with his next words, a tempest in his eyes.

"Show me, Lark. What did those bastard kids do?" I raised my shirt a little, showing the tape and soaked-through fabric had done a terrible job at keeping the wounds on my abdomen closed. My two tunics layered together kept the blood from showing. Father gave a sharp intake of breath when he saw. Wrath continued to fill his eyes and he let out a long, slow breath. I knew that look. That he wanted to murder someone. The problem was he'd have to murder the entire town. Because they were almost all in on it at some time or another.

"I'm so sorry, Lark. You deserve none of this."

I smiled grimly.

"You should know I broke one of their noses. With my fist."

He bellowed a laugh, certainly for my benefit. "That's my girl." He embraced me into a careful hug. I heard a small sound that sounded suspiciously like a sob. But when I pulled back, there was no sign of it. There was a knock on the door, and the telltale sound of squealing hinges to let us know Eldan was here. "Okay, Lark, who's going to tell Eldan he has two patients again?"

I woke before the dawn, unheard of for me. I didn't know when I eventually fell asleep, but it must have been late. I got up and walked to my attached bathroom. My appearance was frightening to say the least: red-rimmed eyes lined with dark circles, hair like a tumbleweed, and blotchy, pale skin. What a complete mess. I decided a bath would be the way to go. I knew I'd have to have another one after training later, but I just needed to feel clean. There was a variety of soaps and many different scents. I decided on eucalyptus and mint, craving something that might get me feeling somewhat energized. I washed slowly, relishing the hot water. I hadn't realized I'd felt so cold, the water thawing me from the inside out. I washed my hair three times over. It took that long to get the remaining blood from my hair I hadn't even realized was there until I saw the tinges of red in the water. I left the conditioner in my hair for several long minutes while I soaked in the hot water before rinsing it and combing through the numerous tangles.

I heard a knock on the door. I tensed. Was it Locke? Breakfast? Locke with breakfast? I decided not to answer, and I heard the door open. So much for locking the door. I was going to have to have words with Locke about that.

But the door closed seconds after opening and I heard the lock click into place. I cast my awareness into the room, feeling nobody within the confines of my space. I took a moment to appreciate the ease with which I did that. It must have been breakfast being delivered. I rose from the bath, rivulets of water pouring off me. I pouted at having to leave the hot water. I donned my dressing gown and saw that breakfast had indeed been delivered. Oatmeal, an assortment of fruits, a tin of honey, and some yogurt topped with what looked like sweetened pumpkin puree. I also saw some breakfast sausage on the side. Damn Locke to Hell, but he did feed me well.

There was another knock on the door. I quickly stood and opened the door to see Aspen in front of me. "Good morning, Lark. How did you sleep?" I glanced at the clock in a pointed look. I still had over an hour before I had to meet him. What was he doing here? He gave me a smile which I didn't return.

"I slept fine. What are you doing here?" My abruptness didn't throw him but his puppy-dog eyes looked sad. It's hard not to trust someone who looks like the fae embodiment of a golden retriever. And it was even harder to be intentionally mean to them.

"Locke sent me to bring you to your new quarters." New quarters? "He apologizes for giving you such small accommodations. It was a last-minute, split-second decision to bring you here and he wasn't prepared. I understand he was going to bring you here at some point, but he wanted to have your rooms ready." Rooms? Plural?

"What if I'm perfectly content here? And why is everyone his errand person? He can't face me himself?" I asked, crossing my arms. Aspen laughed.

"Locke is dealing with a few emergencies in town right now. And hold off on making that decision until after you've seen what's waiting for you. And Locke really does insist we move you somewhere more comfortable. No offense, but this two-room spot isn't big enough for you. You're going to need more room for your weapons, armor, clothing, and anything else."

"I get weapons and armor?" I asked, my mouth hanging agape. They'd give me a weapon to use against them to escape?

"Of course! You'll be fitted for armor later today as my memory serves. And as for your weapon," his eyes glinted, "I guess we'll see what you're good at." I turned to pack my belongings. "You don't need to do that. We'll have someone bring your things to your suite later on." I shuddered, not loving the idea of a stranger rifling through my things. "Does it make you feel better if I'm the one that moves your things?" I nodded after a moment of hesitation. "Okay then, I'll do it after our session later. For now, will you let me give you a tour? Port Azure is really something special."

I followed him upstairs. So this place wasn't entirely underground. Hell's Gate was. Where I was sleeping was. There seemed to be a million hallways we didn't traverse down. My guess was it was originally how they hid when the rebellion was very new. Stay under ground, stay out of sight. Stay safe. But I followed him up a long flight of stairs until we breached a threshold of a large door. I looked around. Windows and the greenery beyond proved I was above ground once again. My breath was stolen from me as I took in where I was. We were standing in a shining atrium with large glass pillars and a domed glass ceiling at odds with the dark gray stone floor, reminding me so much of the Library of Aramithia. The dark gray was continued to a massive, curved staircase leading upwards. Glass refracted the early vestiges of morning sunlight around the room, giving it an ethereal appearance. I walked over to inspect the flawless glass. Upon touching it, I found it frozen. I wrenched my hand away from the sharp cold. It wasn't glass at all, I realized in awe, but spelled ice. Perfect, flawless ice pillars elegantly connected the floor to the ceiling.

I stepped out the main doors to the outside at Aspen's behest. The salty sea air, cool this early in the morning, greeted me. It blended harmoniously in with the pine and spruce from the forest to the south, smelling faintly of alpine. I looked to where the Veinfall mountains nestled to the west. Their snow-capped peaks singing pink and orange in the sunrise.

It was... beautiful.

Port Azure was stuck someplace between encampment and town. There was a mish-mash of permanent and temporary, old and new. Cobblestone streets mixed with compacted dirt, stone, and wood buildings tangled with a few cloth exteriors. But instead of looking decrepit, it looked eclectic. Interesting. I didn't know what my eyes would fall on next. From the doors to the atrium Aspen and I had emerged from, I landed on a covered stone veranda with the steps to the middle of town at my feet. I looked out at a perfect square, much like Loc Valen or Poplar Hollow. To the southernmost wall stood a clock tower, its watchful face looking to the sea to the north. The wall of the building I'd just exited, Aspen told me was dubbed the Citadel. I almost choked at the ridiculousness of that. The Citadel was massive, indeed, with two massive spires looming from it. It was more a mansion than a citadel. A mansion that may have been extravagant ages ago, but now fell on the cusp of disrepair. Maintained well enough to function. The Citadel. I snorted to myself. How pompous. But then an idea nagged at the back of my brain. I began to wonder if it had been a joke, naming it that. Much like how they'd dubbed themselves the Court of Rebels. The Citadel took up the entire border of the eastern portion of the square, green vines taking over much of the aged gray stone of the wall. Time had taken its toll here. I glanced upwards into the windows, looking for signs of life that must surely be there. I saw nothing. The homey scent of baking bread reached me then from a bakery nearby, reminding me of Poplar Hollow. Reminding me of my father. It my heart ache fiercely with profound homesickness.

Tall and thick stone walls rose up around the perimeter of the town, casting much of the perimeter in shade, but also protecting its citizens from the forest just south of it and the terrors that undoubtedly dwelled within it. And keeping me in, I thought with resentment.

Aspen pointed out various points of interest within the Square. Business thrived, even so early in the morning. Much like in Loc Valen, there were merchants at pitched tents with their items, cafes with fae milling about for a warm beverage, and even a blacksmith taking orders from a customer. I didn't know what I'd expected from the rebels. Perhaps stony-faced, angry fae. Bitterness on their tongues and in their eyes. Hostility towards anyone and everyone. But that wasn't what I witnessed. Fae milled about, going to and fro, in a way that so reminded me of Loc

Valen but slower. Calmer. More relaxed. Many were smiling. They looked happy. I pondered the implications of that. This could be reality everywhere if the Barbaric Queen were to fall. I looked around taking in her lack of influence. How happy everyone seemed. Even Poplar Hollow, along the very southern edge of the Court and held away from Loc Valen, didn't seem this happy, though I supposed that had to do with the poverty and being the last stop of the line for traveling merchants. I scanned the fae, taking in every detail. But there didn't seem to be anybody suffering from poverty here. Everyone seemed to have enough. I tried not to think about what that said about Locke's leadership skills. I couldn't stop my eyes from roaming across everyone's face, wondering if I'd see Locke. I didn't.

Aspen told me that further out beyond the walls of the city were the fields that sustained the Court of Rebels. I saw their houses interspersed between buildings and out towards the edge of town, the mountains once again demanding my attention in the backdrop, taking my breath away a moment in combination with the swiftly rising sun. Aspen beckoned me back to the Citadel, citing the remainder of my tour. Despite the chill making me hug my arms to stave off gooseflesh, I was reluctant to go back inside. When we returned to the atrium I noticed a few details I hadn't before. Doors I hadn't noticed before. Aspen and I continued up a few flights of stairs that opened into what seemed to be a residential wing. Aspen pointed out that everyone I'd met so far lived up this way and that I was just joining them. That was a nice way of saying I'd be carefully guarded, I huffed to myself. Well, that would make escaping difficult. We arrived at a set of double doors. Aspen paused, grinning at me before he opened the doors to the most beautiful room I'd ever seen. Clearly the inside was better maintained than the outside? Or perhaps magic was involved in preserving the stone. Or perhaps it was an aesthetic. Because the aged stone walls of the outside were in stark contrast to what was before me.

It had panoramic windows, offering an exquisite view of the sea I'd scented earlier, the beachy tide just north of our current position and of the Veinfall mountain range to the west, the beautiful but unforgiving border between Courts. They reared up in the not-so distance in all their glory from this uninterrupted vantage point. A sunrise was well underway, painting the sky in hues of pink and orange. Like a symphony of color in the sky. At the foot of the mountain, trees waved in the wind, their leaves a staggering red and orange in the early fall weather. Early for this time of year, but this far north it shouldn't surprise me. It was breathtaking.

I finally tore my eyes away from the view to admire the rooms. Its warm-toned wood floor and creamy wall color gave it a calming, cozy feel. It had a nicely decorated seating area with a sofa and two huge chairs perfect for cozying up with a book. A fire in the hearth greeted me warmly. It took a moment before I realized the hearth was see through. Double sided. I walked through the adjoining door to find a bathroom with the same view, all white tile and gleaming gold finishes. Stunning. Luxurious. Way too over the top.

The bedroom also had a fireplace and wall of windows. Light teal and white bedding of many layers looking plush and comfortable. The multiple textures giving it a luxurious feel. I opened a massive closet to find clothing of all types inside: formal, everyday dresses, pants, and shirts, slippers, boots, shoes, all of it was here. I'd never had so much before. My gut fell through the floor. I imagined I'd find it when I went back to Hell's Gate. I didn't do a thing to earn this. I resisted the urge to cry. Aspen out his hand on my shoulder.

"Locke just wants you to be comfortable. You've been through so much, Lark. You deserve this. You deserve to be taken care of. I know you worked hard your whole childhood helping your father." So Locke really did tell him everything. Splendid. "Don't give me that look. We're not your enemy. None of us are, least of all Locke."

"He killed my father!" I snapped at him. "He can try to buy my forgiveness with these rooms, these pretty things, but I can't forgive him. Not for that. He'll never—"

"Why are you so sure Locke killed your father?" It rang odd, the same wording Locke had used with me. And Lenore.

"Because he was searching my father's body, holding the knife that killed him, and was covered in his blood," I seethed. Nobody believes me. Of course, they'd blindly believe the fae that was leading them. Fine.

"You don't know all the facts," Aspen said, looking a bit like a wounded puppy. His big eyes were sad as he took in my ever-hostile demeanor.

"Then tell me all the facts. Everyone seems to have a tough time telling me! If you want my opinion to change, I'm going to need to know!"

I saw the want in his eyes. He wanted to tell me. He opened his mouth, but no words came out. My heart sank. Aspen sighed after a few heartbeats.

"I can't," he finally drawled out. "Locke ordered me not to. I don't always do as I'm told, but I understand Locke's reasons." His eyes got hard and serious for a moment. "And he has a good reason, Lark. I promise. But trust me. Please. And trust him. We are your allies. Your friends. I've seen the way you look at us. At him especially. You can hate us if you want. I'd rather you didn't because we don't return that sentiment, but if that's what you want to do, that's fine. But don't hate him. And of all the fae you have to worry about, you never have to fear any of us. Least of all Locke. You don't ever have to fight for your place here the way you did before. I hope you know that. Nobody here will ever hurt you or disrespect you. Those scars you think we didn't notice? You'll never receive another one from anybody here." I stared at him. I blinked down at my faintly scarred arms. I thought of the scars on my back. I didn't know what to think. What to believe anymore. Aspen seemed so sincere. So honest and open. But I'd thought that before. I've learned my lesson about trusting others. Allowing fae in only set you up to get hurt. Locke just recently proved that. I scoffed a humorless laugh. The clock sounded half passed the hour and Aspen grinned, asking me if I were ready for our first lesson. I doubted it.

Aspen showed me in the closet where my training attire was. I decided on tight black leggings and a black fitted shirt. I wore sturdy, ankle-high boots that should've been heavy but weren't. I braided my long hair back and I was ready in under five minutes. I emerged from the closet, Aspen whistling his appreciation. I blushed.

"Come on then, Little Bird," he said, already walking to the front door. "Let's see what you're working with."

"Little bird?" I scrunched my face in distaste. He grinned as we walked out the door.

"Larks are birds. It fits."

"It's cringe-worthy."

"Then make me stop saying it in Hell's Gate," he challenged. I decided I would more than rise to that challenge.

By the time we walked into the arena, it was filled with the rebel army. Some were sparring with various weapons like I had seen Locke do yesterday. Some were moving too fast for my brain to process their movements. Some were practicing archery, their movements skilled, precise, and well practiced as they pummeled the targets with arrows. I noticed they seldom missed their marks.

There was a magic instruction taking place to the far right of me as well. I saw fae create weapons of ice, conjure massive torrents of water at one another, or blow hot steam. There was the occasional shout of pain, but nobody ever seemed to get injured. There had to be hundreds of fae in this massive facility, and it was still nowhere near capacity, still so much space for additional activities.

Aspen led me to an open area near the weights, which I eyed suspiciously. I wasn't sure what Aspen was going to put me through, but I was certain it was going to suck. The fae in question turned and began going over our new routine. Upon my arrival every morning, I would start with two laps around the room, one in each direction. I would come back to this area and begin mobility stretching, stretching through movement rather than remaining static, to prevent injury. I would then perform light body weight exercises: glute kicks, lunges, sit ups, planks, stair steps, and the list kept going, boggling my mind with all these new terms. Then he would meet me here for our workouts. My mind went blank for a moment, my jaw falling slack. That wasn't the workout? Aspen met my eye with a thoroughly amused grin as he continued his speech, seeming to savor my discomfort.

Failure to do so would result in me being forced to run stairs. I asked what he meant. He gestured at the rows and rows of stadium seating above us. There had to be hundreds of stairs. If not thousands. Running stairs meant you went until you were done and couldn't move any longer. Or you finished going up and down each row once. Which ever came first. I gulped to negate the tight feeling in my throat and chest.

Aspen guided me through my warmup, doing it with me. It was a little insulting, him not breaking a sweat while I was trying to suck in all the oxygen in the room just a few minutes in and trying to ignore the horrid cramping and tension building in my muscles. Before this moment, I'd fancied myself to be in somewhat decent shape. Going through Aspen's routine I knew that maybe that wasn't case. And we were only just getting started.

By the time I'd finished my warmup, I was drenched in sweat and my limbs were a little shaky. I sipped a lot of water, trying to not guzzle it down like I'd wanted to. Aspen had the audacity to look as fresh as when we'd arrived. Aspen went over with me various punches I already knew: uppercuts, hooks, jabs. It felt good to run through some old routines that felt familiar. He went over various counters and blocks. Instructed me on how to read an opponent, and how to maneuver around them. He seemed happy with my form over all. Seemed to be pleased he wasn't starting from total scratch with me. I sagged, weariness picking at my limbs. Aspen chuckled at me lightheartedly.

"We're nowhere near done, Little Bird. Get up." He pulled me to my feet before I could bring my shaky legs under me. "I know you hate that nickname," he said with a wicked grin. "I want you to punch it out of me."

"You want me to hit you?" I asked incredulously. I'd only ever truly sparred with Father. The answering gleam in his eyes forced me to see a different side for Aspen. Maybe he wasn't quite as golden retriever-ish as I initially thought, leaving me wonder if he were completely sane. "I want you to try." He raised his chin as if to offer a challenge and present a target at the same time. "Let's see what you've got!"

I squared my shoulders and crouched down into the athletic stance he'd shown me, my fists cocked and ready. I gauged his stance, looking for the best opening. But I also knew that if presented me with one, it would likely be on purpose. He growled at me to hit him or he'd come for me. I didn't have to wait long before he pounced. He was fast, but I was too. I leapt to the side, quickly recoiling my legs under me. He rushed me, and I punched upwards with him nearly on top of me, lunging upwards with my legs to give me enough power to break through his block. He staggered backwards, surprised by my moves, but I still missed.

"Impressive evasion," he said, his eyes assessing. As if he knew I'd had to evade attacks my whole life. "But I told you to hit me. So hit me!" Annoyance dragged its fingers down my neck and I huffed. I didn't bother crouching again and I ran at him head on. He was expecting it and blocked easily. I narrowly avoided his counterattack, a punch to the torso. I had to figure out a way to open him up. Lateral movement, I remembered with a sting. My father told me a way to break an enemy's guard was to be more unpredictable. Move around. Keep them guessing.

So I circled. Switching my stance often. I faked going in to watch his reaction, his block. I may end up taking a punch to hit him. I decided almost instantly. Worth it. Anything was worth it if I could wipe that smug grin off his face.

I launched myself at him, watching his right side as I beelined towards it. At the first sign of his block, I dug my feet under me, dodged to the left around his block, and launched from there, his face now open. My fist made contact with the side of his cheek at the same time his elbow caught me hard in the ribs, sending me back a few steps. Pain crunched through my side and exploded behind my eyes. I grit my teeth and I grinned savagely through the pain at him. I'd punched him. I got him hard too, a small welt forming on that perfect high cheekbone of his. I expected him to come at me again and I raised my hands, ready to strike again, feeling my ribs scream in protest. I felt my body curl to the side as if to take strain off those ribs. As if to protect them. I felt a moment of fear that he might attack again before Aspen surprised me by putting his hands up in a sign of surrender.

"Well done, Lark," he praised, pride dripping from his smooth voice. He fingered his welt a bit. I winced as I tried to stand and found that my ribs recoiled angrily when I did. Goddess, even breathing hurt. The sharp pain in my side only intensified when I tried. "Sorry about that. Come here." I eyed him wearily as he approached. He gently placed his hands over my ribs and I hissed and recoiled from him. "Trust me," he purred in a soothing voice. I didn't stop him from putting his hands on my sore ribs again. He commented that they felt bruised. I felt a tingle of magic and he blew out a breath. "I gave you two cracked ribs and you barely even flinched. Damn it, Little Bird, that's pretty impressive." Another tingle of magic and I felt the sharp pain become dull. Until it was only a nuisance. I could stand straighter. I could breathe painlessly. It still felt sore, and I had no doubt I'd bruise, but it wasn't that blinding pain now either. And then after another moment, it was gone entirely. I gaped, having no pain and full range of motion again. Aspen must be well versed in healing magic. Healing even cracked bones takes a lot of study and power. He told me to come at him again. I grinned in reply.

We stayed after it for two hours. He showed me how to read an opponent's guard better. He told me how to break someone's guard, and how to flit around them without using as much energy as I did. Someone as slight as me needed to use my speed, he'd said, echoing the words of my father. I felt proud of him. That he'd taught me the basics before. He showed me a few simple attacking and defense maneuvers to try. Some feeling so foreign to me, others felt as easy as breathing. I couldn't help the intense surge of pride when Aspen seemed impressed with me. And I threw myself into the challenge of our lesson. When our lesson was over, Aspen helped me stretch and walked with me to cool down, chatting mindlessly with me as we went. He loved books too. They were a weakness of his. We discussed various titles and he told me he'd helped Locke stock the library for me. He knew some of my favorite books, but he looked forward to seeing my reaction to some of his recommendations. I told him I looked forward to it too. I was surprised by the fact I actually meant it. It was the first genuine smile I'd given since I'd been here, however brief.

The tension in my body was intense. My muscles felt like ropes to the point I was barely able to move by the time I'd climbed the stairs to my rooms and settled into a piping hot bath. I tried to inch down slowly, with a heavy ache settling into my limbs. But I ended up falling into the scalding-hot water when my arms gave out from fatigue. I hissed when the hot water washed over me, burning and turning my skin an angry red color.

But after a few awful moments, the water began to soothe the aches of the day and unknot the tightly laced muscles. I gingerly washed the sweat and grit off of me. I still had a magic lesson with Locke. I frowned. Aspen had confused me today. He told me that we were allies. Friends. Now growing up, I never had much in the way of friends, but I thought you didn't lie or withhold the truth from them. But Aspen said he had a good reason. For killing my father or not telling me why, I didn't know. Perhaps both.

I must have drifted off to sleep. There was a heavy knock on my door and it roused me. The hot water was now barely warm and the bubbles were nearly gone. I heard my name called out. Locke. Of course it was. I looked at the time and realized I'd missed lunch. I'd been sleeping in the tub for over an hour!

I called out, letting him know I'd fallen asleep soaking away my workout pains. He knocked on the bathroom door and asked if I were okay. I told him I was fine and I'd see him in a few hours when we had our lesson. When I finally emerged from the bathroom fully clothed in a similar outfit to my training outfit earlier and my hair flowing behind me, Locke was gone. On my nightstand was a minty-smelling salve with a note:

Apply liberally to sore spots after your workout. It works wonders.

Locke

I didn't need to test my muscles. They still indeed felt sore. I put some of the pleasant-smelling slave on the more tender spots, feeling a warm, tingling sensation settle into my skin, even sinking further lower into the muscle tissue itself, giving relief where the hot water just couldn't. Pure bliss.

I wandered my way around until I found the dining room. That was a nice way to say mess hall. It was huge, ornate, with large tables and benches, ready to accommodate an army. Did the entire town eat together or just those in Locke's employ? Currently, it sat near empty. I wandered, finding my way to the kitchen area, unsure if I should be back here, but my growling stomach urged me on. I looked for anyone who could tell me how to proceed. Where to get food.

"Lunch was an hour ago, wench! Scram!" a scraggly, middle-aged man said from the sink. How had I not seen him? His clothing was brown and dirty not unlike the dishes he was cleaning I supposed.

"I'm sorry, sir," I said, my small voice contrite. "It's my first full day and I missed lunch. Would it be okay if I got something to tide me over until supper? You don't even have to help me. Just show me where and I can do it myself. Even just a sandwich?" I flashed him a charming smile. He didn't look like he was buying it but then, "Your first day?"

"Yes, I arrived here last night. Locke had told me to be at lunch but after my weapons lessons I fell asleep, exhausted. It won't happen again." He grumbled but pointed to the ridiculously large pantry and told me to make myself a sandwich with whatever was there. I thanked him profusely.

I found bread, cheese, and some sort of leftover roasted meat in the fridge. I even found butter. Real butter! It was simple fare, but it tasted so good and I savored every bite. I thanked the man again. He waved me off and grumbled at me to scram again, but his words didn't have the bite to them that they had when I walked in. I checked the time and cursed. I had to be back at Hell's Gate soon. I braided my front pieces of hair into a crown over the top of my head and quickly pinned it in place. I half jogged back to Hell's Gate, my muscles protesting the whole time, making it just in time. I stopped just before the doors and walked in as if I were perfectly on time and didn't just rush here like a lunatic. I tried and failed to calm my breathing as well.

Locke stood alone in the empty coliseum. The place felt enormous with just the two of us here. He looked at me as I approached with a small smile on his face. Not a smug grin for once. An actual smile. My heart skipped a beat and my pulse skittered in response. I scolded myself for being so affected by his looks. His smile didn't falter, but his eyes darkened, his brows knitting together ever so slightly.

"You're actually my instructor?" I asked, my tone coming off surprisingly dry and cool considering how flustered I felt. He shrugged, arms coming outwards from his body.

"Far be it from me to brag about my considerable gifts, it's so undignified, I do so this one time." I scoffed at him as he continued, "I'm the best there is at water magic. So I'm the best to teach you." I didn't dare think about how much I'd learned in the meadow during my stay in Loc Valen.

"That's an ego trip if I've ever seen one. Tell me, how do you and your ego fit in the same room? Even one the size of Hell's Gate? Your arrogance is appalling." He grinned wickedly at me, challenge in his eyes.

"I think the word you're looking for is 'confidence.'"

"I think the phrase I'm looking for is 'go to hell,'" I murmured, my voice thick with revulsion.

"We're standing in a place called Hell's Gate. I'd say close enough!" I glowered at him with my arms crossed. His features softened. It was the first time I'd seen Locke like this since I'd been here. "Look, you can try to beat me up using magic. Try to do what I have planned, and for the love of the Goddess above, try to do what you're told. You can go back to being a pain in the ass again later. I promise I'll make it worth it if you do."

"For the love of the Goddess, I'll go through the lesson if you stop trying to get into my pants again!" He boomed a laugh that went on for a few seconds, making me uneasy.

"I'm sorry," he said in a tone that made me think he wasn't very sorry. "Who said anything about sex? Can't I reward you in other ways?" I felt a blush creep across my face and I pursed my lips, fixing him with a venomous glare. Mortification threatened to swallow me whole. I hoped it would. "But it's good to know you thought of sex with me as a reward. I'm happy to oblige anytime."

"Are you good at anything other than running your mouth? Because it doesn't seem like you have much else to offer." He smirked.

"As I said earlier, it's undignified to brag. Come closer and we'll get this lesson started." I took a few steps in his direction, casting a glance around my surroundings, still finding us to be the only two here. "Seriously, get over here. I don't bite." I chewed my lip before I realized what I was doing, remembering how he very much did bite from time to time. A closed the distance between us to stand next to him.

"Why do I get the feeling this place isn't empty very often?"

"That would be because it isn't," he stated simply. "You're one of the only fae here who hasn't mastered their element. Not your fault," he added in before I snapped at him, "but with early magic training, there tends to be magical outbursts that can cause havoc." I remembered the meadow, when the flames were everywhere. I didn't even remember summoning them. His eyes flickered, as if knowing exactly where my thoughts had led me. "It's best for everyone's safety if we practice alone at first until you have a better handle on your power."

"Won't you get hurt if I have an… outburst?" I tried to keep my voice light and uncaring. An outburst sounded like a good way to get back at him. Perhaps even give me an opportunity to escape. He gave me a strange look that told me he knew what I was thinking but didn't call me on it if he did.

"I can take care of myself, I assure you," he said through slightly narrowed eyes. A warning. He was onto me. I shrugged and gave him my full attention. Ready to finally learn how to wield my magic. One lesson before had me capable of so much. Even if I didn't like the idea of him instructing me, I couldn't deny how far I'd come in such a short time. I couldn't wait to see what else I could do. What I could be capable of. What I could use against him when the time was right. I narrowed my eyes. I was ready.

"First, I want to teach you some theory you may not have been taught previously. About whole magic. Magic not bound to an element, such as healing or shrouding." Like how I could reach out with my consciousness to feel other fae or other beings around me. He nodded. "Yes, just like that. All fae are born with the magic of their court, and all fae have access to whole magic and can all perform most spells to some degree, but everyone is born with different innate abilities. Some fae are gifted at healing as Aspen is. I was gifted shrouding. Some fae are gifted stealth, others The Sight," like Amaya, "and so on. Whole magic has millions of spells we can use for combat or for daily living. You having access to whole magic and all four elements means we don't know what your limits will be. And similarly to how sore you were today from training with Aspen, you need to work up to using large amounts of magic. The well of it within you hadn't been tapped into your whole life. Now it's being used often. Like a muscle, it'll get easier to use until it's as easy as breathing and your stamina will last longer too.

"Okay, I want you to reach out with your mind like you did before. As far as you can." I did so, feeling him on the edge of my awareness. I cast my mind out about thirty feet. It was a strain to go further. He told me to push into it, stress it a bit. Play with that boundary. I gritted my teeth as I did what he asked, all while fighting the mental fatigue. I flinched, feeling an odd stretching sensation in my mind. When I could hold it no longer, I let it go and it snapped back, leaving me panting and gasping for breath. "Very good. I want you to do that every day, throughout the day. Flex the muscles of your power that way, trying to go further each time." I nodded.

"To start, I thought we'd begin with some control exercises. I want you to conjure water like before and hold it into a ball." I did as he commanded, this time coming easier than the last. It took a few seconds to bring water to my hands, and a few more to form a sphere, but I got it. I beamed. "Well done," he purred. "Now make it a square." I rearranged the water as he asked. Then a triangle. The five-pointed star was the hard one. Maintaining one or two points meant letting another dissolve into the center. At one point, I was pretty sure my star somehow looked more like a penis. Locke, to his credit, coughed back a laugh behind his hand, and I, to my credit, didn't drown him where he stood.

It took long minutes of heavy concentration, but I finally got all five points on the star. I released it with sigh and wiped the sweat from my brow. But Locke was as relentless as he was a good teacher. He had me do it again after a moment of rest. I could feel the sucking sensation in my body, my magic depleting.

I made the star quicker this time, now knowing how to hold multiple points of contact without folding the whole image.

"You're a fast learner," he praised. "It takes some people a few lessons to do that."

"I'm not some people." I barked a laugh.

"No, no, you're definitely one of a kind." I flung a few drops of water at him. I regretted it immediately.

He summoned enough water to fill a pond and surrounded us with it, effectively blocking the world away. He held it at bay as I fingered the freezing cold, shimmering water that rose up around us, my face watching in awe.

And then he slammed the full force of it down on me, knocking me on my ass. I came up sputtering and angry and cursing up a storm. He laughed.

"Dry yourself off and we'll be done with our lesson." I didn't even know how to begin. He reached a hand to my arm with his magic he pulled. The water he'd dumped on me lifted off my skin, leaving my skin dry. I got the idea.

In my mind, I pictured my body. I pictured the layers of water on top, and using my magic, I pushed. I didn't know how hard to push, so I pushed hard. Locke looked surprised when I opened my eyes. I was completely dry. I'd managed to soak him and about fifty feet around us. I'd even pushed water that wasn't on me, just near me.

"And that's why we train alone the first little while." He chuckled. I grinned back before I could stop myself. He smiled at me. I came to my senses, turning my back to him and left him in Hell's Gate.

Dinner time felt awkward. There were hundreds of people all getting food at the same time. It seemed to be laid out family-style down the center of each long table and everyone helped themselves. It seemed nobody under Locke's employ went hungry here. But I knew nobody, and I hadn't the slightest clue where to sit. I didn't even see an open seat. Was there a hierarchy? Nobody acknowledged me. I almost left when I heard my name called. My eyes searched the crowd and found Aspen, Locke, and the twins. They were seated with someone I didn't recognize. I wandered over. Now that others had picked up on the royal table acknowledging me, it would've been more awkward to leave now. Their table was separate from the rest, but I expected that seeing as how this table seemed reserved for royalty and their immediate friends. Aspen pulled out a chair, noticeably between Locke and himself in the center of the table. Locke glanced sparingly at me and Aspen encouraged me with his eyes, beckoning me. Everyone at the table regarded me differently. Some with curiosity, some deadpan, and the last one looked downright hostile.

Great.

I took my seat between the two men I knew, which I was certain was by design. Aspen wasted no time in introducing the other at the table, the last Knight of the Rebel Court.

That was Abel. He was the one looking like I was a cockroach and he was about to crush me under his boot. His long, dark hair pinned back elegantly framed his face. All sharp angles and eyes as black as obsidian. They bored into me with a heavy weight. He was very striking with his menacing demeanor and stiff posture. He continued to glare at me as I approached, assessing my every movement. He was practically vibrating with antagonistic energy. Indignation flared brightly within me. I glared back, ready to tell him to shove it.

The sisters I'd met previously were the other two Knights. Lenore and Lennox sat opposite me, regarding me with curiosity. Lenore raised her eyebrows at me as I pulled my chair out. There was no sign of hostility, despite my punching her earlier. I eyed her wearily. All long hair, legs, and unusual golden- hued eyes that sparkled with the conversation around us. They regarded me with interest as I took my seat, making certain to make eye contact with each of them. Lennox smiled warmly at me and asked how my first day had been. I told the story about how I was sore after Aspen's training, so I fell asleep in the bath, missed lunch, and had to beg the nice man in the kitchen to let me make a sandwich to get through. Aspen burst out laughing, Locke regarded me strangely, and the girls grinned. Abel coolly glanced sidelong at me briefly but returned his attention to his meal.

"Nice man? The old man who yells at everyone at any given point?" Aspen said.

"The man who once refused to give me lunch because I was late?" Lennox said, her voice cool at the memory.

"The old man who calls me names all the time?" Lenore chimed in with a hint of annoyance. Wow, this guy wasn't popular. But I'd told them how he was defiantly a grumpy old man, but I asked him politely if I could make a meal for myself and apologized for getting into his hair and he let me. But quite frankly, anyone who called their prince and his knights names and didn't take their shit, I was already a huge fan of. Aspen gave a low whistle while I stockpiled my plate with roasted meat, rice, and fresh roasted veggies that were clearly cooked with the chicken. A warm, savory butter sauce over all of it. My mouth thought it was in heaven.

"I don't know how you charmed that crotchety, cantankerous old man, Lark. Maybe being pretty has more perks than I ever thought," Aspen said making me blush. "But keep doing it. If you can make him less of an asshole, maybe I could sneak snacks between meals again." Locke looked pointedly over at him. "What? I'm a growing boy!" I grinned.

"Only if you share these snacks with me. Then you're on!" I teased. Aspen's eyes glimmered with mirth as he laughed at me and gave me a one-armed hug, leaving his arm around the back of my chair for just a moment. Locke didn't acknowledge it, deeply conversing now with Abel with a clenched jaw.

"Maybe that's your unique talent," Lennox giggled. "Charming cranky old men."

"Hey, if it gets us free snacks, then who are we to contest it?" Lenore piped up and I chuckled again, feeling more at ease than I had since I'd been here. Really not since… The inn, I realized. Everything went to Hell after that. I bit my lip, and right on cue, Locke looked over to me. His gaze descended to my lip briefly and flashed me a knowing smirk. I quickly looked away and busied myself with my dinner, listening to the sparkling conversation around me. Locke even joined in, ribbing his friends with his ever-present sarcasm.

But I couldn't deny that something happened over the course of dinner. That something has shifted, but I didn't know if it was within me or them. Or perhaps it happened over the course of the day. I was listening to the conversation and my anger at being here had lessened. Locke was speaking, telling some amusing story at Aspen's expense. Aspen tried to feign innocence, not that he was fooling anyone—not even me. But listening to the story, I looked at Locke as he was speaking and smiled before I'd even realized what I'd done. His own smile faltered for the briefest of moments but he continued telling the story without missing a beat while I returned my face to that of casual, cool indifference.

When Lenore and Abel were busy discussing another important moment of their day in dramatic detail and squeals of laughter from Lennox and Aspen, Locke's gaze found mine, and to my surprise… held it. Heartbeats passed as his gaze bored into mine with an intensity I found surprising. Something flickered there for the briefest of moments. Something soft. Vulnerability? It was gone before my next breath, but for some reason I couldn't explain, I still couldn't tear my eyes away from his. I opened my mouth and closed it again, my question immediately dying on my tongue. But this heat, this intensity, this crackling energy, wouldn't be fizzling out any time soon. I hated him. Even though I hated him with a fiery passion that would make the Everday Isle proud, I was mature enough to acknowledge that he was outrageously attractive. But I was smart enough not to be ensnared by him again.

I hate him, I reminded myself sternly. With every fiber of my being. I would see him dead. One day soon, when I had control over my magic, I'd repay him what he did to my father. My blood boiled as my mind conjured an image of my father dead, Locke kneeling next him, searching his body, not even cold from death yet. I took a calming breath, feeling my hands heat up. I looked down, realizing my flames were just about to ignite under the table. If anyone noticed, they didn't say a word. I took another slow breath, refusing to lose control or composure. I was more dignified than that.

The only one who seemed to notice I wasn't myself for a moment was Locke, whose gaze still hadn't left me, though I now noticed his features were carefully guarded. As if he knew exactly what turn my thoughts had taken. I hoped he did. The others continued conversing contentedly around us, not seeming to notice the dip in my mood. I broke eye contact with Locke at last, giving him a look of haughty dismissal. A look I'd been on the receiving end of more times than I could count. I refocused my attentions to his friends and the boisterous conversation. From the bits I'd gleaned, Aspen had pranked Abel, and Abel was swearing his revenge in quite the colorful manner. Lennox and Lenore kept score for them. Apparently, this was an ongoing thing. And poor Abel was down by a lot.

But it also sounded like when Abel got Aspen, he got him *good*. It was hard not to chuckle at their easy banter, and it was clear to see how long they've been friends for.

Locke chuckled quietly beside me, a low rumbling sound I almost didn't hear. He looked sidelong at me for a moment, offering me a grin. I looked at him but I felt so conflicted in this moment. I knew he felt it too. I needed to ask if there were a way I should shield my emotions from him. I glared at him. This emotion detector was getting out of hand.

The others kept chatting and jeering each other even as dinner was winding down, but I couldn't concentrate on what they were saying. All I could think about was Locke's proximity. And what a bad daughter I was.

As everyone filed away for their personal time I realized I was tired and was really looking forward to reading, curled up in my chair, next to the blazing fireplace, enjoying the view. Too bad I couldn't get a hot cocoa. I immediately admonished myself for being so spoiled here. I'd never eaten or slept this well. One day. It took one day for me to get used to it. What did that say about me? I quietly walked the hall to my rooms after saying goodnight to nobody, Locke following behind me. Locke's eyes were intense as he regarded me and bade me goodnight. I strictly ignored him, but I couldn't deny the strange look on his face. It was like he was trying to tell me something without speaking the words. But then he cleared his throat and the moment was gone.

"Do you remember the Blood Wraiths?" he asked me suddenly, bringing me right out of whatever trance I'd been in. I nodded, unsure of the change in energy between us. A shiver dusted its icy fingers down my spine, remembering what I'd heard that day I'd met Locke. The wet, snapping bones sound. The clicking. I remembered how I'd hear them scream in the night from all the way out in the Deep Wild.

"Why?"

"I know you're thinking of an opportunity to escape." I did my best to keep my face composed, not to betray that he was absolutely right. He didn't seem fooled. "You should know what you'll face if you attempt to. Even if you got passed the misdirection wards, you have the sea on one border, the mountains to the Air Court on another. And all across the southern border, is the Dead Forest. It's a nesting ground for Blood Wraiths. They inhabit the forest, as do many of the souls who tried to cross it without our permission. Leaving would be a suicide mission, Lark."

"Why are you telling me this?"

"Because I have no desire to fish your corpse out of the forest," he said dryly. "Just stay here a small while, learn your magic, and you can go if you want."

"Do a swear spell," I said. "Promise me that. Right now." Without any hesitation, he softly spoke the words, the tingle of magic surging in the small space between us.

"I promise and swear on Aspen, my second in command, that you, Lark, may leave of your own volition once you have learned to control your elemental magic to the point you're not a danger to yourself or others. I swear until My Lady release me or under pain of death."

I felt the magic snap into place like an elastic on my skin, making me jump. I gaped up at him, not knowing what to say. He actually did it. My mouth hung open a beat, genuinely shocked. He glowered at me. We stared at each other a long moment. My heart was pounding for a reason I couldn't identify.

"Is that all you require?" His eyes were intensely cold and hard, even his face seemed sculpted from stone, the perfect face of indifference. I didn't know how to respond to his question even as I turned it over and examined it in my head from every angle. I opened my mouth to speak, thought better of it, and closed it once again. He looked like he was also on the brink of speaking. An idea struck me. I glanced around us, finding us utterly alone in the shadowed corridor. Without taking my eyes from his, I leaned down, grasped the handle of my knife from my boot, and pulled it to his throat before I had second to examine this half-baked plan further.

All residual humor from his face had disappeared. Any residual warmth had vanished. He regarded be calmly as I dug the knife's edge into his skin. Not enough to break it, but enough that he felt it.

"I should kill you right now for what you've done," I whispered. I poured every ounce of the hatred I felt for him into my glare in an attempt to hide my heart pounding away in my chest, so loud I was certain his Zodiac hearing could pick it up anyway. I didn't know what I was doing. My chest heaved as I dragged air in and out of my lungs, every breath feeling heavier than the last. His eyebrow twitched. His hand came up to clasp mine. His much-larger hand enveloped mine. His calloused hands were gentle. He could easily disarm me, I realized, my body tensing for a fight. I snarled at him.

"So do it," he murmured, pulling my hand closer and nicking his skin. A tiny drop of ruby blood welled and dripped down his neck. I gasped. He exposed more of his neck to me, my heart beat an unsteady rhythm in my chest in response. "Go ahead." His voice rang out, calling my bluff. There was no taunt in his voice, even if there were a speck in his eyes for just a moment.

My hand shook. There was too much adrenaline surging through my system. My nerves thrumming in my body, making me feel twitchy. *Kill him*, I thought. I willed my hand to move. To slice. To end his life the way he'd ended my father's. In my mind, I saw the scene again. My father lying in a pool of his own blood, staring lifelessly at me. Locke, kneeling over him. In that moment, I felt something change within me. The red-hot rage that had been simmering and churning within me since I awoke here had just boiled over. I saw red. My hand twitched. I heard a sharp intake of breath that made my insides twist. A heartbeat went by. I didn't move. Another heartbeat. And another. The only sounds were our ragged breaths. My vision cleared. I saw the shallow incision line I'd made. My stomach revolted, a strange reaction I couldn't explain. The dread that had been slowly filling me had finally come to a head.

"Don't keep me in suspense, love," he drawled out, a hint of a half smirk gracing his lip. His eyes flashed with a dare. "It's killing me more than you are."

My hand shook. I wanted to end it so badly. *Just finish it!* I was screaming at myself. His eyes never left mine. Never stopped searching mine. When I at last lowered my weapon. I watched him release a slow breath.

"I'm not like you," I spat at him. "I'm not a monster."

"I know," he said soberly before his features twisted back into that smug half grin. "Though if you're trying to tell me you're into trying a little knife play, I won't hold it against you." He trailed off, his gaze slipping to the knife still clutched tightly in my shaking hand. He leaned in close, his mouth near to my ear. Every fiber of my body stood on end and on high alert at his proximity. I glared at him, stubbornly refusing to yield ground to him. "Unless you want me to," he finished in that low drawl of his, his breath on my ear. He even had the gall to wink at me as he pulled away.

I huffed my disgust and turned away from him to move into my bedroom. A warm hand grasped my wrist and spun me back around to face Locke's chilling blue eyes.

"If you pull a knife on me again, Lark, you'd better be sure. And you'd better follow through."

"Is that a threat?" I hissed between my clenched teeth. He yielded nothing as his eyes barreled into mine, his face only a breath from mine.

"This coming from the one who'd just held a knife to my throat without provocation. That's rich."

"Fuck you."

"As I've said already, you're more than welcome to," he said in that husky voice of his, that sardonic smirk taunting and infuriating as ever. I wrenched my hand from his. He offered no resistance as I shouldered my door open and slammed it in his face. I leaned against the door, fighting off the feeling of breathlessness. In that moment, I realized it wasn't just hatred for him seething through me. It was hatred for myself. I'd come *this* close to avenging Father and I'd failed. I couldn't....

I heard his fading footsteps down the hall, open his door that I was just now realizing is so close to mine. I settled into my rooms after locking the door. I didn't move for a long time, my heartrate continued to thunder in my chest, refusing to slow. What had I nearly done? I looked down at the dagger still in my trembling hand. My mind was both numb and racing simultaneously. I dropped it, flinching at the clattering sound, breaking the thick silence. I'd nearly killed Prince Cancer. And he'd nearly let me. Why? Just to prove to me that he didn't think I could do it?

He was right.

My disgust at my failure was palpable. I picked up my dagger and placed it under my pillow. My heart fluttered sporadically when I saw the tiniest trace of red on the otherwise spotless silver blade.

My heart finally began to slow, my nerves stopped thrumming as I gazed over the night view before me. I watched the trees bowing in the gentle breeze, allowing myself to be lost to it for just a little while. An escape. If I couldn't physically escape, perhaps my mind could.

I shivered after a long time, feeling the coldness of the room. I looked towards the fireplace as I wrapped a soft, cream-colored blanket around my shoulders. I wandered to the fireplace, an idea, a theory taking root. Excitement thrilled me as I reached into the well of magic inside myself, feeling it respond. I glanced at the fireplace, an idea, a theory, taking root. Excitement thrilled me as I reached into the well of magic inside myself. I thought of fire. Willed it to my hands. The flames answered immediately and enthusiastically, writhing around my palms and wrists. My magic felt like an invisible friend made corporeal. I could finally play with it, interact with it for real.

I walked to the fireplace, stretched my hands out towards it, and pushed my fire towards it, extending it as I might my own hand. To be extreme surprise and delight, my fire obeyed, sparks igniting within the hearth, and sparks of joy within my heart. I still couldn't believe I could use magic. I willed my fire to die down. My flame hesitated, as if not ready to leave the party yet, but it went away again with the force of my will. I grinned. I knew I had so much still to learn, but I was so proud that I was able to do simple things. I couldn't even do those before. I lifted my attention to view the room. I noticed my stuff had indeed all been moved by Aspen, the massive bookcase now fully stocked, including with all the books I'd bought in Loc Valen. On the bookcase was a note:

Start with the one with the red cover—trust me.

It had no signature but I knew who it was. Aspen. An unbidden smile toyed with the edges of my mouth and my heart at the thoughtfulness as I settled into the chair that was like a chair and a half, bringing a soft blanket with me. It was already warm and cozy next to the fire now roaring beside me. From my vantage point, I could see the night sky, the stars like glittering diamonds up above, the silhouettes of the mountains looming in the not so distance. Stunning. I smiled as the sweetest calm enveloped me, chasing away the guilt and the fear and the anxiety for just a moment. I drank in the view again for a long while before I ever even made an effort to crack the book.

Chapter Ten

I tried for what had to be the thousandth time that day to push some semblance of magic from my fingertips. To feel the tingle of magic from my own hand as my peers around me began crafting simple spells: summoning water, snow, and ice and bending them to their will.

Nothing. Not a single magical thing happened at my desk. Even my lunch sat neatly in the corner of my desk, untouched. I glanced moodily at everyone around me, for the millionth time wondering why I was cursed to be magicless. Everyone ate their lunches with their friends, chatting animatedly, while I sat by myself trying to avoid detection. I didn't know why I kept trying to summon magic. I knew better. But hope was sometimes hard to break.

The professor, a mean-spirited fae named Professor Epsilon, conveniently avoided looking in my direction most often, as if trying to forget I existed. She only ever acknowledged me when my classmates got too physical with me and she was left with no other option to intervene or face the wrath of my father. And even then, sometimes she left the room.

"Eat this dirt." Kenna, my most popular tormentor, looked down at me, shoving towards me a container of freshly fertilized soil. I hadn't even heard her come up behind me. The reek of it nearly made my eyes water. "It's the only way we'll allow you to stay here. Poplar Hollow doesn't want you. Think of it as your tax for staying here." I sneered up at her with a dismissive smile.

"Hi Kenna. Do you always carry that around? Because it would explain a lot. Between the smell and your shit personality." She fake laughed and pushed the container until it was directly in front of me. She continued laughing, now in earnest at my disgusted reaction I wasn't able to hide when I caught a glimpse of a worm. The smell was revolting. I glanced to the professor for help but she was determined to avoid looking this way.

"Eat this."

"No," I said, putting strength to my voice. "Go sit down."

"Or what?" She smirked, turning to get the reactions of her now smirking friends, Hilara and Chennai, who flocked like sheep behind her.

"Eat it! Eat it! Eat it!" they chanted, their pitch rising in candor and getting the entire class to abandon their lunch and join in.

"It tastes like chocolate," Chennai cooed with a very serpentine smile.

"Don't be silly, Chennai. She's too poor to know what chocolate tastes like," Hilara pointed out with a snicker. "Now I believe the consensus was that you're only allowed to stay if you eat this. So do it."

I looked them all in the eye, crossed my arms in front of me, and said the words I knew they'd make me regret.

"Fuck off."

Every head in the room turned to look at me, including the professor, turning with a clearly fake look of outrage on her face.

"Lark! That kind of behavior will not be tolerated!" she exclaimed. I was beyond trying to convince her to leave me alone. She knew what was going on. She didn't care. I was magicless. Less than worthless. Not worth helping. "Apologize!"

I looked at her with a carefully guarded expression as I evaluated my options. Not one of those options included backing down. No. I was done running. I was done being a victim. My father had been teaching me how to fight. Today, I fought back.

Today, I stood my ground. "No."

"Lark. Now." Just like a master calling a dog. I rose to my feet at last, stretching to my full height. I glowered at her, my lips loosening into a snarl as I squared my shoulders.

"No."

I stood firm, holding my ground. The professor made eye contact with the fae around me, silent communication passing between them, before she turned her back and walked out of the room. I grimaced inwardly. I knew what was coming. I'd been preparing for this since the last time this happened. Before Kenna could grab the container and force my face to meet it unceremoniously, I gripped the knife hidden in my boot and held it out, willing my hand to be steady. It only partially obeyed.

"I said fuck off." I kept my voice firm. They gave me weary expressions, Kenna's gaze dipping occasionally to my blade, unsure what to do with this new development. It was commonplace that they all have magic to craft weapons for their disposal. I had more than one scar to prove that. This was the first time I dared bring a weapon. A weapon I now threatened them all with. Some jeering came from the class that now crowded in a around us, blocking me in. I made it very clear as I crouched to retrieve my second knife, that I would give them a hell of a fight. And I'd make it hurt.

"If you want to do this," I said, my voice that of pure biting defiance as my eyes scanned potential assailants, "I'm happy to see how many of you I can bring down. I'm betting all of you."

Chennai and Kenna took a bold step towards me. I brandished my blade in response. Kenna's set jaw told me that she would fight and fight dirty. With a sneer, she took another step, when, from across the room, Gael sent an ice dagger aimed straight for my heart. I saw it. He knew I saw it. Made sure of it. I brought my steel blade to the weapon with a flourish, exploding it into icy shards upon impact. I shot him a brief look. He nodded subtly.

He'd never interfere. I knew that. But he knew without a doubt that I would block that attack. A maneuver, a brief display of skill that would make everyone rethink attacking me.

It didn't work.

Seven assailants, two stab wounds, and multiple lacerations later, I stumbled away from school and towards Eldan's cottage, dripping a trail of blood through the street as I went. Though, I thought to myself with a small smile, thank the Goddess that dirt didn't touch me. The tiniest of wins. But a win all the same. The moment the fight started, the container was completely forgotten about, magic becoming the best thing to come at me with. The thing I could do little to defend against.

I took down more of them than I'd thought. The school healer immediately tended to those I'd injured. Kenna had successfully punctured my blade-wielding shoulder, allowing someone else to take me down. But they were the only two of my assailants that I hadn't rendered unconscious.

Before I left the classroom behind, I saw all the blood underneath the pile of unconscious fae I left. It was smeared everywhere, which in turn made me aware of my blood loss. The head rush hit me then. I needed to find Eldan. I couldn't faint. Not here. Eldan was sympathetic, if not horrified, but definitely not shocked when I eventually crashed in a bloody heap through his front door, startling both him and a patient paying for his potion. With a hiss and an insult to me, he promptly left.

"Goddess, Lark! Are you all right?" Eldan leapt up to support me and aid me over to the couch. I coughed, blood spilling over my lip as I did so.

"Yes, Eldan," I said in as dry a tone as I could manage. He returned my tone with a matching expression as he began a healing spell for the leaking wounds. "I usually spurt blood from various places. I'm fucking grand."

"This is the third time this month you've been injured," Eldan said, eyeing me like I might lose consciousness and entirely ignoring my tone. "You're running quite the tab." I heard his real words: What the hell was going on?

I shook my head. The truth is, I genuinely didn't know. I changed everything today. I'd fought back. I'd fought back instead of running away. And I'd nearly won. After today, I knew they'd think twice about coming for me. Today, I felt like I'd won. Because in a way, I did.

I woke to the soft sunlight of the early morning filtering into my room. I yawned and stretched before flipping over in exhaustion. I stayed in my chair curled up by the fire far longer than I had intended to and I was definitely not ready to pay the price. I knew breakfast was soon. Far too soon for my liking. I groaned against the pillow at my own bad decisions but refused to leave the warmth and comfort of my cloud-soft bed. I sank into the mattress in defiance and closed my eyes. A knock sounded at my door as if on cue and I let out a quiet curse.

"Come in," I said, fingering my blade under the pillow but choosing not to grab it at the last second, despite wanting to stab whoever was knocking at my door. Ugh, I already regretted uttering those words. The door opened to reveal Locke standing at my door, a tray of breakfast food in his hands. I raised my eyebrow at him. My eyes flicked to the place I'd cut him last night. I shouldn't have been surprised to see no trace of it. He must have healed it.

"What are you? My delivery maid now?" I asked him quizzically, but with less venom than I'd intended with my residual awkwardness from last night. The image of my knife to his throat came unbidden in my brain. He huffed a laugh, and hid it at my scowl.

"That's not even a thing," he said, striding easily into my chambers and closing the door with his hip. He set breakfast down on the table and made himself at home.

"What do you think you're doing?" I asked him incredulously. Why in the actual hell was he sitting at my table, fixing himself a plate, and looking at me like I was the moron?

"Remember I told you I was going to reward you yesterday?" My skin heated at our conversation. That I thought he'd been offering sex. The widening grin he gave me told me he was remembering the exact same moment and I resisted the urge to bury my head in the pillow and hide. I glared daggers at him, but it only served to heighten his amusement as he fixed himself a plate, looking relaxed and perfectly at ease. "Are you going to eat breakfast or…?"

"Why are you in here?" I asked in a dismissive tone. I didn't want to eat breakfast with my father's murderer. I didn't want to eat breakfast with my damned kidnapper. Dinner with the group was enough. What was his play? He hadn't brought up last night when I…

When I'd tried to kill him.

"I told you. I'm giving you your reward. You're playing hooky today." He flashed me a grin that before everything happened would've made my stomach flop. Instead, my stomach twisted itself into confused knots, and shame flooded me. I held to my belief from yesterday; I could acknowledge that he was attractive and that my body responded to him. Didn't mean I hated his guts any less. I crossed my arms against his attempt at kindness. "If you eat breakfast, I'll take you to what I have in store for you. And I think you're going to be really happy."

"What the hell do you care if I'm happy?" I snapped, rising to my feet and storming towards him. "You kidnapped me!" He heaved an exasperated sigh. He put his utensils down and spun in his chair to face me.

"Is this the conversation we're going to have? I didn't kidnap you, and you know it. You need to get ahold of your magic before you hurt someone, including yourself. Or worse, they'll kill you if you're discovered. I'm saving your life."

"Is that what you call it?" He looked at me, all traces of humor long gone. His jaw set in a firm line.

"Yes, Lark, I do call it that. And I'm attempting to make sure you're fairly comfortable. And don't forget I'm bound by the swear spell."

"Why? Guilty conscious?" His eyes looked pained, but only for a heartbeat before his emotions were hidden from me again. "I'm an assassin. Guilt is a useless emotion for me. Gets in the way of my job and everything I do. Now," he said, setting a plate in front of a place setting he meant for me, "eat. Your. Breakfast." I was about to tell him to get stuffed when my traitorous stomach made itself heard. He laughed and gestured for me to sit. I eyed him with caution as I took a seat and helped myself to a pancake and some scrambled eggs.

We ate in silence. I kept an eye on him at all times, and he had the nerve to look vaguely amused, if not downright bored. As if irritating me were the goal. So I changed tactics and ignored him completely. I refused to let him upset my morning. He wasn't worth anything to me, much less him upsetting me.

He took my plate the second I was finished with it and left the tray outside my door in the hallway for whoever came along and collected it. He turned back to me with a grin.

"Get changed. Wear pants, boots, and whatever you want for a shirt."

"Then get out!" I snipped at him, giving him an expectant look. A slow, lazy grin reached his features as his eyes bored into me.

"Why? I've seen it all already. If you recall..." He gave me a pointed grin, looking absolutely feral. My blood boiled in reaction. How dare he...?

"Yes, I recall!" I snapped at him, looking for something to throw at him. I opted for the utensil knife, seeing how my knife under the pillow was too far away, hurling it end over end with accuracy that even surprised myself. He didn't even flinch, catching the knife by the handle in mid-air before it reached his face, giving me a roguish smirk. "Doesn't mean I don't wish with everything in me that it never happened! I hate you," I seethed at him.

"Good to hear." He scoffed at me, as if I was the one being ridiculous. "Nice toss by the way. And I promise if you come with me, you'll really like what you find. And you'll retain privileges as long as you don't try to escape and to continue doing well in your lessons." *And don't use a knife on anyone else*, were the words he hadn't said. He sounded like a parent encouraging their child to stay in schooling. I huffed indignantly, but curiosity trickled under my skin. What could be so amazing that he thought I'd be this happy despite my circumstances?

"Fine. Let's go and get this over with. Get out so I can change," I huffed, glaring at him for all I was worth. He glared back, showing me his real feelings finally. I knew he'd been putting on a show. Manipulative bastard. Narcissistic. Rude. Arrogant. He finally turned and walked out the door, closing it behind him. I forced myself not to run to the door and lock it behind him. I walked right over to my closet to change. Soft black leggings that hugged my every curve; my fine black boots, each stuffed with a dagger; and a cream-colored, long-sleeved shirt was my apparel of choice. I even donned my mother's green cloak and quickly braided my hair back behind my head before raising my head high and walking out the door, where Locke was waiting soundlessly. He eyed my outfit a long moment before I cleared my throat.

"Is this okay?" I asked, holding my arms out as if for him to inspect. I didn't hold back the dryness of my voice. He nodded, ignoring my tone, and ushered me to follow him. I struggled to keep up a bit, his legs taking long strides and eating up ground faster than my short legs could easily keep up. I knew he noticed because I could see him smirk to himself. Bastard. But when we turned into the light-filled atrium and through the front doors to the veranda, excitement pulled at me. Outside! Fresh air! I inhaled deeply, that brine-and-alpine-scented breeze that greeted me during Aspen's brief tour found me and played with the end of my braid. Though cool off the ocean, my cloak did well to keep my warm enough. The recently risen sun was warm at our backs as he led me through the Court of Rebels.

The square was just as I remembered from yesterday, busy and energetic. It was refreshing to be part of Port Azure, experience it, rather than be held aloft from it. Fae meandered by, smiling as they went. A few tossed me openly curious looks before eventually going about their business. Many eyed me as they greeted their Prince. Locke was ever the gentlefae, greeting every single fae, and many by name. I couldn't say I wasn't impressed and more than a little surprised at how well loved he was.

A merchant selling flowers bowed to Locke and me as we passed by. Before I could tell him that bowing to me wasn't necessary, he presented me with a flower and a smile. Not just any flower; I'd recognize those purple petals anywhere. I accepted it numbly. It was larkspur. My namesake that had grown all over Poplar Hollow. My throat tightened, making it hard to breathe. My mind interpreted it as a sign; I could practically hear my father telling me from beyond the veil to get away from Locke. From Port Azure. My thoughts began spinning rapidly as I thanked the fae in an automatic polite response, and schooling my expression into something resembling calm, despite the anxious churning in my gut. Before I could say anything more, Locke thanked him and pressed a coin to his hand. The man thanked his Prince with another bow and another kind smile to me. He took my hands, stopping them from trembling. I hadn't even realized they were. I began to apologize he spoke first in a soft voice.

"Where flowers bloom so, too, does hope," he said to me with another sincere smile. The words settled over me. I mulled them over a moment before I found myself returning his small smile, thanking him for the flower once more. But the alarms in my head weren't quite ready to cease. I kept seeing Poplar Hollow in my mind, and when I thought of Poplar Hollow... My father, the fire, the blood.... It all came rushing back. Locke also took the opportunity to thank the fae again and excuse us before placing his arm around my shoulders and steering me through the square again, blending in to existing foot traffic.

"Breathe, Lark."

"Wow, that hadn't occurred to me," I snapped, shrugging his arm off.

"Your hands...."

Indeed, the fire runes were glowing under my sleeves, though fire hadn't burst from my skin yet. I then did as I was bade, and took some calming breaths, bringing my mind back to the present moment. I put the larkspur in my pocket, out of sight. I breathed a sigh of relief that the glowing on my arms had muted and stopped. No runes churned under my sleeves. I noted that Locke also looked relieved.

I took in the abundance of fae. They were everywhere. Port Azure may have started as a rebel base, but it had certainly grown into a city of survivors. "Are all these people rebels?" Locke nodded.

"Yes. Those who can and are willing to fight for us, do. Those who can't help in other ways, such as with farming, our blacksmithing, help keep the Court running. Regardless of how they contribute, all of these fae gained a home here in Port Azure," he said with pride. "Every Faerie you see here has either survived an attack from Scorpio's wrath, or is running from it to prevent being present for one."

"There must be hundreds of people here." He shook his head.

"A few thousand now," he corrected me as we walked. I saw small fields to my right peeking at me between buildings, hinting at massive agricultural presence.

"How does Scorpio not find you?"

He chuckled.

"I'm pretty famous for not being in Loc Valen, anyway. I'm constantly on assignment. She thinks I'm scouting for potential seers for her. Even in other Courts.

Occasionally, I have to go back, but I have time right now. As for how she doesn't know about Port Azure; there are so many misdirection and illusion wards up, if you walked through the trees you'd see nothing but more trees. But you'd hear whispers. Voices telling you to run. You'd think you were being chased by the Soulless, which absolutely inhabit the forest. So it's not a stretch. Even if viewed from above, this place looks like forested land unless we allow you to see it for what it is."

"What the hell are the Soulless?"

"It's what the forest to the south of us is known for. Even more so than the Blood Wraiths. The Dead Forest is a miserable place. Those who die in the forest become trapped there. Some ancient magic resides there and refuses to let go of its victims, even in death. So those who pass become nothing more than spirits. Spirits that absolutely despise the living. They're doomed to prey upon them."

Well that was... chilling. Terrifying, actually. I eyed the forest with hostility, as if it might pop a Soulless out to me now.

"That must take a lot of magic," I said. "To keep the wards up. Wouldn't they need a steady supply of magic?" He shrugged.

"Between me and the knights, we have more than enough magic," was his answering reply.

We walked along the mismatched stone streets, towards a building that looked suspiciously like... no. He couldn't... I looked at him in shocked disbelief while he grinned down at me. The most "I told you so" grin was plastered on his stupid face. I wouldn't begrudge him for it this one time as I bit down on a squeal of excitement, my earlier panic momentarily forgotten. My steps felt light as I approached the barn.

A horse stuck his head out the stable window and whinnied in greeting. I stopped dead in my tracks and looked at Locke in question once again. He looked down at me in equal parts amusement and smugness. And he was all parts wide grin as he led me to the sliding barn door.

I inhaled the homey scent of hay and horses, taking a deep breath, finding comfort in the familiar smell, feeling a small part of my soul come out of hibernation as I did so. I patted a particularly eager fellow who was interested in pets and a sugar cube. His soft whiskers against my other palm coaxed a smile from me. For a blissful moment, the storm within me quelled.

He led me further into the stable to a stall and bade me to look inside. I glimpsed his smile when inside the stall was a horse that looked so much like Haven, my heart physically hurt. *Haven...*

The black gelding in front of me looked at me and snorted a greeting. I eyed the white blaze on his face and tall, chromey stockings on his legs in appreciation. He was a big horse and looked athletic. A nice, supple coat gleamed with health.

"Hello, friend," I murmured to him softly. I stuck my hand into the stall, beckoning him come say hello to me on his terms. He eyed me a moment before lumbering over in search of a free treat. As I stroked his ebony neck, his upper lip began to boldly explore my pockets over the stall door, making my smile wider, and even dragging a laugh from me.

"He's all yours," Locke murmured. And my heart stopped. My whole body froze in time. *Mine?* The world stopped spinning for a moment.

"What?" My voice was barely above a whisper, in case this was all a sick joke. Locke grinned.

"Do you want to go for a ride?" I looked up at him in confusion, waiting for the sick punchline. His voice was gentle when he spoke. "This isn't a trick, Lark. This is real. He's all yours." I hated myself for my response, but I'd care later. I beamed up at him and let myself into the gelding's stall, before I remembered that my forgiveness couldn't be bought. But I had to admit, this was a pretty great reward. I stroked his velvet nose first before scratching his ears. Finding a horse's favorite scratching spot was my favorite thing. I smiled as I scratched him with my nails along his mane, his withers, to which he reached around and lipped my leg with that upper lip.

"You mentioned something about a ride?" I asked him quietly. Locke nodded and gestured to a set of tack hanging neatly across from his stall. When I asked for his name, his eyes glittered.

"You get to choose. He hasn't been named yet, though he's earned himself a few choice nicknames." The horse snorted in response, as if to refute his comment. I laughed despite myself. I looked at the way he carried himself. Regal. Strong. Fluid. I knew already that he was going to be a lot of fun to ride. The first word in my mind I knew would be the perfect name.

"Valor," I whispered, stroking his mane. Locke voiced his approval, repeating the name, letting it roll over his tongue.

"I like it." He smiled. I studied the row of stalls, looking for a familiar steed.

"Is Aristocrat here?" Locke grinned again, pointing a few stalls down to the end where gray ears perked up, hearing his name. The name I also gave him.

"You tack up and I'll go get Ari. I'll leave you two to bond," he said as he left me to bring Valor into the cross ties outside his stall. He turned back to me briefly. "And just in case you're thinking of making an escape attempt…" He grabbed my arm and murmured words in an alien tongue. The trickle of ice-cold magic shocked my system a moment and froze my forearm. He pulled away seconds later, leaving a small, strange, swirling black rune on my forearm near my elbow. I was about to screech at him for marking my body without my permission. With black magic, no less. I shuddered. I'd never actually seen Locke use his black magic. I saw the remnants of black magic in his eyes and it left me cold inside. Like staring into a freezing moonless winter's night.

"Remove it," I hissed through my clenched jaw. His eyes narrowed.

"It'll fade by the end of today. It's a tracking rune. So wherever you go, I'll find you, in case you were thinking of braving the forest, which I don't recommend. We ride together, or not at all. Or you can ride with one of the Knights." Aspen, Lennox, Abel, or Lenore. I thought about how I punched Lenore in the face and grimaced. Probably wouldn't be riding with her any time soon. Abel looked like he'd rather be anywhere but with me. So that left Lennox and Aspen. I had no doubt Aspen would ride with me. And he wouldn't put a tracking rune on me either. Leave it to Locke to ruin a perfectly good moment.

I huffed at him and grabbed a brush to groom my new horse. My new horse. A small part of me was squealing in excitement and couldn't help but savor the moment. I pressed my face to Valor's neck and inhaled deeply the comforting perfume of horse. I closed my eyes and for a brief moment I was back home. With Haven. With my father. Back in Poplar Hollow. No Locke. And when I opened my eyes, I saw him. He had the audacity to look at me as if he knew exactly what I was thinking. I flipped him off and returned my attention to Valor while he sighed and turned his to Ari. Twenty minutes later, we were leading our horses to the edge of town along the forest. I eyed the deep tangle of darkly shaded trees with suspicion, which of course didn't go unnoticed by Locke.

"We're not going into the trees, worry not. There's a trail that will take you down to the beach." I released a breath, and my shoulders released tension I hadn't been aware had coiling and reaching into my neck.

I had heard a few screeches of theirs in the night, just like at home. The Blood Wraiths. They didn't sound close, but it didn't leave me feeling comforted, hearing they were out there. Locke's warning regarding the Dead Forest echoed in my mind. Not only did the Blood Wraiths wander the grounds, but apparently the Soulless did too. And Goddess only knew what else. The victims of the forest whose souls were trapped beneath the canopy of the trees, doomed to hunt fae that enter. I had to admit it was a smart way of keeping others from accidentally finding it. Putting a giant and terrifying forest at your doorstep didn't exactly scream "welcome!" I supposed that was the genius of it. Nobody would accidentally find their wards if they didn't traverse the forest first. And who would willingly go into a place called the Dead Forest, with all that haunted it? I couldn't even tell if birds chirped within the confines of the forest's space.

Locke offered me a leg up, and I scoffed him. Valor was taller than I was flexible though, and I led him to the mounting block, where he stood dutifully for me to get on. I gave Locke a hard look that might as well have said *I don't need you!* He shrugged and mounted his horse in one graceful movement. I fought a grimace at his finesse. *Ass.*

He applied the smallest amount of leg and Ari walked along the path ahead of him. I pressed my leg gently to Valor's side and he followed after Ari, needing no further encouragement. I could already tell he was a good boy. My heart swelled each time I remembered he was all mine and I found myself running my hands over his silken neck and murmuring to him. His ears pivoted as he listened, clearly enjoying the attention.

Locke looked back every so often to make sure I was still there as we followed the ill-maintained, slightly overgrown, shady path that sloped gently downwards. I shifted my weight in my seat to take my weight off Valor's front legs. My jaw nearly dropped when the path opened up onto the beach. Not a rock in sight. Smooth white sand stretched a small ways to the water and then the endless horizon greeted me. On either side, there seemed to be miles and miles of beach, lined with trees, the foothills of the Veinfall range beginning in the background, marking the boundary of the Water and Air Courts. Back behind me was the wall of Port Azure looming above me and casting us in shadow. Locke grinned and spurred Ari into a brisk trot, Valor chasing after him into the bright sunlight with a snort. I hated being grateful to Locke, but here I was. But I could keep that feeling to myself.

"Ready to go?" he called over his shoulder after a few minutes. We had just trotted out to the white, sandy beach. The hooves of our horses had just reached the wet sand before the surf when Locke and Ari took off at a gallop, wet sand flying out behind them. Valor's ears pricked forward. He needed no invitation and raced off after them, a wild grin taking over my features. I lengthened the reins slightly to give him his head and turned him loose. The thundering of hooves underneath me, the salty sea air on my face, playing with my hair… it was paradise. This right here was all I ever required to be happy. I set the reins down on his neck and let my arms splay out on either side of me, as if I were flying. It felt like it. I let out a whoop as Valor kicked in another gear. I looked over at Locke, who was smiling broadly as he and Aristocrat matched us stride for stride beside me. Ari whinnied and Valor returned it, but I almost didn't hear over the thundering in my ears and the adrenaline coursing through my veins. It was the most free I'd felt since coming home from Loc Valen.

When we finally pulled up, our faces flushed from the wind and the horses breathing heavily, my mood had brightened considerably. The horses walked in the shallow surf as we turned around and set off at a leisurely walk back home. I could see the small spire of the building that housed me from here but only just. It almost disappeared into the treed background. And it was so much further away than I would've expected. We galloped a longer way than I thought possible. I pat Valor's neck again as he huffed his approval of the run. Ari was also snorting as he entered the surf shallows and he and his silent rider fell into step beside us.

We didn't speak for a long time. I was content to pretend he wasn't there, the giant black spot he was on an otherwise exquisite moment of peace. For a brief moment, I felt unburdened. For a brief moment, the pain and uncertainty of the last few days seemed to be behind me, left behind during the gallop. I knew it wouldn't be long until my ghosts caught up to me, but for now I stared out at the ocean and enjoyed the spray of water on my face. Ari's and Valor's hooves plodded rhythmically through the shallow waves. A taste of freedom.

"You look happy," Locke said at last.

"It's the happiest and free-est I've felt since I've been here," I answered, my tone dispassionate with my reluctance to acknowledge him. I wasn't ready to break my reverie. I knew I should say thank you to him. For Valor. For bringing me out. I knew I should. But I just couldn't bring myself to say the words.

"I'm sorry you're not happy. It's not my intention." I looked over at him finally. "I want you to feel at home here. My Knights do too. You've made quite an impression on all of them. Especially Aspen." I rolled my eyes. He didn't think I was actually going to believe that nonsense, did he? But when I glanced over, I found myself pausing in the wake of something flickering in his eyes I didn't recognize.

"Answer me something." My tone was calmer than I expected. He nodded, awaiting the question he knew I was about to ask.

"Why did you kill my father? No beating around the bush. I saw you holding the knife, covered in his blood. I saw the moment he died. Just tell me why. I want to understand. I need to understand." Locke looked away. For several long heartbeats, I thought he was not going to answer. He finally looked back at me with a deep frown and sadness in his eyes.

"Your father died because he was simply in the wrong place at the wrong time," he finally said, his voice soft. Sincere. His eyes were cautious but imploring as he regarded my reaction.

"So what did he catch you doing?" I prodded, trying to get some sort of reaction out of him that might give me some sort of clue. "What did he call you out on? What happened, Locke?" His eyes raged into mine with an intensity that was brand new to me. It was like he was trying to send the memory from his mind to mine. What wasn't he saying?

"He didn't catch me doing anything. It was simply as I said, wrong place, wrong time."

"Did you lose control of your magic? Was it an accident?" I kept pressing. My temper flared when he shook his head wordlessly. "Why won't you tell me?"

"Have you considered that perhaps I can't tell you certain things? That for your safety, I can't?" His blue-and-gold eyes smoldered now with strong emotions, looking so like the glistening sea beside us. His face was carefully blank as he looked at me.

"Does it have something to do with your curse?" His face pinched and his mouth set into a grim line. There. Finally, a reaction. Okay, curse related.

"Tell me about your curse," I said. His recoiling from the topic was nearly palpable.

"I can't, Lark." My eyes flashed at him and I had to fight hard to restrain the fire that threatened to snake its way around my arms. "It's not that I don't want to tell you. It's that I genuinely can't. I'm trying to protect you."

"I don't think you understand. Have you ever lost someone? My father is the only one I had in my life. Do you get that? My father was the only one that cared about me." Tears welled in my eyes and I bit them back. I refused to cry. Not in front of him.

"I have lost someone," he said softly in a voice that forced me to look at him. "And she was everything to me. But I can assure you, Lark, your father is not the only one who cares for you. You've made an impression on everyone you've met here so far." My world stood still. She? He'd lost a fae he... loved? It was strange to think of the person that might have held his heart. I thought of us at the inn. Not so much the bedding part. How sweet, thoughtful, and considerate he'd been. I could easily see how someone would love that Locke. My thoughts churned and my stomach roiled inside me as I wondered what she was like.

"And did you know what happened to them?"

"Yes. And it doesn't help nearly as much as you think."

"Yet, you won't let me get to decide that," I said coldly. I wondered if it were me or if the temperature actually dropped a few degrees at my tone. "You know what I don't understand?" My tone was biting and I knew I was skating the line. "What makes you any better than Scorpio?" The stricken look on his face he wasn't able to conceal should have told me my question was enough. But I was seeing red once again and I refused to stop. "The innocent people you've killed. I've heard about the demonstrations you led. How would one killer rule better than another? Do you even remember—"

He cut me off with a sound so feral I couldn't even place it. Even Ari sidestepped under him. When he glanced up, his features were contorted in rage.

"Don't ever ask me that again," he seethed, hissing the words through a clenched jaw. His temper reminded me of deep water—calm on the surface, with violently turbulent waters underneath ready to drag you under. His tone was biting as he continued. "I remember the name and face of every single fae whose life I was forced to end. I never let any one of them suffer. Those I could get away with saving, I did." Like me. I knew he wanted to say that. But he didn't. "And who said I wanted to be king? I'm happy in my role. Especially when Scorpio isn't driving our realm to ruin."

"You talk a lot about not having a choice in the same breath as denying mine," I spat.

"What part of 'I can't tell you' are you not getting?"

Anger boiled within me. He murdered my father in cold blood. I watched the aftermath. He killed him. And won't bother telling me why. What had happened that he needed to protect me from? Rage continued to seethe within me, almost becoming an entity itself, fueling my actions. I meant to cast water over him, soaking him in his saddle. But instead, a gust of wind came from my hands and I hurtled him out of the saddle and into the waiting surf.

Surprise came from me at this new element, and he landed hard, taken completely by surprise. Now was my chance to escape! But one look on my forearm as I gathered the reins reminded me he could track me anywhere and bring me back kicking and screaming. And what I'd just done was proof still of what he claimed: didn't have enough control over my magic. Valor danced nervously in place, but I held him there. I reached into my boot and readied my dagger for Locke to attack me in retaliation.

He got to his feet, water dripping off him momentarily. His black hair hung into his face slightly. His wet clothes stuck to his muscular body, putting it on display. I willed myself not to notice. He pushed the water off of himself before he approached me cautiously, as one might approach a nervous horse.

"Do you really think I'm going to hurt you?" he asked. "Do you really think for a second that I would?" Was that hurt in his expression? Surprise, certainly. But I was certain I also saw a flicker of something more raw. But I also didn't miss the hardness of his gaze that told me he would not waver. The resolve on his face spoke of an iron will that would not break, no matter how many times I asked him of my father. An iron will honed over centuries. I knew I wouldn't gather more information from him about my father. I would never know what happened that day and I would never have closure. Lightning flashed in his eyes. Or was it overhead? Wasn't it just sunny and warm? I cast my gaze upwards to see ominous storm clouds the color of charcoal gathering directly over us. And *there!* Another bolt of lightning lit up the darkening landscape around us. The lightning grew more intense, casting everything in stark contrasts of charcoal and white Locke observed in stunned silence for moment. His blue eyes changed to white, the shadows on his face growing stark with each flash. He looked very like the Crowned Assassin like this, and it put me on edge.

"You… summoned a storm?" he asked. I was assuming me. But the hardened way he cast his gaze to the heavens made me think he was having quite the internal conversation with the Goddess. I couldn't tell what he was feeling. So many emotions crossed his features. Amazement. Concern. Shock. And fear. Just for a moment, but I caught it. Prince Cancer, the Crowned Assassin, was afraid for me. Or hopefully, of me.

Good.

Chapter Eleven

The long shadows of dusk kept us cloaked in secret. Crickets buzzed peacefully in the background and a few fireflies came to light up the moment, lovely in direct contrast to being surrounded by mold and mildew and the damp smell of rotting wood in the unused barn held on the edge of town. His hands explored my face, the small of my back, my hips, my waist, his lips on mine in the small, dimly lit space. Gael's hands were warm as they enveloped me, his tongue played coyly with mine. My heart beat unsteadily in my chest. My first kiss. And with Gael. I'd never imagined that being any different. For as long as I could remember, he'd been the only faerie at school that had never been truly unkind to me. And when we were alone, he wasn't unkind at all. His fun-loving personality really came out to shine. A personality I'd grown to like very much.

My hands wandered timidly and with a great degree of uncertainty along his strong arms, his chest, before settling contentedly around his neck, my fingers toying with the ends of his hair. I broke away, looking up at him with a small smile as I awaited my breath to return to me. A smile he returned. His brown hair was soft between my fingers and his golden eyes shone with mischief even in the dark.

"It's getting late. Can you walk me home?" He hesitated. I felt my smile fall away, his dying in turn. No longer were we just two people who liked one another. I was the Noquim, once again. His eyes returned to their usual guarded state. I felt the sweetness of the moment fall away, leaving me with a bitter aftertaste. I thought I'd have more time with him before the bliss fell away.

"We can't be seen together, Lark. My family would disown me if they knew we were together."

"So walking me home is the same as coming out about our relationship?" I quirked an eyebrow. His arms enveloped me again, rubbing soothing circles along my back.

"You know I care about you. You know it's not like that." I backed up out of his hold.

"So what is it like?" I bit back the resentment in my tone. Softened it. But I knew by the stricken look on his face that my message, my meaning, was plain as day regardless. He opened his mouth to speak.

"Yeah, Gael, what is it like?" a third voice interjected. Both of our heads snapped up as one of Gael's older brothers, Bastian, appeared in the last vestiges of light. "You're in a relationship with the Noquim? I knew you were sneaking out to do something stupid, but this? Really?" He laughed as he spoke, as if he couldn't believe the joke. Blood heated my cheeks as Gael hastily broke further away from me.

"Of course not," Gael growled out, quickly. My head snapped to face him, watching as he avoided my gaze. Confusion and hurt battled for dominance within me, and I struggled to keep my face carefully neutral. A battle I knew I was losing based on the look on Bastian's face. "Of course not," Gael repeated to his laughing brother.

"Oh? Then you won't mind telling me what you're doing? Because you're certainly not helping her with homework." Gael didn't even look at me. He shoved his clenched fists into his pockets. He said nothing, his mouth opening and closing over and over again as he considered his words. I had enough.

"What's the matter, darling?" I asked in my most saccharine voice, at odds with the disgust on my face. Bastian's face was so amused it bordered on maniacal. "Are you ashamed of our relationship?" I made sure to hiss those two words through clenched teeth.

"Of course he is!" Bastian spoke up, glaring at Gael. "Tell her, or I'm telling Mother. She's going to fucking murder you. Or better yet, you can suffer the fallout when the whole town finds out." Gael looked at me then, his face paled and full of calm nothing. I looked him in the eye, ready. Ready for him to break the tiny, sole intact piece of me I had left.

"Bastian, don't do this," Gael said, his head hanging and he withdrew into himself. "It's such an overly dramatic thing to do."

"Maybe. But it's pretty funny. It's also just nice to see that you can fuck up once in a while." His eyes snuck between the two of us. Gael gazed at me, looking torn. I decided to make the decision for him.

"We're done, don't worry." I beat him to the punch, ignoring the way my heart shriveled and withered. Hoping my nasty tone hid the hurt inside me.

"Don't tell anyone about this," Gael said, his head swiveled to address both of us. Bastian shrugged nonchalantly.

"You mean you don't want all of Poplar Hollow to know you just got dumped by the Noquim?" I flashed them both a dry look. I raised my voice, keeping my sickeningly sweet smile intact. "Because how bad do you think the fallout of th—?" He slapped a hand over my mouth in an effort to shut me up, the sting of his hand on my mouth in direct contrast to a few minutes earlier when he'd caressed my cheek. Now I knew a red mark lay there.

"If you repeat the sentence to anyone, you're dead," Bastian warned from behind Gael. "Gael is stupid, but he doesn't need to pay forever for one mistake."

"Fuck you. Fuck both of you. You can't do anything worse to me than you have already." I gripped the blade from my boot, a silent warning to stay back. Bastian smirked and conjured to him a sword of ice. Gael's eyes widened but did nothing to stop his brother's advance on me.

"Bastian, stop. She's not worth the effort. Or the bullshit her father will rain down on us when he finds out." Bastian ignored him, his violent eyes locked on me. I sank into a defensive position. "Is it even worth it if she can't defend herself?" He laughed, making my blood chill and the hair on the back of my neck stand on end.

"Oh, Noqium," he said. "You should've kept your stupid mouth shut."

I blocked his first attack. But Bastian was older, bigger, and stronger. He'd been taught how to fight long before I had. He decked me out, knocking my balance wildly off. His second attack was something I couldn't stop. It skewered the fleshy part of my abdomen, my small blade too small to deflect his sword. I fell to my knees, blood filling my mouth. I couldn't even scream, a gurgling sound replacing it. Pain exploded at the wound site. I did my best to stifle the bleeding, but blood continued flowing through my fingertips.

"You can't kill her!" Gael bit out. "Her father will kill us. He's a fucking Crownguard!"

"So go get that healer friend of theirs." Bastian shrugged as my torso hit the dirty ground. Darkness edged my vision as I watched him lean over me, haughty triumph in his eyes. I could do nothing. My body curled into the fetal position, and I writhed in pain.

Every breath felt like death. "Just so you know, Gael just wanted to get his dick wet." He gave his brother a pointed look. "Right, Gael?"

"It's true," Gael said with a flat voice.

"I'm glad you had fun," I bit out, struggling to rise. Gael refused to look at me, his body turned away. My fingers clenched the now bloody dirt in effort to get my legs under me. "Kissing you was like kissing a slug," I lied as Bastian's boot connected hard with my face, forcing the world black.

My new normal consisted of several things that made up a routine. Training with Aspen in the mornings, with Locke in the evenings, and dinner with the group made up the constants. Aspen was a patient but strict teacher, ensuring that every training session pushed me beyond what I thought my limits were. Over time, I'd improved enough to level him back with combinations and to evade many of his counters, which had become a source of pride for me. I wasn't sure when it happened, but I'd grown to enjoy our training—enjoying the ability to lose myself in each lesson, but what surprised me even more was that I was looking forward to seeing Aspen, though I'd sooner die than voice that. But I'd never been happier to see him than the day he presented me with wooden dowels. It wasn't a weapon; I still longed for the feeling of steel in my hands, but I'd felt triumphant and like I'd graduated something when Aspen handed it to me and told me to hit him. And hit him I did.

Locke hadn't ridden with me since I downed him and discovered my air magic, leaving it solely up to Aspen to take me riding every few days. While I was grateful to Aspen, I tried to ignore the sting of Locke's anger. Even if I couldn't ride, it wasn't uncommon to spend my lunch and spare time with him. Just brushing him and being in his presence brought me a temporary sense of peace. One time I brought a book to the barn, jumped up on Valor's back in his stall, and sat reading aloud to him, watching occasionally as his ears whirled to listen. I remembered my heart feeling so full when I began to doze and my balance falling away with my consciousness, and he sidestepped, catching and waking me before I could fall.

My magic lessons with Locke were professional only. Abrupt. There were no more moments where he almost seemed like he wanted to say something and his posture was closed off from me. Good. I supposed it would make it easier to end him when the time came. Still, I had to push down the sting his quiet glare gave me. I held to it, deciding that rather recoil from it, I'd use it as fire to fuel my anger, hoping it would make it easier when the time came to end him.

Locke's demands from me in our lessons grew more daunting, but I rose to each challenge. Like the good little soldier he wanted me to be. I could feel my power growing. It was a force inside me, a beast thrashing in a too-small cage. Once I had a full grasp on it, I could exact my revenge. And if anybody tried to stop me... I formed an ice dagger at Locke's behest and hurled it at the target.

It bounced off harmlessly to the ground and we sighed in unison. The first thing we've agreed on in weeks.

I wrestled with my contempt, both at Locke and my situation. But there was something else I found myself hating even more: me. I realized I hated myself for not seeing what Locke truly was in Loc Valen. A user. A murderer. I hated myself for thinking he would be any different than anyone else I'd known. And while I didn't trust my own judgement, his reaction on the beach unsettled me. When I'd questioned him on the lives he'd taken, he looked genuinely angry. No, I thought. Not just angry. Broken. He'd looked broken in a way that had me wondering if that were the source of the ghosts that so clearly haunted him.

I thought of Locke back in Loc Valen. How charming he'd been. Funny. Kind. I couldn't reconcile that Locke with the one giving me lessons in my magic, aloof as he was, turning and leaving the second our session was over. Part of me mourned the loss of what could have been, and I hated myself for feeling that way. I mourned the ghost of a relationship that wasn't even real, and with a fae that didn't exist. Because the Locke I thought I'd met was not who exists here with me. And I was taunted by that indifferent face every day. I hated that I was so stupid, so gullible, and after all I'd been through already, you'd think that I'd be more cautious.

And when nighttime came around, and I was finally alone with my thoughts was when the despair and grief nearly crushed me. When I cried myself to sleep, only to wake with my heart thundering in my chest and my sweat-slicked hair clinging to my nape from a nightmare. Every time I closed my eyes, I saw my father's dead body and Locke kneeling over him covered in his blood. I saw my father's green eyes wide open, terror frozen on his face. But his eyes never moved, glazed over in death. His blood soaked into the ground under him. Sometimes my nightmare would show everything in a stark red light, making his blood appear almost black, and Locke's face would twist into a cruel smile. Most nights I wept myself back to sleep, the ache in my chest feeling like a physical hole.

I couldn't deny that interacting with the others was a welcome distraction, even if I didn't trust them. Even Abel seemed less openly hostile towards me, though didn't really interact with me, he wasn't openly glaring at me. So that was something. Every evening, the six of us met for dinner, sharing stories of our days. I was content to listen. To sit quietly and observe them all. They seemed content to let me fade into the background. And why wouldn't they be? I wasn't under the illusion that I was one of them. But sometimes I wished I was. And every once in a while, I let myself pretend that I wasn't just their secret weapon.

Every once in a while, I let myself pretend I was one of them.

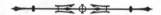

Lennox was bright, friendly, and outgoing. Lenore was dark, witty, and just as outgoing as her twin. Their large, albeit different, extraverted personalities took a lot of getting used to. But I couldn't help but like their energy and their skill at keeping the conversation going at the dinner table any time there was a lull. Lulls were usually filled in by ragging on each other in good humor. Those stories were always my favorite. I sat back, silently enjoying the camaraderie the group displayed. It was clear how deep their bond went as I watched Lenore tell a funny story, earning surprised gasps and chuckles from everyone. Even Abel, who was almost always so stony faced, his smile seemed so out of place.

For the first time in weeks, I noticed Locke's sidelong gaze at me every so often, picking up on my emotions. His expression was always hard to read, but occasionally there was a flicker of emotion I'd catch. Sympathy sometimes. Amusement. Thoughtfulness. Surprise. I refused to let him reading my emotions dull my mood. I refused to let him affect me in any way. I would do his training. I would become strong. And I would end him. Maybe avenging my father would make the nightmares stop. I would make up for my failure a few weeks ago.

"Did you hear Everleigh is speaking again?" Lenore asked the table, pulling from my violent reverie of making good on my threats. Everyone seemed to perk up at the question. My curiosity was piqued.

"That's amazing to hear! She's been through far too much." The reply came from Lennox before she took a drink of her water.

"Who's that?" I asked, my voice quiet. I could tell that my participation in the conversation had surprised Lennox, but she smiled at me nonetheless.

"She came in not long ago, seeking refuge from Scorpio," Locke said. "There are more all the time."

"What happened to her?"

"Nobody knows the specifics. Just that her soulmate was killed by Pisces. That's why she sought refuge here." I felt my eyes widen as I leaned forward. Her soulmate? No wonder she wasn't talking. My heart went out to this fae I'd never met, for enduring a trauma no fae should have to endure. I knew soulmates weren't commonly found, but one supposedly existed out there for everyone. It was said that when one lost their soulmate, the emptiness within them could never be filled again. Like part of them was forever ripped away.

I liked to think that part was utter nonsense.

But maybe there was at least some truth to it if Everleigh was as traumatized as Lenore and Lennox were telling us. The table went silent for a few heartbeats. The lack of conversation quickly became uncomfortable.

"Have we ever told you about the hair dye prank we pulled on Locke?" Lenore asked suddenly, changing the heavy subject after the awkward pause. I didn't miss the mischievous sparkle in her eye. Snickers sounded around the rest of the table, the awkwardness quickly falling away. Locke laughed and shook his head, raking his hands through his hair. Aspen looked like he, too, was choking on a laugh as he reclined in his chair, occasionally tipping back on the back legs. I kept waiting for the chair to tip over, but it never did. I shook my head with a rising smile, leaning in on my elbows for further details and urging her to continue. Lenore, of course, needed no further prompting. She flashed a grin of feigned innocence at Locke from under her eyelashes. Locke gave her a look that said he saw right through her, which only made her smile wider, displaying her perfect, straight teeth.

"Well, you know how his hair always looks good?" I shrugged and observed Locke. He did have great hair. Longer on top with the slight wave to it. Black like a raven's wing, it hung slightly into his eyes in a roguish way.

"He does have better hair than most fae," Aspen chimed in, clapping Locke on the back. "You're so pretty, Your Highness." He batted his eye ashes teasingly at his Prince, causing Locke to chuckle.

"Yes, and if you tried a little harder, You might be... Well, maybe not pretty," he pondered aloud. "Passable to the opposite sex, I suppose" Aspen faked a wounded look.

"I object to your insult, Prince! I do quite well with the ladies."

"You should let said ladies tell you that," I chimed in, smirking at Aspen's fake hurt. Lenore snorted her drink, and Aspen smiled back at me. Locke chuckled again. Even Abel smirked into his cup.

"I thought this embarrassing story was about Locke?" Aspen said, setting the stage for Lenore. Locke scowled without any real venom in it. It looked more like a pout. I brought a small smile to my face before I realized what I was doing. I quickly pulled my attention back to Lennox, who had begun speaking animatedly.

"He was getting ready for some ball or another in Loc Valen," she began, speaking with her hands. I swear she'd be mute if someone tied her hands behind her back and stopped her from gesturing as she spoke. "And you know how he has a thing for his hair." Her smirk got bigger, and Locke's eyes twinkled in amusement and his lips lifted in a mock grimace.

"I snuck in," Lenore took over the story again, ignoring the annoyed look his sister gave her as she twisted her fork in her hand, "while the others kept him distracted. I had bought blue and pink spray-in color. Temporary, of course," she mused. "I put the color in his hairspray bottle." I gawked. He had a hairspray bottle? Cancer, the Crowned Prince and Nightmare Assassin... used hair product?

The thought was so ridiculous I couldn't help the fit of giggles that erupted from me at the thought. "

When he began doing his hair, he smeared the blue and pink in it." Lenore and Lennox burst out laughing at the memory. I could picture it. Locke in his fine clothing, finishing up the final touches to his look, his hair. Only to find the blue and pink haphazardly everywhere. I found I also chuckled hard at the thought of Locke, always so in control, always one step ahead of everyone else, panicking over a bad hair day.

"Her Majesty was pissed," Aspen wheezed through laughs. "He never did make the appearance he was supposed to."

"She wasn't quite as sympathetic as one would hope." Locke smiled wryly, but not without amusement still. "I got my ass kicked, and I got stuck with Pisces's duties as well as my own for a week." I grinned.

Dinner was winding down and people were shuffling out of the dining hall. I began to stand when Locke surprised me by addressing me for the first time outside our lessons in Goddess knew how long. "Everyone is coming back to my rooms for a few hours. You're welcome to join us." He gave me a small, sincere smile that made my heart flutter in my chest. My heart was a fucking traitor, I thought, with venom directed to myself. Aspen or the twins had invited me before, but I'd always said no.

For once I didn't want to go to my rooms just yet. I didn't want to be sad and by myself. I didn't want the night to close in around me. Every experience in my life was telling me this was a bad idea. That it wasn't worth it. And yet…

"Everyone's going?" My voice sounded squeaky as it betrayed my nervousness. He nodded, and I hesitantly accepted the invitation. Locke seemed pleasantly surprised as I walked with him side by side down the hallway to his rooms, neither of us saying a word. I felt my skin prickle at his proximity. I felt the casual brush of the hand against my fingers and I pulled away, feeling heat in my cheeks. It didn't happen again.

I couldn't help but wonder what his bedroom might look like. What *did* an assassin's bedroom look like? In my mind, I pictured black walls with various weapons displayed garishly all over in obsessively neat little frames or shelves. I imagined blood-red furniture to add to the morbid oasis. Maybe some kind of torture cage in the corner. It was so comical I almost laughed, despite myself.

Locke opened the double doors to soft light and the easy chattering of his friends. I glanced around, finding the image in my head and the one in front of me to be vastly different. The layout wasn't dissimilar to mine, breathtaking view and all, but the color scheme was different. My rooms were all decorated with blues, golds, and cream colors; his were outfitted in the finest and most luxurious fabrics in hues of light gray; crisp, clean white; and stark black. Occasionally, there were hints of gold accents scattered throughout the room. Sophisticated. Worthy of royalty. I didn't doubt that those hints were real gold. What struck me about the room was that while it was pristine, it also felt warm. Inviting, rather than the coldness the color scheme should have inspired. It smelled good. Like him. Of pine, musk, and a little of the coals in the massive fireplace. The bookcase he had was lined with books; most had cracked spines, hinting at how often they'd been opened and read. A gold cart with sparkling crystal glasses and a variety of liquors sat next to me, inviting all for a drink. Aspen clutched a glass in his hand as he spoke to the twins sitting easily on the couches, who all glanced up at our arrival. I blinked in surprise as I looked around. Aspen chuckled at my expression from his place by the fire, drawing my gaze.

"She's been in Locke's room five seconds and she already looks disappointed," earning himself a round of chuckling from everyone. Locke gave Aspen a loaded look before turning back to me, his eyebrow quirked.

"What?"

"It's… really nice in here." I felt my cheeks heating at the attention on me.

"What?" he repeated with an amused lilt. "You were expecting doom and gloom?" I shrugged.

"It would fit your doom and gloom personality," I shot. Locke opened his mouth to speak.

"He's the worst assassin!" Lenore chimed in before taking a sip of her wine. "Couldn't even fend off an untrained intruder with how vanilla this room is." Locke laughed and shot her a darkly amused look, which softened slightly as it fell to me when I laughed. He wandered over to where Aspen sipped his drink by the warm fire.

"What kind of assassin would I be if I left my weapons and equipment out for intruders to see." To prove his point, he fished out a carefully, expertly hidden dagger from beneath the mantle. My eyebrows shot to my hairline. If I hadn't watched him reveal it, I would never have known it was there. I looked at the blade as Locke turned it over in his hands with a smug expression aimed at Lenore. It made me now wonder how many weapons lay here in secret. My eyes scanned the room, snagging on any possible nook or cranny, but I found nothing, but I supposed that was the point. The illusion of safety. A tingle down my spine told me that maybe it was the perfect assassin's room after all. And what better assassin was there than the Crowned Assassin? Locke walked easily back over to me with a final grin at Lenore, who stuck her tongue out at him before returning her attention elsewhere, and Locke began pouring himself a drink from the cart.

"What other equipment would you need besides weapons?" I found myself asking out loud. I wished I could take those words back as soon as his bemused grin stared back at me. He leaned in so only I could hear him while the others chatted easily.

"You want to know what equipment I have in my room? Why? You want to know what I'm into?" He winked. I schooled my expression into an outraged sneer. That Goddess-awful grin widened before he lifted his glass of whisky to his lips. The bastard was toying with me. I rolled my eyes at him.

"Here, Lark." I whirled my head around to see Lennox beckoning me over with a wide smile, and a bottle of wine in one hand and two glasses in the other.

Lenore tipped her head my way in invitation too. "Come have a drink. There's plenty of wine!" I turned my back on Locke and my feet carried me over to her straight away. I couldn't deny I was grateful for the escape route. I smiled politely and joined Lenore on the edge of the couch after murmuring my thanks.

"You looked like you needed a rescue," Lennox whispered conspiratorially with a wink. Lenore poured me an extra glug of wine for good measure. I heard, rather than saw, Locke join Aspen by the fire. I ignored him.

"Yeah. Locke's kind of an ass," I said with a grin that grew with theirs. "Thanks."

"You're not wrong," came Lenore's snide comment. Lennox shot her twin a dry look, which made Lenore's smirk grow as she failed spectacularly to feign innocence. "What?"

"I'm glad you finally joined us tonight, Lark." Lennox pulled her attention back to me and smiled warmly. I stared at her a beat, searching for any sign of the deception I was so used to.

"You're one of us now. Whether you like it or not," Lenore said, clinking her glass with mine, her smile chipping away at my residual unease. Aspen confirmed their statements by squeezing my shoulder as he perched himself on the arm of the couch next to me. I smiled meekly at him and he gave me an easy, almost lazy smile in return. My heart squeezed painfully. I wanted so badly to believe in this. That this was real.

But I knew better.

We chatted animatedly through the evening, leading well into the early hours, sipping our drinks. Having dabbled in alcohol only a few times before, I was unfamiliar with the spreading warmth through my extremities. I was also unfamiliar was how fuzzy my head began to feel. But my grin seemed plastered in place for the evening as I felt my remaining shyness fall away. This was what having friends was like. Aspen chuckled at me as if sensing my inebriated state and pulled me into a headlock. I hissed at him and told him vehemently and with colorful language that nobody over the age of ten should be put into headlocks. He gave me a noogie, tousling my hair to hell. I was *so* going to get revenge on him tomorrow in Hell's Gate. I spat venomous promises of violence at him. He had the audacity to laugh at me as I thrashed to remove my head from his grasp.

"I'm just going to tell you that we're going to shorten our lesson a bit. Come to Hell's Gate for eleven a.m. instead. You're going to want the extra sleep."

"I wasn't aware that was an option!" He finally released me from my prison under his arm.

"It is when you're the instructor and you're also going to want to sleep in." He winked at me as I smoothed my hair back out, calling him a not-so-nice curse word under my breath. He grinned wider. I glared at him as he booped me on the nose with his index finger, bidding us all goodnight. He took his leave with a loud yawn. The sisters drained their glasses and also left promptly, citing getting up early for their duties and their own training. And just like that, Locke and I were alone in his room.

I was adult enough to admit that I felt the heat thrumming between us. Like electricity and fire playing along my skin, making every nerve ending stand on high alert. It ignited instantly as the door closed and we were left alone. He stood at the fireplace staring at me as if I were the most complicated puzzle he'd ever seen. I glowered at him and told him to get a picture if he wanted to stare at me. Get a painting done up or something.

"It wouldn't do justice to the real thing," he said, his lowered voice like velvet trailing down my spine. I didn't know how to respond so I said nothing and averted my gaze, eyeing various things around the room that were suddenly very interesting. But he remained looking at me. I rubbed my arms in response. I didn't even notice he'd gotten closer until he was a step away. I could reach out and touch him. His face blank and unreadable. But I was slowly understanding that that was a mask he wore when he wanted to hide whatever it was he felt.

"What color are my emotions?" I asked, genuinely curious. Maybe he could help me sort through the wild feelings stomping around indistinguishably. He paused before answering, his eyes unfocused as he observed my aura.

"I see confusion. Which is yellow. A pale yellow. A bit of contempt, and odd red color. That's good. I like your contempt. I see nervousness, which is orange." He raked his eyes down my body, setting my blood on fire before continuing. "I see lust, which is an intense shade of red, almost burgundy." He smirked and I blushed, looking immediately for an escape route. He tilted my chin up to look at him again, the blue of his eyes bright and focused on me. "You look like the most beautiful sunset."

"What are you doing?" I asked him tersely, my voice barely above a whisper. My heart thrashed in my chest loudly enough I was certain he could hear it.

"What I swore I wouldn't do."

"And what's that?"

"Be alone with you. Pursue you. Want you." His eyes darkened and I knew he was thinking of that night at the inn. Heat coiled lower in me as I remembered too. My chest tightened with anxiety and anticipation and confusion and so many other things that took up too much space, leaving very little room for oxygen. He drifted slightly closer. He was in my space now, sharing my breath. His scent wrapped around me.

"I know you remember last time you bit your lip." His tone was smoldering. Husky. I released my lip, unaware I'd even drawn it into my mouth. My insides melted and clenched together and my toes curled in my shoes.

"You... This is a bad idea," I whispered, more than a little breathless. I felt my mind going blank. I tried to remember why I didn't want this, why I should fight this magnetic pull between us, but my mind couldn't seem to hold a thought for long enough with his face this close. My head felt fuzzy, presumably from the wine.

"I agree. This is a terrible idea."

"This is the alcohol talking."

"I'm absolutely convinced that's true."

"You killed my father." His face changed, but he didn't move away from me. His hand touched my face in a touch so gentle I had to check to see if the touch were indeed there.

"Is that truly what you think?" he asked me. But I knew what I saw. But his voice had the slightest bit of hurt in it that even he couldn't hide, and in my inebriation, I doubted myself seriously for the first time. I said nothing, not knowing what to say. I refused to verbalize this doubt. To verbalize it would be to make it real, give it form. And it would make me a traitorous daughter. But in that moment, I realized that I desperately didn't want Locke to be his killer. The heat between us was raging and begging me to close the distance between us. But what would that mean if I did?

His hand found mine and gingerly placed it on his chest. I felt the pounding of his heart under my fingers, echoing my own. I looked up at him, surprised our encounter was affecting him so.

"You're killing me, Lark," he ground out. My head was so fuzzy. His lips were so close to mine, just a breath away. His musky pine scent wrapping around me. I closed the distance, surprising both of us. I pressed my lips tentatively to his. I wasn't sure what I was doing, but I know what my body and the wine were demanding. He kissed me back fervently, his hands pressing me into his hard body. My control snapped. I needed him. I fisted my hands into his hair. His tongue warred with mine. I bit his lip, eliciting a growl from him, and he clamped my hips down and ground into me, taking the control back from me. I tipped my head back and let out a breathy moan. He didn't falter. His lips caressed my face, my neck, my collarbone, lighting me up from the inside out. He picked me up and deposited me on the bed, him following overtop of me. My legs wrapped themselves around his waist. I whispered his name in wanting. His hands ran up and down my body with a deliberate slowness that tortured me. I ran my hands up his abdomen, his biceps, before settling around his neck, luxuriating in the hard, male feel of him. He broke our kiss with an abruptness that startled me. I could see the lust in his gaze and it swept over me.

"I'm not bedding you tonight," he ground out with some effort, and I felt his dismissal hit me hard like a blast of cold water. "It's not that I don't want to. Clearly." He gestured to the bulge in his pants. Seeing it sort of took away the sting of rejection. He continued as if reading my mind. "I'm not rejecting you. You've been drinking. A lot. So have I. I also got carried away, more than you know." He hit me with a heavy, loaded look. I saw it in his eyes. Because I saw that look whenever I looked in the mirror. Self-loathing. "I'm very drawn to you, but consent matters to me. I don't want you in my bed drunk, only to wake up the next day and regret it. If consent isn't enthusiastic and sober, then it's not consent. But I respect you too much. We can't do this." Goddess damn him. He was right. I knew the alcohol was fueling this tryst. As much as I hated to acknowledge it, it made my heart warm against my better judgement to hear that he respected me. I decided on a single liberty. I kissed him once more. Chastely on the lips. He gave me another loaded look. But for the life of me I couldn't decipher its meaning. I took a deep breath to calm my raging heartbeat and libido. To clear my head.

"Lark..." I cut him off with a kiss, as sweet as the last one. I pressed my hand to his cheek. He pulled the blankets back on his bed, inviting me to spend the night, but not the way I'd imagined a few moments ago.

"What are we doing?" I whispered.

"Things were not supposed to," he said back, turning out the lights with magic. All but the one on his bedside table, casting him in a candlelit glow. "One day I'll explain why."

"If you can't explain that, can you explain something else instead?" I asked, pulling myself to a cross-legged position on the bed, and regarded him with open curiosity. I felt, for the first time since I'd been here, the hatred and anger I'd been harboring for the faerie in front of me had quieted. Caution, mistrust I felt, but for once, no hatred. Even much more flattering emotions were rising to the surface. Emotions I refused to look at too closely.

I was a terrible daughter.

He regarded me wearily and cocked his head at me. "What do you want to know?"

"Why are you doing all this?" I gestured to all around us. "The Court of Rebels. Why are you fighting Scorpio so hard? You're a Prince of the Water Court. What's in it for you, specifically?" The lightning in his gaze made me think I'd said something wrong. The stricken face was so unlike his normal demeanor that I averted my gaze, ready to apologize when his hand settled on my knee in a comforting manner.

"No, it's okay. Perhaps it's time you knew the full picture about me," he said, pinching his furrowed brow before continuing. "I've been around a long time. I've held the title of Cancer a long time. It feels like I've always been the Crowned Assassin. But my job was limited to eliminating threats to our borders. The safety of our Court. Something I do with pride. When Scorpio ascended as Queen, when we were both cursed, she went mad slowly. Her curse forces her to live through the agony of every wound she's ever suffered. Though each wound heals, the pain of it remains forever. That never-ending pain is what drove her mad and it's why her desperation to end the curse is so visceral. Her madness has become her mind's only escape from her reality. She's had many attempts on her life, including by her own hand. She cannot die, but neither can she live." He swallowed. It was difficult not to feel the tiniest bit of pity for the Queen. Agony. Every single day. Torture, day in and day out with no reprieve for five years. That's enough to make anybody crazy.

"You said she wasn't always like that," I prodded gently. He dipped his head in a single nod, a grim smile on his face.

"She wasn't. She used to be kind. Caring. Funny. We grew up together in the Zodiac Guild. I've known her longer than I've known almost anybody else. Including Pisces, who came later. I used to think she was going to be a great Queen. A fair Queen. Just. Until she fell under the curse. She did everything she could to save her brother from illness. It was days from claiming his life. He was her only family, and in her desperation to save him, she turned to the Dark Arts. Black magic. It kept him alive, but at great cost. I tried to stop her but I was far too late. I was cursed alongside her, as you know."

"So why are you stopping her? Were you"—I almost choked on the words—"in love with her? Are you trying to get her back? Is it revenge for getting you cursed? What is it?" His head sunk in what could only be hot shame.

"I did love her. Not in the way you think though. I loved her as family. Like a sister. A long time ago. Before she'd ascended as Scorpio. Before the curse. But she changed. When she was cursed a few years ago, she was no longer the fae I remembered growing up with. Surviving the rune gauntlet with. She's willing to do anything, use anything to get what she wants."

"She has something of yours. Doesn't she?"

He nodded, looking at me with barely hidden vulnerability. And like he hated displaying that vulnerability.

"It's my father. He has a sickness that can only be controlled with a very expensive potion that's administered weekly. I can pay for it, but only the most talented healers can make it, and they're all in her pocket. If I don't do what she says, she'll make the potion inaccessible to him. He'll die without it." For one moment, a single heartbeat, I saw a fae who was as broken as I was. It should've brought me joy to see him this way. But all it made me feel was sorrowful and sympathetic. Before realization hit me like a brick.

"That day you let me go..."

"I defied orders that day. She didn't necessarily know you were there. I made a judgment call. She never found out, to my knowledge, so he should still be safe." He'd risked that for me....

"Can't you portal to them? Get them out? Bring them here? Can we bring in or train a qualified healer?"

"Loc Valen is warded against portals of any kind. Unless Scorpio authorizes it, it cannot happen. I'm not allowed anywhere near them. And I haven't told my family. I wasn't allowed to. Because as long as I remain her loyal attack dog on a leash, my family is safe."

The words sounded bitter passing his lips and my heart gave a squeeze for him. I called him a dog on a leash that first day. I had no idea then how accurate that statement was. But instead of feeling smug, I felt awful for Locke. Not only was his family being dangled before him, they weren't even aware of it. He was suffering alone.

"She's used them to force me to kill countless numbers of innocent people. She's made me into the Nightmare Assassin. But that's not who I want to be. That's not the legacy I want to leave. I don't enjoy being a monster." His words sounded broken by the end, barely above that of a whisper. I reached my hand to his, interlacing our fingers. He gave mine a gentle squeeze.

"You're not a monster," I whispered, surprising even myself with how much I meant those words. It wasn't long ago I was saying the opposite. But I knew full well he only killed when he wasn't able to save them and send them here, to Port Azure. His head snapped up to meet my gaze, surprise registering on his handsome features. He'll never admit it, but I can imagine that's what happened to my father. His hand was forced to save his family. I couldn't say that it was okay. But I could understand it. There wasn't anything I wouldn't have done to save my father. My heart felt shredded into pieces when I realized that while I couldn't accept it now, I could find a way to live with it without it destroying me further. It was as close to closure as I knew I was going to get.

We stayed like that a long moment, our fingers woven into one another's without saying another word. My heart was pounding. I couldn't help but feel like that was the most exposed I'd ever seen him. His mask he usually wore was down, showing his soft features and vulnerability in his eyes on display for me.

"Thank you for telling me," I said softly, giving his hand another squeeze. He squeezed back with a sad smile.

"Tell me something about you." It almost sounded like a question, an ask more than a demand. My mind raced as I struggled to come up with anything interesting enough to tell him. He was a Prince, for the sake of the Goddess! "Tell me about your father. About Poplar Hollow. Tell me about what it was like growing up without magic."

"I thought you wanted to be cheered up, not depressed," I half-joked. "Most of that isn't terribly interesting or entertaining." He cocked his head.

"Try me."

So I told him. I told him how the sun set over the small settlement and casted the red brick buildings and homes in its evening amber glow. I told him how with the forest in the background, especially in the fall, with its vibrant foliage, it was breathtaking. The bridge was one of my favorite places for that. Or if I needed distance, I'd go to the hill that led to the forest and sit there, looking down at the town in the evening sunshine. Sometimes when the wind hit just right, you could smell the market. The fresh bread, various spices, simmering meat on an open flame... Just thinking of it now, I could nearly taste it.

I told him how I'd use Haven as a means of escape from reality. Being ostracized over and over again from the community because of being magicless. The senselessness of that still made me seethe a bit. Especially now that I knew I had more magic than all of them combined. The cool taste of irony felt bitter on my tongue. I told him how I'd learned to fight when my father witnessed the bruises for himself after four of my peers had held me down and attacked me. I'd learned to evade attacks, even magical ones. But I seldom got a hit in retaliation. But according to everyone in the town, I was the provoking party.

I told him how people used to pretend to be my ally, my friend, only so they could get close enough to me to use me when they had need of me. Or to really hurt me. All for sport. That a boy pretended to like me once, only for it to be one big, painful joke. How he'd gotten his friends to pretend to accept me too. Just so it would hurt worse when they attacked me alone in the forest later. I told him how Eldan was kind enough to me and my father and gave me a job as his apprentice a few years ago. He taught me so much, but without magic, I couldn't create potions or use healing spells. I had to do it the tedious way, but he taught me nonetheless. He'd let me use Haven whenever I'd needed. He was family in his own right. My heart constricted thinking of him now, wondering what he was doing now. If he wondered where I'd gone. If he'd searched for me at all.

Locke listened attentively through all of it, nodding at the right moments, looking murderous in others. His eyes gleamed with the threat of violence when I'd told him why I'd learned to fight. The injuries I'd sustained for no reason other than being different. Being easy prey.

"I'm so sorry you went through all of that. You didn't deserve any of that." He squeezed my fingers again, forcing me to realize we were still connected by our hands. His features were earnest as he looked at me. I gave a small half-smile and a shrug. His other hand came up and made me look at him again, with an air of insistence.

"No, I mean it. Magicless or not, heavy on the not, obviously." He half smirked at his own bad joke. "Nobody deserves that kind of treatment. That being said, you're an incredible fighter. You honed your skills well here, and you've learned so much. You're impossibly strong considering how broken I know you feel. But as broken as you feel, you're not. You might be bent, but you haven't broken. Because you're made of stronger stuff than that. You've been forged. Your trials and tribulations were the fires from which you came, strong enough to conquer anything. Especially when after everything they did to you, not only did you not hate them, at least not entirely, you tried to help them as Eldan's apprentice. If I didn't know what true strength of heart was, I'd learn by your example."

My mouth fell open, unable to process his words. A slow smile spread across his features, earnest and genuine. I returned his smile with a shy, sheepish one of my own, my heart singing at his words.

"Thank you." My words were breathy and I averted my gaze again, a blush creeping along my face. He lifted my hand to his lips and placed a gentle kiss on the back of my hand, sending butterflies through my stomach. Or a hurricane.

"Can I ask you something?" I asked him, desperate to change the subject, my cheeks still pink. Locke nodded, his eyes watching me intently from under his lashes. "I want to know about dark magic. You don't have to tell me about your curse. But I want to understand the process of it. What's it like in the shadow realm?" What did my mother have to do to have me?

"That's more than one question." He smirked, though his shoulders stiffened a bit at my questions. "Why do you want to know?"

"Don't worry, I'm not looking to add a fifth element. I'm already the strongest fae around. I have to let the rest of you have *something*." He sniggered, shaking his head at me. I grinned back at him. There was a lighthearted moment before he sobered, bringing my smile down with his. He took a deep breath as if to gather his thoughts.

"Fae are drawn to the idea of the shadows because it's powerful magic. Because they think it can grant wishes in exchange for a curse," he began. "But they don't realize the payoff isn't worth it. It's never worth it. I hate that I have it. I hate the way using it makes me feel. When the runes carve themselves into you… " He sighed. The look on his face, regret and pain laced together, made me want to make him feel better. But I didn't move as he continued speaking.

"There's a spell to access the Echo Isles. Written in the old language. But it's no place anyone should ever visit. And thankfully, very few do," he said, his voice contemplative. "The very light is tinted darker. Many fae have been banished there over the centuries, and you can feel their hate. The weight of it. But the worst part was the Grievling. The master of the Echo Isles." I had never heard of such a creature. At my confused look, he elaborated. And part of me wished he didn't.

"He's the stuff of nightmares. The king of the darklings, those who dwell in the shadow realm. He's made entirely of shadow. His smile was the worst part. It was way too wide, and full of teeth." He shuddered again. He must have been genuinely terrifying if even the Crowned Assassin were afraid of him. "He delves into the deepest reaches of your soul, finding what hurts you. What your worst fears are. And the curse he places upon you is reminiscent of those fears."

"That sounds horrible!" I gasped, squeezing his hand again. The thought of the Grieveling delving into your soul… I could see the pained look on Locke's face. He didn't have to tell me with his words how much it had hurt. I could clearly see it in the lines of his face. "Wait, I thought you said Scorpio asked for the power to heal her brother?"

"She did. She begged the Grievling for powerful shadow magic. Magic that could keep her brother alive. The cost was the curse she was given. A horrible existence. The worst part was that her brother wasn't saved. Not really. The shadows didn't heal him. He's frozen in time, perpetually sick and can't get better, but neither can he die." I didn't have words. Her brother's fate was eerily similar to hers. My father once said that the darkness didn't grant you your real ask. It was always a perverse thing that made you wish you'd never done it at all. I saw now what he meant. Locke's voice softened as he continued.

"As for shadow magic, it's also something of a trap. The magic is tied directly to your soul. The darker a fae is on the inside, the easier the shadows fester like an infection and corrupt that fae's soul. The more you use the shadows, the faster that process happens, but some very strong fae can fight it off long term." Like him? Like Scorpio?

"What process?"

"Death. Once the soul is fully corrupted..." He trailed off, leaving his meaning to sink in. I stared at him, unsure how he could be so calm.

"But what about you? Are you okay?"

He shrugged. "More or less. I'm still here, aren't I?"

I looked at him through yet another lens. He's suffered his curse for a few years. Did he not have so much darkness in his soul? Was he strong enough to fight it off ? For how long? That was a thought path I didn't want to traverse, so I banished it quickly.

"We should go to sleep," Locke said, not withdrawing his hand as he laid down in his clothing on the bed. He gave me a small tug. Not a demand. A shy invitation. Not to have sex, but spend the night. The butterflies from earlier returned, making my stomach feel light and my heart jittery. I tried to force my legs to move to my own rooms, but I found I didn't want to go. I didn't want to move. I was exactly where I wanted to be. Eyeing him with caution, I lay down across from him, our hands still grasped together.

"Locke?"

"Hmm?"

"This doesn't change anything." I was pretty sure I was lying. I wasn't sure, but I was hoping that my racing pulse wasn't from his proximity but the wine. Drinking clearly brought emotions out of me I'd rather not experience or look too much into. I just hoped that he didn't know. I heard a faint chuckle from him rumble in his chest.

"I know. Get some rest. You have to be up in a few hours. And so do I."

I rested my head on his pillow and my eyes closed, searing the image of Locke's handsome face looking at me into my brain. That was the first night I didn't wake up crying.

I woke to cascades of sunshine in the room. I groaned against the rising sun. I pulled the blue pillow over my face. Wait, *blue*?

I was in my own room, my own bed. When did that happen? I tested my body for signs of a hangover. A mild headache. I was pleased that was my only affliction. I deserved so much worse. Eldan and I had created enough hangover tonics and seen the effects of hangovers enough times to know I felt much better than I'd expected. I glanced at the time. Not yet breakfast. There was a note on my bedside table.

I hope you have the sweetest dreams -L

My heart melted at the note, bringing a wry smile unbidden to my face. I contemplated last night as I ran myself a bath. While the water filled the tub, I began a fire to drive out the chilliness of the morning. I flushed, remembering Locke and I last night. What we almost did. Mortification colored my cheeks a vibrant red. I was glad he stopped us from going to bed together. Things wouldn't have gone that far if I weren't drunk. But then there was all the stuff he told me about his family. Why he needed Scorpio out of the picture. I hardened my heart to him, refusing to let it further soften me. But it didn't work. The Crowned Assassin had worked his way under my skin and I could feel him swimming in my veins. I hated it. He wasn't the Crowned Assassin to me. Just the crowned ass.

My thoughts jumbled in my head as I tried and failed to relax in the bath, the steaming water failing to work away my anxiety. The heat failing to unknot the worry in my stomach. Why had I kissed him last night? I recalled his lips, his hard body against mine. Why had I allowed it? I was an idiot. He killed my father, for crying out loud! And yet... I remembered the look on his face last night when I asked me if I truly believed that. I remembered that feeling of doubt. I couldn't imagine him killing someone innocent. For zero reason. What scenarios did that leave me with? A mercy killing didn't fit. There was nothing wrong with my father. My father was guilty of grave offence? It was highly unlikely since his body was broken after the monster attack and then he took ill. He'd been holed up in our cottage. He couldn't have gotten into much trouble. It was possible, I supposed. He had hunted small game for us and was mobile enough for that. I supposed Scorpio could've ordered the kill, which was what I'd thought last night. But how would she have known about him? Which meant one other scenario, if I were to trust that doubt: He didn't kill my father.

But then who did? There was literally nobody else there. And why wouldn't he just tell me? It'd be plausible, I supposed, if anybody else had been there. I had to ask him about it again, but every time I did, he shut me down or walked away. He'd, to this day, never denied nor confirmed it. The thought unsettled me in a way I didn't understand. It sank into my stomach like a poison.

I couldn't take it anymore.

I stopped bothering to stitch the still-bleeding cut in my leg closed. Yet another one that wouldn't scar thanks to the magical balm Eldan gave me when he saw the scars begin to pile up. I smiled grimly and without humor in the stark candlelight flickering throughout the room.

I looked around the room, my expression caught between a sob and a sneer. I couldn't do this anymore. Was my life meant to be such misery? My eyes raked down my body, snagging all too frequently on my now faint scars. Despair and sorrow crashed into me in equal measure and pulled me under the surface. My lungs stopped working as if I were really under water. I braced against it but found no relief. And as I glanced around feeling any fight slither from my body, I realized this time I couldn't find my way out. I hadn't done anything to deserve aside from being born magicless. And because of that, I knew it would never get better. Anywhere I went, I knew it would be the same.

In the silence of the early hours of the morning, I wept. I wept silent tears that soaked my face and fell in thick, fat drops to my bedding. The kind of crying that you felt all the way down to your soul. And in that horrible moment, I knew I was finally admitting defeat.

I made the decision then. And immediately I felt lighter. I felt the weight of the world finally leave my shoulders. It was finally about to be over. I should have felt fearful. Apprehensive. But all I felt was relief.

My tears didn't stop. Not as I gathered my legs under me. Not as I stalked slowly to the kitchen. But the feeling of relief only heightened. It brought a small smile to my face once again as I glimpsed the knife block in the kitchen.

It made a shiver-inducing sound as I gripped it and freed it from the wood. I turned it over in my hands, watching with detached fascination as the blade reflected the light of the single candle I'd carried with me. The only source of light in an otherwise pitch-black home.

I couldn't deny the weight struggling with the now disappearing sense of weightlessness I'd just experienced. The unsettling feeling in my stomach. Would it hurt? Going beyond the veil? Would I be accepted into whatever afterlife the Goddess has in store? Or would I be rejected because of my magicless nature? Would even the Goddess herself send me away—even in death?

These thoughts swarmed me, interrupting my earlier inner feeling of peace. But gripped the knife harder, determined. A moment of pain similar to all the pain I suffer anyway, for everlasting rest. At last.

At last. I wouldn't have to suffer the indignation of my peers. I wouldn't have to fight. Or run. I wouldn't have to look over my shoulder anymore. I brought the knife to my wrist, the steel surprisingly cold, biting into my skin. Not enough to break it. Just enough to coax a hiss from my lips. I remembered that feeling of calm. I latched onto it the way a starved animal latched onto a kill, allowing that feeling to fill me up. I stared at the knife as if in a trance as I readied myself.

The sound of rusty swinging hinges broke me from my reverie and startled me. In the same second, my eyes darted to the source of the sound and saw my father in a sleep-induced daze as he shuffled out the door, no doubt risen by a bladder urgency. His sleepy, half-lidded eyes widened with a sudden alertness when he took in the sight before him. Me in the kitchen with the knife poised to slice deeply into the tender flesh of my arm.

He launched himself forward. I didn't even have time to blink. He was on me, gripping the blade with his bare hand. I heard the grunt of pain the blade wrought from him as he took the blade and threw it with all his strength. It landed hard against the wall on the far side of the living room where it clattered noisily in a loud heap to the floor. "What the fuck are you doing?" my father cried. I could hear the desperation and anxiety and rage all clamoring for my attention. It hooked my attention, making me freeze, my limbs no longer obeying me. I glanced at my now empty hand in despair.

"What am I doing?" I echoed his question in a whisper, my hand feeling empty, bereft of my knife. My peace. In place of the calm and peace, however conflicted it was, all I felt now was numb. My earlier despair wasn't forgotten, though, as it thrashed on the other side of that numbness just aching to reunite with me. "I can't do this anymore." My father looked at me, his jaw tightened on a curt reply. He steadied himself before reaching for me. I didn't resist as I fell into his arms and sobbed, this time loudly as they wracked my body. I poured out my despair. My heartbreak. My loneliness. My pain. All of it. Father stroked my hair and rocked me back and forth, as if I were a child again. And I let him.

"I'm so sorry, Lark." My father's gruff voice found me. So soft I questioned whether I did actually hear him. "I'm so sorry your life is like this. I'm sorry in ways you'll never know."

I didn't know what he meant by that. But I just leaned into him as my sobs continued.

"I don't want to be here anymore, Papa," I wailed, my voice nothing but a pain-filled, pitiful sound. I scarcely recognized my own voice, for once not shielding and masking my feelings. I didn't have any strength left for that, or anything else. Finally, they were laid bare before us both. I felt his shoulders stiffen even further. I saw him clamor for something to say. But what do you say in the face of your own child's attempted suicide?

"I know, Lark. I know. But you're needed. You're so needed. And so loved. Does that not matter?" he asked softly. I didn't answer. I pressed my mouth into a thin line to suppress the tears. "Life has been hard for you. I know it has. But when I look at you, I see someone who is harder still. You're a diamond, Lark. Something that cannot be broken by anything. Not even life. So when life gets hard, I need you to be harder. Stronger. Better. Because you are all these things." I felt his grip strengthen around me then as if he could keep the shattered pieces of me from scattering to the wind. And his already-wobbly voice reduced to a barely-there, strained whisper that hurt what remained of my heart. "I don't want to lose you either. I've already lost your mother. Don't make me watch as I lose you too."

I didn't know what to say. So I only nodded mutely.

"Don't let them win, Lark. Every day you're here is a win. Every time you smile is a victory. Every day you best them at their own game is a well-fought war won. Stay. Keep stacking those wins. Whatever keeps you here. Just please… Please stay." There was a time when those words would've lit the fire of competition in me. Of spite, if nothing else. Now the embers had long cooled to the bitterness of my reality.

I wrapped my hands around my father then, nodding again in silent promise. But that wasn't enough for him.

"Say the words, Lark." It took me a moment. A long moment of silence where I caught my breath. I spoke with a soft, shaky voice.

"I'll stay." And I knew it was the truth. For my father, I would try. I didn't want to. A part of me wanted to end it anyway. But the look on my father's face when he saw me with the knife… it broke something in me, proving to myself that I could continue to break even after I thought I already had. And if for no other reason than to make the only person I loved happy, I would stay.

Even if I hated being here with every fiber of my being.

It was hard not to appreciate how much more fit I was these days, except during the workout. During the workout, Aspen could go to hell. He constantly reminded me when I said that, that we were, in fact, at Hell's Gate, so I was going to have to get more imaginative than that. I made a rude hand gesture at him. I decided waiting for your opponent to make the first move stinks. I flung myself at Aspen, using the techniques he'd taught me. "Fighting was just dancing. Except you have a winner," he'd said to me.

Today I fueled myself with the frustration of last night and I fell on him wildly. He lunged at me. I dodged by leaping to the side, away from the jab he swung at me. I brought my legs under me and countered with a fist of my own, which was blocked easily. I retreated another step as another punch was thrown. We repeated this for a long time. Punch, evade, counter. Aspen every so often baring instructions at me. I felt my breaths coming quicker and shorter. No wonder cardio was such a big deal. I faked a punch and spun into a roundhouse kick that connected solidly with his torso. He grunted and I grinned, smug pride filling me to the brim. It was short-lived, when he swept my feet out from under me and took me the ground. I refused to let him get the upper hand, but my refusal didn't matter much when he had a full guard over me, making any effort I had to defend myself useless. I tried the guard-breaking tactics he'd shown me, but honestly, the guy had at least a hundred pounds on me, if not more, in pure muscle. I huffed out the word "cheater" at him and he barked a laugh.

"Don't be a sore loser. You're actually doing quite well. You've improved a lot since you got here. You'd be a match for a lot of fae now." I couldn't help but brighten at his words. And hammer punched him in the gut as he stretched to let me up, taking him completely by surprise. I laughed as he dramatically wheezed and fell off me, calling me a cheater.

"Don't be a sore loser," I said sweetly, sticking my tongue out at him and plopping down next to him. He faked a glare at me that he couldn't maintain and ended up grinning back at me. I reached over, stretching so I didn't actually have to get up for my water bottle. Now that I was resting, my muscles hurt and were screaming their protest. I hissed as I fully extended my torso to grab my bottle. Aspen smirked.

"How was the rest of last night?" Aspen asked me, with a voice dripping with suggestion, not bothering to be subtle. He raised his eyebrows innocently when I looked at him with poison in my expression. He couldn't know about last night, could he? Locke didn't seem the type to kiss and tell.

"I left not long after you did." *I think*, I added silently. I didn't actually know how long it was before Locke deposited me in my own room and tucked me in. Aspen wiggled his eyebrows.

"And what happened in the meantime?" I glared at him. "Oh, come on, Lark. You think the rest of us don't notice? You two are into each other."

"I won't deny he's attractive," I chewed the words out. "But it doesn't change a thing. He killed my father. I refuse to feel anything positive for him." I could feel the lack of conviction in my words, but my biting tone should've hidden it.

"Refuse all you want, we all see the way you look at him. Love and hate exist on the same coin. And the funny thing about them is that they both require passion. Something you both have. Passion will blur those lines a lot."

"Well, he's made it clear we can't be together in any capacity. We both have set that boundary. So I refuse to be involved with that." You know. Starting now. That didn't stop the small budding hope that maybe one day something could come of us. If nothing else, a peace between us. Aspen's eyes darkened, saddened. He knew, I realized. He knew what Locke wouldn't tell me. "Tell me." Aspen looked up innocently. "Tell me what you know."

"I can't." He sighed, looking deep into my eyes. "It's not my curse to bear." But the moment was soon gone when he stood abruptly and told me our session was over. He told me to go cool down and he'd see me at dinner. Our conversation ended so suddenly my head was spinning.

The rest of the day passed by in a blur. Lunch came and went without issue, as did the personal time I spent doting on Valor. His ears perked up when he noticed me and greeted me with a nicker of affection, making my heart want to burst. By the time I was supposed to have my magic lesson with Locke, my heart was pounding a nervous rhythm. Were we going to ignore everything? Pretend it didn't happen? Or would that ember between us smolder even today?

He walked in finally, apologizing for his lateness. His posture was stiff as I observed him and we began on spell work straight away. I almost sighed. Right back to that aloofness. Fine by me.

Except for some reason, it wasn't.

He gave me various tasks: create hot steam that could burn, scald, or incapacitate an attacker, create ice as far out as I could push it, create shapes using water and fire, the shapes getting more difficult. Today I was struggling with creating a moving, living flame out of water between my hands. I liked irony. I was concentrating hard, moving the shapes, changing shapes, changing the sizing of the shapes that I conjured. Sweat beaded on my brow at the effort, but I was thrilled I was maintaining this. Finally, Locke ordered me to stop. Or barked at me, would be more accurate. I stopped all magic, looking at him quizzically.

"You've done well with your water element, Lark," he said, his voice stiff. Formal. Not the laidback person I'd been dealing with before now. His shoulders never seemed to relax at all as he spoke. "Now it's time to try your fire element. I'm going to run you through similar exercises, but we may need outside help to teach you the inner workings of fire magic. Earth and Air as well for that matter."

"What does that mean?"

"It means nothing right now. Magic is instinctive. Intuitive, to a point. You may already understand your magic on some level. The elixir your father had to you drink is well out of your system and your magic is getting stronger every day. Your control over it is growing as well. Enough that I think it's time we try focusing on your other elements and see what happens."

I nodded in excitement. I was ready to try out my fire magic. I conjured flames to my hand as I had a thousand times. It wrapped itself around my hands, my arms, like a snake, fire runes showing up brightly on my skin. I loved the way fire magic made me feel. Water Magic made me feel strong, like the water slowly eroding the earth, peaceful, and calm. Fire magic made me feel alive. A different kind of strength. It made me feel invincible. Worthy. I readied myself for Locke, unsure of the tasks he'd chosen.

"See those targets?" He pointed to my left to see seven targets all different distances away. Some were twenty feet away, others more like forty. I smiled. I liked where this going. "Hit them. Push your fire magic outward."

I swear I felt my flames dance in my eyes. I was only too happy to comply with his orders. I pointed my arm at the target. Sweat ran down my back. I'd never used my fire magic this much at once before. At least not on purpose. I gritted my teeth and pushed. A line of fire from my hand streaked towards the target like a shooting star. It wasn't particularly fast, but my aim was true. It ignited the target, sending up a pillar of black smoke and flame. I grinned in the firelight. Locke's expression tinged with awe and pride. I opened fire on the other targets, missing three of the six others. The arena filled with pillars of flame where the targets once stood. I admired my handiwork with a mad grin.

"Hell's Gate, indeed," I whispered to no one in particular. Locke grinned, the first sign of emotion today.

"Glad to see it's finally living up to its namesake."

"All we need now is brimstone."

"Well, I can't really help you there, so you'll have to make due with scaring the hell out of fae with just flames," he murmured. And we used our water magic to douse the flames, leaving the arena full of hot steam.

My body was spent, and my well of magic was beginning to drain, feeling very much like water emptying through a drain in a basin. Slow and steady. But I didn't feel tired. I felt energized. Alive. Excited. My body hummed with my magic, an energy I'd never experienced. I wanted to do more, more, more. I realized I was bouncing on the balls of my feet when Locke quirked an eyebrow at me.

"More?" he asked, his eyebrows raised in surprise. I nodded excitedly.

"More."

We spent another thirty minutes running through grueling exercises before my magic fizzled completely out. Hitting objects with flame, Locke made targets out of water close by to us for me to hit. The water would sizzle out of existence as my flames evaporated it on impact. Next I began creating a flame weapon, such as a whip or a sword. Even an arrow. I had to focus hard not to let the arrow burn the wood of the bow. I failed twice, losing us two beautiful bows. I apologized several times, but Locke waved me off, telling me not to worry about it. But even he couldn't hide being severely impressed when I kept the fire arrow contained and loosed it. I whooped in triumph. Assuming my aim with a bow wasn't terrible, which it was, it would be a deadly force. And the thought of never not having a weapon again was comforting. I didn't have to rely on my blades ever again. Between ice daggers and fire weapons, I was in decent shape. I particularly loved the feel of the flaming whip in my hands. I felt strong. Powerful. And the way Locke was looking at me made me think I looked it too.

I practiced fire shapes the way I did my water shapes as well. That part was easier, because the magic worked similarly here. It was just a matter of slight adjustments to my approach with it. My flame eventually sputtered out, my well of magic well and truly empty. But I still felt energized. Locke made a sound that was half laugh and half sigh and suggested we head to dinner and meet the others. As we turned around we saw our friends standing behind us with a cart.

"How long have you guys been there?" I asked. Aspen grinned widely. Lenore and Lennox laughed.

"You didn't even notice us?" I flushed. I really had no idea. I shrugged and offered an apology.

"Tell me there's food on that cart?" I asked, my stomach also joining the conversation. Lennox unveiled today's dinner and all our plates, kept warm by trays. "You know, for a rebel base, you guys seem to have a lot of luxuries."

"We all come from wealthy lines. It helps make sure everyone in Port Azure has enough," Lennox said meekly. It wasn't a brag, just a fact. She didn't elaborate, but she didn't need to. I understood her meaning.

We settled on the podium while we ate together.

"I've never seen fire magic up close. I was starting to wonder if you had the element after all," said Aspen. "Nice to see His Highness wasn't exaggerating."

"So, I can stay in the club?" I smirked.

"I think your chances look good," said Aspen.

At the same time Lennox joked, "You'll fry us if we try to kick you out!"

I laughed and joked about that being the true motivator for keeping me around. Everyone chuckled. But I found that as soon as I made that joke, a piece of it settled into my bones and I wondered if it really were true. Part of the reason they were training me was to help them against the Queen. To start the Uprising in earnest. I was their weapon. But they would want strong ties to me to help ensure I fought for them. Or at the very least not against them. I wondered about their ulterior motives for a long while into dinner. Locke kept looking at me, stealing glances with a worried gaze, as if reading my thoughts. I had *got* to get that guy to show me how to block him from reading my emotions, because this was getting out of hand. He caught my gaze with his, his eyes hard. He shook his head no, a movement so small it was nearly imperceptible. No? No what? That there was no ulterior motive? Or no something else? Before I could ask him, he'd moved on to speaking with Aspen. I realized one member of the group wasn't here.

"Where's Abel?" I asked.

"He said he didn't feel well and had a long day, so he took his dinner to his rooms and is going to bed early," Lennox said.

"He's been doing that a lot lately," Lenore replied. Indeed he had. I was pretty certain it was because he disliked me. I remembered the glare he'd given me from day one. His behavior had been better, though it was clear he'd wanted nothing to do with me. I'd once tried to engage him in conversation and all it did was end in him staring at me as if I'd spit on him. I'd looked away awkwardly. I remembered asking Lennox if I'd done something. She looked just as baffled as I had and said she had no idea what I could have done.

We changed topics to various funny stories from our day. Aspen had been working on the old man from the restaurant and got his first snack today. I laughed, having always been getting snacks, not that I was admitting that. I was an only child. Sharing didn't come naturally. I grinned under my hand. Locke raised his eyebrow at me, a knowing smirk on his lips. I placed my finger on my lips subtly. He inclined his head and winked. I grinned.

Lenore snorted.

"Do you guys want to share that private conversation you're having with the rest of us?"

"Private conversation? Secrets don't make friends," Aspen stage-whispered, giving his best wounded puppy voice.

"Not particularly," Locke growled, while I smirked. Lennox grinned at me in a way that reminded me of a grinning fox. She looked like she knew something I didn't. That was starting to feel like a common theme here.

We finished our meal and stayed out chatting until the hour was late. Feeling happier than I had in a long time I excused myself, kindly bidding everyone goodnight. I couldn't help the calm feeling coming over me. Maybe I could stay here, even after I perfected my magic. Maybe I really had carved myself a place, after all. I had friends. Real friends for the first time in my life. I heard footsteps behind me. I turned and smiled at Locke who was quickly approaching me, his face sullen. I felt my brief calm slip away, my guard going up immediately.

"We need to talk." His voice was suddenly serious, eliminating the last remaining vestiges of my good mood.

"About what?"

"You know what. Last night." He shifted his weight, looking uncomfortable. His eyes beseeched mine for something. He always seemed to talk with his eyes, a language I couldn't understand. But for a moment, he looked torn in two. I had a feeling I knew what was happening. I steeled myself, ready to lose everything I'd gained in my time here. *Don't ever let them know they've hurt you.* My father's words came back to me, bolstering me in that moment.

"Okay. Talk."

"Last night... it can't ever happen again. Whatever this is between us is a very bad idea. And I'm so sorry. Last night was my fault, not yours." He may as well have lanced a hole through my chest. I had no idea why it hurt so much. I refused to acknowledge it or look under that rock. Tears pricked the back of my eyes, but I forced them back, swallowed the lump in my throat, and held firm.

"Fine. Then we're in agreement."

"This isn't a game, Lark. Being with me... it's a bad idea. One that could end badly for both of us. For you in particular. I'm not willing to risk your safety. I've spoken to the Knights, and they agree it's too dangerous." My eyes shot wide at the betrayal. So much for friends, I bit down on the thought.

"So that's it? I don't get to know the details? I don't get any input? You and your friends just make decisions for me? You get to do this whole push-pull thing and think that's fine? Using me for your own amusement isn't fair." His eyes blazed as he looked at me, but he didn't say anything. "Please, just talk to me about what's going on," I implored, trying one last time, a fleck of the maelstrom of emotion I was feeling inside coming through in my voice.

"I can't," he said, his voice final. There was nothing for us. No future. Nothing. And his friends backed him up. I walked away to my chambers, refusing to let the tears fall.

This felt just like the story I told to Locke the night before. This felt just like back home. The time several years ago, a boy in my class, Arin, had said he'd liked me. I didn't believe him and told him to get lost. After weeks of being persistent, and his friends talking to me, telling me how much he liked me and how much they wanted me to be part of their friend group, I finally agreed to let him take me for lunch. For the first time ever, I had friends and someone that liked me. It was my first public outing with a boy, and I was excited. I even had butterflies. He was handsome and well liked by our classmates. Quiet. Reserved. He was referred to as the nice guy consistently. I should've known better.

I was to meet him in the square, where we'd go to one of the little shops to grab a basket and sandwiches and have a picnic on the hill outside of town. He showed up with none other than Kenna, and his friends. The friends that had spent weeks talking to me. Making me think we were friends. All of them ridiculed me for thinking anybody could like me. They'd thrown ice at me. One of the projectiles had cut my face, drawing blood. I'd ran. I'd ran into the forest and nearly got lost in my effort to get away from them chasing me, laughing, and taunting me the whole time. They'd herded me nearly to the edge of the Deep Wild. By the time they'd given up on catching me, I was covered in cuts, some of them pulsing blood. One rather nasty one on my arm needed stitches. I could have asked Eldan for some healing magic, but I refused to rely on anyone at that point. I felt the sting of rejection all over again. I heard Arin's friend's voice taunting me.

"Of course he doesn't like you. Why would you think anybody likes you? You're worthless. Magicless. Get used to rejection. You're going to see it a lot."

I had never forgotten those words.

Those words rang in my head now as I turned away from Locke. It might not be exactly the same but it was hard to not see a few parallels. The contrast between last night and now felt... deliberate. I felt his eyes on me until I turned the corner. My emotions came at me all at once. Anger. Hatred. Sorrow. Heartbreak. Aspen may have been onto something with the whole love and hate, passion being a thin, blurry line that separated the two. Because as much as I hated him again in this moment, there was something else there too that I refused to look at, but it was becoming increasingly difficult not to acknowledge. I stamped it down as best I could.

I made it to my room in time. I closed the door just as the tears flowed down my face. Crying for being rejected so thoroughly by Locke and for being a traitorous daughter. But after last night, I had thought just maybe there was something there. Even if that something were a truce. There was an intimacy I had felt last night that was brand new to me, and in its wake, I found that I didn't want to fight Locke anymore. I had found some form of acceptance here for the first time last night. And today when our friends joined us for dinner in Hell's Gate… it had felt like I might have truly found a place to belong. I'd gotten a taste of what it felt like to be really happy. But now I realized it was the alcohol and my hopeful imagination. Or it was him trying to ensure I stayed fighting for his side of things. Which also led me to doubt the Knights of the Court of Rebels. They clearly weren't my friends. They, too, refused to give me any information. Locke's rejection had brought about an icy freeze of my emotions towards everyone in the Court of Rebels. I disentangled myself from the hope I'd had earlier. I choked on my bitter anger at myself for allowing myself to believe they were my friends. When was I ever going to learn? Nobody was friends with the Noquim.

A half-baked idea occurred to me as I paced my room with a restless energy and I knew what I wanted next. I had control over my magic now. I could take Valor and leave this place. Leave them all behind. Go back to Poplar Hollow. Or somewhere new. The thought should have been exciting, but it wasn't. It felt like an end. Bitterness and dread enveloped me in cold hands as I laughed humorlessly at how stupid I was. I didn't know where I planned on going. Poplar Hollow wasn't much of an option, not without my father. I longed for anonymity of the city again, but I couldn't return to Loc Valen. I had no plan, no clue about what my new beginning would look like. Only that I didn't want to be in Port Azure.

I got up, knowing I couldn't stay here a moment longer. I just couldn't. I didn't know how I was going to get through the Dead Forest, but with my magic largely under control, I didn't hate my chances of escaping. And after this long, nobody, not even Locke, was monitoring my movements anymore. But if I got caught... I brushed off that concern as fast as it'd dawned on me. If he found me, he would have to drag me back here kicking and screaming. And I could do so much more damage than when we fought previously. My flames purred along my veins as if in reassurance of that thought. He couldn't grab me if I were covered in flames. I grabbed the bags I came here with and packed a few sets of clothes. I donned clean clothes for the journey and strapped my sword over my head. I slipped my feet into my boots, depositing my daggers into them. I could summon water to drink and hunt as needed.

There was a knock on the door, interrupting my emotional, half-cocked plan. I froze. Did they know? Was that even possible? I took a breath to sound as though I wasn't crying. To keep my voice from shaking and sounding suspicious.

"Not interested in whatever it is you have to say." My tone was scathing. It should've been more than enough to dissuade visitors. No response other than another, more persistent knock. I cursed at them through the door, keeping my voice hard-edged. The next knock was more like a fist pounding the door down. Genuinely afraid they'd bust down the door if I didn't answer, I cursed and I opened the door a crack. But not before moving my half-packed bags from my bed, and my sword from my back, to the far side of the door to conceal them in case he could see in. I opened the door a crack. I peered out to see Aspen leaning in my doorway.

"What do you want?" My voice was beyond cold. It was the coldest night in winter, freezing you from the outside in. Cold enough to stop your heart. He ignored my tone entirely as he look in my disheveled state.

"Oh, Little Bird," he said, seeing my tear-stained cheeks. I seethed at the stupid nickname. "What did he tell you?" His eyes blazed. He looked angry.

"Nothing that wasn't true," I hissed through my teeth and narrowed my eyes at him, fury and indignation flaring. "Now if you'll excuse me..." I began to close the door, desperate to get him out of here. His foot caught in the door and I pushed against it. A flare of alarm gripped me then, my heartrate picking up. He couldn't come in and see my bags. It occurred to me that I had no idea what would happen if he caught me trying to escape. Would I be locked up? Would I be a prisoner?

"Lark…" His voice was soft. "What's going on?"

"Nothing is going on! I just want to be alone!" I felt my voice raise an octave. I was always the worst liar, and everyone knew it.

"Let me in. I just want to talk. I even have snacks." I heard a rustling that must have been the aforementioned snacks. I even heard bottles clinking. Wine? What the hell was he playing at?

"No."

"Yes." His voice brimmed with what sounded like concern. But obviously, that wasn't the case. Locke and his Knights just wanted to make sure I fought for the right side. He refused to take his foot from my doorway, making it impossible to shut the door. I opened the door slightly to slam the door into his foot, but before I could, he took that tiny opening I gave him and shouldered his way into the room. I walked away from the door to the fireplace, anywhere to draw his eyes away from my half-packed bags by the door, my heart beating in my throat.

"Why do you reek of panic?" he asked, his eyes searching me for any explanation for my mood. "Has someone hurt you? What the Hell happened with Locke?" His eyes scanned the room and found my half-packed bags waiting for me by the door. "Oh," he breathed, looking genuinely sorrowful.

"Get out!" I growled, not knowing what else to do. Tears pricked the back of my eyes again, but I wasn't going to let more of them fall.

"You're running away, then?" he asked. "I'm surprised at you, Lark. I really am. You're going to try to brave the Dead Forest, knowing what's out there?" I didn't answer, I didn't move. I barely even breathed. "Wow. I didn't see that coming." He rubbed the back of his neck.

"I don't belong here. That was made abundantly clear," I snapped at him, not bothering to hide my hostility. "I'll take my chances. I have a solid control over my blade and my magic. That's the only reason I was here anyway."

"I'm really disappointed, Lark. I thought you were made of stronger stuff than that." That comment hurt more than it should have. I steeled myself, placing armor around my bruised heart.

"Not that I give a shit, but what exactly is that supposed to mean?"

"You're giving up. After you said you wanted to get back at Scorpio, who is ultimately the reason for your father's death, by the way." My attention snapped back to him. "She didn't use the knife, but she pulled every string that day. I thought you wanted revenge. I thought you were going to fight."

"I don't belong here."

"You keep saying that. But where exactly do you think you belong?" His eyes were hard on me as he looked at me.

"Anywhere I'm not lied to. Where my emotions are played with. Where I'm not used as a plaything. Anywhere but here," I seethed, every word sounding to my own ears like the breaking of my soul. Forging, my ass. I wasn't forged. I was incinerated.

"What the hell did that idiot say to you?" he breathed, his eyes studying me. He closed the door, blocking my escape, looking at me like I might fall to pieces.

"I already said, nothing that wasn't true."

"That doesn't clarify anything, Lark. Why are you running? And who are you really running from?" I ignored him and continued to pack my bag, refusing to acknowledge him. He walked over to me with that smooth, graceful walk of his and gently but firmly grasped my hands in his. I tried to pull away but he didn't let me. He tugged me closer to him until his arms were around me, a cage I couldn't escape. I hissed, and cursed, and thrashed, in a maelstrom of fighting limbs, but he just held me tightly, taking every hit. "Talk to me, Lark. I'm your friend."

"Like fuck you are." I landed a solid punch to his abdomen. I heard a whoof as he exhaled with the pain, but didn't move. "Like fuck he is. I don't want to be somewhere where all I am to anybody is a pawn."

"Ah," he said, rubbing soothing circles into my back. "I'm not sure what the fuck Locke said to you, but if he insinuated for even a second that none of us cared about you, then I will personally go kick his sorry, stupid royal ass." I huffed. I wanted to tell him he was full of shit. That I didn't believe him. But something about his tone…

"Yes, we obviously want you on our side. We need you, Lark. But mostly we want you here. Who else am I going to spar with? Not many fae keep up with me like you do." He grinned down at me. I looked straight ahead at his chest, though his shirt was now soaked with tears I hadn't even known I'd still been still crying. "But Lark, I can assure you, nobody wants you here more than Locke does." I tried to pull away, but his hold remained firm.

"You're lying." I shook my head.

"Do I need to get the twins in here? Because I'm more than certain they'll be extremely hurt, as I am, that you think all you are to us is a pawn." I looked at him wearily. This whole thing felt familiar. I thought back to last year when those boys befriended me. It felt superficial then. Aspen... didn't. I could clearly see the concern in his glittering green eyes. Eyes like a meadow after a heavy rain. I felt my resolve rattle, but not break. "Fuck it," he said when I hesitated, moving towards the door, but not letting go of me. Our bodies moved together as one, making me feel awkward and uncoordinated. Like the weirdest dance of all time. He moved to my door and pushed a button I didn't even know was there.

Within moments, a body was there, ready to help him with whatever he required. Wow, I hadn't even known that was an option.

"Bring Lennox and Lenore here. Right now. Don't let them refuse. It's urgent."

"Yes, My Lord." He bowed at the waist and was off like a shot down the hall of the residence wing.

Aspen didn't wait a second before closing the door. I shrieked when he picked me up over his shoulder in a movement so fast I felt nauseous. He threw me in a heap on my bed next to my saddle bags, their contents now spilling everywhere.

"What exactly was your plan even? You don't have any provisions. No food, no water, nothing for a shelter.... What are you doing?" I glowered at him, my venom renewed. I refused to answer him. Thankfully, I was granted a brief reprieve when Lennox and Lenore burst into the room, eyes wide and ready to take on anything. In flowy, floral night dresses. It was so ridiculously comical I almost laughed. Almost.

"What's going on?" Lenore griped with a yawn.

"Is everything okay?" Lennox stretched after seeing no immediate danger. But then they both saw my saddlebags and their eyes raised to mine. I inclined my head and gritted my teeth.

"You were going to leave?" Lennox whispered the question, looking like she'd been punched in the gut. Lenore glared at me, the hostility I've been waiting for from her since I punched her rising quickly to the surface.

"What the hell are you thinking?" Lenore's voice raised but wasn't quite yelling. "You were actually just going to up and leave us? Because what? You didn't get your way one time?" I didn't think I was successful hiding my shock as she continued. "Do you realize how much it would hurt us, hurt Locke, if you left? Worse, if you went and got yourself killed in that damned forest? Do you know how fucked the Realm would be? We need you!" I shot to my feet, fury once again at the surface. There it was. They needed me for the good of the damned realm. Back to being a damned pawn. A tool they currently had use for, but once it was done, they'd cast me aside and go about their day.

"That's just it, isn't it?" My anger boiling over, my voice rising in volume to match Lenore's. "You need me for my power. You need me not to fight against you. Well, here's the thing, I'm not fighting against you. I never was. But I'll be damned if I let you pretend to give half a damn about me, just to drop me when it's convenient. Like what Locke just did. I don't belong here, I don't want to be someplace that lies to me about everything. I don't trust any of you." I narrowed my eyes at each of them.

"What the hell did Locke say to you?" Lennox asked, her words echoing Aspen's as she came towards me. Lenore shoved her aside and shoved me back onto my bed, standing over me imposingly with her arms crossed.

"When did you get the impression I pretend anything for anybody?" she asked, fire sparking in her eyes. "What makes you think any of us were using you? We helped you, we trained you, trained with you even. We've drank together. We eat together every night. We talk every night. For fuck's sake, Lark, the first time you met me, you punched me in the face. In the interest of preserving the idea of being friends, I let it slide. But you never apologized for that. That fucking hurt!" she seethed.

I had no idea what to say. My mouth froze on the retort I was set to have. Was she right? Was it them just putting in the work for later, or was it... real? The thought hurt so much more than I could've thought. The fear. And in that moment, I finally acknowledged what had been driving my anxiety today: the fear that if I really let these fae in, I wasn't sure just how deeply they'd be able to cut. If these fae did to me what the others in Poplar Hollow did, I wasn't sure I'd ever be okay after it.

Lennox's calm voice floated to me in direct contrast to Lenore's growl.

"Lenore is angry because she's hurt. Please don't misinterpret." Lennox glanced at her twin as she rolled her eyes in a huff. "In fact, I think it's safe to say we're all extremely hurt by you wanting to leave. We all thought we were friends. We like you. We care. Do you not feel the same way about us?" I didn't know how to answer. Of course I did. I didn't want to admit to anything, fearful of the fallout. Fearful of what came next. I saw the ice daggers in my mind's eye as those fae chased me, mocking me, and I shuddered.

"You really never had friends before, have you?" Aspen murmured from beside me. "Locke had mentioned your town wasn't... welcoming to you because of your lack of magic. But you've never had friends before, ever?" It wasn't even really a question. He knew the answer. I shook my head, hot shame washing over me.

Lennox sat down beside me and pulled me into a hug, letting me rest my head on her shoulder. "What have we done for you not to trust us?" she asked gently, sounding so genuinely hurt I wanted to cry more. But for the first time, I wanted them to understand. I had only told Locke the brief version of the story. I told them the whole of it. How Arin and his friends had deceived me. How it echoed to the secrets here. I told them how Arin and his friends had chased me near to the Deep Wild, hoping I'd get lost in it and not return. If they saw me, there was a flash of ice or steel that ended with me getting a deep laceration. The cuts had been deep enough to cause concern; I showed them what remained of my scars. But the blood was likely to summon some form of monster, Blood Wraiths, in particular.

That day, I thought I'd had a group of fae I could call friends. And I was nearly killed by them. I didn't want to make the same mistake here. I'd spent my whole life fighting. Keeping others out. I let my guard down a handful of times, only for me to end up destroyed in the process, and I knew I couldn't survive it if it happened again. I told them all of this, the tears flowing.

Lennox and Aspen sat beside me, listening intently. Lennox looked as if she might tear up. Aspen looked angry. Lenore did too. She grabbed a bottle out of Aspen's bag and shoved it into my hands.

"Drink."

I opened the bottle of fruity-smelling wine and took a long sip. It tasted as wonderful as it smelled as it washed over my tongue and my senses. Lenore grabbed the bottle back from me, took a swig, and passed it to Lennox. Lennox took a sip and passed it to Aspen before it found me again.

Aspen got up and grabbed my bags. "Can I put these all away now?" I heard the real question. Was I still leaving? I nodded tersely and dragged a long drink of wine from the bottle. How'd it get down to half empty already?

Aspen smiled, looking relieved. Lennox hugged me fiercely. Lenore sat beside me, assuring me that I needed to drink more and there was plenty where it came from. Aspen grabbed the snacks, popping corn and baked salted kettle chips, and brought them over.

"I'm sorry," I breathed, not really sure how to move forward. Aspen, Lennox, and Lenore all embraced me, not needing to say another word. I choked once on a sob as I felt a piece of me that I thought had forever been shattered was made partially whole for the first time in my life.

We spent hours, well into the early morning, talking, the four of us. We laughed, we drank, and we shared stories of how we grew up. Granted, theirs were much funnier than mine, but Lenore particularly enjoyed the story about how a boy tried to punch me once and I ended up breaking his nose. That girl loved her violence. The girls had fallen asleep in my bed. I was thankful it was as massive as it was, or we'd never have all fit. Aspen sat against my headboard, my head on his shoulder. He played with my hair absentmindedly and exhaustion threatened to take me.

"I know it doesn't seem like it, but I promise there's a good reason. It's not that he doesn't want to tell you, it's that he just can't." So we were going to talk about Locke now. Great. That wasn't going to ruin my buzz.

"Does this have to do with his curse?" A sharp intake of breath confirmed it. Aspen didn't respond, but he looked like he was seriously considering his next words. "Tell me about the curse, please."

Aspen looked at me with empathy in his eyes.

"Locke is my best friend, but he is still my Prince. He ordered me not to tell, and I will uphold that. I have to."

I glowered.

"I can't break an order, even for you, Lark. And besides, I agree with him; if you knew, you'd be in danger. And it's not something you can defend against."

"I don't need protecting! I'm not a child. I can take care of myself." He shook his head.

"Not against this, Little Bird. I'm sorry. There's nothing any of us can do, no matter how much we all want to. And believe me, nobody wants to tell you more than Locke. He hates lying to you." I decided I was done pushing the issue. I was done with Locke. I was done with all of it. I just wanted sleep. "Get some rest, Lark."

"Tell my jerk sparring partner I'm not coming tomorrow," I murmured into his shoulder, my eyelids falling heavy as if attached to weights. He chuckled.

"Your jerk sparring partner will make an exception today. Lark?"

"Hm?"

"I'm really glad you're still here. I'd miss my other best friend if you left." My heart filled to the brim with emotion, but I bit it down. I squeezed his hand in response, and he squeezed mine too. Lennox and Lenore were fast asleep next to me. I cried silent tears, and for once, they weren't sad.

Friends. This is what it was like having *friends*.

Chapter Twelve

The next several days came and went in a blur. I threw myself diligently into my training with a vigor I hadn't previously discovered within myself. Mercifully, nobody mentioned the night I nearly left. Not even Locke. I wasn't even convinced anybody had a chance to tell him, with him being gone from Port Azure so often lately. I wasn't sure of where he was going, but my guess was that he was in Loc Valen, maintaining appearances. Or perhaps he really was just avoiding me. I hadn't even seen him for magic lessons either since that day. My interactions with Locke had been almost nonexistent, save for a few brief passes in hallways with unreturned sidelong glances from me, and occasionally during dinner when he was in Port Azure long enough to eat with us. Far too often lately, the seat next to me sat empty, and far too much did I feel the coldness of his absence.

Lennox and Lenore stepped in to assist my training, running me through drills and teaching me combat techniques with magic. Even Abel had taught me a few lessons, though he was a terrifying teacher.

In the mornings I trained hard with Aspen, but even my exhaustion didn't chase away my bad dreams and anxiety. One morning after a particularly miserable evening crying myself to sleep over something I couldn't understand, I decided not to stay in bed with my thoughts. I woke early, even before the sun. I glimpsed through my window the barest beginnings of dawn kissing the horizon. I donned my training attire and walked to Hell's Gate with purpose in every stride, as if I could outrun or outwork the demons in my head. There was nobody in the hallways this early. I marched determinedly to the stands where all those stairs stood waiting for me. I decided today I was going to bring my body to its limit, and maybe tonight I'd finally sleep somewhat peacefully. Maybe tonight I wouldn't find my heart lodged in my throat.

One step at a time, I reminded myself, feeling the burning ache in my legs and my lungs. I embraced it. Savored it. I needed to feel like I was doing something. It took me over an hour, but I finally completed an entire lap of Hell's Gate Arena. Every. Single. Stair.

My legs nearly gave out at the top of the final flight, as if they knew salvation were at hand. I collapsed in a breathless heap at the top, unsure if I would ever be able to move again. I gingerly tried to stretch the cramping from my legs, but the pain that made itself known when I did stopped me in my tracks and stole my ability to breathe. Goddess, I wasn't even this sore after my first training session here. What had I done?

So I lay there on my back, staring at the ceiling, waiting for the soreness to ease in my aching limbs. I didn't know how much time passed. I eventually began to hear voices of fae filtering in to the arena below me to begin their normal routine. I dragged in a deep breath and sat up stiffly, watching for the moment Aspen entered Hell's Gate.

I wasn't kept waiting long. I saw his blond bun and bronzed shoulders slip through the entrance and wander over to the weights section. I watched a few times as he gazed up at the door, waiting for me. I tried to get up. I truly did. But the heaviness and angry cramping in my legs told me I wasn't going anywhere. As I gathered my legs under me, I found I couldn't fight gravity with what little strength remained in my legs. They went boneless, and my rear hit the ground again unceremoniously. I bit down on a curse as my quads cramped, letting me know they were not at all pleased with the stair treatment.

I knew Aspen wouldn't hear me from up here if I called out his name. Not with all the commotion. But I could do something else to get his attention. From my place on the ground, I gathered my magic to me. I conjured a snow ball and hurled it down to him, using a little push of magic.

I missed but it got his attention, and he looked up at me with surprise. I waved. He motioned for me to come down. I shook my head with a shrug. He gave me a questioning look before I saw him move towards the stairs. He was a few minutes before he joined me. He laughed as I grunted that I was unable to move. That I was certain that I was forever stuck in a heap at the top of the stairs.

"Did you run the stairs? All of them?" he asked incredulously. I nodded. "Why?" I shrugged and told him I wanted to push myself today. His look of concern was fleeting as he heaved me to my sore and aching legs. I squeaked as they nearly gave out. "Well, fine, we'll skip the workout portion of our session and just focus on sparring today." *Ugh. Can someone please give me a weapon already?* I eyed them longingly where they hung, ready for whoever wanted to grab them. I could've sworn the sword winked at me and the mace waved.

"Soon." A cajole. "You can't use a blade without knowing how to fight first," he said, reading my mind. "But what about archery? As I recall, your aim sucks, Little Bird. A compromise?" He held out his pinky finger for a promise. I grinned for the first time in a few days at the gesture. A pinky swear. I hadn't done that since I was a child. I stuck my pinky to his.

I couldn't even try to put into words the gratitude I felt towards Aspen. He noticed my excessive limping. My knees bowed in and out unsteadily as I tried to walk in a position that didn't hurt my legs. He stifled a chuckle behind me. I couldn't even turn around to glare at him.

"You look like a newborn calf trying to walk," he said, voice rife with amusement. "Sit down for a second. Let me help you. Otherwise, we'll be here all day."

I tried to sit, but all I really did was fall gracelessly onto my rear end again, my breath leaving me on impact with a whoosh. He smirked at me as he ran his hands down my legs, fingers tracing healing spells as they went. As soon as the magic touched the deep knots in my legs, I felt instant relief. I sighed into the soothing magic.

"Thanks, Aspen," I said appreciatively. He nodded, still smirking. I knew I wouldn't be thanking him for long with that grin. When he finished, I stood, testing my legs. I waited for the aching soreness, or for my legs to give out again. I was grateful to Aspen that their strength had returned, and the heavy stiffness I'd had before had vanished. I would actually be able to participate in our lesson without pain. I turned towards Aspen who was standing in the sparring ring with a grin. Aspen smirked and started walking back towards me, much like a broken marionette, with limbs going this way and that, and lacking even the bare minimum of coordination.

Then I realized he was making fun of me! I burst out laughing. "I did not look like that!"

He gave me a wolfish, toothy grin.

"You absolutely did, Little Bird. And if you disagree, show me how wrong I am with your fists." I smiled back, stepping up, happy to comply. It was odd to punch a fae in the jaw as hard as you could, and for him to whoop and give you a high five. "Now that you can hold your own with the Crownguard, I think you're ready for a weapon," Aspen said with an approving grin, leading me towards the archery station. I felt elated at the thought of holding a weapon again, even if it weren't a blade. It felt as if my life had been missing a sense of focus and control, and I hoped that a weapon would fill that void.

I couldn't stop the grin from spreading across my face as Aspen handed me a bow, chuckling while I turned it over in my hands eagerly. The bow string was surprisingly taut, proving to be much more difficult to draw than I anticipated.

Despite my enthusiasm, archery didn't quite go as well as I'd hoped. To say that my aim was bad would be an understatement; it was abysmal. In an attempt to nurse my wounded pride, I'd blamed the tautness, but Aspen quickly shot that theory down with a derisive snort.

While managing to maintain both his composure and patience, he gave careful tips for every arrow that missed its mark, keeping his spirits high despite my dipping mood. I hung onto his every word, taking each suggestion to heart. I may not have been a natural-born archer, but I refused to let that stop me from succeeding. When I was about to admit I was the worst archer in all of Meridian, an idea occurred to me. Aspen didn't say I couldn't get creative.

I closed my eyes and inhaled slowly, centering myself as I focused on my magic, reaching deep within myself. The wind began to swirl around me in response, whipping the loose hairs across my face. I envisioned an arrow of ice in my hand, feeling the sharp coldness of it as it manifested. A sense of calm settled over me as I took aim, just as Aspen had taught me. I loosed my arrow with a push of my air magic, giving it a boost of speed. A soft light trailed behind my arrow as it soared towards the target, reminding me of a shooting star.

My face split into a grin as it hit an inner ring of the target with a thwack. It wasn't a bullseye, but it was an improvement, and any improvement was worth celebrating. But with one look at Aspen's expression, my excitement faltered.

"What's wrong?" I was unsure of what I'd done wrong; I'd expected him to be thrilled that I finally made a decent shot, not staring at me with a brooding look.

"Nothing is wrong, Little Bird." He spoke slowly, choosing each word carefully. "For you to have never used magic before coming here, it's impressive how much you've learned in such a short time." He smiled softly, but I could still see the concern in his eyes. "I know many fae that are far older and much more practiced than you are that still can't do what you just did."

"So, you're saying that I'm formidable?" I'd hoped to ease the tension with humor, but his dark look and humorless laugh told me that this was more serious than I understood. Hanging the bow back on its rack, I turned to give him my full attention. He shifted his weight uncomfortably, something I'd seldom seen him do.

"To put it bluntly, you are quite possibly the most powerful Faerie in Meridian, and maybe even beyond."

My lips parted in a gasp, taken aback by his outrageous claim.

Ignoring my reaction, he continued, "With your ability to control the elements, the Queen will tremble before you, and rightly so. I just hope that once you complete your training, you will remain on our side."

"What does that mean?" I couldn't help but feel the sting of his words, that he'd even consider questioning my loyalty.

"Scorpio wasn't always this way." He spoke softly, his green eyes growing distant. His words echoed Locke's and for the first time, I found myself wondering how well he and the other knights of the rebel court knew Scorpio before she ascended the throne, before the curse.

"She was beautiful, strong, and loyal to her Kingdom and Court." He huffed a laugh. "Some would even say that she was kind hearted."

His memories of Scorpio did not coincide with our current reality, but that's all that they were—memories. Even with Locke's claim that she had been a good fae before the curse, it didn't change the fact that she was the Queen who had killed countless innocents during her search for a way to end her curse, and took sick pleasure in doing so.

I questioned whether she could ever wash her hands clean of the blood that stained them, or if her soul could break the surface of her sins. Was she worthy of a chance at redemption, or was she buried too deep beneath the tragedy that she had inflicted?

As if reading my thoughts, Aspen continued.

"The curse changed her into who she is now, but there's still a chance that we could help her, at least to some degree." He held me with an intense gaze. "But if you were to suffer the same fate, we wouldn't stand a chance against you. You control the power of every Court, and with that power comes opportunity for great change. I can't help but wonder what you'll do."

Beyond the inevitability of facing Scorpio, I hadn't truly considered my life beyond training. Even if I had, what change was I supposed to enact? Not only did I not possess the education to sit in the throne room discussing political matters, but the end of Scorpio's reign would likely put an end to the civil wars, allowing the Courts to finally be at peace with one another.

Wasn't that ultimately our goal?

Aspen's eyes drilled into me as if he expected an answer I couldn't give. I was pardoned from coming up with something when a fae ran over to us, eyes wide, frantic.

"Lord Aspen." It was odd hearing someone speak so formally to him. I knew he was Locke's second in command, but it was strange hearing his official title. I only knew him as my friend. But I watched as Aspen became a leader of Locke's rebellion, looking every bit as deadly and dangerous as I knew he could be. His eyes were sharp and assessing as he asked the man to speak his news.

"His Highness requests your presence immediately." He looked over to me. I almost snorted at Locke's official title. *His Highness.* I suppressed a smirk. "You as well, my lady." *My lady?* Since when had anyone called me that? I didn't fit the criteria for that title. My surprise must have registered on my face, but he thankfully didn't acknowledge it. He bowed his head respectfully, but never took his eyes off me. "I understand that His Highness has important news, but a word of caution, if I may be so bold; I believe this news may be distressing." I bit my lip as Aspen and I looked at each other. I saw the concern leech into his eyes. I saw his posture stiffen. His jaw clicked. Whatever this was, it was clearly news to him. And it worried him.

I thanked the fae, my hand on his shoulder before Aspen took my hand, and we jogged down the hallway. I assumed Aspen knew where to go. I had never been to this part of the base. We took so many turns I could barely keep track until we came before a double-doored entrance. He didn't bother knocking as he entered, ushering me inside with him.

The room was bare. It held a few chairs, a table with several maps strewn about, and a massive desk, behind which sat Locke, his gaze piercing as we entered the threshold of his office. Next to the desk were two men I'd never seen before. Lenore and Lennox stood in full black armor behind Locke, their gaze sorrowful as they looked at me. Why was armor needed? Was an attack pending? Abel wore his armor paired with his usual hostile glare. One of the strange men appeared to be injured. He was curved within himself, a posture I knew only too well. He'd been hurt in the abdomen. I could see no blood, and he seemed alert enough, though dirty and disheveled. Everyone looked prepared for a funeral. My throat thickened. What had happened?

I felt, rather than observed, Locke's gaze on me. I saw the glowering simmer of his glare at Aspen holding my hand, but it was gone in the next breath. Aspen squeezed my hand in comfort. I squeezed back. Aspen looked as somber as the rest of the party, like he already had an idea of what's going on.

"Thank you both for coming so quickly," Locke said at last.

The two men bowed their heads and murmured in acknowledgement of our arrival, "My lord. My lady." I blushed despite the situation. I was never going to get used to someone calling me that.

"Lark. This is going to be difficult for you to hear. But as this involves you and you've been training faithfully alongside us for the past few months; it's time you're brought up to speed. The Queen, as you know, has been hitting towns, cities, and villages within the Water Court. She's looking for a seer who can tell her how to end her curse. How to determine the individual from the prophecy in the Vale." I paled, guilt driving through me as surely as a blade, halting my breathing in its tracks. *She's killing fae looking for me....* "To tell her who she needs to kill. As far as we know she doesn't necessarily know it's you, yet. But... she hit one particular town today." His voice was grave. Lennox looked away. Lenore bit her lip as she looked at me.

"What town?" I gasped the words. But I knew. In the pit of my stomach, I felt the nausea start. Locke regarded me with what could only be pity but hesitated to answer. "What town, Locke?" My words were barely a whisper. I felt the lump forming in my throat before his answer even came.

"Yours, Lark." The words were a punch to the gut and my knees shook. "She destroyed Poplar Hollow." Aspen put his arm around me, helping steady me. The urge to empty my stomach roiled through me and I fought it. I asked the question I was afraid to ask.

"Survivors?" I felt my voice break "Eldan?" My mind also went to Haven. My heart ripped from my chest at the thought of Haven and Eldan not being okay. And if I were being honest with myself… I didn't want to see Gael dead, despite everything. My grief was a palpable thing in the room. I knew these fae were treacherous to me. But that didn't mean they should die. But I'd be lying if I didn't feel violently mixed emotions dropping in and mixing with my guilt and grief until my emotions were a concoction I couldn't decipher anymore.

"We don't know. That's partly why you're here." His voice was not without sympathy. "We're going to look for survivors now. Bring them back with us. You'll be a familiar face to them, and that is an advantage we seldom have. But if you don't feel that this is something you can do, we will not force you. We will all understand. This will be very difficult."

There was a moment where I couldn't latch onto a single thought. Poplar Hollow had been razed to the ground. All those fae… that for years had hurt me, ostracized me, the fae that had never given me a chance were likely dead. Kenna. Chennai. Professor Epsilon. Bastian. I should've been happy. Jumping for joy. Many would say they got what they deserved. But all I felt was a heavy nothing in my gut. Not numb exactly. A dull heaviness tangoed with static-like anxiety within me. It simply made me want to throw up.

"When do we leave?" My hushed voice was barely above a whisper. But I refused to break. Not here. Not in front of everyone. Aspen tightened his grip on me. I pushed away. I didn't need their pity. I needed to do some good for my home. Or what once was my home.

"Immediately," Locke said. "Go and put on your armor. Lennox and Lenore will assist you. We will meet at the front entrance in twenty minutes." He nodded to the sisters as if to dismiss them. They bowed their heads. They were somber as they guided me back to my rooms, neither of us saying a word.

Lenore was the first to speak once we got to my closet. They helped me don my armor. It was surprisingly light. And fit like a glove. It was a shiny black in color. The chest piece even had places for my breasts to fit comfortably. The chest plate in the shape of wings was one piece connecting to two shoulder pieces with spikes on them. Arm bracers ran along my forearms. A strange, scaled metal clung to my legs. The scales were tough, but small enough to lend itself to flexibility as well as strength. Lennox told me it was dragonscale armor. Completely resistant to tearing, it would protect me against any attack, even magical ones. And rather than feeling uncomfortable, heavy, or pinching, it felt like a second skin. My skin breathed easily as well, to my surprise. I donned my tough leather boots, comfortable and well broken-in for the journey. I stashed my two blades inside by my calves as always. I never realized how naked I'd felt without them, their weight comforting. My father's sword was next. I swallowed the lump in my throat. I'd hidden in in the back of my closet. I hadn't wanted to see it. I forced my tears back again as I fingered the hilt gently before slinging it over my back.

Lenore sang her approval. Lennox told me I looked as fierce as I did beautiful. I tied my blond waves back into a loose braid down my back before we headed out. I couldn't reconcile who I was when I arrived here, versus the armor-and-weapon-clad faerie that stood in the mirror staring numbly back at me, her eyes dead.

"How recently was Poplar Hollow hit?" I asked before we'd reunited with the rest of the group. "How dangerous is this mission?" Lennox gave me a pitying look. Lenore just looked angry. It was her that spoke first as we strode to meet with the others.

"Poplar Hollow was hit only last night. Scouts found the smoldering remains only an hour ago. The Queen's forces must have moved on by now. Still, be on your guard."

"How are we getting there? How did scouts travel from there to here so fast? If we're close to the northern border that's a two-week journey by horseback. And that's not including survivors." The sisters smiled to themselves, as if enjoying some secret together.

"You'll see."

We met Locke and Aspen by the gate of the Court of Rebels, the Dead Forest taunting me, beckoning me with knobby, discolored fingers and an evil grin. Somewhere deep within the confines of the trees came screech sounds that could only have been a Blood Wraith. The shiver that hit me had nothing to do with the temperature.

Locke's armor mirrored mine. The same as the day we'd met. Aspen also changed into his own battle-ready ensemble, but his was dark blue rather than all black. The insignia of the rebel alliance was on his breast plate, his blonde hair thrown up into a messy top knot.

I looked at Locke, really looked at him, for the first time in several days. Even if we saw each other at dinner, we didn't acknowledge one another in any way. It didn't stop me from sneaking glances at him from time to time, but I found his attention was never on me again. I hated how much that hurt.

But now I looked at him with trepidation. Caution. And there was a question in my gaze. What the Hell were we walking into?

Abel came around the corner with something in his hand. Abel's long hair blew on the breeze created by his fast pace and long, angry strides. I wondered if he were ever happy. He deftly ignored me. I spied what was in his hand as he presented it to Locke: a cloudy white stone with runes on it. It was the size of his fist and had the insignias of all four Courts on it. I blinked.

"What is that? I thought I was the only thing in Meridian with all four elements." Abel huffed at my ignorance.

"It's a Jumpstone. A portal. And there are plenty of relics in Meridian that rely on the use of various magics, or can be utilized by all magics. You're only special because you happen to have all four elements and be fae," he snapped at my ignorance and gave me a haughty sneer. Locke barked at Abel for his tone, leveling him with a glare I definitely saw a threat in. Abel did too. He muttered an apology he didn't mean under his breath and turned his gaze away from me in disgust. Lennox shot him a nasty look from under her brows and pressed closer to me. I offered her a wry smile of thanks.

"A portal? I thought portals weren't real? Or at least so rare they may as well not be real." I looked at Locke in shock and awe.

"Jump stones are exceedingly rare," he said, as if reading my thoughts. "Only a few members of various Courts have access. Being the Water Court's Assassin, I need to be able to get to my missives quickly and without drawing attention. This is how I get around. Some of my far-ranging scouts have one as well so they can inform me quickly about all sections of the Water Court. You can only jump to places you've been though, so you'll be the one to lead us there since it's most familiar to you. But be warned. Once we get to Poplar Hollow, it will take time to recharge. You can't just use it over and over in rapid succession."

"How long does it need? Can you give it magic to recharge it?"

"You can, but it'll drain you. It's a risk because you need magic to pass through it."

"Are we done playing show and tell?" Abel snapped with irritation before I felt the ripple of magic through the air. It was a fiercer magic than I'd used before. Where mine was a gentle wind, this was like heavy music pulsing through me, leaving goosebumps behind on my skin and an unsettled feeling in my core.

Locke recited a strange incantation from memory. When I heard the dialect, I had no doubt it was a spell spoken in the old language of the fae. From before Locke, the Zodiac Kinship, and the courts themselves. A passage of pure sunlight opened in front of me. The light churned within itself sluggishly, but still so bright I had to look away at first while my eyes adjusted.

"Think of your home," Locke said to me. "Think of your cottage. See it in your mind's eye as we pass through the portal." He took my hand. I let him. Aspen took his and everyone else fell in line behind them. "You're going to lead us there. But you must clear your head of all other thoughts." It wasn't hard. Right now, all my thoughts were swirling around images of home. I remembered my father and me eating berries and fresh cream in my kitchen. I remembered him teaching me to cook various stews with minimal ingredients or salted meat for the winter. Of him tucking me into bed, reading me a bedtime story as a child. Singing loudly and very off-key in front of the fire, as I giggled and clapped along. I thought of home, when home had felt safe.

The first thing that hit me was the silence. Complete silence. Even birds didn't chirp nearby. And when I opened my eyes, we stood in what remained of the living space of my cottage. The charred remains of it burned to cinders right down to the foundation, though parts of the back wall still stood erect. I took in my former home with a sourness in my stomach. There was little left but char and ash. I wandered through the once modest cottage as we all began to fan out. I looked in my old room and stopped short. There was a body charred beyond recognition. It was barely recognizable as fae, but for the shape of it and the lingering scent of burned flesh. Who was this? How had the scent lingered after all this time? My home burned weeks ago. I gagged and quickly left the room, the scent of burning followed me. Except as I finally looked beyond the border of what was once my home, I realized it wasn't following me. It was all around me. My village hadn't just been attacked; it had been obliterated.

I walked out the back of my cottage in a daze, not fully processing what I was seeing. The sky was gray, and reflected my horror and despair at seeing the sweet, little red-brick cottages torn or burned to the ground. The bodies that littered the streets like common trash, long gash marks from a blade carving into them. Flies circling the wounds of the dead, their buzzing the only sound I could hear besides the ringing in my ears. The stink finally hit my nose. I couldn't hide it any more. I retched.

I cast my awareness out, my mind looking for signs of life anywhere around me. Please, my mind whispered to anyone who could hear me. Please be alive, Someone. Anyone.

I let the tears fall finally, unable to hold them back. The type that fell in silent streams and soaked your cheeks. They cascaded silently down my face as I worked, searching for any signs of survivors. I half-ran to Eldan's house. I found it much like the others, half of it still stood, but it had caved in along the far side, though parts of the stable were still standing. *Haven!*

I ran to the barn, finding all the stalls mercifully empty, the doors fallen open.

She hadn't been slain in her stall. A tiny pearl of relief turned into a huge force when I checked the tack room. Her saddle and bridle were gone. Eldan must have gotten out or been away during the attack! I clung to that hope as I continued to glance around Poplar Hollow. Smoke still heavily scented the air. But so did the scent of rot, burning, and decay. Some sections of the town were still unsafe to search, the buildings still actively smoldering. My mouth tasted like ash as I took in my former hometown, bodies strewn about haphazardly and without care. I'd never said the funeral rite more times than I had today.

I walked the streets, my eyes seeing what my brain refused to process. I saw the wreckage, but in my mind's eye I saw it full of life as it used to be, my brain layered the two images together, making my head ache as much as my heart.

It wasn't long into my search for survivors before I came upon a very familiar cottage, with bile rising in my throat. I stood on the precipice of the door for long moment, my heart hammering painfully against my ribs. I scarcely dared to breathe. When I at last found it in me to open the door, I felt it meet resistance but open with a bit of pressure. Something must have been barricading the door.

When I peeked around the stuck door, I saw what I was afraid of: Gael, Bastian, and their parents. And I saw what—or rather who—blocked the doorway. Bastian's corpse. He was leaning partially against the door I was on the other side of, his head lulled back. He was missing an eye. A huge, bloody crater was visible instead from where I stood on trembling legs. I couldn't walk in. I couldn't do it. Gael lay close to his brother, no more than a few feet away. His eyes were open in death, and his mouth pried open in a silent scream. A puddle of dried blood lay under him, giving me flashbacks to the day my father was killed. Seeing Gael like this… not like this. He was a coward, but he didn't deserve this.

"I'm so sorry," I sobbed, guilt seizing me and making my legs tremble and threaten to give out. My lips tripped over the Goddess's prayer, the funeral rite. I hadn't realized I was crying even harder now. As soon as the words tumbled from my mouth, I quickly turned and fled, knowing I would never scrub that scene free from my mind.

The others were fanned out, checking every body they came across. All too infrequently, I'd hear a shout. Aspen with his healing abilities would tend to anybody we found.

I hated this. I hated that I knew most of these fae. Had interactions with most of these fae. But nothing prepared me for the sickness I felt when I came across the children.

Two siblings, no older than ten, holding each other in death. Their mother mere feet away, her throat slashed, blood long dried around her, and flies made use of her. The stench was unfathomable. A sob wracked my body. I cast my consciousness out, begging for someone to respond.

Then something stirred. My eyes snapped open and I looked closer at the children. The one was definitely dead, the smell and the flies were proof enough even before the stab wounds. But the younger of the two, perhaps nine, was lying under his brother and had no visible wounds. With shaking hands, I reached out for his wrist. And felt a thready, faint thumping of a pulse. My own pulse skittered in response before picking up double time. I yelled for Aspen. I screamed his name over and over until I felt his hands on my shoulders.

"You're going to be okay," I told the unconscious little boy. I gripped his hands as Aspen worked his magic over him, his healing magic glowing green in the dim gray light. His fingers traced runes I didn't recognize into the boy's skin, glowing green before vanishing beneath the surface of the boy's skin. Aspen was sweating, and his eyes were less sharp than they'd been before we'd arrived. Based on the shouts, I figured they'd found two other survivors. He'd done a fair bit of healing already.

"This boy is barely clinging to life," he ground through gritted teeth as he traced more healing runes. "It's a good thing you found him when you did. Go, I've got him." I nodded once and squeezed the little boy's hand. I was content to see him stir slightly, but not regain consciousness.

"Lark! Locke! You need to see this!" Abel called out from back the way we came. I followed the voices back to my cottage.

Burned in to the front lawn was a message I couldn't understand. I also didn't know how I'd missed it before. *Because we didn't go through the front door,* I realized. We walked through the back potion of the house.

"The burning did not fool me."

The burning?

I glanced at Locke. I could tell by his pale countenance that he understood the message. It was the first time I'd ever seen fear, real fear, on his face. His eyes were wide as they flicked to me, his mouth falling slightly open.

"What does that mean?" I asked him wearily. Why did they burn a message in my front lawn? And why did he look so horrified? There was a small moment of silence before he sighed.

"It means the Queen found out about you," he said at last. Despite his face, his voice didn't falter. He finally turned to look at me. "You remember the night your father was killed?" I nodded, not sure if I were ready to hear what he was about to say. I turned towards him, giving him my full attention. "I started that fire to your cottage." My body stilled of its own accord. Ice ran awash through my veins. I felt my head shake as if to refute what he was saying, unable to find words. After a long moment, my gaze pierced him, anger quickly taking the emotional helm. He held his hands out as if to placate me and urged me to listen. "I heard rumors that the Queen knew where to find you. That was what I was investigating before I arrived that day. The time-sensitive errand that held me up. That her current seer saw Poplar Hollow in a vision. She saw your house in that vision, but not you specifically. She was informed that the fae in that house needed to die. Your house. She didn't know what you looked like. But if she thought you dead, she would be forced to move on and either write it off as a false vision or believe that the one she had to kill was already dead. I placed the body of a dead female bandit inside your home and set your home ablaze. I made it look like a kitchen accident. That way, if anyone investigated, they would see a dead girl's body charred beyond recognition and assume it was you. I did it to protect you." It was my turn for my mouth to fall open, slackened from my shock as I attempted to process what I just heard. My mind was stopped for a moment and then all at once it was reeling from what he said. I remembered coming home to find my cottage on fire, flames so high they seemed to lick the sky. Locke set that fire? When after several long moments when I finally found my voice, I scarcely recognized the small, mousy sound, only just above a whisper.

"And what of my Father? Why was he killed?" Somewhere inside me, I felt a roiling rage. But it feels like someone else's. I felt detached from it. I gazed at this rage with disinterest as it snaked its way around me, gripping me as I raised my gaze to Locke, who shifted uncomfortably.

"Your father's death was out of my control," he said, carefully considering his words. I couldn't understand why he still wouldn't tell me what happened. I knew he'd never tell me. And before I threw an ice dagger in his eye, I spun on my heel and walked away, now focusing on my anger. We may need him yet. But once we were back in Hell's Gate, I would be tearing him limb from limb. I felt my anger fester like an infection in an open wound. The first vestiges of pure, unadulterated hatred gripped my heart with ugly black fingers. And this time I wasn't sure they'd let go.

I cast my awareness out again as far as it could go. I felt sick as I recognized the dead, my neighbor, Molly. She had been a kind soul. When my father took ill, she had baked us a small pie, using the berries in her garden, or she would occasionally give us a chicken from her own coop for eggs I found or meat I hunted. She knew we didn't have a lot of coin, but she often shared what she had to make sure we didn't starve. I'd guessed her kindness was towards my father, possibly even my mother more than at me. Her kids weren't as kind. They had taken an active part in my torment, I remembered bitterly. But that bitterness felt empty looking at them now, the fetid wounds to their chests reaching deep. It was hard to remain angry when you looked upon all this death. We didn't find any more survivors. I felt part of me break. These killings had been brutal. I'd heard whispers of the attacks in the realm, but they were seldom this far towards the outer rim of the Court. I couldn't understand the savagery, the ruthlessness, behind these attacks. The senselessness. We had nobody here capable of being a seer. Perhaps there was also a rumor? It was common knowledge that the Queen only required rumors as evidence. Perhaps that's what this was? I tried so hard to make sense of a senseless slaughter.

No. It was like what Locke had said. She'd caught wind that I was here. And when I wasn't…

This wasn't looking for a seer and cutting loose ends. This was a message, both to me and to Locke, whose position as a traitor was now suspected if not outright known, if I'd had to guess. I glanced sidelong at him from where I was. She must have known about me somehow though. Perhaps someone from Poplar Hollow had said that I was gone? I wondered what this meant for Locke's family. I grit my teeth as my guilt threatened to swallow me whole.

This was revenge. This was a message. And this was a warning.

The town spun as my vision darkened for a moment, my mind rallying against this new information. Sobs broke from my lips. All these deaths. They were my fault. I should've been here. It was supposed to be me! I gagged as my trembling knees gave out at last under the weight of my regret and sorrow. *It should've been me, it should have been me!* my mind screamed at me as I railed against this new information that was breaking me. If I were here, I would be dead, but nobody else would be. None of this devastation would've happened.

I heard commotion. Voices behind me, indistinct, but growing louder, close to the square. Raised voices. I turned and followed. Perhaps we'd found another survivor. No. No, these were voices raised in anger. It broke through my desolation as I looked up to the area near my burned-down cottage to find the sources of the voices.

Abel was screaming at Locke, who looked lethally angry. The kind of angry that sent an icy tremor up my spine. He looked dangerous. I saw shadows coil around him, bending light around him, his black runes on his forearms glowing black. Locke was readying himself to use shadow magic! I knew how much he hated using it. Were we under attack? My eyes and magic scanned the horizon, seeing and feeling nothing. But Locke's eyes never left Abel. Abel's eyes glowed bright blue as he yelled. I heard him say Scorpio's name. "She's the reason they're dead!" I heard him shout as I strode closer. I heard the malice in his voice. His gaze fell upon me as I approached with a questioning glance. I hadn't even realized my feet were moving until I stopped next to them.

"Abel, are you okay?" I asked him, taking in Abel's shaking extremities and the cords in his neck bulging. He looked... vengeful. Locke's attention flew to me, following Abel's unblinking glare. His face was desperate as he started to speak. Too late. In a movement so quick my eyes couldn't follow, Abel closed the remaining distance between us and slapped a heavy iron manacle onto my wrists, binding them effectively in front of me. I struggled, unsure what was going on. I cast a bewildered look to Abel, who sneered viciously at me. A strange, nauseating feeling came over me that I couldn't explain, making me feel weak in my knees. Before I could shout in protest, Abel spoke.

"This is all her fault!" he said, his nostrils flaring. His words might as well have been a punch to the gut, knocking the wind from my lungs. His eyes found me again, seeming pleased with his actions. He smiled in the most sinister way that made my skin crawl. I was still taking in the restraints when he grasped my braided hair, knocked my feet out from under me, pushed me face down to the ground, and placed his knee and his weight on my back before I even had time to scream or react more strategically. He grasped my hair tighter in his grip and lifted my head to look at Locke. I couldn't hold back the screech of pain I let out at him pulling my hair so violently. I began to call magic to me, to get him off of me, but felt none. I searched for the shimmering well within me but found nothing. Panic rose within me instead. Where was my magic? My stomach dropped at the same moment I forgot how to breathe. His gauntlet on his free hand came to my throat, a hidden blade springing forth with a sharp metal on metal *snick*. It was deafening in my ear and successfully forced me to absolute stillness. Locke drew his knife in response, eyes blazing with fury, but didn't advance.

"I can slit her throat right here and end this. Don't you give me another reason," he snapped, bringing his gaze back to Locke. Locke had a weapon in his hand but looked stricken. I understood Abel's anger. I felt that same anger towards myself. I closed my eyes, feeling the tears flow. Not for the fact there was a knife at my throat. But because he was right to do so. "Don't hurt her," he said. His sapphire eyes were anxiously scanning me head to toe, and Abel, looking for a way to get me out of this situation. His voice was filled with… worry? Abel held all the power right now, and I knew that didn't sit well with Locke. "Let her go. We can discuss this, but let her go."

"It's too late!" Abel said, pulling my hair and wrenching my neck. The pain snapped me out of my nearly catatonic state. I gritted my teeth against the pain and turned a venomous glare in his direction over my shoulder, refusing to show further weakness. "How many towns like this have to be destroyed? How many lives have to end?" He forced me to turn to look at him. I could still only see him in my peripheral vision but he was smirking. "I'll make sure it's quick." The same words Locke had once said to me, but the look on Abel's face had me seriously doubting him.

"Get off of me!" I snapped, struggling against his ever-tightening hold. "Before I freeze your balls to your armor and rip it off you!" I felt his body shake with a laugh. I spit at him. It landed nowhere near him with his having control of my head, but my point definitely got across.

"I'd slit your throat before you got the chance." His tone was dismissive, as if talking to a child having a temper tantrum. "Besides, have you noticed your bindings on your wrists?" I glanced down with my eyes at the silver glinting there. "I spelled them myself. They lock your magic down. You may as well be mortal. You're in no position to make threats." He gave me a grin that made my stomach turn. But he was right. I reached for the well of magic inside me again and felt myself hit a wall, my magic inaccessible on the other side of it. Every time I tried, the head rush and the nausea returned and I had to bite back bile. For the first time, my heart started to pound, and my breaths came shallowly. Fear. I refused to show fear, but it was plain to see in my reaction to the situation nonetheless. He had my magic locked down, a knife to my throat, and he was getting ready for something. I could feel it in the tension in the air. "And neither are you," he said to Locke, still scanning for a way to free me, real panic behind his eyes.

"The Queen has to kill me herself. You can't kill me," I spat, his attention settling unwillingly on me. I wasn't sure antagonizing the bad guy that hated me while my magic was locked down and a knife was pressed to my throat was the best idea. "It's her curse. That's why she's looking for me. She has to be the one who murders me. If you kill me now, you'll ensure this all keeps happening until someone else like me is born. Who knows how many years that will take? Centuries even?"

"She's right," Locke said. "I was there when the prophecy was read. And so was Lark. The Queen has to be the one to kill her. But that won't happen. At least not in what's left of your remaining lifespan."

"You think I don't know that?" Abel scoffed, completely unruffled. "I don't have to kill her. But I can injure her to where she teeters between life and death, for Scorpio to finish off. There's nothing you can do to save her! They're waiting for me to bring her. Stand back and I won't hurt her further. I'll make sure her death is swift and painless if you let me go right now." His voice raised an octave as he noticed Lenore, Lennox, and Aspen surround him with murderous gazes and their weapons drawn, waiting for any opening Abel gave them. I felt his desperation as well as the knife nicking my throat, drawing a bead of blood to my neck. My scalp screamed, demanding to be released from the torturous grasp Abel had on it. "I'm taking her with me to Loc Valen. Think how handsomely the Queen will reward me when I deliver her," he boasted, full of confidence. Locke took a solitary step forward. Abel's knee crushed further into my creaking spine, further pulling the hair he held in his iron grasp. I hated the shriek he elicited from me. I ground my teeth. Tears prickled at the back of my eyes at the feeling of his hands on me, and I was at his mercy. Mercy I was pretty sure he didn't have. And he was one twitch in the wrong direction from snapping my neck. "You can't stop me. You don't want to risk me hurting her further, do you?" Locke paled visibly, stopping his advance. The blood drained from his face as Abel pressed the knife further into my throat. I bit back the whimper of pain when I felt it cut.

"You'll do no such thing," Locke said, flourishing his blade, a smirk now touching the fringes of his mouth. "Because you're already dead." There was a blinding flash and Abel's garbled response came before I could blink. Locke had disappeared and reappeared beside me in the same breath with his knife in Abel's throat. Abel spasmed around the weapon, his body going tight and rigid. His grip loosened on my hair, giving me room to pull my hair out of his reach while I bucked and twisted my way out from under the weight of his knee. I was disturbed to see the blood, all of it gushing down his front onto me. I bit back a gag as I got out from under him and put distance between myself and him as he choked on the dagger, eyes wide and uncomprehending how he'd lost.

Locke called for Aspen to heal him, dark promises of payback on his lips as he regarded Abel. I looked at Locke holding the jumpstone. That was how he did it, my eyes widening in realization. Genius. He poured his magic into it to recharge it. He just needed a little more time to charge it. He was keeping Abel talking on purpose. Lennox was by my side, helping me to wrench the spelled metal bindings from my wrist. My magic power rallied behind it and hit me like a tidal wave the moment I was free. The feeling of accessing my magic again… it was like being whole again. I didn't understand how I went my entire life without it. It was like missing a limb. And taking that manacle off was returning my missing limb to me. Aspen was using his magic to keep Abel alive, even with the dagger still lodged in his neck. Blood was either leaking or spurting around the dagger at this point. I saw the sweat beaded on his head at the effort. If I could stop the bleeding, I could help Aspen. Fire danced in the background, attracting my attention. A piece of wood had fallen into the smoldering ruin of a building, reigniting the flames momentarily. My eyes were seeing something my brain simply wouldn't process. I blinked as an idea occurred to me. Fire. Stopping the bleeding. Of course…

I grabbed the manacle and put it on Abel, none too gently, and showed him what I was about to do with my fire magic and my blade, while Locke and Lenore held him still while the jumpstone recharged.

"Hey Abel, want to see me do a trick?" I asked in a low voice. I held my flame over the blade and watched it heat the metal. A small part of me relished the look of horror as realization dawned on him. I watched as he struggled to retreat, but Locke and Lenore wouldn't allow it. He was now at *our* mercy. Restrained with his magic locked down. There was a feral part of me that relished in the sweetness of justice. Locke looked at me, practically humming with approval as he understood my plan. He and Lenore held Abel motionless with Aspen still pouring healing magic into him to keep him alive. Abel could only watch as my blade began to turn red, knowing what was about to happen.

"This needs to be cauterized, Abel," I told him, keeping my voice taunting and light, forcing away the feeling of revulsion inside me. That part was hard at war with the angry beast within me demanding payback. My scalp still sung from the grip he'd had on my hair, from where he pulled it. I smiled grimly as I regarded him. Abel's eyes were wide, and a hideous wail left him. I refused to look at the blood pooling underneath him.

There was a warning in his eyes as he glared back at me, gurgling on his own blood. The funny thing about there being a knife in your throat? It makes it hard to talk back.

"What's the matter, Abel? You were all talk before," I said. Locke sniggered as he regarded me, his eyes dark. He looked sort of... impressed? Proud, perhaps? His approving gaze stayed on me while he held Abel still as he struggled. I looked at my now red-hot dagger and inwardly cringed. I knew that what I was about to do was likely going to be the kindest thing that would be done to him once Locke got his hands on him back home. He wasn't the Crowned Assassin for nothing. Locke was well versed in torture, and gauging by the steely glint in his eyes, Abel's hours were numbered.

My blade was red hot, and now almost white hot in the center. It would do nicely. I approached the group, eyes on the injury, trying not to gag at the sight of all that blood.

"Hold him down," Lenore grinned savagely and obliged along with her Prince, each taking a shoulder and a fistful of hair. I conjured my magic again and encased his lower body in ice, heavy and unyielding. I didn't want him to kick either of them. I looked deep into Abel's eyes as I grinned. "This is going to hurt like a bitch."

I removed the knife in his throat, extracting it carefully so as not to cause too much more damage on the way out. The moment the metal was free of its flesh and blood sheath I quickly applied my heated blade. Abel's head jerked and his scream was bloodcurdling as I made contact with his wound. I gagged on the smell of burning flesh and my hands being covered in hot, sticky blood. Worse yet was the smell paired with the sound. The sizzle. The hiss. I knew of several food items that were forever off the menu because of this moment.

I should be disgusted with myself. A part of me was. But a bigger part of me was grimly satisfied that this traitorous filth was being dealt with. He had not only threatened me, but his betrayal affected Locke, my friends, and the entire Court of Rebels. That was what I couldn't find forgiveness for. When the wound was finished closing, I removed my blade, summoned water into a orb, and wiggled my knife through the water, billowing steam rising with the cooling of my blade. I had to keep cooling the water with how bloody and hot it got, and I didn't relish the scent of boiled blood. Aspen took a deep breath and sat down for a moment, absolutely exhausted.

Locke leaned down to look at Abel, who was barely able to breathe, his lungs dragging in small, labored breaths. He was barely conscious. Locke looked into the eyes of the fae who had been his knight. His ally. His friend. Locke's hand closed around his throat, long, deft fingers digging near the freshly cauterized wound. Abel gave a soundless scream. Locke looked more dangerous than I'd ever seen him.

"You hurt Lark." His voice was a low growl. "You betrayed all of us. You think you know pain now. I promise, I'll redefine that word for you. In a way you'll never come back from." Abel's face was the epitome of pure, unadulterated terror. He looked at me once over Locke's shoulder. I should've felt pity. The old Lark would have. But as I looked into his eyes, I felt nothing. No guilt. No pity. He made his choice. I turned my back on the grisly sight of him and took a deep breath. Locke tossed an order at Lenore and Lennox to keep an eye on him while the jumpstone recharged. They were only too happy to oblige, their sneers at Abel almost encouraging him to try something.

I walked over to Locke, who was cleaning the blood off his dagger the same I way had.

"Thank you," I said quickly, not able to meet his eye. "For saving my life." Locke looked up, his glittering gaze piercing, calculating. Ever assessing, no real emotion showed on his face, that mask left carefully in place. His hand reached out gently to my chin and lifted my face to look at him. I bit my lip.

"There's no need to thank me." His voice was surprisingly gentle. "I thought by now you'd know that I'd never let anything happen to you." My traitorous breath hitched in my throat before I remembered how to breathe. But I couldn't hide that my heart was racing.

"I'm so sorry, Lark. I had no idea he would do something like this. I knew he was angry. I didn't see the extent of his anger. And it put you in harm's way. I'm sorry."

I blinked. I tried a few times to say something. Anything. But several sentences died on my tongue before I finally grasped onto something intelligent to say. "You shouldn't feel remorse for someone else's actions, Locke. It's not your fault." He looked unconvinced but said nothing. I sighed, rolling my shoulders to relieve the growing tension in them. "How long until the jumpstone is recharged?"

He shrugged.

"A half hour in any case."

"May I try to charge it?" He handed it over without a second thought.

"Pour your essence into it. It will be easy to establish a connection. It's harder to break. And you'll need to break it if it tries to take too much of you."

"Tries to take too much of me?"

"You'll see what I mean," he said. "You just have to resist its pull."

I looked at the jumpstone in my hand. I'd thought it was stone, but now that I held it, I saw it was like a very opaque crystal. Various runes on it, I knew would light up with magic, glowing as if lit from within. It was a warm, hefty weight. Heavier than I thought. I called upon the well of magic in me and pushed it towards the stone. It felt like a bridge, like the stone had anchored itself to the magic I gave it. I fed it, ushering more and more magic towards it. Until I realized I wasn't pushing anymore. The stone had a latch on my power on its own, not unlike that of a leech with a bloodmeal.

The runes began to glow more, softly at first and then more brightly. It was a wonder how Locke had hidden it from Abel. Another use for massive hands, I supposed. I felt a tug at the well of my magic inside me, like a hose sputtering and continuing to flow. It made me flinch. From somewhere outside myself, I heard Locke tell me, "That's enough," with a note of concern in his voice. I looked at the stone glowing brightly.

"Resist its pull," Locke had said to me, still sounding so far away. Like an echo on the wind. Stopping the flow felt a lot like trying to turn a hose off, but there was no nozzle to do so. The magic was flowing from me, unchecked now. In a growing panic, I did the only thing available to me: I kinked the hose.

It was enough to give me a second to sever the connection. With a gasp, I righted myself. Too much. I threw myself backwards. As I was about to hit the ground, strong arms caught me around my shoulders. Locke looked down at me, impressed.

"You charged it fully, and then some. How do you feel?"

"A little dizzy," I admitted. He chuckled.

"Most people throw up or even pass out doing something like that and you're just dizzy?" He shook his head with a laugh. It sounded almost lighthearted. Almost. "Are you ready to go home?" I looked around me at the decimated remains of Poplar Hollow. Looked at the ruined cottages, still smoldering. I looked at the burn, blackened, blood-soaked ground. The bodies that littered it. I thought of my father. Eldan. Gael. This once was my home. I realized in that moment I would never be back here. I had a new home now. With one last heartbreaking glance around, I looked to Locke and nodded. I was ready to go home. To Port Azure.

We all linked together as Locke led us and a weakly struggling Abel through the portal of light back to Hell's Gate. It was disorienting to blink in one set of surroundings, and blink once more and you're in another set. To breathe a breath in one setting, and take your next in another. The wall sconces blazed brightly, making my eyes blink rapidly to adjust.

"What's going to happen to Abel?" I asked as Aspen half-dragged, half-carried him down a hallway and out of sight. Abel raged against his restraints, but his waning strength was nothing for Aspen and the twins as they escorted him out of sight. I didn't notice the half-mad and terrified expression he bore as he was taken away. He was begging someone to listen to him. Locke's wry grin was enough to chill the very blood in my veins.

"You'll all die if you don't hand her over!" was the final warning I heard from Abel with his ruined voice before I heard a heavy-sounding door shut, and then it was silent. The sort of silence that felt heavy, oppressing.

"Trust me when I say you don't want to know. But rest assured that what you did to him will be the kindest thing that befalls him the rest of his short life." His tone was laced with lethal promise. I barely suppressed a shudder. The wicked gleam in his eyes told me he meant every word of that promise.

"I'm sorry. I know he was your friend." Locke's eyebrow twitched.

"He stopped being a friend the second he made the choice to lay a hand on you." His voice was a hushed but deadly tone. His magic pulsed sporadically around me, like thunder I could feel but not hear, telling me exactly how angry he was. "And now he'll pay for what he's done. And soon we'll get to the bottom of the depths of his treachery. You should go to your rooms," he said, his face softening. "You're clearly exhausted. And you did so well today. I'm proud of you." I wish my heart didn't leap at his praise. I shouldn't have been so excited by it. I wasn't supposed to still be so affected by him.

"Take me to the survivors. I was a healer's apprentice back home. I'm also a familiar face. I can help."

"Are you sure you'd rather not rest? You look dead on your feet." I nodded. "Okay. I'll have some food sent down for you. Follow me. I'll show you to the infirmary." I swear this place was half underground and just a series of haphazard tunnels. The fact that I hadn't actually gotten lost yet was ridiculous, and frankly, divine intervention. There was always another section I'd not seen.

I turned my thoughts towards what was revealed today. The Queen now knew that I exist. Knew who I was. It was possible she knew what I looked like. But time would tell if she knew how powerful I'd become. And how vengeful I was, especially after seeing Poplar Hollow. I'd end her reign and her life in the same blow. For my father. For Poplar Hollow. For Amaya. Locke looked at me with a beat of concern.

The smell of sterilizing agent, stale blood, and death greeted me before we walked through the doors. The only patients here were the three survivors from Poplar Hollow: an old man, a girl a few years older than me whose name I didn't know, and the little boy I'd found. I recognized the older man, I realized with dread. I'd treated him with Eldan for his arthritis. Eldan and I made potions for him regularly so he could work to support his family. A family that no longer existed.

My feet carried me straight to the boy. I took his hand in mine as I assessed his injuries. He had a massive contusion on the back of his head, and multiple lacerations all over his tiny frame. My heart wrenched at the thought of hurting someone so young. So innocent. I looked at Locke. I put my hatred into it. But not for him. I silently swore vengeance on those that hurt these people. This child and his innocent family. I would not let this go unanswered. Unpunished. He nodded, reading and understanding my emotions. I knew he saw the fire in my eyes.

"Let the flames fuel you, Lark. But don't let them consume you." I looked at him and to my surprise, I didn't feel intense hatred that had been actively blooming earlier today. I refused to acknowledge the feelings there too much, but the long-simmering hatred had indeed died down. Perhaps it was my exhaustion, or the intensity of the day taking its toll, but it was true. Or maybe I just realized that hate was a useless emotion. One that didn't serve any purpose. "I can feel your vengeance. Be careful, Lark. Revenge is a dangerous line to walk. But knowing you, I'm confident you'll walk it well." He turned and strode purposefully from the room. I knew where he was going. I grimaced for Abel, even though I knew he deserved whatever Goddess-awful thing Locke had in store for him.

Did he, though? Yes, his actions were abhorrent, but his opinions weren't. He'd wanted an end to the civil war before it started. I could pose that end. My death. I hated to think of myself as a lamb destined to slaughter, but at the right time and by the right hand, but if I were honest with myself, that was exactly what I was. I knew my new purpose in life: to end her curse as her walls fell around her, her armies in heaps at her feet. Then we would end her curse. We would end her.

And peace within the Water Court could begin anew.

Chapter Thirteen

I felt movement by my hands and it caused me to stir. My eyes drifted open just in time to see the little boy's eyes flutter open weakly. I held his hand gently, the pad of my thumb stroking the back of his hand in an attempt to be calming.

"Hi, I'm glad you're awake." The boy's eyes darted around, panic in them. "It's okay," I soothed. "You're safe. I know the horror you went through. But you're safe here, I promise. Nobody here will ever hurt you." The boy's head swiveled while simultaneously shrinking into the bed and pillows, and I knew what he was going to ask before he even uttered the words, my heart aching already.

"Who are you? Where's my mom?" His voice was timid and unsure. Tiny hands clutched the blanket to him, as if donning armor. He looked so small on the too-large bed, and smaller still with the blackened eye that had formed in the hours since our return to Port Azure. My chest hurt at the thought of telling him he was alone in the world at such a tender age.

"My name is Lark. I lived in Poplar Hollow until a few months ago. I was the healer's apprentice. You may have seen me with Eldan." The boy looked at me, no recognition in his eyes.

"What happened?"

"Let's start with your name," I asked with a smile.

"Elias."

"Okay, Elias. I'm afraid what I'm going to tell you is difficult. Are you ready?" He nodded. "Our town was attacked. When we heard what had happened, my friends and I came as soon as we could. We saved whoever we could. You and two others." I knew as soon as I spoke them that I chose my words poorly. I winced when Elias's eyes lit up and I knew he thought I meant his family. I hated myself for what I had to do next.

"Where's my mom? My brother?" His eyes scanned the room and fell upon the other two survivors. Both were still unconscious. His eyes whipped back to me, beseeching. "Where's my mom?" he asked again, more insistently, tears filling his eyes, causing mine to fill as well. Though so young, understanding seemed to settle in him, and he began to cry. I held him to me, giving him room to pull away if he wanted. Instead, he clung to me, his arms around my neck so tightly it was hard to breathe. I held him. I rocked him. I stroked his hair. I murmured soothing words. But most of all, I cried with him. I knew the depths of the despair he was feeling. I remembered seeing my own father's corpse, his lifeless eyes seeming to stare at me. I prayed to the Goddess above he didn't remember the horrors of the attack. A small mercy, but a mercy nonetheless.

I hummed a lullaby. One my father used to hum when I was sick as a child. It was a slow melody. Calm. Peaceful. I felt his racking sobs slow and stop altogether. He listened to the song as it hit its crescendo, and I fell silent again.

"I lost my father too," I said after a few moments. I held Elias tightly, as if I could put together all his broken pieces. But all I could do was show him that he wasn't alone. "Before my cottage went up in flames a few months ago." Or was it only weeks? I'd lost track of how long I'd been here.

"That big fire was your house?"

"Yes. And someone slayed my father. I know how you feel. And I'm so sorry about your mother and brother. I want you to know we will find those responsible. And we will make sure they don't get away with what they've done."

"What's going to happen to me?" I gave him my brightest smile.

"You'll stay here. With us. You'll make lots of new friends, and practice magic, and learn new things." I tried to make my voice peppy, optimistic. I needed him to feel those things on some level. I wanted him to feel hope. Because that was what kept me from the very edges of despair when I lost my father. And he was so young. "You're going to be okay."

"My lady." Locke's captain from yesterday was in the doorway behind me. I prayed he did not bear news of another attack. It couldn't be, I told myself. It was too soon. He looked calm, which I took as a good sign. "His Highness has sent for you. In his rooms. The others have already gathered and are awaiting your arrival." I didn't want to leave Elias.

"Will you stay with Elias? He's been through so much, I don't think being alone is a wise decision for him." He gave me a look of… approval? A gentleness I hadn't seen before. "It will be as you ask, my lady," he said. "I'll personally see to it that the boy was well cared for." I looked at Elias, who was silently pleading with me to not leave him. My heart tore at the sight. I held his hand.

"My good friend here is going to take good care of you. Did you know he's a captain of a whole army? I bet he could tell you some really amazing stories while I'm gone. And I'll come and visit as soon as I can, okay?"

"Yes, my lady," he said, mimicking the captain. My hand brushed his shoulder.

"You don't need to address me so formally. My name is Lark, okay?" He nodded. I turned to the captain. "The same goes for you. Lark is perfectly fine."

He stuttered. "Yes, my l—Yes, Lark." He caught himself, and I could feel him tripping over the words, feeling the strangeness of them. Always so formal. So polite. But for the life of me, I couldn't fathom why people were calling me their lady all of a sudden. Sure, I was friends with Aspen who was a lord, and Lennox and Lenore who were ladies of the Court. Locke was their sovereign Prince. But I was not of noble blood. I didn't have a title. I stood, giving Elias a last warm look and a gentle squeeze of his hand.

"Treat him like your own," I said to the captain, who nodded with kind eyes.

"I swear it will be done. Now go." It should've sounded dismissive. Instead it sounded kind, even fatherly, as he turned his attention to the sad, broken little boy with a smile. I smiled one final time at Elias before I left the infirmary. It warmed my heart to hear the captain begin to regale Elias with stories of mighty kings and queens, of epic battles and monster slaying and kind princesses. Elias hung on every word.

I roamed the halls, getting lost a few times. I had to stop and ask for directions a couple times, getting so turned around in this new area. But I eventually found my way to the familiar double doors of Locke's rooms. I didn't bother knocking as I stepped through the threshold.

Lenore, Lennox, and Aspen lounged in the seating. Locke, as always, in his desk chair. He had a drink in his hand. A burning amber liquid in a crystal glass. The others held something similar. Locke stared impassively into his glass.

"Tell me we're drinking because we have something to celebrate," I said, eyeing up the half-emptied bottle of liquor before pouring myself one. "Please tell me we're not moping over more bad news." Locke looked up at me with his eyes from over his glass. This was seeming less and less like good news. Lennox and

Lenore could barely look at me with their red-rimmed eyes. Lennox sipped her drink while Lenore slugged hers back and poured another in a tight grip. Aspen couldn't seem to look away from his drink, his mood pensive at best. You could find more cheer at a funeral. "What's going on? Where is Abel?"

"Abel is dead. He'll never lay a hand on you again. He got a death worthy of his atrocities." Locke's voice was hard and sharp when he spoke. The rage I'd seen in his eyes when I'd seen him last had not dissipated, but intensified. The almost static-like flickers of his power railed into me, into all of us, making my hair stand on end. I knew his wrath wouldn't be quelled any time soon either. Abel's betrayal had cut him deep, even if he didn't want to admit it. I shuddered. "And he has been a bigger traitor than we could have ever anticipated." Locke started, "He wanted to turn you into the Queen, yes, but not to end the civil war within our court." An angry smile twisted his features before he downed the rest of his drink and poured another. "He was going to use you, and turn all of us in to gain the Queen's favor. With me casted as a traitor Prince, he was trying to become the new Cancer upon my death. Too bad the Zodiac Guild would never allow someone from outside the guild to become a Zodiac. Someone who hasn't even undergone the rune trials. But that was his plan. Sell us out and become royalty. That's how the Queen found out you didn't die in the fire. He's been communicating with her." My blood ran cold. My thoughts stopped forming. I felt my mouth gaping like that of a fish trying to form the words.

"Wait, is there proof?" Locke looked at me with a patient expression.

"Between mine and Lenore's interrogation techniques, he sang like a canary." I knew without doubt that interrogation in this case, meant torture. I had to suppress a shiver as I looked away. "He told me his plan in exchange for mercy. He got it. But I promise you this, Lark, he suffered for what he tried to do to you." My heart sped up, beating inconsistently. I wasn't sure how to respond to that.

"How were they even communicating?" I asked.

"A combination of carefully crafted letters that were spelled to dissolve into flame once read, and the occasional secret meeting via jumpstones. Those days when we thought he was eating dinner in his rooms? Gone. We coaxed a long, and thorough, confession from him." Aspen took a long glug from his drink at that moment, as if the horrors of the interrogation were a lot to bear, even for someone as steadfast as he was.

The way Locke's eyes darkened... The intermittent flickers of raw emotion; Locke looked frayed and dark, and the shadows I found there drifting wickedly in his gaze made me want to curl into myself, and I couldn't help wrapping my arms around myself in response. The gravity of the situation hit me then. I couldn't quell the horror that came with the realization of what Abel had done. Had tried to do. These fae were his friends, and he would've seen them slaughtered? For what? For political gain?

My heart went out to Aspen, Lennox, and Lenore. Even Locke. I could see their mixing emotions. This betrayal had hurt them all.

"So the Queen is coming here?" I asked, trying to calm my heart rate. "She knows of the rebellion now. Who heads it, its forces, its location?" I almost couldn't force the words past my lips. But I felt a small sliver of relief as Locke shook his head.

"That's the Goddess's one mercy. She doesn't know our location. She doesn't know you can actively wield three of your four elements. She doesn't know the size of our army. We found that correspondence in time before he sent it. But he's been talking to the Queen for weeks. She knows now what you look like. There will be wanted ads all over the realm for you. He's been using tidbits of information to gain the Queen's trust. Buy her favor. Try to bargain with her for Cancer's position. She knows I'm a traitor. I doubt I'm a prince anywhere but here right now."

I put the liquor to my lips and slugged the whole thing back, wincing as the burn warmed my throat and belly. I poured myself another.

"What of your family?" I asked him. He shook his head, not looking at me.

He looked straight into the amber liquid in his glass.

"I don't know." His voice had taken on a desperate edge, revealing the depths of his horror at last. Of his fear. I resisted the urge to hug all his shattered pieces together. I knelt before him, taking his hands in mine and squeezing. His sapphire eyes were dull from the trauma of today. I rose to my feet, anxiety squeezing my chest. I wanted to help but I had no idea what to do.

"Is there anything I can do right now? For any of you?" Lenore and Lennox enveloped me into a tight hug. I felt how heavily this weighed on them. I held them up after putting my drink down. I wouldn't let any of us be alone. Aspen looked angry. He was always in such high spirits. Always smiling. It was a different side of him indeed to see angry Aspen. Locke looked at me and his gaze softened a little. I remembered how he sparred with Aspen. I remembered the smile on his face. I released the girls and slugged my drink.

"Get up, Locke," I said to him. My voice held no room for hesitation. He reluctantly stood, tossing a questioning glance my way. I took his hand and led him down the corridor, down the stairs, past fae dwelling the hallways who watched us go, to Hell's Gate. Once inside the empty arena, I whirled on him. "Fight me." He looked at me with weary confusion. "Don't hold back. Not for me. Let's go." He needed an outlet. I thought I did too. He didn't get what he wanted from Abel. He looked angry. Murderous. I could feel the wrath-fuelled energy coursing off him in waves.

And I was calling him on.

"You're sure about this?" he asked with hesitancy. He would know exactly how good I was at sparring. Aspen had been reporting my progress to him weekly since my arrival. And probably discussing it daily in addition. But I didn't want him to hold back. I needed this too. I felt my rage, my helplessness, my guilt screaming inside me, begging for any kind of release. And I saw the same echoing in him. I knew that look in his eye. Because it was in mine.

"Just don't let up because you're fighting me," I said, lowering myself into an easy fighting stance the way Aspen had taught me.

"I won't injure you," he said. "And we can stop at any time."

"Just fucking try to hit me already." I flashed him a dry grin. The one he returned reminded me of a predator baring its teeth.

We squared off then, me throwing the first punch, which he easily blocked and followed with a knee to my abdomen. I was able to roll with it, mitigating the blow while my fist made contact with his face. Surprise registered on both our faces. I didn't think either of us actually expected me to get a hit, certainly not right away. I utilized it to my advantage and threw another combination at him, all of which were evaded or blocked. He countered, blindingly fast, but I was getting better at seeing these fast strikes and I evaded them, though not without difficulty. There was no banter. No sarcasm. Just fight.

We sparred like that for what seemed like eternity. Sweat poured off my body with the effort it took to keep up with him. My fists hurt. I might have cracked a knuckle in my left hand. But neither of us was winning over the other. Sweat dripped into his eyes. He was trying to bring me to my knees, and I kept just out of reach. Evading or countering each attack with a blow of my own.

Until he swept my leg out from under me. I fell hard to the mat and he pinned me to it with his body, his forearm to my throat, winning our match. I glared up at him as I struggled to force my lungs to breathe, and all of my protests were stopped at my lips when I saw the familiar heat churning in his gaze. There was a pregnant pause where neither one of us said anything, just feeling that heat simmer. My thoughts began to scatter to the wind under his gaze. For a moment, I couldn't tell if my heart were racing or had stopped altogether.

"I can't stop thinking about you and I hate it," he growled low in his throat, before crushing his lips to mine. The sun rose then. It must have been the sun that engulfed me with this heat in me, over me, between the two of us the moment his lips landed on mine. There wasn't even the slightest hesitancy. Not from either of us. His lips were demanding and passionate, and I found myself matching that as I yielded to the sun I now realized was within myself. I held to it and burned up in its fire. My lips demanded from his, took from his as much as his took from mine. And all I knew was fire and urgency and longing and something... something else I refused to accept or acknowledge.

The moment his lips parted from mine with a sharp intake of breath as he struggled to drag air into his lungs, that sun set. That sun set below the horizon of my conscious thoughts, taking with it the heat, leaving me stranded in a dark, bitter, and frigid place.

A place of anger.

When he rose up on his elbows fully, my sense came swimming back to me in disproportionate segments. And as much as I wanted this, as much as I could finally admit to myself I wanted him, I wasn't going to do this just because he was feeling sorry for himself. I put a hand on his chest, and he yielded, moving off of me. I saw the question in his eyes.

"You don't get to tell me we can't have a relationship, and then do that when you feel like shit," I spat at him. "That's not fair."

"You're right," he said stiffly.

"And the fact is, I can't stop thinking about you, either. And I fucking hate it. Because you've made it abundantly clear that you don't want me. And I refuse to be your toy you dangle for your amusement when you feel like shit." My tone was angry, accusing. And I saw something burning in his eyes. "Besides, isn't the reason we can't be together because I have to die?" I guessed, putting words to what had been dancing around in my head for some time. Horror flashed in his eyes before the anger did.

"You know damn well I have no intention of letting you die." His voice was calm, but with an undercurrent of seething rage. His posture was tense, even more so than when he'd been sparring with me.

"No, you just need me to die at the right time. Isn't that why you want me to train so hard? So I stand a chance of dying before the Queen but taking as many of her supporters as possible?" I knew I was being cruel. I couldn't stop myself. Even with the flash of pain in his eyes. "So that we can break down Scorpio's defenses and I can die at the right time, and you can swoop in to kill her?" He approached me, grabbed my braid, and forced me to look at him, his face very close to mine.

"You know that's not true. Don't forget I can feel your emotions. You know without a doubt that if we go down, we go down together. I'd gladly give my life for you. And I will not let you die, not now, not tomorrow, and not in our final battle. I've done everything in my power to prevent it thus far!" he snapped. Prevent me from dying? What had I been in danger of since I'd been here other than Abel? I shrugged out of his grip with an indignant huff, my temper flaring. I turned my back to him and walked out of the arena.

I sank into the inviting foamy bubbles and steaming hot water, so hot it nearly scalded me. I welcomed it as the water reddened my skin. I sighed as the heat seeped into my aching muscles. My neck was sore from Abel wrenching it by my hair. I shivered despite the warmth at the horror of yesterday. The fear I'd felt when I thought Abel was going to kill me. When I thought it couldn't get worse, it did when he was a traitor, about to deliver me to Scorpio. He was going to betray Locke and the Court of Rebels. How close all this came to being under siege.

And then there was my reaction. I had cauterized his neck wound. I had taken pleasure in his suffering. What on Earth did that say about me? I wanted even to regret the pain I'd caused him, but I couldn't. I hated myself for how I felt, but he'd deserved it for trying to betray Locke, my friends, and our Court. I felt a savage need within me to protect them at all costs. I also needed to figure out when I'd started calling the Court of Rebels *my* Court. And not just a court. Why I cared as much as I did. But I knew why. It wasn't just Locke and the Knights. It was fae like Elias, and the captain who so tenderly tended to him after I was summoned. It was fae like the grumpy old man who let me steal snacks occasionally. It was the fae who oohed and awed at my magic during my lessons with Locke and saw it as a sign of hope. It was the fae that trained so hard every day for their cause, or those survivors desperately just trying to hang on to a sense of hope, of normalcy, of safety. Fae who'd never hurt anyone, were guilty of nothing, but ended up a victim of Scorpio's wrath nonetheless. Fae like Everleigh, who'd escaped here after the death of her soulmate. I sank deeper into the water to my chin, as if the hot water could drive away my swirling, opposing emotions. As if the hot water could help me sort it all out. I loosed a sigh, knowing it couldn't, but settled on the idea of finally picking up my book again that Aspen had recommended, hoping it would serve as my escape from my current warring emotions.

I'd reheated the bath water twice in my refusal to leave, my skin well pruned. I took my time dressing in a shirt and yet another pair of my soft cotton leggings, of which I seemingly head a never-ending supply. I lived for the tingle of magic in my fingertips as I summoned the fire that began to blaze in my hearth, casting my room in a cozy glow, the perfect juxtaposition to how I was feeling. I no sooner had curled up with my book on my favorite chair—the one in front of the fire and the windows with the lovely view—when a knock came from my door, soft and hesitant.

The back of my head hit the back of the chair as a wheeze of irritation came over me. I just wanted to be alone. But against my better judgement, I called for the knocker to come in, too tired to get up and open the door. The door opened and Locke stood before me, leaning against my door frame.

Before I could tell him where he could shove off to, he spoke.

"There's been another attack," Locke said, his voice gravelly. I finally took a good look at him. His eyes were wide. Haunted. Dull. He looked disheveled, as if he'd been wandering around with only his own demons for company for days on end.

"Where? So soon? What's she looking for?"

"It's a place called Frostfall. It's where I grew up." Realization dawned on me. *His parents...* I felt a flash of sympathy I stubbornly refused to acknowledge.

"Where are they?"

"I don't know." His voice... it hurt. This wasn't the same Locke I sparred with earlier. Or the one who saved me from Abel in Poplar Hollow. Not the one who kissed me in the library of Aramithia. Not the one who bantered with me during my lessons with him. This Locke was sullen and weary. His eyes looked sunken in, the dark circles beginning under them. His color was pale. The way one looks when they think their family has been obliterated.

Once I would have mocked him. He'd killed my father, it was only justice and karma at work that his should die as well. But all I felt was his numbness, the horror of loss fighting for dominance behind it. I stood quickly, ready to aid the fae I once swore to kill.

"I wouldn't ask you to come with me if I didn't think I'd need your help," he said to me as I began putting my armor back on, starting with the dragonscale pants directly over my leggings, and shoving my feet into my leather boots.

"You couldn't keep me from being there," I said sincerely. His family was innocent, no matter if I thought their son was a Goddess-forsaken ass. "Are the others ready?" He nodded.

"Yes, but Lark, there's something you need to know." I looked at him while pulling on my chest plate and bracers. I still couldn't get over how light and movable my armor was. "I think this may be a trap. Scorpio attacks both of our hometowns in a matter of days? It doesn't seem coincidental. I need you to be ready. And I'm giving you the chance to back out." His eyes met mine with clarity for the first time since he'd been in my room. I glared at him.

"I don't care if it is a trap," I growled. "I'm coming with you. You look like Hell so I imagine someone will need to cover you in a fight." I muttered. He gave me a dry, humorless half-smirk that faded quickly. No banter, no witty remark, no comeback. I tried to ignore the worry that was settling into my bones. Because I knew the look on his face well. It was a look I wore for months after my father was killed.

After he killed your father, I reminded myself for the millionth time silently.

His face fell further as if he'd heard my thoughts. I tied my hair quickly into its trademark braid, keeping it out of my face. I stuffed my daggers into the compartments of my boots and prepared to sling my father's sword over my head. I paused. I supposed it was time to call it my sword now. I fingered the hilt hesitantly before strapping it behind my back. *My* sword.

"I'm ready."

He nodded. "Then let's go. The others will be waiting."

We arrived by jumpstone to another smoldering ruin. A sight I got my fill of previously. Smoke nearly choked me trying to enter my lungs. I suppressed a cough as I surveyed our surroundings. There was nothing left. Fire had reduced everything to cinders and ash, right down to the cement substructure.

It clearly used to be a peaceful, charming little village. A stream of cold water passed through the heart of the small town of Frostfall leading to a small pond on the edge of town. Steep cliffs shaded the area from either side, forming a near-perfect horseshoe around the settlement, giving me the feeling of being in a bowl. It probably protected the town from the elements, but I couldn't help feeling like a caged animal, my hand itching to draw my sword. A forest loomed ahead of us to the north. But now this place was little more then a village that had been razed to the ground. Bodies littered the area, bloodstained, the pond red. Locke looked them all over, saying a small prayer to the Goddess over them. We split up into groups and searched for survivors. Aspen and the twins took the south portion of the town, Locke and I took the north.

"This was your home?" I asked with confusion. I had always assumed he'd grown up in Loc Valen.

"My parents realized my power at a young age. They applied for me to receive training under the Zodiac Guild. They're the counsel that ultimately decides who gets accepted into training." I nodded, remembering reading that during my time in the library. "Who is strong enough to lead our realm. I was chosen quickly and taken away to Loc Valen to train, and once it was complete, I competed for the position of Cancer." His eyes were far away in a memory before blinking back to the present. "The rest is history."

I cast my awareness out, looking for any signs of life. A beating heart clinging to life, a stirring consciousness, anything. But I found nothing. Like in Poplar Hollow, it was eerily silent. No birds chirped, and with the cliffs around us there was no real breeze rustling the trees. It was silent aside from the occasional pop and hiss of a still-burning fire. This attack had been recent. Locke and I both knew what this was. This was a message to Locke from Scorpio for his supposed treason. Locke's countenance grew more worried as we passed by corpse after corpse; none of them were his family. And unlike last time, none of these poor souls had managed to survive. Their wounds were clean cut, deep, and atrocious. They were efficient. This was a mass execution. And there was no place for any of them to go surrounded by cliffs and forest. The town enclosed by cliffs that had likely shielded them from the harsher elements had also been their downfall. Nobody could get out, especially not if the lonely road to the south—the only entrance to this Goddess-forsaken place—guarded. This was full-scale slaughter.

A frustrated howl came from Locke, as he kicked… something, sending it flying. It clattered and rolled, landing several feet away. I could feel his despair radiating off of him in waves. I rushed to him as he fell to his knees, his head bowed. His hair fell over his eyes, hiding his face from view. I followed his gaze to find… nothing. I'd expected two new corpses. Perhaps Locke resembled his mother, glittering blue eyes dull and lifeless now, and black hair caked with mud. Perhaps his father next to her, his strong jaw slackened in death. But there was nothing. My knees hit the dirt beside him, unsure of how to proceed.

"What is it?" I asked.

"They're not here." His voice was a whisper followed closely by a strangled sob.

"Isn't that a good thing? This was a slaughter. We don't want to find their bodies. Maybe they escaped."

Locke looked at me, eyes dull, but something churned in their depths. "Or Scorpio has them." I heard him break at last. I couldn't take it anymore. I didn't know how to help. I didn't know how to ease his pain. I didn't even want to admit why I wanted to. I reached out and tugged his body to mine in an awkward hug. His head tucked under my chin as I held him a moment. I felt him freeze.

"I've got you," was all I said. I held him tightly enough that I imagined squeezing the shattered pieces of his heart back together. He hadn't been allowed to see his family in five years. He'd done all he had to keep them safe. To get back to them. And to save the Water Court as a whole. And he'd done it mostly alone.

Not all alone, I reminded myself. Aspen, Lenore, and Lennox had been there for him. And Abel, before everything that happened. I felt yet another crack in the armor I'd erected around my heart. I shuddered against it, fought against it, but it was there. I was helpless. The Crowned Assassin was well under my skin, not that I'd admit it to anybody other than myself.

Aspen and the twins were walking towards us, obviously unsuccessful in their attempts to find survivors.

A laugh tickled the edges of my awareness, making my arms fall back to my sides. A laugh I didn't recognize. It was soft, so soft I thought it was in my imagination. But Locke's head snapped up and I knew I wasn't the only one who heard it. His features instantly giving way from weariness to understanding. To rage. My head swiveled looking for this new fae. I followed Locke's gaze and I saw him. I scrambled to my feet and drew my sword, my mouth feeling dry. This is it.

A battle. A *real* battle.

"It's so nice to see you again, Lachlan. You're at Court so little, I was wondering what's been keeping you so busy of late." A smooth voice drawled. It crawled over me, made me shudder. I looked up. Atop the cliff sat a male presence. He sat as if he were lounging and watching the sunset, legs dangling over the cliff, elbows resting on his knees, and a giant grin highlighting his high and sharp cheekbones. Not someone I immediately knew. He had pale hair, disheveled and the color of moonlight. His relaxed posture showed that he clearly didn't view any of us as a threat. His arms glowed black, I noticed. He wore his shadows like his plated armor. Black shadows writhed like darkness given corporeal form around him. A toxic miasma of black magic.

"Pisces," Locke hissed. "I wondered when you'd show yourself."

Pisces. So he was the other Zodiac. I bit the inside of my cheek as my blood ran cold. The irony wasn't lost on me that once I had hoped it was Pisces I ran into in the Vale, not the Crowned Assassin, and yet here I was, ready to defend the latter from the former. I grit my teeth at the savage look on Pisces' face. He's in league with Scorpio, helping her to break the curse. He's been helping her eliminate towns. *Maintain order and justice,* they had called it. He was the one doing most of the killing. So Locke was right. This was a trap. A perfectly laid trap he knew Locke couldn't resist. Because if he came alone, he could capture him, and

I was sure he guessed I would come for him. Or if we all came, he could kill them and take me to Scorpio. Either way, he won.

"Awe, Lachlan. Cancer was always the most sentimental of us water signs." He addressed me with a steely glint in his eye that made me straighten my spine. I glared up at him. "Were you hoping for a family reunion?"

"Where are they?" Gone was the undone Locke that was barely holding it together in my arms. This Locke was back in control of himself. His seething anger palpable likely even from Pisces' position above us. If he were sane, he'd run. Run like Hell itself was at his heels. Because the rising darkness I felt in Locke was the kind of darkness you couldn't cage for long. Aspen and the twins arrived beside us, hissing and drawing their blades. I was surprised that Pisces had come alone. My eyes flicked to the only road in and found it empty. I cast my awareness out, further than I'd managed before. My mental muscles tore at the effort, but I found no signs of life. Pisces really had come alone. Was I missing something?

"They're with Scorpio." He chuckled. "Your mom is hurt that her only son hasn't returned to them in so long." Locke's eyes flashed and so did my magic. Fire erupted around me, bringing Pisces' gaze back to me with mild interest. My red-hot temper flared at how blasé he was about killing all these innocent people. For Locke's family. And for what? A message? Revenge? What was his play?

"You'll pay for what you've done!" I yelled out to him, stepping up beside Locke and staring Pisces down. My flames were now coiling around my body, setting me awash in the hellfire that matched my fury. It begged to be set upon Pisces but I reined it in, a silent promise in the hiss and flicker of the flames. His head cocked to the side as he regarded me with keen interest. Something else flashed in those eyes so filled with grim amusement: recognition.

"I see you have a new pet. Put a leash on her for now. My interest is with you first before I begin my business with her." He directed a hand at that lonely little road between the shelf-like cliffs, beaten up over time and ill maintained. And a dark shadow emerged there like a curtain, blocking our escape and sealing us in. I glanced around us, seeing only cliff on either side of us and the trees just to the north of us. When I brought my attention back to Pisces, he cocked his head with such nonchalance it made me grit my teeth in a withering scowl. Locke was also stiff beside me, poised to strike at any moment. He took a protective step in front of me. I had felt the tingle in the air as he called his magic to him. "I'll have fun with your little toy later. Have you broken her in yet, or do I get the honors?" He turned back towards me with a wild grin that made me want to be sick. "And then you belong to Scorpio. How does it feel to be so important? That the fate of a ruler—nay—an entire realm rests upon your shoulders?"

"I belong to no one," I ground out. He chuckled in response.

"Your death will save our Queen a lifetime of misery. And of course, the Water Court as a whole. And yet you choose to remain living. If I didn't know any better, I'd say you were quite selfish." His words tore right through my chest, my mouth agape. The words I'd been struggling with for months now. It must have shown on my face. My doubt. My hesitation. The self-hatred I'd been grappling with for being alive. "Oh darling, did I hit a nerve?" His voice was full of mock sympathy. "Because you know it's true. Every breath you continue to take is a travesty. But not for long."

"She's not going with you!" Aspen finally found his voice in the fray. He looked at me. "Don't listen to a word he says, Lark," he implored me, eyes full of honesty. "Nothing about you is selfish."

"Yeah," said Lennox, stepping up beside me. "We have a plan. Trust us," she bolstered me. Pisces laughed.

"How will that plan go once you're dead and Lark is in my hands?" he asked. We pointed our weapons. "Oh, there's no need for that. I'm not going to be fighting you." He chanted a few words in an alien tongue I recognized from Scorpio in the Yemerian Vale, the language of black magic. Of old magic. He pointed at Locke and the shadows rushed toward him. His own magic rushed out to form a black shield, absorbing all light for a just a moment. For that one moment, all there was, was Pisces' shadows rushing to Locke, and Locke attempting to fight them off. But Locke didn't use his black magic enough. Pisces clearly did, because it broke through without much effort and enveloped Locke, whose piercing screams were enough to break something within me. He fell to his knees, mouth still open in a silent horror. I forgot the danger we were in and I rushed to his side, falling to my knees with him searching, grappling for how I could make things better. For the first time in my life, I had no idea what to do. No plan. I didn't know how to fight this. And that scared me almost more than anything. Almost. The shadows disappeared. No—not disappeared. They were absorbed. Like they'd entered Locke's body.

"Meet your opponent, Court of Rebels." Pisces gestured with a mocking flourish. He was grandstanding, clearly one for theatrics. "I'm so going to enjoy this. I wish I'd brought snacks. Want to know the best part? The spell I've put on him means he'll attack the one he loves most. He'll kill them unless I stop him. It makes so much less work for me if he brings her to me. And he'll destroy any who get in his way." I looked at Pisces, my thoughts and emotions jumbled together, flitting through me too fast to decipher.

Locke growled, breaking the relative silence. But not like anything I'd heard him do before. This was lower. Rougher. More animal. I tore my gaze away from Pisces to see changes in Locke. His eyes were growing darker, the cerulean blue nearly completely eclipsed by swirling black. His jaw was clenched so tightly I could see his muscles popping out.

Lenore stepped out from behind me, placing her hand on my shoulder.

"You need to get some distance." The tension in her voice made my stomach fall through my body in the most sickening way. She sounded almost afraid. And that was terrifying. Lenore wasn't afraid of anything. Everything was afraid of Lenore. If my attention hadn't been so closely trained on Locke, I might have noticed her soft footsteps prodding slowly behind me, getting closer.

"Run," Locke whispered suddenly. His voice was rougher than usual. Darker. Edged with a pain I couldn't put a name to.

"If the spell makes you hurt those you love then I'll keep you from harming the twins and Aspen," I said on my knees with him bracing his shoulders. I implored him to trust me. I could handle him. I thought back to our sparring earlier and doubt flickered. "I won't let you hurt them," I promised.

I could hear him grinding his teeth so hard now his jaw was clicking audibly. His fingers dug into the dry earth, the dirt fracturing and giving way under his considerable strength. He looked up at me, the torment in his eyes flashed despite the darkness seeming to leave him in some sort of haze. My heart cracked for him.

"I love *you!*" he growled out, words barely discernible through his clenched jaw. I could see the wracking of his body as the spell he was under demanded he did its bidding. Bidding his mind was wildly thrashing against. But for a long heartbeat, my eyes met his, and I saw the honesty there. My mind began reeling. The thought was nearly incomprehensible given everything that had happened. But I was determined to help him when, in a movement too fast for my eyes to follow, he shoved me away from him, using his elbow. I landed inelegantly on my backside a few feet away with a hiss. I didn't miss the claws of shadow erupting from his fingers. A chill trickled down my spine. That was new. "*Run!*" he howled in anguish. "I can't fight it much longer, Lark. Get out of here!" Aspen appeared from somewhere behind me, moving into action. He gripped my wrist and flung me to my feet.

"Run, Lark!" he cried and he propelled me forward towards the forest's edge. "And don't look back! We'll keep him off you." I wasn't even sure where I was supposed to go. But that was the point of Pisces' little game, wasn't it? The inevitability?

Another animalistic growl came from Locke, this one deeper still, more guttural. I wasn't even sure if he were even fae anymore. When his head snapped up to appraise his surroundings, his eyes were now black and veined with red; the dark magic had taken root and was firm in its hold over him. I risked a glance up at Pisces. He was thoroughly enjoying the show, sitting up on the sheer cliff with a smirk that showed he knew he'd won.

Not if I could help it.

I turned and sprinted to the forest, Locke lunging at my sudden movement. Aspen body-blocked him, pleading with him to come to his senses. To remember me. That I loved him. I cringed, my chest heaving and feeling tight at hearing the words aloud from someone else. I refused to acknowledge that further right now. I forced my feet to move me as far and as fast as I could towards to cover of the tress, trying to quickly come up with a plan. Any plan.

I had to find a way to get to Pisces. I didn't know what it was—call it intuition—but ending the spell and saving Locke would only happen if I defeated him. Defeated a Zodiac. Defeated someone with more years of sword training than I had years on this earth. By a lot. I prayed to the Goddess above that Aspen had trained me well, and under the cover of the trees, I began planning my ascent to the monster above. I could hear Aspen taking a beating from Locke and it took everything I had to block it out. I heard a scream. One of the twins, no doubt, was seriously injured. I had to hurry. My friends depended on my success. No pressure. I looked at the cliff face with wide eyes. There were no vines to climb, nor ledges to scale. The cliff face had to scale at least thirty to forty feet high in the shortest areas. I looked to the trees. How close did the tree tops come to the height of the cliff? No matter where I looked, the trees were too short, their sturdy branches that would support my weight wouldn't reach high enough for me to scale it. But I had to try something. Maybe I could blast myself up with air magic. Get as high up the tree as possible. I'd lose the element of surprise, but it was my best shot. Pisces most likely thought I was hiding like a coward in the trees. There was another shriek of pain. I gritted my teeth against the flood of images of my friends being hurt, or worse. I forced myself not to picture them like my father when he was killed. Instead, I took that fear and my outrage, and it let it fuel me.

"Let the flames fuel you, but not consume you," Locke had said to me yesterday. I intended to use that mantra as my lifeline.

I climbed. I climbed as fast as I could, one limb in front of the next, ignoring my protesting muscles, and continued pulling myself up the tree. I was still ten feet short of the top of the cliff top when I reached the end of branches that could easily support me. The one I was currently easing myself onto swayed and bowed under me, causing me to curse under my breath and fight to urge to vomit. Or look down. I knew from experience that I was fine with heights until I made the paralyzing mistake of looking down. The branch creaked louder and I stilled. My heart hammered. I didn't even dare to breathe. Another loud groan from the tree. I grasped the branch above me, just in time. The branch under me snapped and fell an uncomfortably long distance before hitting the forest floor. My heart leapt into my throat as I swallowed, suppressing a scream as my legs dangled and pedaled uselessly in the air. I tried hopelessly to find another foothold, any foothold, as the branch I now held began to bow as well.

I hoped the Goddess was listening as I prayed for help. I looked for a solution, but there was nothing. My best hope was to try to fall onto a lower branch. Or use my air magic to soften my fall, but my control over my air magic was temperamental at best. Sweat dripped down my neck as I waited with bated breath for the inevitable breaking of the branch, my heart beating in my throat. On a whim, I tried casting my magic out. Any magic. I didn't know what I was hoping for, but it was better than sitting here, waiting to die. I felt the strangest click deep within me I hadn't felt in a long time but I couldn't place.

A familiar tingle came around me and I felt sturdy under my feet again. A new, sturdier branch had grown out of the trunk, large enough to support me. The branch I currently held no longer bowed. Golden runes swirled over my skin. It took only a moment before I realized what I'd done.

I'd finally unlocked my earth magic! That feeling was from when I'd knocked Locke off of his horse when I discovered my previous elements, I realized. I pressed my hands experimentally into the cliff face. It gave way immediately to sturdy hand and footholds leading upwards. I glanced up at the footholds, looking like the steepest, sketchiest-looking staircase of all time. I began my ascent with trepidation but renewed vigor. I knew a different kind of terror waiting for me at the top.

When I pulled myself to the top, my eyes went right to my target: Pisces. He clearly wasn't expecting me; his attention was focused on the mayhem below him. The coppery scent of blood made its way to me from up here and I had to resist the wave of nausea. I knew time was of the essence. I heard the screams of battle, the cries of pain. I flinched but sunk into a crouch and forced my feet forward. I had to do this for them. I snuck soundlessly; my dagger unsheathed from my boot. I'd slit his throat and be done with it. A few feet to go. I was getting closer and my luck held; he still hadn't noticed me. I crept up to him, my hand held him fast in place by his hair and dragged my dagger across his throat. No blood came. Nor was there a scream of any sort. It was a deep cut. There should be an arterial spurt of blood. But none came. He simply disappeared from sight. There one moment, gone the next in a wisp of black smoke.

A throaty chuckle came from behind me. I spun, dagger ready to defend myself, to see Pisces—the real one—standing there with an infuriating smirk on his face. My heart sank. Of course it wouldn't be that easy. Of course he knew I was coming.

"Sorry about the confusion, sweetheart. I just really wanted to see if you had the gall to try to kill a Zodiac." He grinned wider, drawing the darkness around him again. "I admit, I'm impressed by your ingenuity getting up here and your willingness to slit my throat. Being trained by an assassin has obviously given you a backbone." An unsettling thought broke through my focus. Pisces created some sort of doppelganger? I wasn't aware magic could do that. Perhaps it was a special talent of his, but gauging by the black shadows that had erupted from the wound I'd inflicted, it was shadow magic. I was starting to think the limits that applied to elemental and rune magic either didn't apply to black magic or the limits were very blurry. The distinction between possible and impossible became indistinguishable.

"I'm glad it wasn't you," I said with a smoothness that I hoped hid my unease. I drew my sword, re-sheathing my dagger at my side. My two daggers remaining secret in my boots. "Slitting your throat would be too quick for you. You don't deserve the mercy of a quick death," I spat. "What I'm going to do instead will be far worse!" I wanted to lunge for him. To knock that slimy grin off his face. But I took a steadying breath and allowed myself a brief moment to assess him. Pisces was a Zodiac. He was immortal. He had decades, if not centuries, of training. I couldn't afford to take risks here. I narrowed my eyes at him, but he attacked before I'd concluded my attack plan.

Pisces launched himself into the fight like it was his lifeline, his sword slashing at me in an arc that would break any block I made, so I had to keep my feet moving. Forced to constantly be on the defense and evading meant it was impossible to land any attacks, no matter how small. Pisces laughed as he rained down more assaults on me, forcing me to keep moving, driving me in circles around him. Before long, I was panting, and there was one attack I couldn't quite evade in time, though my blade was able to mitigate the damage. The blood on my exposed upper arm of a deep cut I couldn't yet feel ran down and dripped at my feet. First blood to him. I growled.

I could still hear shouts of pain below me. Yells, and the occasional scream. It took all of my control not to look down at the people I cared the most about.

We traded blows, my exhaustion becoming apparent to my aching limbs. He seemed to be more energized as he fought, as if he were feeding on my sorrow and anger and desperation. I blocked a lighter attack from him, gritting my teeth in frustration. It was time for me to take the offensive. I wasn't getting anywhere like this. I countered another devastating blow, the clanging metal screeching in the air. I reached into myself, tugging on my water magic, sending a flurry of ice daggers in a wide arc towards his face. They sliced and exploded on impact, leaving him in a cloud of ice crystals. *Yes!* I'd made direct contact!

Pisces looked up at me when the ice crystals cleared, a trickle of blood running down his temple, but it seemed that he'd somehow shielded himself from the brunt of it.

"You want to play like that, little girl?" Magic whirled around him as he inclined his head to stare me down. As if to savor my reaction. He created a whip made of ice. It was a million small, interconnected crystals that were as beautiful as they were deadly. I remember Locke had shown me how to do that. It was difficult to maintain, due to it having so many sharp spots connected together to form the whip. But each tiny section was serrated and could cut like a scalpel. I eyed it wearily. He slashed out with it. I didn't move, a smirk on my face. I summoned fire from my veins, it spat and hissed, a wall of flames between he and I. A wall that melted his ice, rendering his ice magic useless.

"Remove the spell on Locke," I said, the flames of Hell surging and twisting around me. I stepped forward, brandishing my sword, my flames protecting me from his water magic.

"No, I kind of like seeing him destroy his friends. And once he's done with you, you'll be only just hanging onto life. And then Scorpio will end you. It's all so very dramatic. I'll make sure Locke gets to see the whole thing. Remember everything he did."

"Why? Why are you doing all of this?" He shrugged, but the sadistic smile on his face was answer enough. Because he wanted to. Because he loved causing pain. Relished in it.

"Do you want to know what's so funny, Lark?" he asked me.

"I feel like even if I say no, I'm going to have to hear it anyway," I snapped.

He raised an eyebrow in response but kept talking.

"You've thought this whole time that Locke killed your father. And he let you believe it, didn't he?" I didn't respond; the thrashing of my heart against my ribs must have given me away nonetheless though. "What a self-sacrificing idiot." He laughed. "It's almost too good!" Was he saying what I thought he was saying? My father...

"Are you saying you killed my father?" My voice was the grim calm before a winter storm: cold and insidiously deadly. He inclined his head, a savage glint in his eye. A challenge.

"And if I am?" Fury unlike any other seared its way through my veins. My vision bled red. I trembled with how hard I held the leash on my magic. With the weight of what he'd just said. With the renewed need for revenge, bitter on my tongue. For months I had believed, or mostly believed, that Locke had killed my father. He'd let me. Everyone had let me. Why? Pisces, the monster in front of me, killed him. Pisces killed my father.

"Then you just signed your own death warrant," I said, my voice chilling in its calm. I lunged at him at a pace I'd never reached before and slashed with my sword, over and over again. He parried and evaded as we fought. But something had changed, I realized as I kept my blade swinging. I had taken control of the fight and put Pisces on the defense. There was no taunt in his eyes now. Just madness. I felt my anger and frustration mount as he continued to dance out of reach of my blade, or parry at the last moment. "Why?" I demanded between blows. "Why did you kill my father? What good did that accomplish?" He darted away to get some breathing room. I let him.

He shrugged.

"A seer had given us a vision of a house in Poplar Hollow and told us that a fae that lived there needed to die for the cause. Your father was the only one there when I arrived. I didn't know you even existed or else you would've been dead too. When Abel first contacted me, all he said was that there was more than one fae in the house. I guess fae is singular and plural. When I returned, I found the charred remains of a female body. I assumed it was you. But then Abel informed me that you were alive, well, and training with the rebels. I guess I got pretty lucky. I finished the job Cancer was too weak to do. He tried to save dear old dad, if that's any consolation. But I'd left as soon as my task was done. Some of us have important business to attend to. But, and I can't stress this enough." He grinned widely at me, his eyes wide. "It was fun."

I think I screamed. I couldn't be sure with the blood rushing in my ears blocking out most sounds as I rushed him. My sword hit true this time, surprising us both by slicing though his bicep when I broke through his block. He let out an enraged cry as my sword was reddened from his blood. And before he could recover, I threw myself at him, desperate to take any opening he gave me.

In a force of black magic, it was like hitting a battering ram, throwing me backwards onto the hard ground with a yelp. When my head quieted, I realized I was dangerously close to the edge of the cliff. I realized my sword was at the bottom of the cliff as he crouched over me. He had discarded his sword and made a shank of deadly smooth, sharp ice. He held it over my neck, the promise of a cut throat in his eyes, wide with excitement. I grasped his wrists, desperate to keep the blade of ice from finding its home in my flesh, my muscles screaming at the effort. I was holding him off, but I could feel myself losing the battle. It was only a matter of time. He was going to injure me here. I knew he wouldn't kill me. That was for Scorpio. He'd deliver me bleeding and injured like a Goddess-sent gift. And then I'd lose my life. If Pisces hurt me now, it was over.

I risked a look down over the cliff to see Locke engaged with both Lennox and Aspen, all of them bleeding. Locke was attempting to make it up the cliff to me, but Aspen kept knocking him down, forcing Locke to turn his aggression onto him and Lennox. Lenore lay a few feet away, a puddle of blood under her. I couldn't tell if she was breathing, if she was alive.

I heard my scream of rage this time over my pounding heart. My hand diverted course from my grip on his wrist. I had to hold him off one-handed for just a second. But he didn't know about my second dagger hidden in my boot.

I pushed outwards with my air magic, forcing him backwards just enough. He snarled and closed the gap quickly. Rolling slightly to the side, I let his momentum carry him forward. I used my only chance. I unsheathed my dagger in my boot and in the same movement plunged it between his ribs, under his stiff leather breastplate. Once. Twice. Three times. Before he threw me off of him over the edge of the cliff with a vicious roar. I heard my name be shouted, I thought by Aspen, as the ground rushed up to meet me. I heard screams from around me. I heard my name yelled out again. I shielded my face with one hand and threw the other out and *pushed* with the last of my magic. With everything I had left.

Air magic swirled to life, responding to my dire situation like an old friend. From my outstretched hand, a blast of air erupted, slowing my descent. Not enough though. I felt the snap in my arm, and for a moment, my body yielded to the pain. For a moment, there was only the agony in my arm as I screeched.

A yell came from above me. Pisces screamed in pain at the wounds I had delivered to him. I saw the blood from here. I gave a savage grin of satisfaction. Good. I hoped it hurt. I wished I could be up there to twist the knife. I hoped he'd die but I doubted we'd get that lucky. I looked at my friends to see Aspen and Lennox next to a facedown and motionless Lenore. Aspen screamed my name, his arms outstretched for me.

"Lark, get to Aspen, now!" Locke cried out. "I'll be right behind you." I didn't even register the relief that the spell was broken. We ran like hell, me clutching my broken arm. I almost fell as Pisces roared in fury, sending a wall of shadow on our heels. I didn't know what would happen if it touched us, but the eerie screaming and voices that were coming from it made me certain I didn't want to find out. I pushed my feet faster, propelling myself as fast as I could go. I dared a look back to see the shadow right behind me. Locke gripped my good arm and ran using his Zodiac speed and strength, bringing me to his chest in a movement I never would have thought possible. We reached our friends just in time, the jumpstone charged. The last thing we heard was Pisces furious cursing and vows of revenge before we all toppled into the courtyard of Port Azure.

My screaming heart straining against the confines of my ribs and my rapid breathing were the only sounds I'd heard for a long moment. When I finally caught my breath, I took stock of my friends. Lennox was screaming for the aid of a healer while Aspen poured his healing magic into an unconscious Lenore. From my position on the ground, I called her name. She didn't move. I still wasn't sure if she were breathing. I tried to gauge Aspen's expression. He looked desperate as he made room for the healers and worked with them to try to save Lenore. I tried to get to her, but Locke laid a hand over my chest at my collarbone. I could hear his voice but I couldn't register the words.

"She's going to be okay. Just let the healers work."

Within Locke's eyes were a maelstrom of heavy emotion: shame, sorrow, and anxiety swirling together with the fury of a summer storm. I almost sobbed with joy seeing his eyes those clear blue sapphire eyes I adored so much. Not a hint of black left.

"Are you really okay now?" I asked, my voice tentative. I looked him over. He looked like hell. He was covered in cuts, his hair was matted with blood, and the haunted look in his eyes was beginning to look permanent.

"I'm fine." His eyes dipped to my arm I was clutching to my chest. Now that the danger had passed, it began to throb painfully, demanding the attention it so rightfully deserved. "But you're not."

"We need to help the others," I said, once again attempting to move my body over to where Lenore was being treated. My body sagged in relief when I saw her suck in a deep breath as she stirred. Her eyes remained closed, but I could see the steady rise and fall of her chest from here. He increased the pressure over my chest, keeping me still.

"She has all the help she needs right now." The roughness of his voice made my heart hurt. His head bowed in shame once again. He'd done this. It wasn't his fault. I knew how hard he'd fought it. I could see his guilt in his slumped posture and hanging head. In the press of his lips and his deeply furrowed brow. I clutched his shaking hand firmly in the grasp of my good hand, hoping to convey words I didn't have right now. He squeezed my hand back weakly.

Slowly and gingerly, he coaxed my broken arm from me, eliciting a hiss of pain. He apologized before sending a wave of healing energy through me. It felt weirdly cold, but it took the pain away. It even seemed to take down some of the swelling initially. I cocked my head.

"I thought you couldn't use healing magic."

"I can. But it's nowhere near as effective as Aspen's. I can't mend a broken bone but I can take the pain away," he said, not looking at me. I watched as Lenore was hauled off by the healers to the infirmary. Lenore was seriously injured, nearly killed if the amount of blood I'd seen underneath her was anything to go by, to save me. To give me the chance to escape. I wasn't even sure how to thank someone for that kind of selflessness. Aspen sank to the ground, looking too exhausted to move. I inched toward him and Lennox and tugged Locke along until we were sitting in a circle, all too exhausted to move. We were sitting so close all of us were touching. I was grateful for their proximity after the intensity back in the glade.

"I was so afraid I'd lost you guys."

"You were supposed to run," Locke growled. "Why didn't you run?" I glared up at him.

"You'd still be under that stupid fish's shadow mind control spell if it weren't for me," I snapped. Aspen laughed, diffusing the rising tension.

"She's got a point. She saved all our asses tonight from the stupid fish." I smirked as I remembered Pisces screaming when I stabbed him. Not once but three times. My petty satisfaction filled me. Locke looked at me as if knowing and returned my grin half-heartedly. But the pride written plainly on his face was shining. Aspen and Lennox, too, looked proud of me when they asked what had happened on the cliff.

So I told them. I told them how I'd gotten up there, earning gasps and excited cheers when they learned of my Earth magic. I told them of my showdown with Pisces. I told them how I'd stabbed him three times, and that was when he threw me from the cliff to the hard rocks below. I was able to soften the fall enough with my air magic, and the rest they knew. I left the part out of my discovery of my father's true murderer. After everything, I wanted to tell Locke about that alone. And there was one other thing I knew was going to come up in conversation. The reason I had to run was because he loved me. And he would destroy everyone to get to me. I didn't understand how that was possible. Unless it was another of Pisces' mind games. That made more sense to my mind.

But still, I couldn't squash the tiniest part of me that hoped. Even after all the rejections. Even after he'd lied to me, though for the life of me I still couldn't fathom why. I still hoped. And I was so disappointed in myself for it.

Aspen recuperated enough that he could finish healing my broken arm, the angry red slash on my arm I'd forgotten about, and the many cuts to my body. There were more than I'd thought. Pisces had done more damage to me than I'd realized. But I did more, I reminded myself with a sneer. But I wasn't naive enough to think he was dead. I knew better than that.

Aspen told me how proud of me he was for my fighting. Tomorrow we'd start on weapons and combat training.

"You've really proven yourself," he said with a proud smile, clapping me on the shoulder. "It's time to get into the harder stuff now. I think you're ready."

"The stuff we've been doing is what you call easy?"

I washed the blood from my skin and hair. It took several applications of soap before I finally felt clean. My hands may have looked clean, but I swore I could still pick up the scent of Pisces' blood on them, making my stomach heave. Restless and unable to sleep I paced my room despite the late hour. Though I knew my body was exhausted, my brain couldn't stop moving a mile a minute going over the events of the day. I couldn't get Locke's words out of my head. He'd admitted he loved me. But I had no idea what that meant. I knew I'd see him tomorrow, and I had a feeling it was going to change everything, and I wasn't convinced it would be for the better.

But I knew sleep was going to evade me long term. I grunted, realizing I didn't have any clean leggings. So I slipped on a casual-looking dress and shoved my feet into a pretty pair of slippers and wandered the hall to the infirmary. I only got misdirected—I wouldn't say lost—once. But I quickly righted myself. Smelling the sterilizing agent and hopelessness assured me I was going the right way until I made it to the same double doors as before.

I opened the door and walked inside, scoping the sick bay for Lenore. She wasn't hard to spot, her small frame looking even more shrunken in against the white bed, white walls, and white floor. Her blond hair still had dried blood in it. I walked quietly over to her and sat with her, reaching for her hand. She must have had injuries even magic couldn't fix immediately, and I wondered if dark magic could do that. I'd have to ask Aspen tomorrow.

Lenore stirred, making me freeze. I didn't want to disrupt her sleep. She needed rest more than anything. But her eyes fluttered open and rested on me.

"How long have I been here?" Her voice sounded raspy.

"Just a few hours. Would you like me to get you some water?" At her nod, I filled a glass by her bed with the pitcher on the table. I used my magic to cool it for her before giving it to her. She sat up and took the glass with thanks.

"Are you doing okay?" I asked. "Why aren't you healed?" She hesitated before answering.

"Locke was under a spell. He was set to destroy us by any means necessary. He impaled me with a spear made of black magic. Black magic wounds take longer to heal and require more care. Some you can't treat, but I guess I got lucky. Thus…" She gestured to her accommodations. "I'm okay," she said and I realized my face must have looked horrified. "It's not Locke's fault. And I'm glad you got a few shots in at that bastard Pisces. He's always been a nasty piece of work." I smiled a little for her sake. "Why are you really here?" she asked me. I looked at her in surprise.

"I was worried about you. Aspen told me you were staying here. I couldn't sleep, so I wanted to check on you."

"Who are you really avoiding checking on?" she said, cutting right to the chase. Her sharp gaze cut me down to size, as always. She squeezed my hand. "You saved all of us today. But mental scars aren't something you can heal away with magic. Go to him. He needs you, even if he won't admit it to himself."

"I don't know if I can." Her face softened, something I wasn't aware Lenore could do. Maybe she was given really strong potions?

"You can. He loves you, Lark. He has since he's met you. You didn't see what he was like before you, but I do. He's happier with you in his life. He's been able to let go of some of his guilt with you. He seems... lighter. More free. And you know he feels guilty for what happened to me. To all of us. We still don't know where his family is. So frankly, let me go to fucking sleep, and you go to him." There was the Lenore I knew. Crass as ever. I giggled at her tone and squeezed her hand. She implored me to go one last time as I left the infirmary.

My legs carried me to his door all too soon. I wasn't done rehearsing all the things I wanted to say. I raised my fist to knock, but I couldn't bring myself to do it, instead placing my open palm to the door. I didn't know whether to knock. It was late. He was likely sleeping. Like I should be. I turned and walked back down the hall in the direction of my room. A soft click from behind me stopped me in my tracks and sent my gut freefalling through my body. I turned to see Locke standing there looking at me, eyebrows lifted in mild surprise.

"I'm sorry, I didn't mean to—"

"It's okay," he said, his eyes not leaving mine. That electricity that always seems to be between us shot through me on cue, thrumming wildly in my veins. If I weren't already restless, I was so wide awake and alert right now, as if struck by that crackling lightning. "Do you want to come in?"

"How did you know I was here?"

He gave me a dry smile.

"I could see your indecision. So much so, I could feel it through the door." He gestured for me to enter, leaving it up to me if I wanted to.

I hesitated. Because whatever was said tonight would now change everything moving forward. I didn't know if I could do that. But I thought back to what

Lenore said. How he'd lost so much today. My heart bled for him and my feet were carrying me to him without me making the conscious effort to. He closed the door behind us and it all felt very final. But instead of anxiety, I felt a strange sense of calm.

"Pisces told me you weren't the one who killed my father," I blurted. Locke stopped moving. His whole body coiled and tensed. The very air in the room seemed to stand on ceremony awaiting his reaction. "He killed him. So now I'll ask you: why did you let me think it was you? Why did everyone let me think it was you? What was the point of me hating you?" Locke looked torn into pieces, like I might as well have ripped his chest open. Evidence of a visceral pain was easy to see on his face. And he tried to hide it but I saw it too—fear.

"What the hell are you afraid of?" I snapped, my voice raising an octave. I caught myself when I saw his flinch and took a deep, steadying breath. "I'm sorry. I didn't come here to yell at you."

"Why did you come here?" His voice was weary, cautious.

"You lost your family today. I of all people know how that feels." My voice was soft as I took a step towards him. "And I saw your face when you saw Lenore. I saw you break. I know you remember what you did when you were under the spell. But it wasn't your fault. It wasn't you."

Locke laughed without a trace of humor, raking his hand through his raven-colored hair before training his eyes on me.

"It was me though," he said, his voice breaking a bit. I stepped towards him, aching to do something to make him feel better. "I lanced my black magic through Lenore's chest. I only just missed her heart. I almost killed her, Lark. And what scares me even more is I was more worried about what I would do to you." His eyes were filled with warring emotions. "I would have killed you. Not that Pisces would have let me. He would have let me leave you in tatters to deliver to Scorpio. And I wanted to. Aspen, Lennox, and Lenore got in my way. They stopped me. But the only thing on my mind was you." I wasn't sure when I stopped breathing, but my lungs began screaming for oxygen. I dragged in a long breath while I waited for him to continue. He looked me dead in the eyes.

"I can feel your emotions. So I know it's too late to try and save you from this. I can't keep you in the dark any longer," he said. Before I could ask what he meant, he continued. "The spell he placed on me was a dark magic spell. Very hard to use. That's why when you hurt him, the spell broke. He needed his magic to heal himself, rather than control me. The spell that forced me to attack the one I love most. And my bloodlust was centered on you." He gave me a pointed look and I felt my heart stop before picking up again at a pace I wasn't sure was sustainable.

"Are you saying—"

"Yes. I'm saying I love you." A dry smirk was on his lips. "I have ever since I saw you in the Yemerian Vale."

"Why are you saying these things like they're bad?" I asked. His face continued to speak of inner torment I didn't entirely understand.

"Do you remember the curse put on me trying to stop Scorpio from using black magic?" I nodded. He took a steadying breath before speaking. "The curse was that I would only have one true love in my immortal lifetime. And I would love her deeply and limitlessly. But when she loved me back, she would find her days limited. When the fae I love falls in love with me, she's cursed to die." My world shattered around me. I couldn't hear, feel, or speak. I watched Locke's lips move as he spoke, but I couldn't process further what he was saying. But I could lip read. He kept saying the words "I'm sorry" over and over again.

"That's why you let me think you killed my father. Why you let me think you used me in Loc Valen. It's why you continued to reject me." My voice was a hushed whisper. "So I'd hate you. So I wouldn't love you. Or at least the monster you pretended to be. You were trying to keep me alive."

He nodded tersely.

"At least I know I'm not a terrible daughter," I mused, drawing a confused look from him. "It wouldn't look good for me to be in love with my father's murderer." I knew he obviously knew from my emotions. That was likely the only reason he was telling me the truth finally. But the sharp intake of breath and joy on his face made my heart leap. A fraction of a second later, he seemed to remember that my loving him wasn't the end goal, and the broken expression on his face crushed me. He looked at me as if I were already dead.

I felt a tingle deep within my body followed by something snapping in place. I flinched. That must be my new curse, locking itself into place, assuring my destruction at some point in my relatively near future. I shuddered. He strode purposefully forward towards me, closing the space between us. He drew his arms around me at last. My arms came around him as well. The armor I'd erected around my heart shattered at last, taking with it the last vestiges of anger. It felt like home, being with him like this. Without the guilt. Finally, the restlessness that had plagued me all night ceased. This was where I needed to be. In his arms.

"I love you," I whispered again, the words feeling strange on my lips. I'd never said those words to anybody. There had never even been anybody remotely close.

"I'm sorry," he whispered, his breath in my ear. I turned to kiss his cheek. I placed my hand on the other cheek and pulled his face to mine.

"We'll find a way out of this. For now, we have one another for the first time. And this isn't exactly how a lady wants to be treated when she confesses her feelings finally," I said in a half attempt at humor. It brought a small smile to his lips a breath before he kissed me. It was soft, sweet, and spoke of two broken fae finding each other against all odds. But fate had a strange way of working.

"I love you," he whispered against my lips, holding me tightly. His arms around me tightened, his palms gliding over my back. "I've wanted to tell you for so long. Every day you hated me was like a second curse." I squeezed him tighter.

"I'm sorry," I whispered. "For everything. Wanting to escape, hating you, being a general pain in the ass." A chuckle racked his body and shook me.

"You are definitely that." He smirked, the tiniest hint of mirth in his eyes. I took his hand and kicked my shoes off. I led him to the bed before kissing him again, my lips yielding to his.

We slid under the covers together. I rested my head against his shoulder, and he wrapped both of his arms tightly around me, kissing the top of my head.

"Making you hate me was the hardest thing I've ever had to do." I looked up and stared into his eyes so he would see the truth of my words.

"I'm not sorry. If I die tomorrow, in a week, or in a year, you will have been worth it. We will have been worth it." I felt a small shudder break from him. I knew he didn't believe that. Part of him still saw himself as the Nightmare Assassin. As the killer of innocents. I knew he saw the blood on his hands. I knew he hated what he'd done. "Let's just enjoy tonight. Just once, I want to fall asleep and wake up to you." He nodded, planting another kiss on my forehead.

My eyes drifted shut and it took mere moments for me to fall into an exhausted sleep. As I drifted off, I heard him tell me he loved me once more. I slept with a smile on my face. It was the happiest I'd been in my entire life.

I woke to rustling in the sheets next to me and warm sunlight filtering in through the windows. I stretched as I opened my eyes, immediately finding the source of the rustling looking down on me, his head propped up on his hand.

"Creep," I muttered with a smirk. He grinned, bringing a lightness to me I didn't even realize was possible.

"Only for you." He leaned forward to kiss me. I had to marvel at how it was so easy being with him like this. As easy as breathing. Except for one small black detail. The curse. I kissed him back, dragging my hands through his sleep-tousled hair, messing it up further as I smiled against his lips. "Good morning," he said to me with a voice still husky from sleep that ignited a fire in me. I eyed his sleep-mussed hair with obvious approval. "I could get used to this." His easy, toothy smile was sweet, unhindered in the sweet moment between us.

"So could I." I bit my lip, watching his eyes flash. I reached up, my hands, my fingers tracing the outlines of the swirling dark blue runes on the considerable swells of his biceps, his pecs. My gaze dipped briefly, taking in the hard plains of his abs, though I didn't trail my hands that low. Not yet. I marveled at the hardness of his muscles. How solid he felt. He grinned knowingly down at me, not the least bit shy. One side of his smirk rose higher than the other, a single canine peeking out at me. I smiled bashfully up at him from under my lashes.

"Like what you see?" His voice was low as he winked at me. My face flushed.

"Not particularly." My tone did not fool him for even a moment. He huffed a laugh against my neck before planting a kiss there, sending a small shiver down my spine. He snaked his arm around me, still chuckling low in his throat before he whispered into my ear.

"I never knew you to be a liar, love." His voice grated on that last word in such a way my toes curled. His toothy grin was incredibly infectious. I reached up and kissed him. Slow and sweet. The way I'd ached to for so long before last night. His lips moved unhurriedly against mine. My hand came up to cup his cheek. His arms tightened around me. Home. This was what home felt like. The only place I wanted to be. But I felt the black rot within me, a heavy and unwelcome weight I had to get used to. The curse. The only darkness on an otherwise perfect morning.

"Not to ruin the mood or anything, but can I ask something?" I asked after I pulled away. He nodded; his expression unguarded but cautious.

"Can you tell me anything else about your curse? Our curse now, I guess," I corrected myself. I hated the frown now replacing the easy expression he'd had earlier. "Does it give any specifics? How I... die, or when? Any loopholes, by chance?" I tried to keep my voice light, but the edge of anxiety crept in, hijacking that thought a bit. I didn't think I'd fully processed all of this yet. Or perhaps I wouldn't be so cavalier about this. I was going to *die*. Locke shook his head.

"There isn't much in the way of specifics, I'm afraid. That's partly why I was in the Library of Aramithia that day in Loc Valen."

"Did you ever get to looking? I don't remember you doing much reading when I saw you there." Amusement flashed in his eyes as we both remembered the same thing; him irritating me, and our first kiss.

"I did later. There aren't a lot of books on black magic. Not a lot is known about black magic, or curses for that matter. And if that information existed in the library, Scorpio would have sniffed it out by now. She's been trying to break her curse every minute of every day for five years." I could see his anxiety spreading behind his eyes, though he hid it well. "Something I suppose I'm going to understand better now. the best chance I can think of is you falling out of love with me," he mused.

"Nope. I'm afraid you're stuck with me. You lost the receipt and you can't return me." My attempt at humor had the opposite effect. His face tightened.

"How can you be so relaxed about this?" His voice didn't falter, but I could see the unease on his face. The guilt he carried.

"Because right now, there's nothing to be afraid of. And you know I'm going to fight like hell to stay with you. If I die, I want my death to mean something. And if it has to happen, if Scorpio kills me, then my death will save the realm. If I do cross that Veil, you should remember that you're worth it. I'm not afraid of the curse."

"I am!" he hissed. His voice didn't raise, but somehow it felt like he was yelling. My gaze snapped to his. He paused, raking a hand through his jet-black hair. "I love you. Losing you might be the hardest thing I'll ever have to deal with. And beyond that, you don't deserve the fate that will befall you just for loving me. You deserve a long, happy life filled with love, and life, and vivid color…" He trailed off, heaving a sigh. "When I was cursed, I'd never been in love. At least, I thought I had been, but when I met you I realized… I'd never felt about anyone the way I feel about you. I assumed love was a fleeting thing for most fae. Superficial. I have felt true love before in others, but it's rare. It's only seen in soulmates. I've never been in love before. I thought I had been," he repeated, eyes slightly distant for a moment. I wondered for the briefest of moments who he meant. It stopped seeming important to ask when he continued.

"But then I met you. And I swear to you on everything I am, I'm going to find a way to spare you. I'm not going to give you up to the Veil without a fight." I could see in his eyes how much he meant every word. I almost told him not to make promises he couldn't keep. Promises were a strange magic. Breaking an accepted promise meant a curse of a different kind. I didn't accept his promise as I spoke to him. "Soulmate," he breathed with a hint of wonder. My heart pounded. Is that what we were? Was that even possible?

"You think we're soulmates?" I asked, finding my voice sounding breathless. He nodded.

"My curse specifically said I'd love you and no other for as long as I live. Is that not your definition?"

"I love you, too," I told him earnestly. I watched his eyes light up, before his face fell, as if remembering that us being in love was what cursed me. I cupped his cheeks gently and bade him to look at me. "I'd love to make you feel better by telling you I don't. That I could stop. But I could no more tell the stars not to shine at night," I said. "I could cover them with clouds, but they'd still be there shining for when the storm cleared." He kissed me sweetly then, his lips capturing mine as a single tear ran down his cheek. I wiped it away and kissed that spot the tear had vacated. I felt the depth of emotion he'd been holding back, and I wondered how I'd ever thought he'd been indifferent to me at all. I wondered how I'd avoided my own feelings when they were this big. This loud.

After a moment and a shuddering, sobering breath, he seemed to have collected himself. He smiled down at me with a real, genuine smile. One of my favorites that made my heart trip over itself. I hated in that moment that he could hear my heartbeat with his exceptional hearing.

"Who knew you could say such pretty words?" He grinned.

"Who knew you could be such an ass even when you're not actively trying to be one?" He snorted a laugh.

"And yet you're still here."

"It would appear so." I rolled my eyes at him, but couldn't stop the grin from finding its way to my features.

"Because I'm just that irresistible." He winked at me. I burst out laughing. "You're… something, all right."

"I'll take that as confirmation."

"It didn't matter what I said, you'd take it as confirmation," I accused.

"I can neither confirm nor deny that statement. It's the biceps and fancy hair, isn't it?" I laughed and rolled my eyes at him.

"Too bad all your brains are in your biceps," I murmured without any punch to it. He grinned, remembering my insult to him the day we met. "And really, you only have fancy hair because of your products!" I winked.

"Alas, it's true. I'm a fraud!" He chuckled.

I felt the way I did when we were at the inn in Loc Valen. Peaceful. Easy. He seemed so unroyal. Not like a Prince at all sometimes. This was one of those times. He wasn't the Crowned Assassin. Not Prince Cancer of the Water Court. Nor was he the Prince and leader of the Court of Rebels. He was just Lachlan. My Locke. The fae I fell I love with. He was kind. Strong. Selfless. And he loved me. The fae I would do anything to protect.

He kissed me then, slow, and easy and sweet. But I felt an undercurrent of something urgent within him. My body reacted to it instinctively, yielding to him. I felt something warm coil in my core. I knew he felt the charged tension suddenly between us, because he drew back and looked into my eyes, the question in his now heated gaze. I nodded and pressed my lips to his fervently.

His lips were hot and relentless against mine, and I matched his pace and enthusiasm perfectly. His fingers slowly traced the curves of my body, in direct contrast to the feverish pace of his lips now slanting over mine. It drove me wild. I bit his lip and soothed it with my tongue as he'd done to me many times before. He ground against me, revealing the hardness of his body and his arousal. A soft moan came from me as I ground my hips back, in eager anticipation of what was to come. He chuckled against my lips.

"Just as greedy as I remember. Slow down. I intend to take my time with you." A trickle of anticipation and something else ran through my body and settled in my core. Of promises I knew full well he could deliver on. He spun me around so he could torturously remove the ribbon tying my dress, still wrinkled from sleep last night, to my body. "I want to see this dress on the floor," he whispered roughly in my ear, making my insides clench together as it opened. I took my arms out of the short sleeves and it was gone. Locke had seen to that. He discarded it to a puddle on the floor, leaving me only in my underthings. He bit his lip in appreciation, his eyes raking me before trailing kisses down my body to my collarbone. It wasn't fast enough for my liking.

"Please?" I tried, biting his lip. In a blink, he had forced my body underneath him on the bed and had me pinned under his weight. I felt like I was never going to get used to his Zodiac speed.

"Oh, you'll beg. Don't worry." His voice low and full of sensual promise that made me shudder against him. His warm breath by my ear sent cascades of goosebumps everywhere. I whimpered, wanting to touch him too, to relish in the feel of him. I wanted him now. But with his weight on me, I couldn't move. He used his knee to part my legs as he kissed me fervently, as if he might die if he didn't. Once again, his kisses trailed down to my collarbone, his one hand holding him up, his other snaking across my abdomen upwards towards my breast. I arched into him, and he took advantage, reaching behind me to unhook my bra and throwing it somewhere across the room. His hand came back to palm my breast before his mouth replaced it, his tongue circling and toying with my nipple. I moaned and fisted my hands in his hair, bowing into him. His hand trailed lower down my body again. Light touches, slowly moving downwards to where I was aching for him to be. I tried to buck my hips to encourage him to move faster, but he chuckled against me, and pinned my hips further to the bed.

"Do I need to retrain you, Lark?" He tsked.

"Yes," I breathed without any shame in my voice. The approving growl I got from him told me that it might just happen. "I need you," I ground out, my voice sounding heady. "Please." His fingers dipped down to trace the outline of my panties, palming me from the outside. He groaned in approval when he found them soaked through.

"You do need me," he said teasingly, trailing his fingers over me before finally sliding my panties off. His fingers slid across me once, twice, sending a shudder through me before finally he plunged two fingers into me. I moaned his name loudly, along with an expletive at him finally giving me what I wanted. What I'd craved from him for so long. I wasn't quiet as he pumped me, and I could tell it wouldn't be long before I found my release, the hot pressure deep within me already beginning to build. His tongue still toyed with my nipple. Finally, his palm roughly hit the center of me with each pulse of his hand. It was quickly my undoing. I shuddered with his name on my lips, my release surprising me with its intensity. Fireworks exploded behind my eyes. My body hummed in appreciation. When at last I looked up, I knew he wasn't anywhere close to done. I bit my lip.

He kissed down my body now, licking, nipping as he went. He was still taking his time driving me mad, his fingers still stroking me through my aftershock. When his tongue finally dragged up the center of me, I cried out. I looked down at him feasting on me. Enjoying me. I panted his name as his fingers pushed into me once more, replacing his tongue. He grinned up at me as his tongue hit that one spot at the apex of my thighs at last. Where I was silently begging for his tongue to be. He started so light, so teasing, I thought I'd go mad. I whimpered, a plea for more.

"Fuck, Lark. You're just as good as I remember," he groaned, making me light up from the inside. Making me want to detonate.

Looking down my body, I saw his eyes take on a primal essence before his tongue slowly, expertly, circled the apex of my thighs. I felt the pressure inside me already beginning to build again. My hips bucked at the sensation, my flesh hypersensitive. He pressed his hand over my hips, effectively stopping my movements. I whimpered and cried out as he continued his tortuous ministrations. I was completely at his mercy with him controlling the movements of my hips. My breath quickened again as he drove me higher towards oblivion. I moaned at each deliberately slow flick of his tongue. His fingers fucked me fast and hard, and I saw the wicked gleam in his eye. He was enjoying this. I was rising higher and higher and teetering right on the edge. I was shaking.

"Come for me." The husky command in his voice did me in. I loudly followed his command. I called out his name as I fisted my hands in his hair as my body spasmed. He let my hips move then and I ground against his tongue. He groaned, letting me ride out my release, his fingers and tongue driving it onwards and prolonging it entirely. When I finally stopped moving, finally catching my breath, and came back down to Earth from wherever I'd been, I felt him get up off the bed. I realized he was wearing far too many clothes. I smirked at him. He wasn't the only one who could dole out orders.

"You need to undress. Now," I said to him, no room for debate in my voice. He raised an eyebrow but conceded. I sunk to my knees before him as he removed his shirt. I caressed his thighs as I waited for his pants to be removed. I bit my lip, looking up at him. "I once told you my mouth wasn't just for sarcasm. Take your pants off and I'll show you." I loved the growl I got in response. I loved the effect I so clearly had on him. When he finally sprang free, I realized I'd forgotten just how much of him there was. I started slow. Torturously slow, as he did to me. Licking his sensitive head, swirling my tongue around it. I dragged my teeth ever so gently over the head of him. I felt his hips flex in response. I looked up at him sweetly. "What was it you said to me? 'Stay still. Or I stop,'" I ordered. The heat in his gaze almost made me combust. My lips parted and I pushed his length into my mouth, bit by bit, slow at first but picking up speed. He hit the back of my throat, and each time I fought a gag until my reflex stopped. I could see him trying not to move. He tried. But with every flick of my tongue, every time I dragged my tongue down the underside of his sensitive shaft, I had him flexing his hips into me, groaning my name. But then play time was over. I gave him a heated look, showing him how much I was enjoying this. Until he pulled out of my mouth. And lifted me onto the bed again, this time on my hands and knees.

"You want this, Lark?" he ground out, positioning himself just outside me, sounding just as needy and breathless as I was.

"Yes," I moaned. "Please. Please, I want you."

He smacked my ass once and pushed himself inside me inch, by inch. I swore at the feeling of it. He didn't move as I adjusted to the fullness inside of me, giving me the time I needed to adjust. When I felt my inner parts of my relaxing into him, I ground against him, letting him know I was ready. It didn't take any more encouragement than that. He slowly pulled out of me, and swiftly filled me, sending me reeling. He did it once more, grasping my hair in his hands, tugging slightly. I wanted more. I begged for more. He gave it to me, at last.

His pace was brutal. Feverish. I didn't even realize I was screaming until his hand let go of my hair and came around to cover my mouth and muffle me. I gritted my teeth in an attempt to lower my volume, but the cascades of pleasure he was giving me made that difficult. Once satisfied I wasn't going to wake the whole wing, his hand left my mouth and migrated down to the apex of my thighs, which was now extremely sensitive. He tapped it a few times, sending blinding sensation through me before circling it with his finger, and I was falling again, his name on my lips. My body sagged, exhausted. Nearly spent. Nearly.

But he still wasn't done. He was ravenous. But so was I. When he pulled out of me, I whirled on him, taking him to the bed and pinning him beneath me. I wasted no time in lowering myself onto him. I moaned at the angle of it this way. The depth. And he was letting me take control. I rode him slowly at first. Deeply. He hissed and swore.

"What is it you want?" I asked him, mimicking the way he spoke to me. He smirked up at me. All cocky male satisfaction as he gripped my rear.

"I want you to ride me harder. Faster. Or I'll make you." His breathy voice betrayed how affected he was; it was my turn to be smug. I had a feeling he would make good on his threat. But I obliged him. I rode faster, I rode harder. I took him deeper. I was losing myself to the feeling again as we found this new rhythm. I felt a familiar pressure building. There was no way I could fall again. But my body had other ideas. Suddenly, Locke dragged me forward by my hair to kiss me. He gripped my hips and drove upwards hard into me, once again regaining control. I buried myself in his kiss, losing myself. I moaned into his mouth, that pressure building to its peak. I begged him to make me fall over the edge one last time. He thrusted savagely into me in an insistent command to do so. I had no control over the scream that ripped through me as my vision went fuzzy when I obeyed him. I clung to him as he rode me through it once again. His thrusts became impossibly harder still as I felt him swell inside me. He found his own release as he called my name. I rode him through it this time, the aftershocks of my release squeezing him gently through it. He rolled us over so I was beneath him, and he pulled out of me, giving me a chaste, sweet kiss. The exact opposite of everything we'd just done. My cheeks flushed. And I fought the urge to cover myself. Which was ridiculous. He'd seen everything already. He smiled at me and kissed me once more.

"I'm going to run you a bath. You deserve it," he said, his eyes touched with sin as he smirked at me. "Besides, I think you're going to be a bit sore."

"Only if you join me in it," I said, smiling at him. He grinned as if the thought hadn't occurred to him.

"How could I resist?" I felt my cheeks flush again at his words. My eyes darted down, though there was a small smile on my face. He tipped my chin upwards so I had to meet his eye. "You are beautiful," he said, punctuating each word with a kiss. "You are incredible." He kissed my forehead. "I can't believe you're mine." My cheeks may as well have been flames for how flushed they were. He leveled me with a pointed look. "I love that a few compliments have such an effect on you. But it worries me that nobody has told you these before. That you don't believe them." I shrugged awkwardly, unsure what to say. "My new mission in my life is to make sure you believe that you're the beautiful, kind, smart, capable, funny, incredible fae I know you to be." I didn't know what to say, at a complete loss for words. I kissed him, putting all my love and appreciation for him into it. He kissed me back just as tenderly. He broke the kiss and turned towards the bathroom. A few moments later, I heard the water run and he emerged in a bathrobe. I wrapped a blanket around myself.

"What? I want a bathrobe!" He laughed as he produced one from his closet behind me. White, crisp, clean cotton. It felt like luxury on my skin as I donned it. I grinned at him in thanks as we walked to the bathroom. I was sorely in need of a bath. I could feel that my gait was a bit wider as I walked. If he noticed, he didn't say anything. But he was definitely looking self-satisfied by something.

I looked at the tub, intended to check the temperature, and saw the foamy surface, bringing joy to me at the luxurious-looking suds.

"Bubbles? You put bubble bath in?" I looked up at him incredulously. He grinned with a shrug.

"I may be a man, but I'm not an animal. There may also be a potion for healing sore muscles in the bath." I looked at him skeptically. "What? You think I don't get sore after sparring particularly hard? And don't think I didn't see the way you were walking a minute ago." He winked at me as I flushed. I splashed him. He barked a laugh. I disrobed, with my back to him, and settled into the water, the heat already doing wonders to relieve the tension from the last few hours. I moved forward in the massive tub to allow room for him. He slipped in behind me and I settled against his warm, broad chest. He wrapped his arms around me, scooping bubbles onto my shoulders and rubbing the soap into them in a light massage. I sighed, leaning into this touch.

I felt my eyelids get heavy. I relaxed against him, head lolling to the side. I could feel the smile on my face as he kissed the top of my head.

"I love you," I whispered before the world fell away.

I knew I was dreaming. I was absolutely aware of it. I was in the middle of a vicious battle. Bodies lay strewn at my feet for what seemed like miles, the ground slippery with blood. I saw Locke and another armor-clad fae I recognized as Pisces engaged in heated combat, swords and magic alike flying into the fray. Scorpio whirled on me. She had a weapon in her hand. A sword. I looked down to find myself with a sword too. She spat at me about how her curse would finally end. She could finally rest. Finally, be herself again. She launched herself at me, an angry, conceptual snarl on her lips. Something changed the moment her blade crossed with mine.

"The time is now," a voice whispered, familiarity touching the edges of my awareness, but dancing away whenever I tried to grasp the memory of whose voice it was. And suddenly the dream rearranged itself. Scorpio was straddling me, my hands frozen to my sides with thick ice my magic couldn't seem to break. My well of power was empty. I had no way to fight back. Her hands were around my throat. I couldn't breathe. My lungs began to scream for air and I knew this was it. My time had come. I thought to my time with Locke, wishing desperately that we'd had more time. All I could hope for at this point was that my death counted. That it mattered. The fringes of my vision became darker as Scorpio boasted her victory with a sneer. I heard Locke calling out my name from somewhere far away. I whispered his name. How very fitting that my last word would be his name. I smiled, knowing that the curses would die with me. That Scorpio wasn't going to win. Locke would end her. My vision went dark and I felt my heart stop beating. I was dead.

Suddenly I was looking at myself in third person, though nobody could see me. I watched as Scorpio wrung the final vestiges of life from me, bruises forming on my neck.

I felt something break deep inside me and I knew the curses had shattered. I watched Pisces laugh as Locke fell to his knees screaming for me. How his scream seemed to be the only sound despite the war around us. How poignant his heartbreak and devastation. Tears formed in his eyes as I watched, bringing tears to my eyes as well. I watched as Locke stumbled in his effort to get to where my destroyed body lay motionless.

"The time is now," the voice repeated, more urgently this time. I looked within the confines of my memory as I watched the scene, looking desperately for the owner of the voice. A few heartbeats passed and realization steamrolled me.

Amaya.

She had said she would help me when things turned dire.

I looked for Locke and spotted him running to my body where it lay at the Queen's feet. A storm gathered around us, lightning flashed in his eyes. He screamed. Lightning hailed in the sky crashing to the earth around us. And then a jolt hit my body. Seconds passed. But I didn't take my eyes off my body. The me on the ground suddenly took a gasping, ragged breath, green eyes opening wide with terror, and a soundless scream on her lips.

"Lark!" Locke was shaking me awake. I shuddered awake from my dream. I looked up a Locke, who was looking at me in concern. "Lark, you had a nightmare."

"I'm okay," I said. "In fact, I'm better than okay. I think I found a way to save me. A loophole in the curse. One that can save me and stop Scorpio."

"What?"

"Locke... I think I found a way to save me, and end all of this."

A Message From H. L. Hamilton

Hello! And thank you so much for picking up *Of Curses and Contempt*. This is my first book I've ever written and it's a joy to be able to share it with you. I hope you enjoyed the story so far as much as I enjoyed writing it.

If that cliff-hanger made you mad, take heart! Book two is on the way!

What's a first book without a cliff-hanger, right?

If you'd like teasers for book two, feel free to follow me on Tiktok @H.lHamiltonauthor. I'd love to interact with you! I'm also toying with the idea of bonus content for those of you who love Lark and Locke as much as I do.

Dedication

This book is dedicated to so many incredible people. The list is not a short one. First, my parents for believing I could do this when I didn't. Thank you, Mike and Lisa. For everything. The best parents on Earth.

A special thank you to my best friend, Nikole, who is immortalized as one the characters in this duology. I bounced more ideas for this book off her than anyone else. I'm forever grateful.

To Kat, who helped me so much through this entire process, and became such a close friend along the way. This book wouldn't be what it is today without you.

Bella and Kayla, your kindness, help, understanding, and enthusiasm is beyond incredible. I'm so grateful for you both!

And last by but no means least, to Justin. The love of my life. Who put up with me writing nonstop for months to get this book finished, and gave me so much inspiration I love you. Thank you.

Printed in the USA
CPSIA information can be obtained
at www.ICGtesting.com
LVHW041609161123
763837LV00102B/144/J